"IF THEN is a love story, the history of a marriage, a topical meditation on the end of capitalism; best of all, it is a bone-deep, blood-sweet British fantasy, naive and ingenious as William Morris and as warpedly nostalgic as Richard Jeffries' *After London*. It is also the only intelligent book ever written about the technological singularity. As disturbingly hyperreal as any Pre-Raphaelite painting, IF THEN imagines what the end of history really will really look like."

Simon Ings, author of Wolves

"Sumptuously written, with prose that glitters with a dark lustre like a Damien Hirst fly collage, intricately plotted, and a satirical point as sharp and accurate as the scalpel of a brain surgeon: De Abaitua operates on the smiling face of the present to reveal the grimacing skull of the future."

Will Self, author of The Book of Dave

"*The Red Men* is a breathtaking novel of ideas."
i09.com

"De Abaitua's extraordinary fictions, scientific and otherwise, emerge from a deep and mysterious understanding of culture, and show it to us in a new light."
James Bridle

"*The Red Men* is an exciting and confident debut."
Strange Horizons

"This near-future literary thriller is remarkably prescient... it is De Abaitua's pinsharp observations of human nature that make this an uncomfortably standout read for me."
Sarah Higbee

MATTHEW DE ABAITUA

IF THEN

ANGRY
ROBOT

ANGRY ROBOT
An imprint of Watkins Media Ltd

Lace Market House,
54-56 High Pavement,
Nottingham
NG1 1HW
UK

angryrobotbooks.com
twitter.com/angryrobotbooks
Bellum se ipsum alet

An Angry Robot paperback original 2015

Copyright © 2015 byMatthew De Abaitua

Cover by Raid 71
Set in Meridien and Gotham Black by Argh! Nottingham

Distributed in the United States by Random House, Inc., New York.

ISBN 978 0 85766 466 2
Ebook ISBN 978 0 85766 467 9

Printed in the United States of America

9 8 7 6 5 4 3 2 1

For my children

"The front cannot but attract us, because it is, in one way, the extreme boundary between what one is already aware of, and what is still in the process of formation."

Pierre Teilhard de Chardin,
THE MAKINGS OF A MIND

"Today's truths become errors tomorrow; there is no final number."

Yevgeny Zamyatin, ON LITERATURE,
REVOLUTION, ENTROPY & OTHER MATTERS

IF

1

Whatever he was, he was not quite a man. The bailiff found the soldier hanging off a coiled bank of barbed wire running through the heart of Blackcap farmhouse. The soldier did not seem to feel pain and struggled in silence to free his arms and chest from the metal thorns. Though his features were well-defined – a blade of a nose and dark brows – the eyes were mindless, the mouth loose and undirected. No, not quite a man.

The soldier bucked urgently against the new, coarse-cut wire, opening up a bloodless wound: his skin parted along a seam on his forearm, revealing pulpy flesh threaded with spokes of tightly-packed crimson seeds like a pomegranate. The bailiff grasped the hard pale sheen of the soldier's wrist, just above the wound. The soldier's uniform – overcoat and pack, a light khaki tunic with two breast-pockets, woollen trousers with a safety pin through the waistband, puttees and hob-nailed boots – smelt of damp earth and the chemical cleansers of the assembly line. He wore an armlet marked with two red letters: *SB*.

The bailiff knelt down and stroked the soldier's close-cropped hair as if calming a child crying in the night.

"My name is James," said the bailiff.

Then James pressed his right boot against the wire and

gently lifted the struggling soldier off its spikes. Once free, the soldier turned slowly on his back, readjusting, realigning. James clambered over the wire and onto the soldier's chest, reached into the tunic and found a pair of bandages, then set about binding the wound. There was neither a flicker of thanks nor relief upon the face of the soldier, his eyes merely agitating at the speeding clouds overhead.

James tucked the bandage back into the soldier's pocket, then noted, tied around his neck, a pair of identity discs: a brick-coloured circle and green hexagon threaded with knotted string and imprinted with the name of J HECTOR. In Hector's backpack there was a blank sketchbook, a tin of watercolour paints, a coarse blanket, shining tins of iron rations, a primus stove and a water bottle. The water bottle was full and James offered it to Hector. His lips inclined toward it. He drank. Water was necessary, it seemed. James hauled Hector to his feet. His clothes were sodden with dew, a sign that he had been on the wire since before dawn.

A sea fret drifted over the downland. James pointed to where the bowl of lush green curved upward to the ridgeline. He began his ascent and motioned for Hector to follow. The soldier did not respond.

"Who made you?" asked James.

Hector's chest rose and fell. He breathed like a man. He drank like a man. He looked like a man. But inside he was pith and beads.

"Did the Process make you?"

No answer. James looked back across the quiet valley. He had seen some things on his patrols of the Downs, but this was new. At least he thought it was. His memory was full of holes.

It was six miles back to town but only four miles across to Glynde. From there he could take a route through the woodland to the Institute. Alex Drown would be interested in the soldier. He would take him to her.

He tried pushing Hector forward. The soldier stumbled on for a few steps then stopped and half-turned back toward James. The will of the Process could ignite within the soldier at any moment: he should drive Hector forward now before resistance rose within him. But James was loathe to show such violence, even to a manufactured man. He believed in kindly discipline, the fatherly appeal to reason, although he had no children himself. He and Ruth had not been so blessed.

James returned to the ruined barn, found a rope, and tied it around Hector's midriff to use as a leash. He climbed toward the escarpment, yanking at Hector to follow him. The soldier stumbled and fell forward without bringing up his arms to protect himself. James would have to carry him. A fireman's lift. James was tall and broad, sixteen stone of muscle and one stone of fat. With the soldier slumped uncomplaining across his shoulders, James staggered to the top of the chalk ridge.

Radio masts lay fallen across the western track, broken into thirds and rusting into the earth. He lay Hector down and went inside the relay station to check for signs of the evicted. The previous week he had evicted three people from the town and sometimes they did not get very far. The relay station was empty.

His patrol route followed the ridge down to the river, then along its course north into town. Hector had been caught up in the south side of the wire, and so must have come from the direction of the coast. James shielded his eyes and gazed out to sea: three long tankers laden with scrap and containers idled at anchor, waiting for a berth in the port. The new owners of Newhaven had found a use for their acquisition: the port was busier than when it had been inhabited by people. He had not been to

Newhaven since the Seizure. His memories of that night were mercifully vague: faces screaming in the spotlights; his giant iron hand peeling back a roof to find a family huddled in their beds; raindrops quivering on the porthole; the silence afterwards; rusting hulls rocking in the oily waters of the harbour.

James headed down the steep old road toward Firle village. The tarmac was cracked. The scent of a colony of wild garlic, clustered in the dappled sunlight at the foot of an oak, reminded him of past trips to the village, before the Seizure, when paragliders rode the thermals rising up Firle Beacon. The view from the air was different now. Ancient and modern ruins merged into one another: the faded road markings just visible through the hawthorn, the mounds of barrow and iron fort, the rotten thatch of a country pub and the flyblown carriage of a lost commuter train, and then the great old houses with their fortified estates, the reservoir, the woodsmoke rising from the encampments of the foresters, and Lewes itself, his home, protected.

The broken road skirted around the edge of the Firle estate. The cottage doors were painted green to mark their ownership by the viscount and his family. Children played in the gardens and in the street. A girl of about ten years old, with straight blonde hair, followed him as he walked; she cartwheeled first with two hands, then with one.

When he paid her no attention, she called out, "Who's the man on your back, bailiff?"

She wore a homemade gingham dress and was barefoot. She wore her hair in a ponytail tied with ribbons made by his wife. Many of the women wore their hair that way as it concealed the stripe.

"His name is Hector," James replied. He lowered the soldier to the ground.

"Is he hurt?"

"Yes."

"So why doesn't he cry?"

"Because he's not quite a man," said James.

"He looks like a man."

"He's not as heavy as a man. Somebody made him."

"Like a doll?" asked the girl.

"Yes."

"To play a game with?"

"Perhaps."

"My dad found one in the river," she said. "He wasn't a real man either."

"When was this?"

"Last week. He was dressed as a soldier man too."

"A soldier from the olden days?"

"From the First World War," the girl corrected him, taking pride in her knowledge. "We all had a look at him. He was different from this one. Chunkier."

"Is your father around?"

"No, bailiff," she shook her head. All the children lied to him: the angle of her left foot, pointed inward, the adjustment of her hair over her right ear, her scrupulous effort not to glance back through the avenue of overgrown sycamore, were all signs for him to sift.

"Where is your soldier now?"

"They took him to the Institute tied to a wheelbarrow. Is that where you're taking this one?"

"Tied?"

"The soldier didn't want to go. This one seems not so alive."

"The Process is weaker in the valleys. Where are your parents?" He felt responsible for the girl now and didn't want to leave her out alone.

"Don't you remember my name?" she asked. "We met at the lido. Your wife is my teacher."

"I don't have a very good memory," he confessed.

She looked concerned.

"Are you sick?"

"I had an operation," he explained. "It had side effects."

"You had an operation to make you the bailiff. We learnt about it at school."

"You know a lot of things."

"My name is Agnes," she said.

Hector stirred. The soldier ran one hand along the hobnailed sole of his boot, recalling the sensation of the earth beneath his feet.

"He's like my cat," said Agnes. "He's with us but he's alone too."

"He's part of the Process," said James.

"Why?"

"I don't understand the Process. I just follow it. The Institute will know what he is for."

James bent down and heaved Hector onto his shoulder; the body had grown denser, and palpably heavier with presence. Time was running out. Agnes, idly chewing the ends of her long straight blonde hair, watched the bailiff struggle down the lane, the dappled light through overhanging branches playing upon the face of the soldier on his back.

At the railway line, he rested and lowered Hector to the ground. A rictus had formed on the soldier's face. James balanced Hector's head on his lap, and worked the rictus away. Under the massaging of his fingers, the facial muscles relaxed, and the soldier took a deep breath, in the same way that a real man would do after the passing of a crisis.

James took out the soldier's canteen and tried a sip of his water. It was faintly fizzy and doctored. Hector reached up for the canteen.

"Do you want this?" James searched Hector's face for signs of volition. The hand hung there, waiting. He pressed the canteen into it. The soldier took a sip, his lips tight around the spout.

Smoke from the fires of the blacksmith of Glynde rose wispy black against the soft green of Mount Caburn. James checked the rope was secure around Hector's midriff. He jogged down the railway cutting, the soldier stumbling after him.

The Hampden family still occupied the grand house of Glynde Place and their tenants in the surrounding cottages worked for the Institute much as laymen and laywomen had for the monasteries; acting as intermediaries between the secular and the sacred. With the railway closed, few outsiders came to the village. Cattle milled around the abandoned ticket office and the cricket pitch had been turned to allotments. The bailiff was known to the men and women digging in the field. Their evasive expressions paid James his due.

The blacksmith, smoking a roll-up cigarette in his yard, was the only one to catch his eye; a proud man whose choice of craft had once seemed quaint, even perverse. Not anymore.

"Is that a soldier, bailiff?" The blacksmith wiped his oily hands on his apron, squinting through cigarette smoke.

"Have you seen more of them?"

The blacksmith nodded. "I heard them marching down the lanes at night. The wooden wheels of their carts on the road. I took them for spectres, but the viscount reckons they're made men and come from the factory out by Newhaven."

"I saw ships, big container ships waiting in the bay."

"Raw materials for the assemblers." The blacksmith was a weathered tall man in his late fifties, cynical and houndish, with deeply scored features, bloodshot eyes and swollen fingers that indicated a neglected medical condition.

"The Process can make anything from a pattern but I'd be out of a job if it started making things that *original*." The blacksmith wiped the oil from his hands with a rag and appraised James from head to toe.

"You're not using the armour, bailiff?"

"Not today."

"Is it broken again?"

During the Seizure, James had stood on this very grass, forty feet high in the armour, pistons hissing, iron fingers fashioned from digger's claws, gearwheels turning in response to his every gesture, his voice an amplified fizzing bark, and asked the blacksmith for help.

"I keep the armour for evictions."

"What if you run into trouble?"

"Have you heard of any trouble?"

"A few of the people you moved on from Newhaven came back." The blacksmith pointed out the villagers working the allotment. "That family walked all the way from London. We took them in. There's some work here, and some food."

The soldier's leash tightened and James staggered back a step.

"He wants to get back with his comrades," said the blacksmith.

"Let me show you how he is put together."

James yanked the rope hard so that the soldier sprawled once more on the earth. Quickly, James sat astride him, removed the bandage, and by the force of his thumbs parted the wound. The blacksmith whistled, set his cigarette aside and reached into the gash with the tip of a penknife, prising out one of the crimson seeds embedded in the man's flesh. He held it up to the sunlight to observe how the light swirled within its translucency.

"A polymer seed. He's been specially grown. His face is very individual, isn't it?"

"His identity discs give his name as J Hector. Do you think he is a copy of an actual soldier?"

"His body is very slight. He's about five foot nine, isn't he? The Tommies were small men. As to whether he is a copy of somebody who actually lived, the Process has to work from an existing pattern. That means something or somebody who existed. The Institute will know for certain."

The blacksmith left sooty fingerprints upon the soldier's cheekbones. He slipped the seed into the breast pocket of his overall and offered James a drink. James declined. He had to push on to the Institute. It was only a matter of time before the Process made the soldier unmanageable.

2

Ruth was also on her rounds, with the afternoon's deliveries folded into a large oilcloth bag: dresses, tunics and children's pyjamas of her own design, and a ball of the brightly coloured hairbands that the women of Lewes could not get enough of this autumn, a ribbon strengthened with wire. The ribbons were used to hold a ponytail down so that it lay evenly over the *stripe*, the mark of the Process that ran from crown to nape.

This stage of her life felt more embodied, if that made sense, than her life before the Process; now she had to walk to meet and talk to people, and be accountable there and then, and trade things that she had made with her hands, rather than the sly interaction of the screen. Of course, she felt the ache of wanting to pull out a phone to check her messages – and saw how, during a lull in conversation, other Lewesians would move as if to take their phones out to alleviate the tedium of presence – but the sacrifice of the screens was no great loss.

In the morning she taught at the primary school and after letting the children loose into the field to play in the roots and branched webbing of the kiss-kiss tree, she undertook her role of seamstress; she made nice things for younger children – babies and toddlers – and their mothers, her tape measure girdling lithe bodies as gossip was ventured over a chipped mug of warm herbal brew, Ruth mostly listening and nodding, taking one pin at a time from between her lips to mark a seam. Sewing itself was done at night, by candlelight. There was no domestic electrical supply so she used a hand-cranked machine set up on a table next to the draughty sash window of their flat above the Needlemakers. Her grandfather had been a tailor, and when she was growing up, he had lived with her family. He kept odd hours too; she would wake in the middle of the night, hear him shifting around in his rooms, smell his lit cigarette, then fall asleep again to the whirring of his electronic sewing machine and the click-clack of its pedal.

She worked at her hand-cranked machine while James came and went in the living room, unable to settle in the two or three hours after dinner that formerly would have been occupied by television and internet. She was peripherally aware of him as the mechanical teeth of the footplate pulled the fabric under the foot and into the stitching action of the needle; he moved from room to room, or rested upright in a wooden chair, one eye half-closed, one boot off, half-asleep. The half they left her with.

The making of things was important to her. James, in their pre-Seizure pomp, made corporate loops for an agency. She remembered how important it was to him, the deadlines and the *soshul* metrics, and so by extension how important it became to her that these loops were persuasive and liked by the right people. She worked as the manager of a library in Hackney, running up and down three flights of stairs to attend to the needs and complaints of staff and customers. In the final year the customers were in a right old state; she opened the doors at nine and they barged into the library to secure its resources for the day, men and women of every ethnic mix, eighty-ninety people by five past nine, the library full at ten, using the computers to look for work, appeal for benefits, run their secondhand car business or church group, or in the case of one particular woman and her three children, living in the library as a refuge from the spread of evictions. As the Seizure approached, London's population was sorted and re-sorted, and her library filled up with the remainders of that calculation. Not customers but *sufferers*. She could not always understand what they were saying, what they were so urgently showing her on their screens. The drop-in shelter opposite the library closed down, A&E started screening in-patients, and before she knew it, one morning she went to open the doors of the library and there were two hundred people outside, almost a mob, spilling back from the pavement and out into the street, overlooked by the balconies of a new hotel and an empty ziggurat of flats.

On her rounds, she preferred to walk around Lewes via the twittens, the steep high-walled alleyways that ran betwixt and between the old buildings of the town. These old ways were quieter and more private; on the high street, she had a vague sense of the other Lewesians judging her and James. Under her role as schoolteacher, she was accountable to every nutty parent and she accepted that, but the feelings of other townspeople toward James was not something she liked to articulate, even to herself. She took no pleasure in it; they feared him, and pitied her. Also, there was an air of playacting on the high street, a let's-pretend of community life that offended her truth, the moral compromise she had accepted as her lot. As if the choice to submit to the Process had not been a last resort but a way of life they had all long strived for and finally achieved.

She knocked discreetly on the wooden gate of the Radcliffes', and then flicked up the latch to let herself in.

She had a cap for their infant son, made the previous evening out of her allocation of jersey cotton. She always put jersey cotton aside for the newborns because it was stretchy and soft, something comforting for the child to grow into. The cap was her own design and included a hand-stitched leaf with red and orange cotton, autumnal colours, so that the parents could always recall the season of his birth.

Ruth called out to see if anyone was home, and waited in the large and overgrown garden. The house was over three storeys and had been allocated to the Radcliffes and another two couples, one young, one much older, forming an ad-hoc extended family. Clearly they had failed to negotiate who exactly – in this setup – was responsible for the garden. She was aware of a heady floral perfume, and was wondering what the source of that scent was – jasmine? Or something richer? – when the man of the house (Laurie? Larry? She never quite caught his name) came out to greet her. She showed him the baby's cap. Could she try it on the child, to check the fit? No, she could not. He explained that the baby was with its mother. They had walked out to the Institute.

"His stripe?" said Ruth.

"We followed the instructions. Gave him the injection, cut his hair, and then gave it forty-eight hours for the cells to form. But it doesn't look right. The cells are uneven in size, and they're still growing," said the baby's father. He was fuzzy with sleep deprivation, unshaven and uncombed and untucked. Younger than James, his hair a crowd of contrary brown curls.

"We've had a few cases of that over the years. I'm sure the Institute will be able to fix it." She remembered the purpose of her visit. "Can I leave the cap with you?" Laurie or Larry accepted it from her, turned it over in his hand, his feelings equally reversible: on the one side, he appreciated the care she had taken in making this gift for his newborn son, and on the other, anguish at the fear and pain caused by the striping.

"I'll come by in a week," she said. "And I know that when I do, your son will be fine."

It was not an empty reassurance. After the injection of the new cells and initial discomfort of their formation under the scalp, people were, by and large, fine. With some grooming, the stripe could be concealed, forgotten about, except in the private moments. Closing the gate behind her, she wondered what the next stop was on her rounds, and found herself touching her stripe, felt the hundreds of tiny folds and ridges under her scalp, the rough discoloured skin on the back of her neck and at the top of her spine. An odd odour came away sometimes; in the twitten, she caught a whiff of it on her fingers, a yeasty concentrate, sour and fungal. She got on her tiptoes, reached over into a neighbouring garden, and plucked bay leaves from an overhanging branch to wipe her hands clean.

The twitten brought her into the ornamental garden of the old hotel, a sloping lawn terrace with a southward view to the Downs and the quiet lanes of the A27. It was noon or thereabouts, and on the lawn Jane Bowles was organizing the preserving and pickling of the produce grown in the allotments. Rows of jars laid out in the sun, using the natural disinfectant of strong sunlight, the best way to dry the jars after they had been scoured with hot water. Jane gave a quick wave to Ruth as she passed by, then continued instructing two men carrying hot jam pans. That was the thing with Lewes life. You bumped into people. And she bumped into Jane more than anyone, their friendship a string of chance encounters. They had organized something once – an afternoon in the bitterly cold lido – but the date did not deserve repeating: the

Bowles had children, and they did not, and James was not easy to be around, if you were unaccustomed to the way his presence drifted in and out.

She taught one of Jane's children, blonde Agnes, precocious but polite enough. But then all the children were precocious in one way or another, one of the benefits of the stripe, and living among the kiss-kiss tree and the other natural forms made over by the Process. What had begun as a last resort had become an ongoing experiment in human potential.

Ruth watched the two men in undyed burlap tunics pour the jam carefully into a jar: a berry jam, red and thick and translucent in the pan that, when it ran, turned amber in the sunlight.

"I'm impressed," Ruth said to Jane. "A very organized operation you have here."

"I used to be a project manager," said Jane. "Making apps." She shrugged, made that sigh and shrug that Ruth recognized as one particular to the people who had accepted their losses in the Seizure. "Today I make jam and pickle vegetables. Over the weekend, I organized the children into picking gangs and set them a competition as to who could bring back the most fruit."

"Did they go far?"

"We let them go outside the wall. As far as Glynde. Your husband kept an eye out for them."

Jane admired Ruth's homemade dress, muslin with a printed white whorling pattern that grew denser toward the hem, puffy sleeves and a frill around the neckline, matched with a black and white wired ribbon in her ponytail. Jane was wearing a pinafore dress made by the Process, thick burlap like the men's tunics, too heavy for this weather. Jane's stripe would register her elevated body temperature, the nagging discomfort of the dress, her irritated adjustment of the straps and this data would inform the next iteration of dresses. But, for now, too hot.

"Were you always a teacher and a seamstress?" asked Jane.

"Neither. I ran a library."

"One of the first to go then."

This remark annoyed Ruth.

"Not at all. The worse things got, the more that people needed the library. And then we were Seized."

The emotion of that day returned to her, the fury and the sickening helplessness. Redundant, she was texted a number to call for help but the helpline was a labyrinth of misdirection, appeals and further promises, all broken, never intended to be kept. Her customers were irate; she stood with them in the forecourt of the library, locked out, and still they asked for her help. Not asked. Demanded it, shoving their mobile phones at her, failing to understand that she was one of them now. It was so primitive what was done to them, a simple exercise of brute power under the guise of necessity. They took what the administrators offered to resettle, and their landlord got somebody else in. James said the signs were there for them to see. He knew from the way the Prime Minister assured the people that their property rights would be respected, and that no one would be forced to part with their assets, that it was over. Property market falls in China. Russian aggression in the Ukraine. Flash crashes every hour on the stock market – the rumbles of an oncoming storm.

Ruth had stood on their porch brandishing a large kitchen knife in her small hand, weeping. When you are a small woman, you rely on the rule of law to confer the authority and respect you deserve. She would not live without it.

Jane, sensing that Ruth was on the verge of tears, offered her some bread with warm jam. It tasted good. In the first months of the Process, they had been forced to survive on the weave of proteins and gloop of carbohydrates that it assembled. The nuances of good fresh food were beyond it. The patterns for the manufacture of an apple were incomplete.

"That's nice," whispered Ruth, staying quiet, not wanting to sob.

"I wonder what the Process makes out of our grief," said Jane. "How does it respond to our sadness?"

"By making us feel better."

"But how can it do that?"

"We do keep bumping into each other," said Ruth.

"I'm sorry I upset you," said Jane. Her smile was uncertain. There was a lingering suspicion in the town that it was unwise to upset the bailiff or his wife, as if their emotional wellbeing carried more weight than others when it came to tipping the scales of eviction. Ruth assured Jane that no harm was done, but that was not enough. Jane would worry about this slight for the rest of the day; it would nag at her at four in the morning up until the next announcement of the names of the evicted.

It was important that they made this life work. Perhaps the Seizure would not last forever, and the rumours of a coming restoration were true. Perhaps it would even fall to the people of Lewes to lead the way in that restoration, as a model town, with their new ways of living with the Process. In which case their cooperation was vital. When she accepted the stripe, she did so not only because it represented survival at a time when survival was at stake but because James had persuaded her that if this experiment worked – and it was an experiment repeated in other modest towns across the world – then cooperation with the algorithm represented hope of sorts.

She hefted her oilcloth bag onto her shoulder, said goodbye to Jane, and continued on her rounds. Of course

Jane would not be evicted: the good mother of two healthy children. No metric of happiness could possibly benefit from the removal of someone like that.

Ruth walked up the twitten toward the motte-and-bailey castle at the heart of the town, strong and timeless atop a raised earthwork. The main street was quiet. The air was cool under the shadow of the keep. She walked up a cobbled path toward the Bowling Green. What did the Process make of her sadness? She knew what James would say: that the sadness was merely blue data and the Process would sort out the accompanying stimuli that caused the dip in sentiment, and so find a pattern to rectify it. But he was just the bailiff, and in all likelihood merely repeating what he had been told at the Institute.

She turned down a twitten, and here the shift in temperature from warm afternoon to bright cold evening was palpable; the surrounding hedges were overgrown, and the high branches of the trees entwined to form a dark green archway overhead. The twitten wall had crumbled back into a yard, forming a gap. The gap led into a small garden that had run to tall nettles, and contained a shed with a rusty corrugated iron roof. She felt a prickling in her stripe. There, padding slowly across the undulations of the roof, was a drone fox, sniffing left and right. Its brown pelt had not grown back where it had been striped, and its left eye was bloodshot, the eyelid swollen and half-curled in. Birdsong overhead, the distinctively arrhythmic jazzy birdsong of the Process; the sensation in her stripe changed from a pickling numbness to a fluid oozing, neither unpleasant nor unknown to her, the nodules giving up their temporary form to release their data. The drone fox shook its head as if to rid itself of an annoying fly or embarrassing memory, and then it stumbled, the legs on its left-hand side buckling under the weight of its body. Its flanks shivered, and the prickling in her stripe abated. Whatever sadness she felt had just been absorbed into the Process.

3

At the end of the village, the track was thick with overgrown honeysuckle bushes and hawthorn trees, with blackberry and rose bushes stripped of their fruit and hip. Hector stumbled through the branches and fell forward onto his palms. He glanced up at James, right hand grasping the rope, their gaze locked.

James offered his open palm. "We need to push on. Not far now."

The soldier pulled harder at the rope, a second experiment in volition. James took out his woodsman's hatchet, and removed the glinting edge from its leather sheath.

"You must stop struggling."

The soldier's eyes ranged around, ignoring James and the head of the axe, attending only to the equation of war in the ether. James heard it too, like a voice from a burning bush or a greeting from a strange animal. The implant partitioned his mind so that some thoughts came from outside of himself, from nature or machines. In this instance, the thoughts seemed to come from between the sun-flicked branches of an oak tree, and they concerned the mathematics of conflict, calculating the correlation between the lust for vengeance and the number of casualties or the vigour to fight against the loss of territory.

The crimson beads threaded through the soldier smouldered and he leapt at James, grappling his waist, so that they fell together. James felt a rush of heat from the soldier's skin; crimson beads melted to form blood, and the blood soaked through the bandages.

The two men struggled hand-to-hand. During the Seizure, James' only relief from redundancy had been his civil defence shifts. He knew how to subdue another man without causing unnecessary hurt. The Process fought like a roach on its back, poorly and unfairly, and could accidentally take an eye or sever an artery. James had to be careful. He hoisted the soldier up with ease, turned his face from his chemical breath, and threw him through the thicket and onto the greensward.

James climbed over the dry stone wall and drove Hector across the field, and then down into a wood. With the rope trailing behind him, the soldier was caught up in the momentum of the steep decline; he stumbled, and then fell head over heels over head. The bailiff followed at an implacable lope. The signal of the Process was weaker in the valley. After each fall, the soldier struggled to get up again.

The Institute lay somewhere within the wood. The old landmarks were concealed beneath unchecked growth. The sheep trough was familiar: a circular concrete divot holding a shallow mirror of rain and a reflection of the morning cloud. The edge of the grounds was marked by a wall of crumbling brick sheathed with grey lichen; it had been broken, here and there, by roots and branches. James heaved the soldier over the fallen brick, then scrambled after him into the wood.

The tall larch and beech trees made a vaulted ceiling. The light scattered by the leaves reminded him of the coloured patterns thrown by a stained glass window. He found serenity among the cool indifference of trees. A muntjac deer, small, with haunches higher than its withers, glanced at them through coppiced trunks, then darted away at their approach. James stepped through a bone-white configuration of fallen branches. So much dead wood. The soldier's blood solidified into crimson beads, and his expression grew heavy and docile. James hauled him through the bronze mulch. There was no fight in him anymore; the semblance of humanity caused by that outburst of will and determination was gone, and he had returned to his factory setting of diffident automaton.

The wood sloped downward. Smoke rose from a charcoal burner's camp pitched beside a stream. The kiln gave off its tarry trail. James dropped the soldier under a tarpaulin strung over a cooking fire and called out a greeting. Two grubby children in the brushwood watched but did not answer.

Hung from an iron hook stuck into the earth, a dixie pot boiled on the campfire, a stew of muntjac bones, nettles and cobnuts. James waited for the charcoal burner to emerge from his cat hole, and soon enough the man came out of the woods, adjusting his braces and wiping his hands clean upon a wet leaf. He greeted them with mannered courtesy. James inquired about the condition of the Institute. The charcoal burner shook his head.

"We don't go there anymore." He took a pocket knife and stirred the stew, poking at the venison. "They used to take two dozen sacks from me a month," he gestured toward the charcoal kiln and its lid of earth sections, strewn with bluebells and fern fronds. "Then about a year ago, they stopped coming out to meet me. I went to speak to the woman who runs it, Ms Drown, do you know her?"

James nodded. Alex Drown. The woman who had overseen his implant and made him into the bailiff.

"She told me they wouldn't be needing any more charcoal. Said they had made other arrangements. Bullshit. But I have learnt to mind my own business. Do you have any tobacco?"

The man mimed a pinch, his lean face streaked with charcoal, his collarless shirt ragged from being washed on river stones and dried on a branch. James shook his head.

"Does he have any snout?" The charcoal burner gestured at the soldier, who sat upon a log with his head bowed. The soldier did not respond.

"Your friend is very quiet," said the charcoal burner.

"Have you seen other soldiers in the woods?"

He shook his head. "It's not often I get to talk to a gentleman like yourself. When I go into town they aren't so friendly since the crash."

"The Seizure," corrected the bailiff.

"Is that what it's called now? The Seizure?" He speared a piece of venison and chewed over that thought. "The people in the Institute – I mean, the people who are left there – they're not really people anymore."

"In what way?"

"Ms Drown warned me not to return. That the staff and the inmates had been experimenting on one another. They were carrying them out on stretchers."

"Experimenting?"

"Poking around in *here*," the burner pointed to his own narrow skull. "I saw a figure through the windows of the great house, naked, about seven foot tall, and something wrong with his head. They do operations there."

"I know," said James, running his fingers through his hair. "Have you seen anything recently?"

"My sons went out there. You know what children are like. Wouldn't listen. They listen now. They came back shivering and white. I would move to a different wood except my kiln is here and the stream is good. A man gets lazy."

The charcoal burner tended to his kiln, dousing the conical pile with water so that it did not burn too hot; steam rushed forth and then slowed, drifting upward among the tall larch trees. The stew boiled away on the dixie.

"How are things in town?"

The charcoal burner was keen for gossip, for some connection with society. James thought of Lewes as he had left it that morning; quiet and self-contained, wood fires and malt steam from the brewery mingling with a curious mist. Lewes had been established over a thousand years earlier to take advantage of its situation: from the top of the Norman castle, a sentry could see seven miles south to the sea, west to Firle Beacon, and north, along the river to the chalk pit and the approach along the disused railway line. The town had two hearts, one high up by the castle, and the other lower down, in the lee of a chalk cliff face sharking free of the undulations of the Downs. It had been easy to erect barriers at each of the points of ingress, securing Lewes against any incursion of the evicted.

"The town has everything it needs," said the bailiff.

The charcoal burner gestured around at the woods.

"Except freedom."

"It has freedom."

The charcoal burner tapped the top of his head, meaning *the stripe*. "Matter of opinion."

James asked for directions to the Institute.

"Follow the wood down, and then turn west at the weir. That will bring you to the old house from the direction of the gardens. You'll have more visibility that way. If you follow the walls then you will end up in the bunkers around the back. That's the way my sons went. I would avoid that. You're welcome to stay for some stew. My wife will be back soon, and she'll be sorry she missed you."

"Perhaps upon my return."

The burner and his boys watched James go, pulling the soldier along behind him, Hector's face fixed in a thousand yard stare.

James followed the directions down to the river. At the shallow bridleway, the glide of the river appeared to reverse against the consecutive drags of stepping stones. In the lee of each stepping stone, the water bubbled and cohered into memory pools hemmed in by the swirl of the current, memories that were inseparable from the current yet appeared – if only briefly – to belong to an individual rock.

He had spent time at the Institute, first undergoing the implant, and then recovering from it. It had seemed the only way to get through the Seizure with any quality of life. He and Ruth had done very badly out of the collapse, and prior to that, the crisis. And then events accelerated.

No, James corrected himself, acceleration implies forward movement. Events lateralized. Events networked.

He had argued with Ruth about the meaning of the Seizure. She insisted that it was plain theft and exploitation. They argued about the onset of their obsolescence, what had been lost, what would never be. They argued about the state of the world before the crisis, or the collapse or the Seizure. James believed that they had been deluded as to the true nature of their society, whereas Ruth believed that the future they found themselves within was a lie, and that the past, and the way they had once been together, was the truth.

Throughout their arguments, events continued to slide sideways, in the same way that if he stood on the bank staring at the river's flow, it seemed as if the bank was moving backward while the river remained motionless.

Humans are astonishingly adaptable. A few years living within the Process and already it seemed as natural to him as the river's progress to the sea.

The soldier went splashing through the cold water of the bridleway; his features had the potential to be cunning, even demonic, if intelligence returned to them.

He hauled the soldier along a muddy path and through the trees he glimpsed the gothic castellations of the Institute: the roof with its eighty or so chimneys, the east wing covered with autumnal ivy, the west wing a turret and great Round Room. Between him and the house, there were three hundred yards or so of meadow ending in a haw-haw, and then a low courtyard wall. It was as if the Institute was below sea level, in a muggy stilted zone, with mosquitos in the air that made the scar on his scalp itch.

The foundations had been laid in the ninth century for a priory. The house had undergone a major renovation at the end of each of the previous three centuries so that it was a patchwork of architectural fashions covered in crimson lichen and vines. Time was fermenting here, becoming an intoxicant. The moon was high and so was the sun. He took the soldier by the hand and they walked together across the meadow. Atop the turret of the Round Room, taut silver sails rigged at oblique angles monitored the ether. Behind the windows, strange shadows passed to and fro.

He stood at the door and shouted Alex's name, then tested the handle. The door opened onto a hallway, a muddy black and white tiled floor interspersed with buckets and chamber pots to collect drips from the leaking roof. Murmurs and whispers came from a bright side room, and through a crack in the doorway he saw the painful movements of a tall and half-naked figure.

But it was Alex Drown who met him at the entrance of the Round Room. Her right eye was entirely bloodshot.

"James. You've come back."

"I've brought you something." He helped Hector into a seated position on the tiled floor. "I found him trapped in some barbed wire on the Downs. The wire was new."

She inspected the soldier, opened the pockets of his outfit, rooted around in his backpack, and looked inside his mouth and his ears.

"I'd say this one was made from archive photographs, reverse engineering from descendants, and something weirder."

She registered the name on the identity disc. "Has Hector been livelier than this?"

"He took a swing at me outside Glynde. The villagers said they had found other soldiers and brought them to you."

"We have half a dozen now. But Hector seems different, as if made from a more detailed pattern."

"Pattern from where?"

"Something weirder, as I said." She grinned at him. Her dark hair was short and ragged, cut by herself in the reflection of a grimy mirror. Her trouser suit had blood stains upon the collar. He noted the vinegary odour of stale female perspiration. Two villagers dressed in boiler suits and frayed grey lab coats arrived to take the soldier away.

"It's good to see you again, James."

"Your eye," he said.

"I know. Upgrades. We should never have augmented the hardware."

He didn't understand.

"The implants," she explained, reaching over to him, feeling through his hair for the scarred intake on the back on his skull. "We should have confined ourselves to hacking the software and not dabbled with the wiring. You live and learn. Every time Omega John upgrades me, my eyes bleed, my fingernails fall out and I lose my sense of balance. Will you join me in the Round Room?"

The Round Room was in a state of benign neglect. The dome of the rotunda was covered by a mural depicting characters from the history of the Institute. The other walls were slick with damp and the paint sloughed off them in silvered waves. Alex perched upon the edge of a heavy dark wooden desk and huddled into her suit jacket against the draught from the sash window frames.

"Do you mind if I ask Omega John to come in on this meeting?" Remnants of corporate dialect remained in Alex's speech. Before the Seizure, she had worked for a technology company called Monad.

An awkward half-naked figure, the same one that James had glimpsed on the way in, walked into the Round Room. He wore a bedsheet like a sash. Skin and bone iterated in a massy cauliflower-like clump at the base of his bald head. Perspiration welled on his sunken spotted chest. The arms were as pallid as wishbones, the shoulders like knuckles. He ran a dry tongue over chapped white lips before speaking.

Alex said, "No one understands the Process as well as Omega John."

Some parts of his body were young, some were old; he bared his strong white teeth in weak acknowledgment of her boilerplate praise.

"I think we've met," said James.

"When you had your implant. Time has been unkind to me since. I'm between longevity treatments." Omega John had a passive singsong voice. "The soldier you brought in, John Hector, was in the 32nd Field Ambulance in the Allied campaign against Turkey in the Great War, known variously as the Dardanelles campaign, the Battle of Gallipoli, or the Çanakkale. Hector landed at Suvla Bay in August 1915. He was a stretcher bearer. History tells us that he survived the campaign, but that is all. The other soldiers delivered to us also wore uniforms consistent with the landing at Suvla Bay but only two of them prior to Hector are the simulacra of particular men."

Alex clarified, "The first four were generic patterns. Like toy soldiers."

"Are you suggesting the Process is playing war?" James asked.

Omega John inhaled sharply. "You've spent too long in the town, bailiff. You are succumbing to the community's anthropomorphizing projection. The Process is a set of algorithms. It does not play."

Omega John wound the bed sheet tighter around his attenuated body.

"The unending Process reconciles the strivings of individuals within a framework of mutual benefit. Nothing more."

"Why has the Process not supplied you with clothes that fit?" asked James.

"We try to keep our needs outside of the Process," replied Omega John.

"Would you like my wife to make you an outfit?" asked James. "Ruth is a very good seamstress."

Omega John treated the offer with disdain, instead asking, "Does Ruth still mark the winter solstice by dangling the broken casings of mobile phones from the window frame so that the Process will not overlook you?"

"It doesn't mean that we believe."

"The Process requires neither your belief nor your observance. Just because it watches over you, it does not mean that it cares about you or even understands what you are."

"Who told the Process to make these soldiers?"

"No one programs the Process. It uses its data set to anticipate future need."

"We don't know why the Process is concerned with the First World War," said Alex quietly.

"There is precedent," continued Omega John. "The Process has created historical simulacra before. Last year, at a Process point in Totnes, in place of the expected allocation, a Methodist congregation and minister from Boston on August 26, 1873 were recreated in living detail. Then, on medicine day, the Process point contained the skin tent of the Reindeer Chuckchi people of the Kolyma district, early twentieth century. My first thought was that these simulacra were due to unusual agglomeration of needs in the town. Human desire is multifarious and liable to mutation. Bad input leads to bad output. However, I am coming round to the theory that prolonged exposure to human behaviour is introducing cognitive algorithms into the Process."

"It's becoming more like us?" guessed James.

"As we become more like it." Omega John took deep satisfaction in this thought.

"Artefacts such as the soldier – anomalies that seem superfluous but must meet some obscure buried need – provide an excellent opportunity to study the Process," said Alex.

"And people, too," said Omega John. "The Process is entirely responsive to people. It monitors and meets the needs of the people within it. Once sufficient data has been gathered on their past behaviour, it can infer, with increasing accuracy, future outcomes, future lives. People are evicted before they can create problems. The question is, does the Process manipulate the data set – that is, the people – to meet future needs that we are not yet cognizant of?"

James could not follow Omega John's reasoning; he was distracted by the malformed and botched arrangement of skull at the back of his head.

"What have you been doing to your brain?" asked James.

"I have undergone forty-eight procedures," said Omega John. "Twenty voluntary, twelve of them vindictive.

Fifteen were subsequently corrective; one, performed a long time ago, was particularly traumatic. My former rivals in the Institute took puerile delight in rearranging the regions of my global workspace."

"His mind," clarified Alex.

"And these pranks–" he pronounced the word with weary contempt "–had physiological side effects, particularly in the regulation of hormones."

"You're doing brain surgery for a joke?" asked James.

Alex's eyelids flickered, and she put her hand up to stop that train of thought.

"It's play, James. One of the characteristics of augmented intelligence is a love of play and the use of games to access insight."

"Is that what happened to your eye? Did someone play with it?"

"Without upgrades I would be out of the loop. As a manager, I have to be able to comprehend the research that goes on here, and the adjustment to our working practices brought about by augmentation has produced palpable gains in our understanding of the Process."

"And potentially even how to interact with it." The excitement that Omega John took in this prospect was evident in the way his fingers dithered.

"But the augmentations have left us physically deficient. That is why Omega John and I would like you to help us."

"I already have a role within the Process."

"We are not asking you to alter your role as bailiff. We want you to look after Hector, monitor him, report back as the Process gets stronger within him."

"It might be dangerous."

Alex took his hand. "It will be dangerous for everyone if the Process continues to produce these simulacra. An army will exceed the carrying capacity of the surroundings."

"What do you mean?"

"She is suggesting that the Process may utilize local low value resources in its recreation," said Omega John. His clarification did not help James' understanding, and noticing this, he wearily attempted the obvious. "We don't know how big its war will get. It may use the town and its inhabitants as raw materials."

Alex gripped his hand. "Omega John calls me irrational but I have a feeling that these things have a tendency to get out of hand."

"It is only when things get out of hand that they get interesting," said Omega John. He gathered his sheet around his emaciated marbled form. "Look after John Hector, bailiff. He is very important to us." Omega John made painfully slow progress from the Round Room.

Alone with Alex, James asked her what the Institute intended to do with the other soldiers that had been found

"Nothing," said Alex. "Not until you've spent some time with Hector. The soldiers are beyond the influence of the Process here. To study the Process' intentions in creating Hector, we need to observe his behaviour. Take him back to Lewes. Keep him close. Tell us what he does."

She led him out of the house and up a path to the Orangery where orderlies drank tea and the soldiers sat around despondent on long benches. There were four generic faces in a row – the toy soldiers she mentioned – and then a gap, and then the simulacra of individuals. Alex introduced two of them. Father Huxley, priest and archaeologist, and Professor Collinson, attached to the 32nd Field Ambulance. Neither stirred with recognition when Alex mentioned their names. James sniffed Collinson: Pears soap, dust, coffee and the sea. Every hair of his moustache had been effortlessly and automatically rendered. To think that Omega John scorned Ruth for her instinctive worship of the Process, when it could replicate the bodies of the long dead!

"These two men also survived the war," said Alex. "Might be a pattern. Too early to say."

"Would Hector have served alongside them?"

"Yes, Omega John said they were in the same ambulance. He's very knowledgeable about the war. I wanted to send you away with all three of them but Omega John reckons you will struggle to control even one."

Dusk in the walled garden, the air soft and coarse-grained, the shaggy cascade of ornamental conifers beside a faintly luminescent chalk path. The orderlies laid blankets around the shoulders of the manufactured men, seated dutifully on benches gazing out of the windows of the Orangery. With their ounces of volition, the men drew the blankets close around themselves.

He wondered about this gesture, a faint of echo of the way soldiers might behave, exhausted by battle and taking refuge. He turned to Alex.

"How does the Process make men with such accuracy?"

Alex was pouring tea into a china cup; she paused, studied him, one eye mute with blood, the other clear and questioning, and was about to answer when Omega John arrived, the wheels of his bath chair rattling over the paved entrance. His personal staff corrected his Russian fur hat, pulling it down over the bandages strung around his enlarged cranium. Amused by Alex's hesitation, Omega John answered for her.

"The men are made from sperm and blood. According to the alchemist Paracelsus, if sperm is left to putrefy in a horse's womb for forty days, then nourished with the arcanum of human blood, it will grow into something like a man."

Omega John wore a sheepskin sleeping bag that covered him from nape to toe, with thick tartan sleeves, from which jaundiced wrists and hands protruded. His orderlies wheeled him to their table.

The air in the Orangery cooled. Through the windows, evening stars appeared between darkening clouds. The orderlies waited at the periphery of the room. Drawn from the laypeople of Glynde, village life and the work of the Institute had been entwined for generations. They were protective of Omega John, as if servicing and prolonging his life imbued their existence with greater meaning.

The authority in Omega John's voice had been broken into many pieces and then reassembled. He talked like a man crossing a rock desert of fissures and cracks: with hesitation, dithering at each turn, then wearily leaping on the next point. The waxy sheen of his skin made him seem close to death, yet his teeth were much younger than his larynx, and new hair burst through the bandages here and there like strong gorse.

"My colleague in the Institute, Sunny Wu, is a forger of flesh, an expert in the Chinese skill of the counterfeit." He coughed violently, and accepted a handkerchief from his orderly. "Sunny Wu grew a living replica of his wife's body, though I suspect it was not from his sperm; she would never have allowed that."

The old man's laugh sounded like kernels being sieved.

"It is from Sunny Wu that the Process acquired the design of a manufactured body."

"But their minds?"

"Yes!" Omega John raised an index finger. "How to forge a mind? Impossible!"

Alex demurred. "We've simulated people before."

"Using digital technology." His pronunciation picked apart the bones of that phrase, leaving only his contempt for it. "Digital was a diversion, a distraction from the real work at hand."

A thought occurred to him, and his hand fluttered for James to come closer.

"How to communicate an experience directly, you see, from mind to mind – that is my life's work."

"Is it possible?"

"We've always known it's possible, bailiff. The Institute has had many successes in that area. The problem was how. The brain is not a transmitter. Simple as. And yet nonetheless the phenomenon exists. Observe. Alex, serve the bailiff some tea."

From a blue teapot, Alex poured him a cup of white tea, the prized first picking of the leaf, she explained, too subtle for his palette until the aftertaste of jasmine, and then, after another sip, he discerned the initial stages of the flavour, experienced it retrospectively.

Omega John worked his thin lips as if he too were savouring the tea, eyes closed, those long fingers playing the sound of the flavour upon the air.

"Yes, jasmine. I can tune into your implant so that your sensations are communicated directly from you to me."

James was sceptical. "Can you read my mind?"

"No. Vivid sensations, strong emotions, a powerful image. The implant puts you and I in harmony. Try something more personal."

He remembered Ruth, sobbing, the kitchen knife in her hand. She had reopened the library to chair a meeting about the potential for change offered by the crisis. Invited community leaders, turned her face to mankind and spoke with optimism against the turmoil. The meeting was broken up by the new police. A gangster policeman swaggered up onto the stage and took the microphone from her, feedback flooding the sound system. James fought his way through the crowd toward his wife. She was arguing with the gangster policeman; he did not bother to respond. From the stage he pointed out the cameras monitoring the crowd, reminded them of sanctions against illegal behaviour and ordered them to disperse. Later, in an argument over the worth of resistance, her shirt off, in her bra and skirt, Ruth picked up the knife to demonstrate the seriousness of her commitment, and the gesture was so futile, he realized that her anger was so heavy, it would crush her.

Omega John gazed at James, and then awoke from his reverie to the dryness of his mouth, the stiff numbness in his fingers.

"A powerful image of the humbling of a woman," he whispered. "Your wife, Ruth. Ripe with emotional content. Alex also has an implant. If you wished, you and Alex could share the same dream through me. Would you like that?"

Alex was gazing sideways at him, interested in his reaction.

"My implant is there solely so that I can perform my role as bailiff."

Omega John laughed. "Of course! Letting you dream would be letting a hammer design a house!"

At his request, they moved their tea party out to his garden, the orderlies carrying the table, chairs and tea set. The grounds of the old house were expansive; junctions were marked with sculptures, curved evocations of natural shapes in iron and wood, and there was a maze and a secret grove strung with lanterns. The lawn turned downhill toward a tidal estuary, the waters flowing back toward the house like a cat coming in at night, bringing a brackish air of mud and life's fresh rot. Omega John's garden consisted of terraces of vegetable beds, a winding path of Moroccan multicoloured tiles, and a Victorian hothouse containing an outsized biomass of rubber and banana trees, steam curling around their little party, water dripping from above. Omega John stopped at the fruit trees; with a short sharp knife, he cropped starfruit and mango, the former tart and sour, the latter sweet, for the party to pass among them. He did not eat himself, pleading "a quite impossible digestive system", but insisted that James and Alex sample the fruit so that he could taste it by proxy.

They left the hothouse through a covered passage and came into the high netting of an aviary.

"The beginning of my collection," he said. A tall tree rose to the top of the aviary, its branches smooth as carbon rods, their configurations unnatural in the way they bent back toward the trunk.

"A tree router. You may remember at the beginning of the Process that we planted one of these next to the school."

James sidled next to Alex, "Is this your work?"

"A collaboration between my employers and the Institute."

With two strong wing beats, a large rook settled on a near branch, its black eyes registering their appearance.

"He sees you," said Omega John. "The stripe stores that impression, and then it is carried through the router tree to the computational matter."

"Where is that kept?"

Omega John shrugged.

"Here and there. We dispersed it to ensure redundancy. Alex is the expert on that."

"Distributed computing. There's no centralization in nature, either. We're exploring correlations between the digital and biological. Some of them are merely analogous but significant findings indicate that, operationally, we can move data from one to the other. My employers tasked me with safeguarding their proprietorial algorithms in the event of failure and noise in the digital network. The Seizure was that event. I'd been tracking the work of the

Institute for a long time; they always seemed close to finding a way of running algorithms on a biological substrate, but they had a number of setbacks."

Omega John snorted humourlessly at this veiled reference.

"But it's more than a backup. Shifting our intellectual property into the biosphere has accelerated its evolution. Biofeedback is so much more granular than user behaviour."

The rook, having measured them with its regal gaze, gnawed briefly at the smooth rod of the branch, then flew up to a higher vantage point.

"We've restored the algorithm to its native habitat." Omega John's lips were dry, and he held an empty hand up into which an orderly placed a drink carton. "Biological processes are inherently algorithmic, designed by nature to solve computational problems across all levels of life: molecular, cellular and at the level of the organism; you, the rook, and then a group of organisms, your town." He could not puncture the carton with the sharp end of the white straw. The orderly performed this tiny act for him. Omega John took a single sip, shook his head, and handed it back. The fluid leaked out of the corner of his mouth, and had to be dabbed away.

"Nature uses algorithms to model the cost of behaviour in terms of energy. The biological sphere of our world is designed to compute. In nature, the mass behaviour of organism is an equation designed to arrive at optimal use of resources."

Their discussion became too technical for James; he knew it was for his benefit, that they hoped to impart some understanding of his situation so that he could perform his role within it. In all his visits to the Institute, all the way back to his convalescence when he was first fitted with the implant, he had never been to this part of the grounds. He pointed this out. Omega John sighed.

"The appearance of Hector is – as Alex used to so tiresomely say – a game changer." His contempt for the idiom of digital business was the closest he came to humour.

Alex said, "Making soldiers is not an optimal use of resources. It's more like a peacock's tail, a display of redundancy to advertise fitness to potential mates."

"Like art or war," explained Omega John. "We need to study the Process further, to catch up, as it has exceeded the limits of our understanding. That is where you come in."

"We want you to understand the importance of our work," said Alex. "In terms of the future."

He had long since lost interest in the future.

The path ended in a low white picket gate and fence, beyond which there was a single apple tree, a wicker chaise longue and a rusty hookah.

"My private garden. My sanctuary," said Omega John. His orderlies helped him to his feet. He bent over and knocked the gate off its latch, and shuffled in his sleeping bag to the chaise longue. "My work with the Process does not afford me as much time to think as I would like. I've been dallying with Paracelsus, a hero of mine. He was an independent thinker, a wanderer and iconoclast. He moved through colleges, dissatisfied by them all. He served as an army surgeon. A noble position to take, the healer amidst the war."

He beckoned to James, and then pointed out a small trowel to the bailiff.

"Dig," he commanded. "Dig here."

James ran his fingers across the soil, and finding earth with some give, he dug into it with the trowel, then set aside a section of soil.

"You'll have to reach inside," said Omega John. "Do you feel it?"

James slid his fingers into the mulch and, finding nothing other than soil and leaf matter, he set himself to lean deeper into the ground. His fingertips brushed against something smooth and dreadfully organic.

"That's it," said Omega John. "Careful now, reach in with both hands and bring it to the surface."

He dug in with his other hand, and grasped both edges of the thing, and it sagged in the middle as he lifted it up. Brushing aside the soil, it was a large organ of some sort, too large for a human, he guessed. He passed it over to Omega John, who located a stitched seam; he untied a knot, and unlaced the catgut so that the organ parted neatly, revealing a massy bloody interior. The smell of something fetid and fungal.

"Closer, look."

He felt thoughts reach out from his implant, the god stuff, the wisdom that came from without. Omega John was still talking about Paracelsus, how true wisdom lay in the discovery of the latent forces of Nature, but what he was showing James, what James saw wriggling in the horse's womb was a private vision: he saw tiny white homunculi, seven of them mewling with foetal features, their feet fused in a lazy tail; nestled in blood, the sperm of Omega John growing in his garden.

4

Hector stood naked and at ease in the bathroom. James washed him by candlelight, dressed him in a pair of homemade pyjamas, then led Hector to the cellar and lay him down to bed. In the weeks since they took him in, Hector's hair had grown out into dark curls, his haunted gaze relaxing into a casual tired regard.

Market day was bright and cool. The moss on the brickwork was white with frost. The stalls set up around the war monument ran along the connecting thorough-fares of Market Lane and School Hill. He stood behind his front door, at the bottom of the stairs, and listened to the town go about its business; everyone was so polite, almost reverentially so. The subtle nod of recognition that passed between the folk. A talent for forgetting is necessary to maintain civility. James stepped out of his house and into the throng, with Hector following dutifully behind.

The sounds of market day: hooves skittering cautiously upon cobblestones; the to-and-fro of barter echoing under the brickwork arches of the bell tower; the creak of burdened cart wheels. Produce was laid out on the pavement, root vegetables on upturned palettes attended to by the Dutch farmer from Welsummer. He couldn't remember her name. She was gnomish in three layers of woollens and a blue woollen beanie, black trousers tapering to sturdy boots. Three times outsiders had squatted at Welsummer, and twice he had chased them away with appeals to their good sense, only for the squatters to return in greater numbers. When the Process selected them for a third eviction, he went back in the armour and that was that. They were outsiders and one of them died under his iron tread. The farmer did not speak to him when he passed her by; her rough hands paused in their task of sorting bundles of rosemary and her gaze, rustic in duration, followed Hector.

Not all of the stalls were useful. Some townsfolk were there just to be part of something – the old men with broken suitcases full of foraged toys and bruised apples, the grey-haired women selling the surplus of their communes: old Coke bottles of bitter cider, hand-printed pamphlets, nettle jam and circuit boards. He sought out Piper's lad and his wares of dressed pheasant, squirrels and skinned rabbits. James bought two brace from the boy, noting his swollen fingers, bloodied from gutting, as they whiffled through the livid green notes of local currency. At the end of the transaction, James touched his heart to indicate his satisfaction and the lad did the same.

He walked the orderly line of repairmen with individual placards detailing skills offered and services required. This was residual behaviour, rendered unnecessary by the Process. Their skills and availability would be sorted algorithmically and bartered accordingly with other townspeople and their labour; that was how the Process generated the core work schedule for the town, and gave meaning to labour that had become meaningless. But the market had a role to play that was more than trade. It was a social occasion, a chance to get out, to see and be seen. The metrics of happiness required old rituals, old ways of doing things, and so time was set aside within the work schedule for the townspeople to make their own trades.

A repairman, bald and heavy, his stripe glistening with sweat, risked an ingratiating stoop before him.

"Do you have any little jobs you need doing around the place? I'm up this street next week repairing the roof of the town hall. It'd be no trouble." And then the bald man whispered, "It's free to the bailiff."

James ignored the offer, and went over to where Ruth stood in line with the other seamstresses. Her samples were slung over her arm: dresses, children's clothes, shirts and hair ribbons. He touched her hand, noting the calluses upon her fingertips, how they seemed so much older than her face; her hands were aged by all the midnights she spent at a table under the sash window, working her hand-turned sewing machine by candlelight. When the machine was hot with work, it gave off the frazzled lint and tobacco ghosts of its previous owner. She kissed him and then steered him away. His presence intimidated potential customers and she was intent upon securing a trade on market day.

At the war memorial, he pulled Hector to him so that they could read the names of local casualties of sundry wars. The longest entry was from the First World War.

"Here are the names of the dead, from your time."

Hector's pale grey eyes gazed obediently at the lettering and the numbers.

"Do you remember the war?"

Hector was close to finding his voice, his throat and mouth worked in anticipation of speaking.

"Do you remember anything? Why are you here?"

No answers to his questions, not yet.

They were interrupted by a woman in stout boots and a long brightly-coloured felt coat, of similar stature to James and therefore considerably taller than the stretcher bearer. This was Councillor Edith Von Pallandt.

"Is this him?" asked Edith, putting her hand upon Hector's clavicle so that she could appraise him. She gestured to her husband to come out of the crowd so that he too could examine the manufactured man. Baron Von Pallandt had shaved his grey hair close to the scalp to accentuate the raised central ridge of his stripe.

"What is your opinion of the stretcher bearer?" she asked her husband rhetorically.

"Not good, Edith."

"We need to talk about your soldier," she announced.

"He does not belong to me," said James.

"He lives in your house. He eats your food. He does eat, doesn't he?" For a vegetarian, her smile was distinctly carnivorous. "You are responsible for him. We live in a very delicate state of balance." Edith held both hands out palms flat, weighing out invisible forces. "When you consider who we have lost, we must be very careful as to who we gain. Have you found more of these soldiers on your patrols?"

"I have not been out since. The Institute told me to monitor Hector so I keep him with me at all times. I am afraid that if I take him back to the Downs, the Process will come on too quickly and we will lose him without learning anything."

"What do you hope to learn?"

"I am only doing as the Institute requested."

"Their request makes sense. You are our most qualified individual when it comes to the inhuman."

She didn't expect him to respond to her sarcasm and instead put her hand upon his arm by way of coercion.

"We are due another list of evictions." Her fingers pinched at her necklace for comfort.

"Already?"

"Yes. We thought we had reached a stable state but it seems not."

"We believe your soldier is the cause," said the Baron. "He is the new element."

The market day crowd pushed between them and against them. Edith put her hand up to indicate that they would speak no more of it in public, and he agreed to visit the council soon.

All the people of Lewes came into town for allocation day, keen to discover what the Process had in mind for their future. Would there be a box allocated to Hector too? If there was, did that mean the Process had intended all along for him to become a member of the folk? If Edith was right, and Hector was the cause of the increase in the number of evictions, then surely reason would dictate that Hector's name would be on the next eviction list. He shivered at the prospect of receiving the list; as Edith hinted, the dictation of the list was one of those moments when he was inhuman.

As noon approached, the people gathered down School Hill. James found Ruth among them. She shared her gains with him – a gallon of barley wine in exchange for two smocks, an agreement to unblock the waste pipe in return for running repairs to a family's clothes – and then, anxious for the allocation, they fell in step with the quickly moving crowd. Hector walked between them and Ruth took the soldier's hand.

"How has he been?"

"Something in him wants to speak," said James. Edith's remark, her hint that he was inhuman continued to nag at him. It was the way she did not expect him to respond; either she considered him slow-witted or perhaps she did not believe his feelings were of any concern.

"Was I ever like Hector?"

"When?"

"In the months after the implant." He remembered his room at the Institute, how Ruth had knitted a pair of gloves at his bedside throughout his convalescence. Every turn of the needle brought another part of him back into the pattern of his self.

"You were scattered. It took a while for you to come back. I was knitting you a pair of gloves and they were ready before you were."

"I remember the feel of the gloves on my hands and Alex explaining to me that the gloves were not part of me. Did I give up too much to become the bailiff?"

"Change is part of life."

"Edith said there will be more evictions."

Ruth looked at the ground. "It's so hard to know what is right."

"She said that I was inhuman." He put his hand on his wife's shoulder. "You will tell me, won't you, if I stop being me? You promised."

Her eyes quickly brimmed with tears, and she nodded quickly and wiped them away at the same time.

At the bottom of School Hill, the market day crowd merged with the men and women trooping in from the outlying estates and villages, their particular district denoted by the patterns upon their baggy knitted jumpers: yellow and black for Nevill, the black and white of Cliffe, the red and black of Southover, the purple and black of Glynde, and so on, as far afield as the blue and white of Isfield. Children rode on the back of empty carts, the whites of their eyes shining in lean dirty faces. Ruth's hand tightened around his. They found their place among the people and walked over the bridge and to the allocation point.

Outside the old supermarket, peeling posters showed bleached photographs of bygone normality, goods and prices, smiling faces, times of plenty, the strangeness of the lost everyday. Even the markings of the car park – sigils depicting family units and disability – evoked a peculiar nostalgia. The building was a low single-storey warehouse,

shuttered and silent. The people at the front of the crowd
settled at the entrance, and the rest fell into an easy
dawdle. He tried to remember what it used to be like here
but he had almost no specific memories of shopping, just
so many dreams of unthinking gliding automation.

The shutters rattled up. The aisles were organized
according to district and then, within that scheme,
alphabetical order of family name. Stacked upon the
shelves, the transparent boxes holding each citizen's
allocation from the Process. The marshals supervised the
people as they filed in and took what had been provided
for them. The boxes were transparent so that each person
could see what another had been given. The boxes
contained some local currency, with the rest of the
contents specific to each citizen, usually raw materials for
their work – new tools, medicines, ammunition, and, in
Ruth's case, yards of cloth and cotton thread. The Process
aggregated the needs and desires of the townspeople for
clothes, scored them alongside Ruth's requirements, and
arranged barter of goods and services accordingly.

The town's currency was for discretionary goods, a sop
to the lost pleasures of shopping. In addition to barter, the
workload also included tasks involved in the upkeep of the
town: which repairs to perform or supervise, repairs to old
buildings and new ones, water supply and sewage, fences
and security posts. Every man and woman had their
allocation of tasks in maintaining the infrastructure of
Lewes. Then there were envelopes holding private
communications from the Process. These were two or
three lines of typescript offering solace or advice on
personal matters, consisting mostly of quotations of
commonplace sentiment with the occasional aberrant
glitchy phrase.

Ruth showed him the cloth that she had been allocated,
white linen for the gowns of lamentation, and yards of

black crepe, black silk and black lace.

"Were there instructions?"

She nodded. Her mouth was small and set. He asked her what the instructions were. She shook her head.

He looked for Hector's allocation, scanning through the shelves set aside for his district. There was no sign of a box for the stretcher bearer; he did not require much by way of food but his presence did upset the fine balance of their allocation. The shelves were mostly empty and a few townsfolk, dissatisfied with their lot, wandered the aisles in memory of the days when there was a manager they could complain or appeal to. He liked to collect his box last so that any curious townsperson could check what he had been given and know that the bailiff did not receive any special treatment. Perhaps Hector's box had been put with his allocation.

He was connected to the stretcher bearer in a way that he hadn't considered before. He could be blithe in that way, too quick to adapt to the new normal. The stretcher bearer had been lying on the wire when he found him. On his patrol route. His planned patrol route. The Process knew he would be there. Knew he would find the stretcher bearer. The Institute had asked him to look after the stretcher bearer so that he could be studied, but perhaps he'd already been given those very orders. Hector's presence in his life suggested that a change in his workload lay ahead, perhaps even a revision of the role of bailiff itself. He had thoroughly adapted to being the bailiff – no, more than that, he had given up so much of himself to live this role that change could only be negative judgement on his performance.

The townspeople assumed the role of bailiff was a position of power and responsibility. They were half right. He was certainly responsible. Patrol was easy, being tall and strong and brooding protectively around the town.

But Eviction Night took an increasing toll on him, the kind of losses only he would notice, numb patches in conversation where he simply didn't know what to say. Some memories had been amputated, their experiential content mussed up and obscure, but their emotional content remaining as a sharp and persistent pain like a phantom limb. And he noticed that he wasn't funny anymore. He used to make Ruth laugh and could always bring her back to him with his sad funny blue eyes. The implant affected his sleep patterns and he had aged dreadfully around the eyes, the skin around his ocular sockets shadow-stained and wrinkled.

He came to the shelf where normally he would find his transparent box of goods and tasks. But the shelf was empty. No box for Hector, and no box for James. He stared numbly at the absence, then looked on the shelves above and below, and around the back. Not an oversight, not an accidental omission, but part of a forming pattern. A pattern of absences, hollowing him out.

5

The caretaker and his team cleared away the remnants of market day, shovelling up rind and manure, their breath steaming with the exertion of the work. The caretaker chivvied on his work gang, and then, catching sight of James and Hector on the opposite pavement, bobbed his yeoman's head deferentially, his stripe visible through his hair's thinning ranks.

"Where are you off to, bailiff?"

"On my way to the moot to get my orders, Terry."

Terry appreciated his pragmatism.

"You do what you have to do."

Terry took a tobacco pouch from his dungarees and rolled himself a cigarette, picking out bits of leaf. He licked the papers and raised his eyebrows at Hector.

"How is the stretcher bearer working out?"

James put his arm around Hector and brought him close.

"You were in the army, Terry. What do you think?"

Terry shook his head. "They were brave lads, the stretcher bearers. They went under fire to get the wounded out of the front line and back to the aid post. But as to what he's doing here, it's well beyond me."

Terry took them to the top of a twitten, one of the

narrow steep alleyways twisting inside the town, secretive trenches of flint and brick walls. From this elevated aspect, he pointed a few miles south, beyond the old road and the floodplain, drawing their gaze to a distant stream of smoke rising from two thin chimneys in Newhaven.

"Another new factory, and it's been running day and night these last three weeks."

"I saw it from Firle Beacon."

"Who's out there?"

"No one as far as I know. I evicted them all. It's the Process."

Terry shook his head at the prospect and lit his cigarette. The tobacco smelt faintly of bourbon, the smoke a bluish speech balloon in the cold air. Terry had talked about his tobacco plants many times, how he grew them in the shed, cropped the leaves before first frost, pressed them with house bricks, shredded the compact lump with a kitchen knife then dried the long hairy strands to his own particular taste.

"If you'd have told me that this is how I was going to spend the rest of my days..." Terry didn't finish the thought, out of superstition. People had grown superstitious about complaining. In the aftermath of the Seizure, complaining was socially unacceptable, an indication, James felt, that the town was maturing. Whinging was a symptom of powerlessness, and within the Process everyone mattered, everyone had a role to play.

The stretcher bearer reached out and took Terry's tobacco pouch from his top pocket. The men watched as Hector casually peeled out a paper, lay a hairy trail of homegrown tobacco upon it, then rolled and licked the cigarette tight in one quick movement. Terry lit a match for the soldier, the quick flame echoing off the flint walls. Hector, cigarette between his lips, closed his eyes in bliss. He smoked quietly and withdrawn, the whites of his eyes fierce in sunken orbits. Terry went to speak but James hushed him: this was new behaviour. The act of smoking produced an expression akin to contemplation. Hector joined them in gazing across the night to the distant factory.

"Being high up makes the signal stronger," guessed Terry. "Have you tried taking him to the top of the castle?"

They crossed the high street and passed through the gatehouse. Hector overtook Terry at a jog. With athletic verve, he leapt over the dry-stone wall onto the hallowed grass of the bowling green. The way he walked and smoked, his cocky manner in looking back at Terry and James, was that of a young man in his early twenties; his walk changed from the exhausted trudge of the trench rat to a deliberate Indian step, in which each foot was placed, toe first, upon the earth.

The bowling green was three hundred years old, the dip and rise of its turf an echo of the waveform of the Downs. Hector found a spot and sat down cross-legged.

James climbed over a low wall and Terry followed.

"Hector…" began James.

Hector opened his eyes and said, "I will not fight."

James crouched close to the soldier's sharp features. "Fight who?"

The stretcher bearer spoke in earnest to surrounding phantoms, as if he addressed the Process itself.

"I will not fight," Hector said with conviction. "But I will serve."

"Who will you serve?"

"I will serve this land but not your country, I will serve the people but not their rulers." He finished smoking his cigarette. "I am not afraid of anything and I will not fight."

Terry took off his jacket and lay it across Hector's narrow shoulders. "The lad's a pacifist."

"Why is he in uniform, then?"

"Some of the conchies were sent to the front as stretcher bearers."

"It doesn't sound like he was sent to fight. More like he volunteered."

"It makes no sense." A note of anger in Terry's voice. "Why, when we're all on the bones of our backside, build something as complicated as a man? It's not like we're short of people."

"Careful," said James.

Terry turned away, and kicked at the turf, composing himself with a couple of brisk pulls on his cigarette.

"It's not a crime to ask why. I don't complain. I do my tasks. But this way of life will end, just like the old ways ended. A government will take us back, and want a reckoning. If we go too far, then we won't be able to come back."

He wondered if there could ever be a reckoning for what had happened during the Seizure. For what he had done. Or rather, for what had been done through him. Evictions, theft, violence. The implant made him into an instrument of the Process. He had wanted to ask Ruth if the people were afraid of him. If she was afraid of him.

Oblique winter sunlight filled the narrow main street. The silhouettes of prison chimneys against the darkening Western Downs. To the east, the night advanced over the ditches and burial mounds of Mount Caburn. The town huddled within the lie of the land.

Hector finished his cigarette and was silent. They waited for him to speak again but he did not. James pulled the stretcher bearer to his feet. Terry asked the questions that had been bothering him: what did the arrival of the soldier mean? Were there more soldiers to come? Would he be evicted?

"There will be answers," said James. "But there may not be answers for us."

The moot was in the Town Hall. Terry left them at the door. It was no place for the likes of him. James led the way by candlelight, down dark, damp corridors, Hector padding behind, their approach sending mice skittering back into the skirting boards.

They came into a gaslit room where a few men and women, the ombudsmen of the estates of Lewes, were whispering as they waited for the evictions to be announced. The ombudsmen were dressed in their district colours: a burly biker from Cliffe in a black and white neckerchief; a former office worker from Southover in red and black stripes with a smuggler's hooped earring, a sign that with the Seizure the man had returned to undergraduate ways; an elderly couple in red military tunics who spoke with the confident enunciation of barristers, and so on, through each of the seven districts of Lewes. Individual names drifted in and out of James' recollection; some days he woke up in Lewes and could not remember the name of anyone in the town. The ombudsmen were reluctantly deferential to him, muttering "bailiff" as he walked through the room. He did not acknowledge them. He noted the prickling suspicion and resentment the ombudsmen showed toward Hector, then closed the wooden doors behind him.

Edith Von Pallandt convened the moot with rote phrases.

"Nothing is decided in this council. This moot exists solely for us to bear witness to the unfolding of the Process and to share our experiences." The introduction complete, Edith peered over the edge of her half-moon glasses at the bailiff and Hector. With remission, her hair had returned in long curls, and she had dyed it with a preparation of henna and indigo. Her nose and chin were strong, her eyes motherly and turned down at the ends. She was not a leader, she would explain, if asked to perform as one;

rather she was a catalyst, or a conduit.

The meeting opened with a polite discussion of the latest allocation, the orderly manner of its passing, the usual suspects who had dared to appear dissatisfied with their lot. Joe, the doctor, spoke about the health of the town, the status of the sick, the number of the dead and the newborn. The death rate – after an initial spike during the Seizure – had bottomed out and the health of the town markedly improved.

Joe, bald and youthful, explained, "I don't know whether it is due to the medicine that the Process manufactures, or the more active lifestyle of the town, or even a consequence of closer community bonds, but we don't see the same incidence of physical or mental illness as before. Take our rehousing of young families in the larger houses of older residents; the drop in depression among the over-65s directly correlates to that policy. Before the Seizure, most of my pensioners were on antidepressants. Not anymore. The community life is like a placebo. It has a positive effect but we don't know exactly how or why. I suspect that if we could extract the nature of this benefit from the Process it would change how we organize societies."

"So this is a sane town," said Edith.

The doctor could not tell if she was summarizing his conclusions or questioning them. "It is a healthy town," he replied. This pronouncement caused him discomfort, and when the attention of the others moved on, James saw a twinge of shame on the doctor's face.

"Is the sanity confined to Lewes?" This question came from the head of schools, Carla. The dark, sallow indentations beneath her eyes were a contrast to the doctor's clean-shaven vigour.

"It's a difficult comparison to make," said Alex Drown. The receiving of the eviction list required her expertise.

She had showered and brushed her hair into a boyish swept-aside fringe.

"The value of the data grown here far exceeds that of the rest of the country. Lewesians are so minutely observed, known so deeply and broadly by the Process, that crude categorizations such as nationality no longer hold sway."

"Meaning?" asked Joe.

"Meaning that in the rest of the country the government organizations that used to collect this kind of data are gone, and that ways of storing and analyzing that data are compromised," continued Alex. "The digital datasphere is polluted and, while some digital networks thrive in quarantine, any attempt to make them open and free again brings about undesirable outcomes: all noise, no signal. As my colleagues are fond of pointing out, these days the cloud is full of thunder but no lightning."

Joe's face remained immobile, waiting for clarification.

Alex smiled, "Meaning you won't be getting the internet back any time soon, if indeed it still exists in the form that we remember it."

"Has anyone been to London lately?" asked Edith.

James said, "One of the evicted families is working out in Glynde. They came back from London."

"I like to hear stories of London," said Edith. "Any news of its misfortunes would reassure me that we made the right decision."

"A character flaw of yours," said the baron, stroking the hand of his wife.

"London is too big to fail," said Alex. "Everything and everyone will be sacrificed to preserve it."

"If you are looking for trouble, then go north." This from Angus, the *douanier*, keeper of the border. Angus also had an implant. Both he and James were big genial men who, under the control of the implant, had committed violence on behalf of the community. No guilt and no bias, that was the genius of the system. When James evicted families he was not in control of his actions, and was a mere vessel for the will of the town. When the *douanier* set fire to an encampment that strayed too close to the perimeter, or beat back weeping mothers with their babes in arms, he did so blank-eyed.

"I heard that Middlesbrough failed to reach its reserve price," said the *douanier*. "They have a month before the deadline and then they'll be put into special measures."

The *douanier* picked up news of the outside world from the people who passed by. Radio signals from outside could not penetrate the atmospheric soup of the Process.

"Are we to expect more migrants at the gate?" Edith asked him, although her glance paused pointedly at Hector.

"If it's a cold spring," said the *douanier*.

Broad-shouldered and powerfully muscled, the *douanier* was a genteel enforcer; before the Seizure, he had been a silversmith. It was Edith's idea to call him the *douanier* rather than the town guard, or the man-at-arms, or the bouncer; the gentility of the French word made the act of exclusion appear more refined. An advantage of the implants was that, once the necessary violence had been performed, men like Angus and James returned to their identities as reasonable, biddable citizens. In the afternoons, the *douanier* repaired jewellery, his great strength focused upon tiny acts of beauty.

"People keep coming," he said, sadly. "We give them sandwiches and send them on their way."

The baron leant back and nodded sagely. "And if they do not accept the sandwiches, your implant takes over and the Process delivers the necessary force. The Process spares you the moral responsibility of your acts, and spares us from living in fear of you. The quality of people can thrive, whereas in the past we merely cultivated quantity. This is the purpose of the Process."

Baron Von Pallandt luxuriated in committing this heresy against his long-lost liberalism.

"I don't think that is the purpose," said Alex Drown.

"Are you going to lecture me?" The baron appeared amused by the prospect. "You sold us to the Process, you can hardly complain when we take pleasure in it."

"I don't object to your evident delight. I just don't believe in your interpretation of the Process."

"What insight can the Institute offer us?" replied the baron. Before the Seizure, Edith and the baron had actively prepared for social collapse, had forearmed themselves against it, and been arrested for foretelling it on the streets of London; that they enjoyed being proved so thoroughly right was hard to ignore.

"I don't believe the Process is refining the inhabitants of this town and discarding the materials it cannot work with." Alex adjusted her glasses. James noted that the bloodstains had been scrubbed out of her collar.

"Aren't we ignoring the obvious?" said Edith. "The reason everyone is so healthy is that the Process predicted who would fall sick and evicted them in the first months."

Joe nodded. "The Process discovers illness before I do. Before the patients themselves. It knows our fate."

"The Process is an iterative, incremental framework for human interaction powered by complete access to everything we feel, say and do," Alex reminded them. "And, yes, Joe, it is predictive. It monitors, learns from and anticipates our needs. The Process is partly composed of algorithms and associated data sets that evolved under the pressure of the needs of billions of consumers, salvaged from the internet and transferred to our biotech. The first algorithms of mass observation screened humans for outliers, specifically patterns of behaviour associated with terrorism. It was our genius to use those same methods to screen for behaviour that was social positive rather than social negative, and use it to reinforce that behaviour."

"And we need eviction to enforce socially positive behaviour?" asked the baron.

Carla was shocked. "Eviction is not a need! Children in my school have lost their parents. Nobody needs that. Who could need that?"

"Not such a sane town, after all," said Edith.

"I don't understand your argument." The baron turned his long weathered face back to Alex Drown. "That these people are cast out of their homes for their own good? Or that our town needs the prospect of punishment – no matter how arbitrary – to function?" The question had the soft 'g' and trilled 'r' of the North Brabant accent, a remnant of the baron's childhood on the family estate in Eerde.

Alex said, "The Seizure was a response to the declining value of labour among the majority of people in the West. Put simply, we needed to find, for people like yourselves, an alternative mechanism to markets for meeting needs and driving production. Lewes was fortunate because, while the value of the labour of its citizens approaches zero, the data that can be harvested from you and used to refine the Process has a reasonably high value."

"We are *interesting*," said the baron.

"But not in the ways that you would like to be," said Edith.

Alex Drown continued, "The Process is constantly evolving. We've established thirty-four behavioural patterns within the Process consistent with algorithms that were extant prior to the Seizure, some from financial services, dating agencies, retailers, market research, some from national health monitoring, some from national security agencies of various nations, one from our own lifestreaming and experiential tagging project, and so on. But new patterns are emerging."

The baron slapped the table with mock amusement. "So how can you be confident of its intentions? Oh, excuse me, I forgot. I must not speak of intentions. That would be teleologically unsound of me, wouldn't it? What would we do without the Institute to counsel us on our flawed ways of thinking? Let me try a different tack: what does the Institute make of the appearance of this stretcher bearer?"

"The bailiff is monitoring the soldier for us. We await his report."

The council turned to James and Hector. Edith gestured for James to come forward. He stood up but Hector stepped ahead of him to stand in full attention before the conference table. The doctor inspected the physiognomy of Hector, testing the plasticity of his skin, the resistance of his flesh, the ridged sinews of his forearms. He sniffed around the chest, and peered into the pupils.

"This is an obscenity," said Joe. "To expend such resources in times of austerity is a moral offence."

"Art is never a moral offence," announced the baron.

"You approve?"

"I do," said the baron. "The Process has become an artist."

"The appearance of this soldier makes a mockery of our sacrifice," said Angus. The *douanier* had relatives on the other side of the fence, scattered in encampments throughout the Downs; James had not needed to evict them because the implant prevented Angus from letting them through the gates.

Edith sought more opinions from around the table. The manufacture of the stretcher bearer may seem to be an affront to the virtue of frugality, but to question the Process was to return to the whinging of democracy, and that made them uneasy.

"He speaks too," said James.

Alex leant forward. "He actually spoke to you?"

"He said he was a pacifist."

Edith was moved by the thought of a pacifist soldier. She came around from behind the table to take Hector's hands in hers.

"Poor, poor boy," she comforted him. He did not respond to her touch.

From the other side of the door came an urgent knocking and a plea to know what was going on in the meeting.

"The ombudsmen are impatient for the eviction list," said James.

"They want to be put out of their misery," said the baron.

Edith let go of Hector's hands. She opened the doors to the ombudsmen. The room filled up with the representatives of the districts, and they were, with one exception from Southover, Lewesians who could trace their ancestry in the town back four or five generations – at least. By contrast, the council was mostly made up of outsiders, people who had chosen to live in Lewes rather than being born into it.

The *douanier* secured the door while James seated himself before the ledger of the evicted, fountain pen in hand. Alex and the doctor set about preparing him. Alex whispered an unlocking sequence into his ear while the doctor took out his syringe case and administered neuroceuticals to make the data flow more easily.

Edith, the incorrigible old hippy, took James' hands in hers as the Process began. He heard algorithms in the heft of the table and flickering in the gaslight. The implant made him into a pantheist, aware of the spirit in each and every material thing. The moon defined and initialized the beliefspace of the algorithm. And as his mother used to say, If beliefspace = 1 then mutate_with_inf (candidate, beliefs, minmax) else halt. If g is greater than or less than six then halt.

Decoherence.

G drew its value from the number of stars visible through the small black window in his bedroom and from the first vector of the last known location of his mother.

Def update_beliefspace.

The substance of his consciousness and the stuff of the universe were revealed portions of the absolute. Godstuff flowed out of the implant and his fingertips trembled with interconnections between himself, other people and the land. The approach of something transcendental. A shell explosion is a flash of inspiration. The undulation of long grass in the night wind. A father's intemperate chastisement of his son. A man in short trousers and a hooded jerkin walking alone across the Downs, whistling a hiking tune. The vast current of things. The trenches to come, marks in the earth where the future will break. Interconnections vaguely apprehended. Deeper than the soul of individuals lie thoughts too vast for language. Evil will excavate the truth more rapidly than Good. A dirge sung over the ruins.

He was staring into Edith Von Pallandt's face and she was afraid.

Mutate a factor and run the algorithm again.

The names of the evicted flowed from his pen. A quick act of automatic writing, his hand moving steadily, one name to a line, twelve lines in all. Ruth's needles knitted him together. It was over, the implant shut down and the tendrils of god stuff slithered out of him.

The ombudsmen shifted anxiously: they had been drawn from the ranks of truculent and sceptical dissenters, chatboard trolls, market gossips, and barroom nihilists whose role was now to witness the giving of the names.

The room was heady with their beefy odour of homemade soap and damp woollens.

Twelve names in the ledger.

The Cliffe ombudsman cried out.

"But this one is a child!"

There, his finger on the page, smudging still-wet ink. Agnes Bowles. She was to be evicted along with her parents and her little brother, Euan.

"She's ten years old!"

"We can't evict children!" Carla was beside herself.

The vast thoughts and scattered images and sense of interconnectedness faded, and he came to in the garishly-coloured room, where he registered human stink and sweat quivering on moustache hairs. People. After the state of grace, he always felt mournful and misanthropic. They asked him what they should do about the child. Surely they could not follow normal eviction procedure. The town would never accept it. The Process had to be questioned. But there was no love in him for anyone and he just wanted to go home. Edith tried to detain him, but he shook her off and warned her away.

James and Hector went outside onto the high street. The evening was cold and still, the street illuminated by high burning braziers. Alex Drown was waiting for them.

"The soldier is a pacifist," she said.

"He said that he would not fight."

"You and Hector are part of an ongoing thought. We must think of him in terms of yourself, your connection to him, what the Process is trying to communicate through that contact between you and him."

"Under the influence of the implant, I saw images of the war."

"It's coming," she said.

"Are you staying in Lewes tonight?" he asked.

She shook her head.

"I will walk back across the Downs."

"It's five miles across dark country. You're not afraid to be out there on your own?"

She looked back at the town hall, as the ombudsmen filed out, and then up at him.

"There's plenty to be afraid of here, bailiff."

6

Ruth resented making men's clothes. She put her arms around James and took his chest measurement then withdrew when he returned the gesture. On her wrist, she wore a small cushion of pins, a sign that he should keep his distance, that she had no patience for him right now.

The choral gowns of lamentation, a dozen hooded linen ghosts, hung in a line across the living room, their breasts rent during the last eviction and requiring repair. She inspected each gown in turn, and, with pins between her lips, made quick notes with a small pencil. It was the week before eviction and everyone had a job to do. The black silk and lace remained untouched in its transparent box.

After James cleared away the lunch plates, Ruth went down to the communal kitchen to put in her loaves and check the stockpot. The kitchen in their house was small with only a firebox for cooking and an improvised vent that let in the cold. Narrow and with broken chipboard, the kitchen had been designed for heating up ready meals after a day at the office, for whipping up fairy cakes or grilling fish fingers, not for baking bread, preserving fruit, hanging game, fermenting cider, cultivating yoghurt, and all the other cooking techniques they employed.

Sensing her annoyance, James boiled water upon the firebox and made tea from a hedgerow leaf bound in a small stained muslin sack. She drank a mouthful and gave the rest to Hector. She was cross. No, not cross. To describe her mood as cross would only annoy her more. She could not forgive him for the names that had appeared on the eviction list.

"I know the Bowles family," said Ruth.

He said nothing.

"Agnes is beautiful and bright and her brother, Euan, who is four, is blond and very serious. The family made sacrifices during the Seizure and accepted reallocated housing in Malling even though they owned a nice place in the centre of town. The father, Tom, built a wooden shelter at the school so that in the summer the children could have lessons outdoors. How will we survive if we evict a family like the Bowles? It makes no sense."

He was staring out of the window, drinking his tea.

"What are you saying?"

"The Process is supposed to create absolute fairness. But can you give me one good reason why the Bowles family are to be evicted whereas any number of frankly useless individuals are still here?"

"What are you saying to me? What do you expect me to do about it?"

"You've met the family. At the lido. Do you remember?"

"No."

"It was last summer. We had a picnic. You bought us popcorn. Their boy, Euan, kicked a ball at you. He wanted to play."

"I don't remember them," he said.

"Then there must be something wrong with you," said Ruth.

Through the window, an unharnessed horse loitered in the empty street. He wondered where the rider was. Ruth would not be receptive to him changing the subject. Snow was coming, and he anticipated waking up tomorrow to discover the horse and the town erased.

"Do you think there is something wrong with me?" he asked.

"I'm tired," she said. "Is there something wrong with you?"

"You are angry."

It took her a moment to master herself. "You told me anger could get me evicted."

"That's just something I say to keep the peace. No one knows what makes a difference to eviction. Apart from the obvious. Do you remember Mr Farncombe? A debtor. And a bad heart. He clearly had to go. Do you remember how he chained himself to the radiator? I had pull the whole room apart."

"You remember Mr Farncombe, but not the Bowles?"

"I remember all the evictions. It is a very vivid time for me. The adrenalin, the confrontation, the strangeness of being there but not being in control. I almost tore Farncombe in half because the Process hadn't registered that, when I took hold of him, he was tied down."

"He might have considered that a mercy."

"Not at all. The *douanier* told me that Farncombe's friends from Brighton came and got him. He's holed up with them in an old hotel on the front. There is always life after eviction. The Bowles family will be fine. Somebody on the outside, some old friend or a lord who wants a young family on his land, will take them in."

"If it is so hospitable out there, why did Farncombe chain himself to the radiator? Did you ask yourself that?"

"He was afraid of change."

"Should I tell Agnes not to be afraid?"

"Tell her not to resist."

Ruth returned to her sewing machine. With one hand,

she spun the mechanism and with the other, held the
linen gown so that the needle completed the seam, and
sealed off their conversation.

No one is indispensable.

His boss taught him that, a long time ago, when he first
worked in an office. He never quite believed it, always felt
there was something exceptional about his insight and his
talent, right up until the point they dispensed with him,
and then with his boss. He went on to teach business to
students, or was it genetics? He was not nostalgic for the
lost age of jobs; in retrospect, it seemed an arbitrary sorting
mechanism for his class. They made nothing but money,
and towards the end, not even that. He heard of a bank
that fired all its clients because their algorithm could make
more money without them. People ceased to be a vital
component of the economic system. To call what
happened next a collapse or a Seizure was to speak from
an anthropic perspective. From the point of view of the
financial instruments themselves, the system was thriving.

The Seizure was a long time coming; like dementia, its
progress was marked by mood changes, problems with
reasoning and memory loss. The wobble, the General
Strike, the crash, the recovery, the second crash, the
collapse, the hope, the end of hope, the chaos and then
Seizure: it lasted for so long that it was normal right up
until *it really wasn't anymore*. The government sold
redundant regions of the nation for private development
and he helped maintain order. An archipelago of
prosperity arose. Islands within an island. He didn't sleep
much to begin with, kept awake by wine-deranged
financial calculations at four in the morning, crazed escape
plans, the rigmarole of anxiety. During sleep, the mind
sorts through the flotsam and jetsam of the day to decide
what is worth committing to memory, and what can be
discarded, and with broken sleep comes broken memories.

No one is even necessary.

Lewes was one of the land assets acquired by an Asian fund algorithm. Alex had been tasked with the experimental transfer of the intellectual copyright of big tech into nature, and put together a deal with the Institute. She explained it to him on numerous occasions but all he remembered was the phrase "black box bio-technology".

"Does this mean we now live inside the black box?"

Bioware for the townspeople was a condition of the contract, the stripe for all, and the implant for a few. He volunteered because he was strong, had no dependents and because he prided himself on his adaptability. He questioned Alex Drown at the very beginning, when she was advising the council on their decision.

"The Process will make a fair society," she explained. "Instead of using market forces to distribute goods to meet needs, the Process monitors the lifestream and physiological condition of each individual within it, and then manufactures and distributes the required goods. The overriding imperative is fairness."

"Can you define fairness?"

She could. "Fairness is composed of over a hundred and twenty metrics; these are simplified using Fourier transforms into a short stream of numbers, and then the Process monitors and nudges these metrics when they exceed or fall into unacceptable levels."

"Into unfairness."

"Yes."

"What if we want to come out of the Process? How do we do that?"

"The contract is very clear. The town has to see the Process through to its next iteration. There is no get-out clause. If the Process is interrupted in its beta phase then the asset loses value."

"By the asset, do you mean the town?"

"The asset is the people and the land unified with the Process. Each component of the asset, on its own, is of negligible value."

"Is there someone we can appeal to, if we get desperate?"

"The Process," said Alex.

"What if I change my mind?"

"Irrevocable decisions form character, James," said Alex. "It's a hard decision but by your age, you should have used up all the easy ones."

After the procedure, he awoke in the Institute. His scalp itched with the implant. Alex tuned him into the Process; he felt a surge of heat at the base of his skull, and staggered around the overgrown lawn of the stately home waiting for his head to explode.

The window of their flat, set on the curved corner of the building, was exposed to the winter gale. It was cold to the touch. In the street below, the horse turned and turned again then set off with deranged resolve down Market Street. He put on another layer of clothes and spent the evening under blankets on their burst sofa rereading novels by candlelight, while Ruth concentrated upon the sewing machine.

The next morning, he went to prepare the armour for eviction night, and took Hector with him. They walked down the hill and into the Phoenix estate. The development of the estate had been abandoned in the Seizure so half-built new homes and shopping units coexisted with rotten warehouse timbers and the weed-strewn backroads of light industrial edgelands. The sky was low and secretive, and snow bunched in the gutters and spilt through the broken roofs of the yards. James made deep footprints, Hector did not. Ruth had traded a quilt for a herringbone tweed overcoat for the soldier, although it was too generous for his trim frame. Hector wore all the clothes they had given him under and over his uniform, so he had four pairs of socks on his feet, pyjamas under his khaki tunic and slacks, and his balaclava topped with a beanie hat. From his pack, he produced a canteen, took a swig, then offered it to James.

"Are we talking again?" asked James, as he accepted the canteen.

The soldier waited for him to take his drink.

The previous night's snow had frozen into ridges and treacherous fissured patches. Their boots crunched through it until they arrived at a concrete bunker half-buried in the earth. Snow curled over the edges of its slab roof like a layer of fat. Through his gloves, James felt the stinging cold of the iron padlock.

The men walked down rough concrete stairs and ducked under a low ceiling to reach an inner chamber forty feet deep, a dark cylinder lined with shelves from the bottom to the top. The torchlight revealed – suspended in the centre of the cylinder – an enormous hand with three sharp, flat, iron fingers. The hand was attached to a rusting girder that in turn ended in a ball-and-socket elbow joint. The beam flashed up. The heart of the armour was a harness with a porthole or colloid for visibility. The beam flashed down. The armour was mounted on two extendable legs.

James hoisted himself up and climbed over the central cage to the shoulders of the armour, about thirty feet up, and started its diesel engine. The engine whimpered, turned over, whined and knocked. Spotlights set high on the armour flared then died off. James cursed, hitched a torch between his ear and collar bone, then dug out a drill bit and a spanner. The pump was off by one timing belt groove. He tightened it and tried again; the engine started without knocking. Climbing over the head of the armour, he released the bolts on the bunker roof. It was frozen shut. He tried to force it but it was no good. He climbed

back down and went outside to clear the snow and chip
the ice from the hinges so that the roof would shift.
Nothing mechanical worked first time.

With the roof off, he could work by daylight. The engine
ran on biodiesel brewed by the town engineers and came
in two varieties, viscous rapeseed oil or the tallow made
from animal fat, which crystallized well above freezing.
The central body piece of the armour was created in the
factories of the Process: it was a structural battery, a mould
of nickel-based battery chemistry and steel. It was
waterproof, which was vital as sometimes the armour had
to lunge through rivers to extract people reluctant to be
evicted. With the engine running, the armour could power
its hydraulics and any appliance he plugged into it – in this
case, a heating coil to thaw out the tallow.

While he waited for the fuel to liquefy, he tried to
engage Hector in conversation. The soldier was biddable if
not responsive; he understood speech but his manner was
dilatory, drifting in a state of mind somewhere between
trauma and narcotic daydream.

"I want you to talk to me, Hector."

The soldier shifted his boots in the snow. The fumes
from the juddering exhaust smelt of popcorn.

"On the bowling green, you said that you would not
fight."

The soldier removed his balaclava. The way the tip of
his long nose hung over an ironic curl of his smile was a
sign that he was prepared to speak.

"I will not fight," said Hector.

"Who are you?" asked James.

"I will serve," said Hector. "I must bear my share. But I
will not fight."

"Who are you?" James repeated his question.

The soldier squinted at him.

"Sergeant John Hector. Have we met before? Yes, in

Limerick. You were one of the fellows in the barracks. Give us a coffin nail."

James did not know what to say.

"Do you have a smoke?" continued Hector. "You are dense, old man."

James fetched an old pouch of Terry's homegrown tobacco stashed among the tools. Hector rolled himself a cigarette and offered the pouch back to James. He shook his head.

Hector coughed, stirred his boots in the snow and walked across the yard toward the river. The Ouse was muddy and low, the bank slick and treacherous. His reflection swayed on the brown river, a thin neck and narrow head atop the overcoat. This stretch of the Ouse was tidal and the clay colouring deepened with the shallowing of the river through the afternoon.

"Where do you come from?" asked James.

"The Westmorland Dales, in Levens," said Hector, and James could hear the accent. "My father is a painter. My mother is dead. Her father was a Magyar so I have Romany blood. Father's from Quaker stock. I didn't sign up right away. We argued about it. I wanted to serve so that my beliefs would be witnessed by the misguided men who fight. I wanted to show that I'm not afraid."

"Of what?"

"Of shipping out. We're under orders although who knows where to. They issued us with pith helmets so perhaps Egypt. Or India. Joe Smith heard a rumour about Japan. What do you think?"

James did not know whether to play along with the delusion or to confront the soldier with the reality that he was out of his time.

"The Dardanelles," said James, remembering what Alex and Omega John had told him about John Hector's service record.

"The Turk? I must read the Koran. But you didn't answer my question: are you afraid?"

James thought of his old life. "I was afraid for so long because I believed fear was a way of controlling the future. But it's just a way of holding onto the past."

"You sound like my father," said Hector.

"If your father is a pacifist, then I am nothing like your father. Did you see the armour?"

"The ironclad? I did. Like something from HG Wells. Does it go?"

"It goes. I can't exactly think straight when I am connected to it."

"I don't imagine any of us are thinking straight. What is its purpose?"

"It's our weapon."

"Why does the town need a weapon?"

"The armour replaces the police. It responds to the will of the people. It is a kind of democracy."

"Democracy is a swizz," said Hector. A disc of river light glinted within each of his pupils.

James went to check the thawing of the tallow. He turned off the armour engine, swilled the fuel around with a stick to aid the melting of the fat crystals, then climbed down into the cage and felt the armour hum around him. The vibration of the engine made his teeth chatter and the mechanical noise was annihilating in the close underground chamber. He slid his arm into the exoskeleton and twitched a fingertip but the mechanical finger did not respond, and that was how it should be. The armour was not his to command. It was the instrument of the will of the Process. He checked the coolant levels, the ventilation and the heat sink, ran diagnostic tests on the electrics and picked brick from out of the pedrails. Maintenance complete, he shut the armour down, slid the roof back into place, and secured the bunker.

Hector was still at the river's edge. He stepped lightly around the frozen mud to peer into a drainage ditch.

"See, down there, a pair of gadwall ducks!" He squatted down to get a better look at a wading bird with long red and orange legs. "And a red shank. The floodplain is a good breeding ground for them. Look at his great dipper's beak!"

From his pack the soldier took out a flat tin of watercolours, a sketchbook, some HB pencils and a nimble sable brush.

"When we were out in the Clare Mountains on training days, I'd always find something picturesque to paint. I could stalk a heron for hours."

He sat cross-legged on the snowy bank, overcoat underneath the seat of his trousers, sketching the red shank as it walked alone through slime and the buttery mud.

"Why is democracy a swizz?" James asked.

Hector concentrated upon his drawing. "I simply do not believe in the idea of the nation. Democracy invariably leads to war because politicians stir up patriotic feeling to get elected. I will serve my fellow man but I will not serve the nation."

The young man drew nature deep into his lungs.

"This will be your first time in combat?" asked James.

"Yes. My soldiering has been endless drill at Basingstoke and Limerick. This will be my first time out."

"Do you remember the day that I found you on the wire?"

The soldier did not respond. The question was not part of the pattern.

The men walked upriver. Hector enthused about the wildlife; at Halmsey weir, watching a swan's glacial drift against the speeding current, he remembered a day out at Lake Windermere, when a swan had attacked a chocolate-coloured Labrador.

Friesian cows milled in the low, boggy plain between the river and the raised earthwork of the railway line. Upriver lay the chalk pit of Offham, the gatehouse of the *douanier*, and the town perimeter. They stopped at an islet in the river. It was riddled with warrens. Under the trailing skirts of a maudlin willow, dun rabbits nibbled and loped, enjoying the protection of the river's course.

"I grew up in Levens," said Hector. "Just before sundown, I'd take a boat out to watch the light break on the mountain's edge, and feel alone on the water. I was a lone wolf, still am really. There are too many people in the army for me. I don't mean you, old fellow. I respect you. It's the commonplace man of the barracks who bores me: the office boys and the city clerks and the shop assistants. Little chiefs in suburban villas brooding on kismet, asking themselves: will I die on the battlefield? What will become of little me, will it matter when the sorry lot of me – all my ideas, because people are just a collection of ideas, aren't they? – soak into the earth?"

He stopped. At his feet there was a dead rabbit, its skin sunken and sallow, the legs and paws lying at full stretch as if the animal had taken one last leap.

"Look there, in the eye sockets, ladybirds! Isn't that the strangest thing?" The eyes had rotted away and in each of the gummy orbits, two brightly coloured, spotted bugs turned this way and that, seemingly confounded by these bone craters. Hector crouched to peer closer, then offered his index finger as a way out. They were not ladybirds. Their antennae were too long, and the head was an array of lens and grille.

If Hector noticed the manufactured quality of the bugs, he did not admit it.

"Are ladybirds lucky, do you think? Two of them."

The ladybirds relayed data back to the drone birds, which fed into the tree routers, from which the numbers were cast up into the Process; if a phenomenon could not be measured by the Process, then, effectively, it did not exist.

Hector fell silent beside the river. James took his arm. "Come," he said, "there is someone we have to meet."

The two men retraced their footprints in the muddy slush. Downriver, snow-covered roofs gathered in the lee of Lewes Castle. Overlooking the river crossing at Pells, a church tower, a steep terraced street, and a child's playground. The river's course, tamed by sedge and bullrush, diverted into a lily pond. They passed the lido and then across icy fields around the back of the allocation point. Hector had reverted to his default silence.

Children were out on the streets of the lower tier of the Malling Estate, and at the bailiff's approach, they scampered away from their creation: a snowman with square armoured shoulders and a horned head.

The men walked up the steep Malling Hill until they reached the outlying terraces of the town flanking the road in from the east. James found the house he was looking for: the house of the Bowles family. Friends and neighbours milled outside with parting gifts of food and equipment. He watched from across the road. Chests and boxes of possessions had been loaded upon a cart, a sign that the family were not intent upon resistance. He wondered if they had made contact with outsiders, if they had a plan for what would happen once they passed through the gatehouse of the *douanier*. He steadied himself against a lamppost. Around its trunk and overhanging broken lamp, the Malling residents had strung dead mobile phones and broken pieces of circuit board, a superstitious offering to disrupt the Process. He stood across the road in a brown windcheater and ancient combat trousers, an unarmoured and untethered man. A snowball scuffed the lamppost. He looked around for the person who had thrown it. No sign.

He crossed the road. The line of well-wishers cringed and averted their eyes at the approach of the bailiff.

"Is the family home?" he asked. A second snowball arced through the air and popped against the side of Hector's head. Suppressed laughter from the line. The soldier took a step to balance himself.

The man of the house came to the door. He was tall, wearing a blue linen shirt under dungarees, with brown curly hair, powerful long limbs and the taut skin of an outdoor worker. The round grey frames of his glasses were created by the Process as was his belt of titanium tools. Over his shoulder, the narrow hallway contained more boxes and a little boy curious to discover who had come to the door.

"I am the bailiff," said James.

The carpenter was appalled. Then angry.

"Why are you here?"

He should have known the name of the carpenter. Ruth had mentioned the names of all the family. But when he reached into his mind for the names and came back empty-handed, he felt an unpleasant greasy sensation in his stomach and fingertips.

"I came to offer my sympathies. And to hear what plans you have for living outside."

The carpenter's hands were large and rough. He took hold of Hector's collar and, striding out of the house, dragged the light lithe soldier over the yard and into the road, then threw him down onto the frost.

"Why him? Why does this thing stay and my children go?"

The carpenter kneeled beside Hector and gripped his skull. "The soldier is an error message. And yet not only do you ignore this evidence of malfunction, you take it into your house. You choose this error over real people."

The carpenter released Hector's head. The soldier

dragged himself to the gutter, rolled over, and got slowly to his feet.

The carpenter came up close to James' face.

"The Process issued me with a new set of tools only a month ago. Why do that if I am dispensable?"

James waited silently. He would never attempt to justify an eviction.

"You want to know my plan? I'm staying. I have a role to play in this town."

"Never make the mistake of believing you are indispensable," said James.

The carpenter did not expect to be criticized. He rounded on the bailiff. But James could not be intimidated.

"I'm sorry. I really am."

"Give me one reason why it should be us?" The carpenter gestured back to his family and there, stood in his door, was the girl Agnes. James recognized her. She was the girl who had spoken to him when he found Hector on the barbed wire, the girl who did cartwheels first on one hand then on two. Before the Seizure, he and Ruth had planned to have children. After the implant, it couldn't happen. Children were strange to him; he knew that he was meant to feel something for them, that the young were more important than the old.

The carpenter turned to accuse the line of neighbours outside his house.

"Can anyone give me a reason why it should be us?"

Every face held a reason why the Bowles should be evicted although none had the courage to speak it.

Turning back to James, the carpenter put his hand to his chisel.

"What if I were to kill you now? It's not like I have anything to lose?"

"You have nothing to lose," admitted the bailiff, "but they–" and he gestured to the line of friends and neighbours "–would lose everything if they did not stop you. And someone else would take my place, and they might not be so honourable as to come up here, unarmed, to tell you to your face that I hope you leave us without violence, that you understand that your best hope is to conserve your energy and keep our goodwill for what awaits you outside. So I ask you again: what plans have you made for after the eviction?"

"My wife's brother lives in Saddlescombe. And the rest of the family are in a reservation in Wales."

"But you plan on staying."

"Even if you drag me out of here by my hair, I will come back for you."

James was indifferent to the threat. "I only evict people. Exclusion is a matter for the *douanier*."

He was done. With Hector trudging after him, James walked back down Malling Hill, paused, then lashed out an arm at an incoming snowball.

7

Eviction Day began with the firing of a maroon rocket from the turret of the castle. The detonation echoed down the narrow twittens, scared the rooks from the tall trees, and sounded deep within the fathoms of ten thousand dreams.

In the bathroom, he turned his head to the profile and shaved the hair that had grown around the puckered canyon of the implant, shedding tiny brown and grey snippets of hair across the curvature of the porcelain sink. The tattered collar of his boiled vest, the tooth powder of chalk and peppermint oil followed by a mouthful of salt water – these were good clean habits. Solitude was a virtue, friendship was a vice.

In his gut, he felt a twinge for the armour, a craving that was almost ulcerous. The pain passed quickly. The urge was reminiscent of the restless desire of Saturday nights and he returned to Ruth in search of distraction.

"I went to see the Bowles family. The carpenter attacked Hector and called him an error message."

"What else could he be?"

"Hector is significant. Hector spoke to me."

"He hasn't said a word to me." Ruth lay still under the covers. "He looks so fragile."

"From his point of view, he hasn't been to war yet. He's not a soldier, just a lad."

"He's a machine."

"I don't see him that way. Maybe I'm too close to the Process."

James took down a transparent box from a high shelf and put it at the end of the bed. Inside the box was his second skin, his private armour. The iron exoskeleton locked up in the underground cylinder belonged to the town; this armour, a tough flexible vest of scales, had been tailored to his body. The exterior of each scale was a ceramic plate of silicon carbide which rode on a supple, tough internal layer of collagen fibres. Each fibril of collagen was bound into a doweling and then stacked in cylinders resembling the densely packed bundles of collagen fibres in the connective tissue between muscles and organs: the fascia. If a knife or bullet cracked the tile it would not penetrate the collagen layer. And if they came at him with hammers, the impact from blunt instruments would be absorbed by shear thickening fluid, a mixture of nanoparticles of silica in polyethylene glycol which would be transformed by the energy of a blow into a rigid shield.

Also in the box, a cushioned helmet that had been moulded to the shape of his skull. The helmet of the iron exoskeleton was decorated with the colours of the districts, and bore the dents and burns of the Seizure. That armour performed a social function. This more intimate armour – crafted in one piece, and modelled upon the arapaima of the Amazon, a giant fish that in the dry season was forced to bask among piranha – was a supple love letter to him from the Process.

Ruth hitched her knees up under the blankets.

"How are you feeling?"

Acid scorched his stomach lining. His temples were urgent poles either side of an unpleasant lightness of mind.

"I just want to get it started," he said.

"What are you going to do about the children?"

"I will evict them as I evict everyone whose names appear on the list."

"If you evict Agnes, it will be difficult for me."

"At the school?"

"It will be difficult for me to love you."

He laid the vest of scales upon the bed, and ran his fingers over the individual ceramic plates to check their integrity.

Ruth looked closely at his face, reading the impulses distorting it.

"I love you, but what you are about to do is evil."

There, she had said it: evil.

"Are we evil?" he asked. "Is this what evil looks like?"

He turned the vest over and tested the fibrils of collagen by stretching them.

"Could you stop the eviction of Agnes, if you really wanted to?"

"Could you, when you are swimming underwater, force yourself not to surface for air? Yes, in theory. But in practice, you give in to instinct for an instant, and then you are on the surface, gasping."

"It's very Old Testament. The sacrifice of the innocents. I wonder if we are being tested like Abraham with Isaac?"

"Alex Drown says that we must be wary of projecting our old ways of thinking upon the Process. It is not God. It is not our father. It is not government."

She got out of bed. She wore a long flannel nightie and her dark hair was tied up so that he could see the discoloration of the stripe at the top of her spine.

"I wish I could argue with someone about this. With you."

"We're not responsible for this, Ruth. We can only be human, and try to survive."

In the living room, the grime on the windows softened the morning light. Hector was waiting for them at the dining table. James inquired if he slept well. No answer. They ate porridge together, and the elevation of his blood sugar alleviated his physiological cravings for the armour.

On the table, James spread out a map of the town marked with the locations of the houses of the twelve evicted. In preparation, he had visited each of them to gauge their resistance. Most assured him that they were resigned to their fate and would be joining the procession. But Francis Sacks was going to be trouble. The Von Pallandts had never forgiven Sacks and his family for their takeover of the allotments in the early days. No doubt Sacks had plans for his eviction. Hiding places. Ambushes. Homemade explosives and hostages.

He was restless to go out but it was not safe for him to do so. Not without his private armour. Something nasty might be planned for him. A knife in the back at the market stall. The carnival atmosphere of the day encouraged people to behave as if their actions had no consequences. Alex, travelling into town over the Downs, would have to take precautions too.

"Do you feel it?" he asked Hector. "The anticipation. The fear."

Hector ate porridge methodically, silently.

His cravings for the armour came in waves; the peaks tightened his throat and made him feel like he was not inhaling enough oxygen, and in the troughs he was weak with relief. The implant was a silvery presence at the back of his mind.

Ruth put her hand on his wrist and stopped him from scratching at the portal.

"Oh Ruth. Is it always like this? I'd forgotten. Why do I always forget?"

"Try to remember what it was like before you were the

bailiff," she whispered.

His old self had been deluded and self-important, and then he had been redundant. A greasy cautious silence met his pleas for work. Everyone could see the collapse coming but no one spoke of it. The truth was considered to be pollution. The economy exhausted its most vital commodity: the future.

No, he would not remember it.

The Process took care of him now. His craving peaked again.

"This addiction to the armour is cruel," said Ruth.

"I could ask Alex to cut the implant out of me."

A look of fear crossed Ruth's face.

"You said that I'm evil." He looked to her to tell him how to behave, how to be comfortable among people. His upbringing had been deficient in socialization. He had been son to a mother who hated men, and he had never known his father. When he was informed that his mother was dead, over the phone, by an estranged sister, Ruth had to persuade him to attend the funeral. Without social instincts, he relied on systems to tell him how to behave.

"It might be evil," admitted Ruth. "Or it may serve a greater good. How are we to know?"

He needed her because he was incapable of acting according to a moral sense. His pragmatism was, in turn, a quality she relied upon. If James refused to perform the evictions, the implant could override him anyway, and they would lose everything for nothing. Like last time. But to cast out children – she would never forgive him.

He said, "The children are just being put outside of the Process. It might even be for their own good."

"If you had ever spent time with children, then you would not be so phlegmatic about it."

"I'm the bailiff, Ruth. The system was designed so that I have no choice in my actions."

Ruth washed, dressed and quickly put on her coat. She was late for school. She kissed him on the forehead, and said, "When you get to the Bowles house, look for me."

Hector's silent face tracked her exit.

Their flat was the upper floor of a converted nineteenth century needle factory, allocated to them for its centrality, overlooking the winged angel of the war memorial. The rest of the building was a communal kitchen. Below, across the cobbled factory gate, trestle tables served bread and soup for the workers securing the town for the eviction.

The caretaker, Terry, supervised a large crew of men, women and children as they boarded up windows and put buckets of sand along the parade route in case of fire. Posts and string marked out where the crowds could stand, leaving plenty of clearance for the armour to pass through the narrow streets.

Every citizen wore their district colours and conversation thrilled with the sense of occasion. A rumour spread that the *douanier* had already sighted the distant progress of the totem from Black Cap. The rumour drifted across the town, to the workers of the Paddock, overseen by a rueful pair of piebald horses, and up the avenue of grand Edwardian houses, past the blackened gap where the Walington sisters had torched their home rather than give it up. Here three or four young families, strong and simple yeomen, now occupied each house in return for working and protecting the paddock, the largest of the town's dozen allotments. With the thaw came wheelbarrows of contorted squash, bags of strong mustard leaf, and the unearthing of parsnips and artichokes.

Ruth ran down a steep twitten as the church clock chimed nine. The sound of children singing from the nearby school house. Her class ran through their lamentation rehearsal as they waited for their teacher.

In the playing fields, under the shadow of the kiss-kiss tree, Sylvia, a tall girl on the cusp of adolescence, read out her essay on eviction to the youngsters:

"Once upon a time, the grownups used to go far away every day to earn money, for without money you did not have a house or food or clothes. As time passed, the grownups went away for longer and longer and the money they brought home was less and less until finally there was no money left. Where did it all go? Money wasn't a thing like clothes or parsnips. Money was a promise. And too many people broke that promise so people did not believe in money anymore. The grownups everywhere realized they had been cheated but even the cheats lost out when no one wanted to plough the field or teach the class or even stop the bad men. All over the land, grownups argued about what to do. Except here. In Lewes, the grownups had a plan because they were the first to know that change was coming.

"Every home used to have a window into another world. A wicked monster took over that world and so we had to close it off forever. But before the gate was shut, we rescued the angels of that world and put them in a special place so that they could watch over us from the kiss-kiss tree, and help us with our school work, and to make sure that everyone gets what is fair. We have to work hard, and do our bit, and stick together. But every day cannot be a happy day. The frost comes late and kills the vegetables. People get sick. People get cross. We can't hold onto everyone. Sometimes we have to let people go. And it's alright for us to be sad that they go. And they will be sad too and sometimes very cross. We make sure that we say goodbye and they are sent away to help other people make places that are as safe and beautiful as Lewes."

The children listened to her with serious little faces, and then asked questions about the monster and the other world, and whether they would be sent away, and why the angels chose one person and not another. Sylvia, the best student in her class, answered each question as truthfully and tactfully as she could.

The kiss-kiss tree had been a pine tree planted at the beginning of the Process, one early January. The branches shed their needles and became brittle and bare. Then, in spring, a miracle: new sap flowed through the tree, its viscosity glinting with information. New branches sprouted quickly from old, an array of smooth wooden rods gently piercing the sky. The trunk accelerated upward. The bark grew thin and torn. Roots broke the earth in every direction, some as thick as fibulas, others tendrils forming a skein of interconnections laced through the top soil: all were warm to the touch.

By late May, the tree was as tall and wide as a house. The pine needles glinted like filaments. The children liked to play near it. Ruth watched them flock to the kiss-kiss tree during break, and the birdsong provided individual counselling from the Process. Classes were easier to manage than they used to be, the children got on better, although this could equally have been due to their parents being around more, the tighter community bond, the change in diet and exercise.

Ruth arrived at the school. The grass was long, the markings of the football pitch stirred in the breeze and distant trails of vapour rose from the root system of the kiss-kiss tree. The morning dew evaporated, the moisture hissed and the soil charred. She noticed that the structure of the branches had changed: the radial spokes emerging horizontally from the lower part of the trunk had fallen away, with the growth clumping in the higher upper third of the tree. This central growth was a misshapen pentagon of livid green webbing, and branches radiated out from each of its points. Suspended in the heart of the webbing was a woody nucleus. The children climbed the mutant branches of the kiss-kiss tree and played games in its shadow.

Ruth took the register. She skipped over the name of Agnes Bowles. The class spent the morning finishing their costumes for the eviction parade. Sylvia asked her teacher if she had heard about this year's totem. The question attracted the general curiosity of the class.

"What has been made for us this year?"

"The farmers say the totem is very big. Much bigger than in the past."

"How does it move, miss?"

"It moves in the same way that a tractor does, Maisie, and it is controlled by the Process."

"Does the Process tell the people what to make?"

"The Process chooses the totem and machines make it."

"Why don't we have machines to make our costumes and our banners too?"

"Because by making things ourselves we are made into better people."

The children did not understand. They waited patiently for her to explain.

"Humans make tools. Some animals make tools too. The making and using of tools is important for developing language, how we think and speak. If we do not make anything, it affects our thinking."

"How does the Process choose what it makes and what we have to make for ourselves?"

"Well, there are lots of things it can't make. It can't make petrol or food – at least, not food that is nice to eat. Equally, it can make things that would be impossible for us because its machines build in layers of atoms rather than having to carve a shape out of wood or stone."

"My dad says the Process gives us what we need. But I never get what I need."

"It's not Father Christmas, Alexander. It must balance all our wants and all our needs. The smartest children are the ones who can control their needs. If I was to put a plate of cookies here, and tell you all that you could have one cookie now, or two cookies later – which would you choose?"

The children conferred and laughed. Two cookies later, of course.

"But if they were real cookies, freshly baked and right *there*, then I know that some of you would not be able to wait. Waiting is a skill you have to learn. The children who can't wait are the children who fail. You must control desire. Making things yourself, understanding how much time and effort goes into everything we have, is part of that control."

"Miss, if it is so important for us to make things ourselves, why do we let the Process make us anything at all?"

"That's a good question, Sylvia." Ruth sat on the edge of her desk. "The answer is that we're still becoming who we are going to be. When I was your age, no one really had to make anything much because other people who lived far away made everything for us. To go suddenly from not making anything to making everything would be too much. People would be unable to cope. The Process helps us make that change to a different way of life."

Alexander asked why the name of Agnes Bowles had not been read out on the register. Ruth was blindsided by the casual mention of the child's name, and the insoluble problem of her eviction. Her body experienced the dilemma as a precipice, nervous flutters in her fingers and toes, predatory shadows swimming through her day.

Sensing the upset of her teacher, Sylvia chastised Alexander.

"You shouldn't talk about the evicted. The bailiff is teacher's husband."

The boy realized that he had a mistake, and afraid that he too might be taken from his home and his class, he started crying. Ruth put her hand on his head to reassure him; his stripe was warm to the touch, the nodules seething with distress. And she was the cause of it.

James had said that they were not the cause of anything but that was no comfort. She had wanted to make a difference at the library, in the early days of the Seizure, and had been slapped down. From one point of view, she had been taught a lesson in powerlessness. But it was really a lesson in brutality – and it taught her nothing that she did not already know. Hopelessness was safer, she had allowed herself to give in to the ease of being irrelevant.

Agnes' name on the eviction list presented her with an impossible choice; damned by either path, she had become listless. The way a mouse tortured by a cat gives up, and lies still, its furry back shaking with the violence of its heartbeat.

Ruth reassured the children. She told them that the evicted always found new homes, but the sound of her own voice was as absurd to her as it was to them, and fear spread among the class. Alexander sat on his own with his head between his knees, weeping, and could not be brought round. As she moved from one emotional child to the next, Ruth glanced out across the playing fields and there, under the kiss-kiss tree, Hector was meditating, eyes closed, head tipped back, his legs crossed and palms resting upward on his thighs, as if straining to hear a distant music.

James said that he had spoken with Hector, chatted with him about his upbringing. All winter they had harboured the stretcher bearer in their home, yet he had never spoken to her, nor to anyone else, as far as she knew. It was impossible to make a decision if you tried to reason it all out. You just had to act according to your conviction.

She asked Sylvia to look after the class. Ruth told them to write down words associated with eviction, on the promise they would talk about it afterwards, and then she was through the fire doors and outside, running across the school field.

The sight of Hector sitting under the tree was strange because adults so rarely went near it. She stopped a few yards short, bent over to catch her breath. He did not respond to her. It was unnerving, because he so closely resembled a person and yet lacked the palpable charge of human presence.

"What are you doing here?" she asked.

She chewed her lip, giving him an opportunity to answer. His silence angered her.

"Wake up and be a fucking human being!"

Her self lagged behind her anger, like a mother picking up after a destructive child. The heat of the kiss-kiss tree was in her stripe: the smell of charred hair and scorched grass.

"You spoke to my husband. So speak to me. Or do you not speak to women?"

He was wearing a singlet and canvas short trousers; eyes closed, his chest rising and falling with meditative breathing, his flesh so pale as to be not quite human, his skin a fabric sealed in one section over his body like a laminate shell, or stitched together like a coat. Made from a similar fabric as her stripe, although without the dense packing of neural cells. Hector was a thing made from a pattern; so, she wondered, from where did the Process get that pattern? A random page from human history or something meaningful, something chosen? She strode forward, took his hand in hers.

"Are you the Process? Were you sent here to communicate directly to us?"

He did not attempt to free his hand from her, but

nothing in his expression gave an indication that he was aware of her touch.

"Or are you just an error message?"

Hector lowered his head: a mass of black curls, no stripe because he was all stripe, bio-engineered cells flickering with data – the data of what people said or did around him and even what they suppressed; what they chose not to say, that too could be inferred. A spy in their midst, like the fox she had encountered on the corrugated roof beside the ruined twitten. She had accepted the stripe because people like her had no choice: that was the lesson of the Seizure. That was why they called it the Seizure – it was the moment when meaningful choice was taken away from the majority of people, as their labour lost its value, and they could no longer sell their time, so they had to sell emotions, relationships, access to their bodies. It had felt like the end of the world, but it wasn't. Her humiliation was familiar to the men and women who came into her library, first or second generation immigrants fleeing variations of the Seizure in their own country. The Seizure was not an apocalypse but the moment an advancing front had finally caught up with her.

Hector took up his backpack. From it he removed books: a copy of the Koran, the Bible, *The Golden Bough*, Blavatsky's *The Secret Doctrine* and pamphlets about Rosicrucianism. She picked up a novel called *With the Adepts*; the frontispiece indicated it had been printed in 1910, and the binding and paper were undoubtedly old and aged. Unlike the fabric of his uniform or tins of bully beef, the books had not been recently manufactured. Hector had acquired them from somewhere, perhaps from within the town. Or they had been given to him.

"I will not fight," said Hector.

She dropped the book in shock. The stretcher bearer looked up, not at her, but at some invisible interlocutor.

"I will serve," he said. "But I will not fight."

Serve but not fight; it was some kind of message to her, a way of refusing. The aura of her uncertainty passed into the kiss-kiss tree. Sorrow became data, individual suffering a value in the great ongoing algorithm, a negative value to be corrected through the thing that gave her pleasure or by removing the source of her anguish altogether. The Process was responsive. Could a sufficiently large reaction against the eviction of Agnes prevent it?

There was still time. A couple of hours until the parades began. Edith was the closest the town had to a leader. Ruth left Hector sitting under the kiss-kiss tree with his books, and ran to the bottom of Keere Street and Southover Road. Edith lived over by the lido but she was more likely to be on her rounds, fulfilling her role as councillor. Ruth headed up the steep cobbled Keere Street. The houses were strung with district colours, elderly residents in their gardens, curious at her agitated state. They all knew the names on the eviction list, but had put the matter aside as the responsibility of the bailiff. He would perform the necessary but unacceptable act, and bear the consequences. She wanted to shout out to them as she ran by: *we can stop this*. Gaining the top of Keere Street, she ran out into the high street, gasping, searching for any sign of Edith. The townspeople passing by regarded her with faint alarm, and one older woman asked her if she had lost her child.

"Have you seen Edith?" Ruth asked her.

"Is Edith your child?" The old woman had the tick and whirr of a damaged mechanism, her scalp yellow and stripeless through the wispy aura of her white hair. Severe curvature of the spine. Too needy to include in the Process, yet not evicted. It made no sense.

The shops were boarded up in preparation for Eviction Night. People were keen to get ready for it. Late afternoon, school would soon be over. She was breaking her promise to the class. But Hector had spoken to her, and therefore the Process had spoken to her. Suggested a way of resisting. Jane Bowles was her friend yet she had not seen her since the eviction list was announced. Because it was easier to let the waters close over them. If she cared so much, then why had she not visited the Bowles family, to commiserate but also to ask of them: *what can I do?*

There, coming out of the town hall, she recognized Baron Von Pallandt, directing the caretaker to secure a tribute of produce to the mantel of the building. She composed herself, and walked briskly over to him, inquired as calmly as she could as to the whereabouts of his wife, Edith.

He was jaunty with her, a tone she found patronizing.

"Is your husband armoured up yet?" asked the baron. He seemed amused at the prospect.

"I don't know. I make myself scarce during eviction."

"Why on earth do you do that?"

"The implant makes him crave the armour. The hours beforehand are agony for him. It's nothing I can help him with."

"You should make an effort to say goodbye to him."

She shook her head. That was not their arrangement, there was no need for goodbyes.

"Have you been down to Cliffe?" he asked.

She admitted that she had not. The baron and Terry shared a meaningful look that they were not about to explain to her.

"Edith is visiting Blue Raven," he said, "to discuss the recording of this eviction in the Kinlog. You'll find her there, if you hurry."

The residence allocated to Blue Raven was on Cuilfail, an estate of large houses situated on the hillside overlooking the heart of the town. She had to pass through Cliffe. The ombudsman had sealed off the narrow street with the traditional anti-bailiff banners: no eviction, we stand as one. The very sentiment she wished to inspire. She interrupted the work of the ombudsman to ask if he really meant it, this resistance. He ushered her away, and when she pressed him on the point, grabbing a handful of his black-and-white hooped jumper to shake some truth out of him, he admitted flat out that he would not speak to her, the wife of the bailiff, not on Eviction Day. His gaze wandered from her; she turned and saw three smugglers hauling a banner from the back of a cart. It was new. One she hadn't seen before. It showed the armour in silhouette, the horned head, its enormous tracks, the iron pincers, all on fire, and overhead a legend embroidered in copperplate script: *Put death in your diary*.

She hiked up the steep winding road into Cuilfail. The houses were sat back in private groves; unique architect builds, sprawling bungalows, burrows glistening with solar cells. She came to a gatepost topped with a carved blue raven, its eye a golden star. It was an artist's garden. Nature bloomed within the shells of old technology: washing machines in which roses poured out of the porthole, a flatpack desk with vintage monitor and keyboard, Anglepoise lamp and printer set up on decking and overlooking the town; the malty smoke from the brewery that was slow to shift in the valley; the high castle and its webbed trees; the surrounding puzzle of narrow streets and twittens.

She knocked on the door and was met by a friend of the artist, an androgynous woman with boyish blonde crop, sensuous lips and an angry flat gaze. Ruth asked if Edith was there, and so she was led through the house. Large hardback art books on low tables and art itself; on one wall, the torsos of four different women sculpted from transparent cellotape. The patterned carpet rendered the lost artefacts of digital glitches in its coloured weave: pixellation, buffer wheels, error messages. Pre-Seizure art, a mixing of authentic craft materials with digital immateriality, and newer pieces gathered from the Process: functional grey moulded chairs and storage units displaying malformed objects that had appeared in the allocation, grey figurines in which the head and feet were joined in a loop, a jacket in which the back was covered with hard plumage, a glass apple with grey resin core.

The androgynous woman stated the nature of these objects.

"Errors."

Ruth did not know how to respond, she suspected that anything she said would only confirm the woman's low opinion of her. She tried introducing herself.

"I know who you are," the woman said, and then reluctantly, as if etiquette were another form of oppression, she admitted to her name: Jesse.

The back of the house opened into a bright studio, with a lectern, easels stacked in the corner, and various canvases lying askance and covered with bedsheets. Blue Raven was working at a table easel, Edith standing before her, clearly stopped mid-sentence at Ruth's appearance, then electing not to resume her side of the conversation. Ruth had not met Blue Raven before. Like Jesse, she was much younger than Ruth in manner and attitude, if not in years; a black woman, vibrant and questioning, her talk riding the current of her fast-flowing thought. Words positively churned out of her. She wore her hair in long dark braids. Had freckles across her nose and a plain black band on each of her long fingers. "My wedding rings," she said, "since we are all brides of the Process." This observation deviated into a reminiscence about the days of dating by app, the platonic nature of her love for Jesse, and the absurdity of maintaining a marriage *at their age* under the war conditions of the Seizure. She insisted Ruth make herself comfortable, and that tea would be served for her, although the prospect of making it seemed too involved in that moment, and Jesse was certainly not there to make the tea, rather her role was to stand around *reminding me of my responsibility as an artist*, in a round-necked monochrome top and skintight knee-length black shorts. And so the offer of tea was deferred. On the easel, there was an ongoing sketch of the town life, and a sheaf of scrawled notes. Set up next to it, animal skin was stretched on a frame waiting to be cut into pages for the Kinlog, Blue Raven's record of life under the Process, an illuminated manuscript, *something that will last this time*, she explained – most of her art had been lost in the Seizure, overwritten or corrupted by *the loop*. In memoriam of this loss, Blue Raven had made this loop the subject of her first work *post-Process*.

Edith interrupted the artist, "I don't think Ruth is here for your retrospective."

Ruth got onto her knees, and bowed her head. This supplication shocked Blue Raven; Edith was impassive, regarding it as a cold stratagem.

"I've come to ask for your help. Both of you." She turned to Jesse. "All of you."

The artist seemed touched by her abjection.

"I think we can stop the eviction," Ruth said. "The Process is responsive to us. All we need to do is to make it aware that enough of us don't want this eviction to go ahead."

Edith turned and walked over to the lectern. She removed the Kinlog from its wooden box, set aside the pigskin cover, and turned the vellum pages until she reached the one she was looking for.

"You and your husband were not part of the original set. So there are one or two aspects of our history you may not be familiar with." She brought the book over to Ruth. The page she had chosen depicted the first Eviction Night. Blue Raven's script described the chaos: families fighting at the gates to prevent their loved ones being evicted. This conflict formed an illustrated border around the text and its central image, of a man lying dead on the street, a cudgel in his hand, livid blood sheathing his face: the first bailiff.

"Our way of life is the result of trial and error. You should consider yourself fortunate that you were spared the first year of error. Crimes were committed that only today will we see a reckoning for. When we agreed to sign the town over to the Process, we knew we had to be striped. We gave up our homes, let ourselves be resorted into an optimal formation. But we did not sign up for eviction. The terms of the agreement left no room for dissent. But, what was the worst that could happen?

"On the first Eviction Night, the people of Lewes stood together and chanted and protested against the removal of our friends and family. The gates fell. Gangs had walked over from Newhaven to protect the relatives they had here, and the experiment seemed poised to end before it had even begun. The bailiff was remorseless, as he had been made to be, and the mob killed him. Might have been someone from Newhaven, or someone from Lewes, the crime was never confessed to. The people who should have been evicted remained in place. They no longer received any allocation, and our food supplies were irregular anyway, before the Process took over the farms. Factions formed. The Process allocated a new bailiff to the town. It had to be an outsider, someone who wasn't already compromised. Your husband."

Ruth reached up, and turned the page, and there was a drawing of the armour driving the people out of Newhaven, James' first act as bailiff. The mass eviction of an entire town. Blue Raven had painted the armour as it bore down upon the wailing despair of a crowd. The port town had been sold and the people had not been included in the deal. By the time James went in, water and power supplies had been cut off for two months, the sewage had backed up, and no support was forthcoming from the administration. The sale had to be honoured. The debt would be paid; more was at stake than Newhaven.

"Why did the Process not respond to your protest?" asked Ruth.

Edith sighed, and placed one hand upon her missing breast.

"We don't know *why*. My husband thinks it is because we unconsciously desire and need eviction, and that the Process is responding to that primeval urge."

Ruth slapped the wooden floor hard with the palm of her hand.

"No! We can influence it."

"The child," said Blue Raven. Edith glanced at the artist, warning her to be careful of her next remark, but Blue Raven was unbiddable.

"Edith thinks I should not include the child in my pages," said the artist.

"I merely reminded you of your responsibility to the people of this town," replied Edith. "When the Seizure ends, we may slide back into democracy, in which case the Kinlog could be used against us."

"Art," said Jesse. "We are responsible only to the truths demanded of our art."

"We need to rally support," said Ruth. "You're the closest this town has to a leader."

Edith recoiled from this suggestion, and responded fiercely.

"Don't call me a leader. I have no power. No influence in all this. That is the point. You people come to me over and again, expecting me to do something, but we have moved beyond leaders."

"You prefer this way of life?"

"Don't we all? Were you thriving in the old world? I was dying from cancer. I'm not cured. I'm not stupid. It's only remission. But my treatment under the Process worked, in a way that it wasn't working before."

The artist pulled her braids to her, inspecting their length, or perhaps merely so that she could fling them back when she stood up. "I'm not sure it's any different now. We have exchanged one form of powerlessness for another."

Ruth interpreted this remark as support for a dissenting act. "The eviction of Agnes is a chance to marshal discontent and use that collective will to influence the Process."

"We don't what is good for us, as a species," said Edith. "We were on the verge of destroying the planet. The Seizure bought the Earth some time. The Process could be the way forward."

"At what cost?"

"What cost would you not pay to save the world?" Edith leafed through the Kinlog. "Why did you not come to me after Newhaven, or the September Exodus, or any of the hundreds of people your husband has put outside the town gates? Because it's a child, I know. I have children of my own. It fills me with sadness. But if you attempt to direct events with your own hands, then you will bear the consequences of that act. It will all fall upon you, Ruth."

"The Process sent me a message," said Ruth. She got up off her knees. "I wanted to stop the eviction. Desperately so. And then the Process sensed this need, and the stretcher bearer spoke to me. He said that we can serve but we don't need to fight. Don't you see?"

Blue Raven smiled, and took up a piece of paper and a pencil.

"Those exact words?" she asked.

"Yes," said Ruth.

"No, not those exact words," said Edith. "He said, 'I will serve but I will not fight.'"

Ruth agreed: yes, those were the actual words.

"The stretcher bearer spoke at the council," explained Edith. "And he used that phrase. It's part of his pattern. The words are not for our benefit, they have no bearing on this situation. We're all in the dark, Ruth, as we've always been; but we've got this far because of the Process, and so we must follow it through to its completion, otherwise we lose everything. Oh, you poor, poor soul."

Edith stood and took Ruth in her arms, then sat her down upon the grey moulded sofa. Blue Raven finally served tea in vintage china cups, and reminisced about boyfriends she had misplaced, while Jesse spoke about the injustices of the old world and the moral clarity of the *tabula rasa*, the ethical component of extinction, the justice of the fall. Ruth heard them but did not listen; the tumblers of her decision continued to turn, she would find a way through this impossible situation.

Edith offered to walk with Ruth back down to the town. As she left, Edith reminded Blue Raven of the consequences of her art.

"I think you should depict the events of tonight honestly and in the way you think is right. But you should be prepared – if there is a resumption of England, and the administration turns its attention to our little town – to rip out the page concerning this evening and burn it, shred it, bury it in the deepest hole you can dig."

By late afternoon, the streets were dismal with rain. Hector stood beside the war memorial in his uniform, gazing long

at the two angels of aquamarine bronze sat at the base of
the obelisk, with the third angel, Victory, offering a garland
from its peak. Rendered in gold lettering, the legend THIS
WAS THEIR FINEST HOUR. Hector regarded the names of the
dead and the passing faces of the living with growing
interest, watched over by James from the distant window
of the flat.

James was ready to go, hours before time. He exercised
to shake off some of the nervous anticipation and failed to
get a hit from his homemade tea.

He succeeded in passing an hour.

Hector remained beside the monument.

What was Hector doing? Was his every act determined
by the Process or had a series of instructions been planted
within him that, as he interacted with other people and
the environment, produced what might appear as will?
Was his behaviour revealing of the intentions of Process,
and if so, could James figure out what it meant? Merely
by standing next to the monument, Hector was changing
the town's perception of him. You could see it in the way
the Lewesians lifted their heads to acknowledge him as
they walked by. Some of the old men even put a hand on
the soldier, nostalgic for a war they had never known. All
the pity and the mourning and the hopeless courage of the
war became, by simple association, the property of Hector.
James felt the idea forming in the Process: the Lewesians,
anticipating the communal experience of eviction, drew
strength from the precedent that such sacrifices had been
made in the past to safeguard the collective good.

James retrieved the armour of scales from the
transparent box. He had wanted to wear it from the
moment he awoke. He abraded the graphite texture of the
helmet between his index finger and thumb. The feel of it
only heightened the cravings. His body swooned with the
memory of full integration with the Process: fragments of

being interconnected in all their complexity and contemplated from a position of invulnerable bliss.

His back felt strong and straight from his exercises. He slid himself into the armour and the bracing pressure of it against his muscles felt right.

The bright yellow plaster of the house fronts were streaked with rain. He set off down the hill, walking quickly, fists clenched, toward the inbetween place of the Phoenix estate. He was alert to potential threats: a rattling movement from a garage; a fleeting reflection in a pool of rain; a figure descending the fire tower overlooking the river.

A small woman in a long coat.

Alex Drown.

"Where is Hector?" she asked.

"Standing beside the war memorial." James gestured back up the hill. "Placed there by the Process like a chess piece. I was hoping you'd be able to tell me why."

"It's not simple cause and effect, James. In a network, causality is distributed across space and time." She gripped his strong forearm. "How do *you* feel?"

"The cravings get worse every time. Can you fix that?"

"Addiction is a feature, not a bug."

"Does your implant come with an addiction?"

"The Institute works in project cycles and part of our working practice involves a burn list in which we work intensely to resolve each of the outstanding tasks. It is my cognitive burn down. I long for that stage of the project. During it I experience complete focus. I forget everything else: this town, personal hygiene, even my daughter."

"How is your girl?"

"I visit her when I can."

He unlocked the bunker and they went down into the dark. The strong smell of diesel, the dusty shelves of oily tools, the lingering fug of the leather padded supports – these were musk to him. He unbolted and slid aside the roof. From her inside pocket, Alex removed a suede case containing her instruments. He climbed into the sealed box at the heart of the armour and uncovered the porthole so that he could see out.

"Ruth asked me if I could stop the evictions, if I wanted to. Is that possible?"

"Well, Ruth doesn't understand you the way that I do," said Alex.

After the procedure, Alex had helped with his convalescence. He remembered long afternoons sat in a wicker chair on the terrace overlooking the lawn, with the backgammon board in front of him, the pieces stacked in their opening positions. He understood the rules of the game but he did not know how to play, that is, the will to win had gone. The procedure on his medial orbitofrontal cortex subsumed his desires and made him more receptive to the will of others. Alex's job was to cultivate just enough will within him that he could act but not so much that he acted contrary to the will of the Process. The procedure made him a good listener. Over the board, across successive games, she confessed her story to him; an alcoholic mother and alcoholic father, who left when he turned sober. She had been carer and coper. Tough, motivated, but lonely. As troubled as his own upbringing. It never occurred to him to initiate a sexual relationship.

"What happens to me when the implant is active?"

"The implant imitates anaesthetic. It degrades the connections between neurons so that the network of consciousness loses integrity. Pathways of your mind fade like rainbow bridges. Unlike anaesthesia, the interruption in consciousness does not shut down control of your body. The implant then replaces the degraded parts of your consciousness with a network of its own which connects you directly to the Process. Once two networks mesh then, unlike anaesthetic, you regain consciousness."

"It's like being carried on a wave."

"Partially. A wave that goes forward and then ripples back, perhaps. Networks are distributed across space and time, and so are we. Software imitates biology and physics: from the smallest quantum events of your consciousness to the formation of stars."

He said, "You bamboozle me."

She took that as a compliment.

"Could you take the implant out?"

"If the implant was a little metal seed in your head, then we could take it out. But it is so much more than that. The implant is a tool we created. You imagined a model of yourself in the image of that tool. Then you delegated control to that model. That you continue to distinguish yourself from the implant is merely a habit of language."

"I see things under its influence. I call it the *godstuff*. It's part of me."

"It's true that you're not entirely responsible for all of your actions."

"I will never be free."

She put her hand on his arm. He was so much bigger than her, and her knowledge of the world was so much greater than his; the imbalances in these respective proportions really turned her on.

"Freedom is not important. We are interconnected. We don't act alone. So don't feel guilty."

She stood on tiptoe and kissed him. Her kiss sparked the implant into life and the gap within him was filled with swarming calculations and visions. *Godstuff*. He staggered.

Alex whispered, "Sometimes I wish I could hack into the Process, and make you do what I want."

She unwrapped a pair of blue polythene gloves.

"Can I stop this?" he whispered.

"Your decisions are made six seconds before you are aware of them. What you think of as free will is post-rationalization. You live in the past, James."

"No second thoughts?"

"Your decision has already been made. Don't waste my time with excuses."

She gestured for him to kneel. He did so, and inclined his head forward, exposing the scar of the implant. She applied anaesthetic gel, and then cut away the growth of skin and flesh until the portal was clean and clear.

8

Here comes the godstuff, flowing in and filling him up. His blood is thickly luminescent with ecstasy and his head is a starshell. The dialogue-in-silence – *James*, the name of that dialogue was *James* – is shunted aside by icons of the Process: the black box itself, then a triangle thing that rhythmically enunciates decision trees, the square of white hot instincts, and two circles of action conjoined in a loop. He thinks of the circles as – respectively – the golden orb of human decision and the iron ring of machine decision. The circles move slowly toward one another until they line up to form the porthole of the armour. It's Eviction Night and all systems are on.

His breath steams the colloid. Its transparent gel shimmers then is clear again. Cold dusk. Strung up in the heart of the armour he hovers in the pose of da Vinci's Vitruvian Man, in two places at once, hands touching the circumference of the iron circle and the edges of a white square. And such emotions! The godstuff thrills every cell that it connects with: the cells in the grass and the brick and the soil and the steel and the stars, the cells in his heart and his tongue, his balls and amygdala. Godstuff sluices around the canyons and contours of his fingerprints so that he can touch other points within the network:

Ruth walking with the crowd by the river, holding a child's hand in her own, a grip he feels from both sides – the safety that comes with being led, the responsibility that comes from leading; Hector is out there too, turning from the monument to observe the approach of the first banners. Alex Drown slumps against the wall of the lockup, blood tears streaming down her left cheek. She told him that when the implant was dormant he was as slow as everybody else, existing six seconds after the fact, stuck permanently in the past. But to the godstuffed bailiff, limbs stretched out and bound into the armour, he owns the *now*.

He apprehends the townspeople as a lightcluster, the larger lights proceeding toward the centre, with smaller points at the eastern and western borders, lights conjoined to others by vertices so densely interwoven as to take on physical form, the heavy light of need and desire.

The crowd lines a narrow street of teetering shop fronts and bowed houses, wearing outlaw masks. At the round house, smugglers emerge from Rotten Row with their faces concealed by handkerchiefs printed with skull-and-crossbones, their stripes covered by whatever has come to hand: a straw boater, a potato sack, a tall top hat.

He comes at them through a house, iron horns to the fore, charging through brick and plasterboard and furniture. His claws rent aside the exterior wall and his head spears through the roof. The tiles ripple aside, and the crowd are screaming, fleeing; their hearts accelerate his heart, the fear of the prey feeds the lust of the predator. The musk of cordite, woodsmoke and acrid paraffin. The first eviction wants him, it pulls and pleads. But who shall go first? The thief, the poor or the child? The triangle thing pushes out least worst outcomes. The iron ring of the machine decision pulses on, onward, on. The back of the armour is a pipe organ of heat exhausts and amplifiers. He

screams the name of the next to be evicted – Francis Sacks
– and veers southward toward Cliffe.

The families of Cliffe run alongside the armour, led by
their swordswomen and the smugglers in woollen black-
and-white hooped jumpers, holding aloft burning crosses
made from petrol-soaked rags and wire frames. Children
scamper through the graveyard of St Anne's Church,
between headstones on tilted ground. Mischief men whirl
sparking strips of rookies overhead and they explode in
flurries of red tickertape, rattling the windows, scaring the
drone rooks out of the router trees. A mucky-faced
smuggler with golden teeth holds aloft a red flare, its
guttering bloody light soaking the fleeing crowd.

At the war memorial, the crowd divides, most turn left
down Market Street toward the fire site and Malling, but
the people of Cliffe turn right toward their defences. The
decision trees blink rightward, and along that path he sees
Cliffe's preparations against him: a rook's eye view of the
ombudsmen preparing the road for his arrival, a peek into
a shed in which men fill barrels with hot tar. At the centre
of the conspiracy, a man to be evicted, Francis Sacks. Part
of the game. The game of his death. There is not enough
of him left to care.

Hot in his harness, blinking at the sweat stinging his
eyes, he senses Hector nearby, the stretcher bearer a
luminous emptiness within the black box of the Process.
High up the memorial, leaning among the statues of
angels, Hector perches in his stretcher bearer's uniform,
knapsack slung over his shoulder, the godstuff roiling
around him like a worried sea, waves of data reaching to
catch him if he were to fall. The decision trees turn their
branches toward Hector. The golden orb resonates. He is
not an error message. He is source code. Hector climbs
gracefully down the monument and then he is lost in the
crowd, and James feels that loss keenly.

The procession heads downhill. The armour is locked down for this part of the ritual. A children's choir move to the front, wailing up and down the scales, the banners of the lost rise up like sails on rigging, accompanied by the incessant scraping of iron barrows against the road. Red smoke from the flare ribbons past the porthole. The children rent their gowns of lamentation.

The mischief men whoop and skitter in and out of his legs, and a Molotov cocktail erupts off his flanks, the fire curling out, sparks rushing upward.

A barricade at the bridge, shadows huddle behind it. With a whirring and grinding action, he raises himself up to his full height, turns his blank faceplate to the crowd, crushes part of the barrier beneath his foot, and scoops up the remains in his claw, casting the burning structure into the river. A few yards of no-man's-land between himself and the enemy line. A tot of rum is passed along that line for courage, and then godstuff and blood and fire shake the armour. In tug-of-war teams, the smugglers bring down shop fronts upon his shoulders, and walls collapse into the back of his knees. He swings in his harness, battering back and forth against the interior. Cog-teeth trapped, the mechanism buckling against its own arrested urgency. The iron ring flickers. Instinctively, he turns to free himself, sees smugglers skipping over the red roofs, releasing flaming barrels of tar from their traps, barrels that skid across the roof, flicking the tiles aside and then hit the guttering, overturn, and spill bursting violent blooms down upon him. He raises great iron talons in alarm and is silhouetted against stormy corona. They have him.

The air scorches his eyes and throat. It's not so strange to be in the armour once you've grown accustomed to the otherness of the body. He spits with anger onto the porthole, and saliva boils away on the hot colloid. Not enough warning from the black box. On its slanted surface, he had glimpsed some of the preparations of Cliffe against him, but not all. A tingle of fear becomes a tolling, he feels – in his coccyx – his body revolt against the trap. A white square hot with survival instincts. He gets down on one knee and the walls fall over him, and then he crawls out, head first, Molotov cocktails splashing against the faceplate. The smugglers aim for the head even though it is empty. Their mistake. He gets to his feet, takes a step forward and the road splinters between his toes, and his leg sinks up to the calf in earth. The heat extractors whine and the industrial brass section on the back of the armour sounds a bugle charge, a factory whistle and a foghorn's warning. Stuck midstep: if he goes forward then his next step may also sink into the ground, whereas if he turns back, then he will be wallowing in the fire again, risky if the diesel in the armour gets too hot.

A smuggler's face appears at the porthole, and then the man hammers at the colloid with a crowbar, trying to prise it open. This is why he has to be inside the armour: to concentrate all their hatred. The dull impacts of bricks and boots upon his back. The smuggler is pushed aside by another, and they press a banner to the porthole; it is a painting of the armour on fire, and a copperplate legend reads *Put death in your diary*. The decision nodes and chance nodes burst ahead, and he sees four paths to his death. His death is not an end node. Chance and decision explode onward from his death. The war will speed over the Downs. The town will be broken down into particles and then resewn into armaments and bodies to run the war again. He moves back along these outcomes to this moment of decision, this moment of chance. He pivots on the trapped leg, heaves his free leg forward, then it goes right through the surface and into the trench below. The porthole is level with a golden-toothed smuggler. He thrusts a searing poker into it. The colloid bends and warps inward around that hot point, and James kicks back, the harness swinging him away from danger. Every way he looks, the outcome is death. Ridiculous. He will decide, then, how to survive. He pulls his elbows up sharp and lets himself topple forward, smugglers diving aside, the armour smashing through the false road and fitting tightly into the trench beneath. Cold soil smears up against the colloid, the hot skin gives off a stifled hiss. The smugglers bring the remaining houses down across his back, burying him underground.

The trench is a line in time and space, a boundary on the edge of territory into which men disappear.

Black smoke steams from the wreckage. The smugglers hitch scarves over their mouths so as not to inhale his carcinogenic stink.

The iron ring blinking, the white box pulsing to restart brain activity. Never. Never has he encountered such resistance. He gazes into the black box, wondering *why is the Process doing this to me?* The godstuff has withdrawn, leaving him with the smell of fear, strong and hormonal, inside the armour. Inside his own body. To lie inside the earth like an exhausted root, to take his place in the grave, it feels right. The mob killed the bailiff before him, clubbed him to death on Eviction Night. He wonders, *is it my role to die?* He twists in the harness but the armour does not respond. It needs the godstuff, the implant that turns him on. The iron ring blinks but does not engage. Stalled. The air turns sour. He bangs his head against the porthole to knock some sense into the tech.

Godstuff flows up through the earth, a concentrate of ideas, a sweet mercury that seeps between proton and electron, passing easily through the armour and filling the void within him. He clears his vents with a fierce blast of air, and then the armour heaves itself out of the trench, horned head breaking up through overlapping sections of shop front, smugglers darting forward to press it back into the grave. But it can't be stopped. Eviction cannot be stopped. On, the iron ring commands him, on!

His floodlights fire up and rake across the smoky faces of his attackers. He finds his voice in a whine of feedback that makes the crowd wince and retreat. This has gone on long enough. The black box pings up the location of Francis Sacks. He reaches down into a twitten and scoops up Sacks in his claw, then cuffs him out into the street. Sacks' family regroup and he leans over and gives them horned sound and fury, then turns back to Sacks.

"You are Francis Sacks?" he asks.

Sacks shakes his head. James appeals to the crowd.

"Will anyone vouch that this man is Francis Sacks?"

Blackened hands rise slowly in the dim street. Then Sacks is pushed forward by the others, his bald head matted with blood and dust. He rants and shouts at the crowd, then pleads with them, then attacks them. The floodlights expose bruised and mottled faces writhing in a brawl. Sacks can take any man in a fair fight but this is not a fair fight. The men and women of Cliffe club their neighbour to the ground, then offer up his unconscious bulk. James gestures for the cart to be brought up.

Eviction Night: one down, eleven to go.

The town is a gyre; the castle and the keep the high centre, the stacked cottages circulating around and about, curtailed by the rise of the Downs. The high chalk cliff on the easternmost side of town is a luminous white thorn with drone birds nesting in its black veins. He loves the shape of this land. Strides over it as one of its giants. Startled electric blossoms of fireworks in the sky, festive ordinance mortared out from the fire site, that old playing field beside the glimmering slack of the river. A light cluster of townspeople gathering there, Ruth among them, stripes syncing for the communal experience of the unveiling of the totem. The totem is massive this year, something the size of a house covered in tarpaulin and trundling slowly across the Downs on pedrails, down through the town, to be unveiled with full ritual at the climax of the evening. Smugglers bring up ladders and swords, preparing to cut the ropes on the tarp.

He coheres in Southover during the eviction of the Aukett sisters, the elderly women holding each other's hands as smugglers help them up onto the cart. The next one will be tough: three evictions in Landport. The Landport lads are notorious for poaching game from the Firle and Glynde estates and their women are always breaking curfew. He expects trouble. Raw trouble.

From Eridge Green Road, he calls out the names of the evicted, his amplified bark echoing all the way across the estate and down to the river. Abandoned toys on the pavement. He taps gently on a window with his iron claw, moves onto the next house, rakes the front wall aside to expose a box bedroom, a frilly duvet, a white wardrobe. He flips the bed over but there's no one there. He places his claw onto the bedroom floor and applies incremental pressure until the house comes apart in his hands, a set of arbitrary divisions within space.

The river cry the drone rooks, they are hiding in the river. Vague outlines of people hunkering in the reeds, stifling their fear. He walks right into their ambush and they come at him from behind outcrops of marsh grass and from under the overhang of the river bank and from out of the muddy river itself, an enfilade of gunfire severing hydraulic lines and cabling. A bullet ricochets inside the armour and *thunks* hard into a ceramic plate on his private armour, his second skin. The floodlights on his shoulders spark out. He ignites the flares in his horntips, and charges forward into the Landport resistance, scooping people up to the left and right then tossing them aside winded, bleeding, wailing with backwards bent limbs. He doesn't feel their pain but registers it as multicoloured data. The resistance gives way and then it's just a matter of chasing down the evicted; he finds one hidden under an overturned skiff, another climbing up a bridge, the third a woman accepting her fate, eyes closed, hands raised, like a child wanting to be picked up by their parent.

The carts are brought down for the wounded and for the evicted. He senses Hector again, the stretcher bearer working with the town doctor, to dress wounds and administer pain relief. The godstuff swarms and coos around Hector.

The guns are new. He opens up the colloid to inspect one, the barrel, handle and trigger guard assembled from one smooth grey piece of hard resin. The barrel was cracked, good for only one round. Process made. A new addition to the ritual. His attention shifts to the black box, asks it *What are you doing in there?*

He crosses the river at the Pells, his hooting and clanking echoing in the timber yards on its banks. His long shadow falls over Malling Field. He must cross the fire site to perform the final eviction. A crowd of thousands wait on his approach, hushing one another so that, apart from the eerie crackling of the bonfire, the field is quiet. And then a mischief man lets off a string of rookies, and James flinches, thinking it gunfire. He turns his enormous blank-faced horned head toward them and there, deep in the crowd, is Ruth, data tags whipping in her wake like kite-tails.

His memories of her are indivisible from the patterns she has made in the Process: her comforting hand placed upon the head of children, the satisfaction her dresses gave her customers, quantifiable through admiring smoothing gestures over ironed linen. The townswomen knew that she was conflicted, afraid of what her husband had become yet needing his protection, a bargain familiar to the people alive after England's fall.

The armour arrives at the fire site. It is the signal to unveil the totem. Smugglers on tall ladders either side of the giant structure cast the rigging aside and the night wind lifts the tarpaulin away.

James presses his face to the colloid, and it shimmers itself clean so that he can get a better view.

The totem is a colossal cube of earth fifty feet tall and twenty feet wide containing a half-buried head, the prominent features of nose, brows, cheekbones and chin breaking through the top soil. A man's face. Skin pores dry with earth, the lips pale and chapped, as if the face had been thrust forcefully into the ground and then slowly turned over. A dead man. A dead face. *His* face? Hard to tell from this distance. Smugglers hammer iron pegs into the great cheekbones and through the scalp and into the skull, threading rope through the pegs. Heave! A great pull, a great straining, and then the face slips out of the earth in sections, landing in the bonfire and scattering a swarm of fireflies up into the night. Charnel smoke chugs from it, black and foul, blue flames leaping through eye sockets and out of the nasal bone. The totem was a prophecy, the node at the end of all possible outcomes: *death*.

He turns away from the bonfire, under the iron conviction that it is time for the final eviction. He will remove the Bowles family from their house. He sets off across the field at a steady pace, a misty drizzle coming in off the Downs, the shadows of a crowd parting before him.

The godstuff seethes with calculation, and if he puts his ear to the black box he can just about hear the chuntering of old code. An equation from the deep past. The symbols are dusty and smell of professorial self-assurance: Let F stand for the freely willed vigour to war, H the highly motivated vigour to war, let T stand for tender emotion or pity, let Z stand for anger, and having exhausted the modern Latin alphabet, we must turn to the Greek: let lambda ( ) stand for vengefulness, let mu (µ) represent pain, and omega ( ) stand for fear. The black box expands, a slanted rhombus of shadowy silken quagmire. The blackness is not a void but dense code overlapping in three dimensions until all white space is covered. Equations of human behaviour are unsatisfactory because free will is indeterminate, its magnitude will have to lie within a limited range. How to symbolize the indeterminacy of whether a person tries to perform the eviction, or actively resists the eviction, or makes no effort at all?

How to reduce the indeterminacy of free will.

The fire site crowds run to keep up with him. News of armed resistance at Landport spreads among the people and one of the guns is held aloft as proof that the Process wants them to resist the bailiff.

The godstuff settles around a modest terraced house, a steep garden, and a man standing in the doorway, Tom Bowles, father and husband, the carpenter with new tools in his belt. They had spoken at the lido together, James remembered that now. How Tom coaxed his young son Euan into the cold water. The boy was so proud of his own courage. James did not resent Tom's fertility, even though the Institute sterilized him when they put in the implant. Alex explained that fatherhood would bias the bailiff, and eviction required total impartiality if it was to remain plausible to the townspeople. It was also Alex who instructed him in the iconography created by his implant during eviction: the decision tree and its symbols – the iron ring, the black box and so on. The implant did not control him; when it was active, he and the Process were one consciousness. We are networks, that was how Alex put it.

The carpenter has to shout to make himself heard over his gobbling diesel engine, "We're not leaving!" The rest of the Bowles family watch him through the dark downstairs windows of the house; Jane Bowles clutches her son to her, while Agnes' serious young face is set apart, watching him intently.

The day at the lido with the Bowles family. He went to get popcorn for everyone and Agnes came along to help as he had a distracted air suggestive of someone who might struggle with the sweet or salty options of a popcorn order. While they waited to be served, he talked to Agnes as if she were an adult because he didn't how to talk to children.

She was curious about his implant. Was it different from her stripe? He knelt down and parted his hair so that she could see the scar. Then she shook her ponytail aside so that he could see the particular pattern of her stripe.

"Your stripe only goes one way," he said. "It outputs your feelings and wellbeing. Whereas the implant goes both ways. Input and output."

She considered this with a serious expression.

"So you can feel what other people are feeling?"

"Yes and no," he said. "The input shows me what they are feeling but only after those emotions have been turned into data by the Process. So I don't feel it."

"So the Process tells you what to do?"

"More than that. When the implant is running, there is no gap between me and the Process."

"Do you like it?"

A good question.

"I prefer it."

"You prefer it to being you?"

"Yes, but that's our secret."

He understood, then, that children do not belong to the parents. They are not possessions. They belong to everyone and everyone belongs to them.

James gestures for the cart to be brought up. Two

smugglers in harness haul it through the crowd, grim-faced in anticipation of the dissent of their fellow townspeople. A communal *hiss* and a single shout of "shame!" The rain swirls over their heads. He wants to identify the troublemakers, haul them out, make an example. The way the gangster police had dealt with Ruth during the library protest. If you raise the stakes involved in resistance then the majority of dissenters will fall away. It's a cruel urge. He wonders at its origin: did that thought originate within the white square of human instincts or the iron ring of machine logic?

His voice is the voice of God run through a filter, a glaring command as terrifyingly out of proportion to the human voice as the armour is to the human body, distorting in both the high and bottom end. The Bowles' house is a matchbox to him, he just wants to open it up and give it a shake. Tom Bowles turns around and commands his family to stay where they are, to not give into the fear. The carpenter can barely be heard above the armour because he is one measly single human voice.

James commands the Bowles family to come out into the street, and places his claw lightly against the arbitrary divisions in space that constitute their house. Tom mutely shakes his head. But from the back of the house comes Jane Bowles, with her two children, making the pragmatic choice, striding head down across the lawn. Their pain flares up and is absorbed into the black box.

The iron ring seethes. The code within the black box is reconfigured by new input. Free will within a limited range. He makes a decision. The colloid peels away, his limbs are released, the headpiece clicks back, he unhooks his harness, and puts his feet deliberately upon the ladder taking him out of the armour. The implant begins the long cycle down.

He gets out of the armour. The crowd is obscure to him. He can't remember their names. He retains faint echoes of insight, the patterns that a moment ago were so clear to him. Then he remembers to look for Ruth. *When you get to the Bowles' house, look for me.*

She is standing beside the cart. He puts his hand out to her, a gesture that both acknowledges her and warns her to keep her distance. The story of their relationship. She looks at him with such sadness. She has never looked at him like that before. Her expression makes him hesitate. He does not know what it means.

"Why did you get out of the armour, bailiff?" Tom has something inside the door frame, the edge of his left foot is pressing against it for reassurance. A cudgel of some sort.

"I didn't want to pick your children up with my claws," says James. "I thought this way I could–"

"You thought? You don't *think*."

Tom shakes his head to convey how foolish the bailiff has been, how unwise to give up the advantage of the armour.

"Please," says James. "Please get into the cart."

"When will the evictions stop?" shouts the carpenter. The crowd shift at this appeal to their self-interest.

"Eviction works," says James. "It's the only way that works."

"It doesn't work anymore."

"We've all lost somebody," says James.

The carpenter has a bitter, disbelieving expression.

"You're trying to persuade me to accept the eviction of my family by appealing to my sense of community? You've all lost your minds." The carpenter reaches for the object concealed by the door frame. It is a gun, James notes, one of the new guns. Tom brings the barrel up to waist height.

"The Process wants you to die."

The gun fires a single shot, it has a distinctive sound, a

concussive hoot, like an enormous blowpipe. The bullet hits him all over the chest, and then he's on the floor. He explores the impact with a tentative dithering hand, and discovers the shattered tiles of his private armour, damage radiating outward from a central strike, the force dispersed across his entire torso by the collagen ribbing.

The carpenter flips the rifle and cracks the butt of it against James' head. His helmet takes the brunt, he sprawls on the rain-wet path. The carpenter turns to the townspeople and beckons them forward to deliver their own portion of retribution. Hesitation in the ranks. The carpenter removes a scratch awl from his belt, grey-handled, another tool of the Process. He kneels on James and uses the point of the awl to dig around the shattered section of the armour. The underlayers of fibre are resistant, but his face is exposed. Tom slaps James, and disturbed by his own violence, he steps back and beckons the crowd onto the bailiff.

"The Process wants us to kill," he says. "We've killed before."

James gets up, makes it onto his haunches. Tom bolts forward and pushes him to the ground then stabs at James with the awl, who gets his arms in the way. The white square of survival instinct is a faint afterglow. Ruth screams.

She hoped for resistance to eviction but not like this. Ruth has been too simplistic in her interpretation of Hector. The stretcher bearer stands on the cart, repeating his assertion that he will not fight but he will serve. Only Ruth notices him. She is so scared that she can't master her thoughts. It's unbearable to see all these good people set against one another. What did Hector mean, *to serve*? That he would bear witness to the war, join its general suffering but not fight, not contribute to its vigour.

She sees it in Tom's eyes, a pure moment of fear and

hatred. No calculation of consequences, his hand holding the awl, a hand he keeps out of James' reach, poised to stab, and then he jabs hard into her husband's side, and at his wrists, and when James tries to defend those vulnerabilities, then Tom goes for the face again.

Ruth turns to Jane Bowles, grabs her hands, pleads with her to see reason.

"We don't want you to go but if this carries on someone is going to die."

Jane shakes her head, says numbly, "We're staying."

Tom looks at his wife. He looks to Jane for permission to murder. Ruth knows that feeling of desperation, to stand with a kitchen knife ready to make a futile violent gesture.

"I'm going to make this easier for you," says Ruth. And then she walks over to the children, takes Agnes up into her arms, a child she has taught in class, a child shivering in the rain and the night, kisses her on the cheek fiercely, and then lifts her up and places her onto the eviction cart.

Tom hesitates. In his fear and hatred, he has left the children exposed.

This hesitation is all the time James needs. He levers Tom off him. The carpenter bolts for his children, toward Ruth, grabs her by the throat but he can't do it, he had not prepared himself to strike this woman. James pulls the carpenter aside and throws him into the crowd. The townspeople try to restrain Tom but he pushes them away and comes at James, yet he's so obvious and old-fashioned and the bailiff is ready this time.

James strikes the carpenter hard on the solar plexus, and he stumbles backward and lands heavily on his backside, breathing in shocked whooping gasps.

Agnes cries to see her father winded and humbled. In her distress, she cries and clutches her shirt because she feels the ripping in her heart. Witnessing her daughter's distress, Jane climbs onto the cart without a second thought, and takes Agnes into her arms, then looks back to her other child, and Ruth is already with him, lifting up the son Euan to place him on the cart too. Agnes reaches over to her brother and brings him into the sobbing huddle of the family.

James offers the carpenter a hand up. Tom refuses it, gets to his feet, and hauls himself onto the cart to be with his family.

The last cart of Eviction Night is led through the streets of the town then up the Offham Road toward the gatehouse of the *douanier* where it joins a line of other carts bearing Francis Sacks and the injured of Landport. The smugglers tether the carts to horses, the animals are spared the rookies and tumult of the night. The *douanier* intones an old prayer then waves for the opening of the gate at the edge of town. The horses trudge forward, the old cartwheels jolt and turn, and the evicted are led away into the Downs.

9

The next morning, at the weekly allocation, James and Ruth waited until almost everyone else had gone before wandering the dishevelled aisles together in search of their boxes. In her allocation, there was a swimming costume and a stout pair of walking boots. But there was still no box for James.

Hector had not been seen since Eviction Night. The *douanier*'s men claimed that he had passed through their gates alone, in full uniform, as if marching off to war. His departure only added to the sense that his role in the town had been fulfilled and that role had been connected to the fateful decision they had taken to complete the eviction of the Bowles family.

In the evening, the Von Pallandts held a post-eviction party at their painted house, throwing open the yellow front door so that the guests could flow easily from street to house and out again.

Edith wore a pale green robe over a dark green dress and her hair was gathered up to reveal a slender neck and a garland of apple blossom. She had an oval face with a forceful jaw which she feminized with an outpouring of auburn curls, completely obscuring her stripe. She was luminous with late spring.

The crowd were older than James and Ruth, a different generation.

"This is how we renew ourselves after the wounds of eviction," said Edith, to her gathering in the street. "This is how we heal." Her smile was nuanced with self-awareness; to talk of healing was a cliché, she admitted that. But life required cliché. Had she not healed? Had she not come back from the dead? Yes, she had. In remission there is no time to waste.

"Our roles change. Who knows what tomorrow will bring? We must always be guided by the needs of the present. And today, we need to heal."

Her husband, the baron, poured James another glass of dry, potent cider from a demi-john.

"Some need to heal," whispered the baron, "but others need to drink."

James did not argue. The baron filled then refilled his glass until James felt drunk and unmoored.

"How was eviction for you?" he asked James.

"I am still piecing myself together."

"Eviction Night was a revelation." The baron gauged James' interest, and despite finding none, pressed on regardless. "All my life, I've studied the religions of the world and longed to be part of something greater: the collective unconscious, the oneness, the great flow. Last night we were minnows streaming through the oceanic mind."

He was dressed in shorts and sandals that exposed the knotty arboreal ridges of his calves and feet. Yoga made him slender and graceful. He brought his hands together in satisfaction.

"And you were connected to it. You must have insights you can share."

Ruth had put Agnes onto the cart. She had taken the evil onto herself.

"Something *was* communicated to us," said the baron.

"I don't think so."

"You couldn't hear the message, James, because you are the medium."

On tiptoe, the baron reached up to the branch of an apple tree, pulled it close then plucked off its white and pink blossom.

"What is nature saying to itself with this blossom? How can we listen to nature as it is naturing?"

James swayed slightly. The baron took it as a sign of interest. He wiped the blossom from his hands.

"The Process is in the background, always listening and monitoring. On Eviction Night, we glimpse its true concerns. It has its own obsessions. They are stranger than anything that exists in man or in nature."

The baron itched the white arrowhead of his beard.

"I believe the Process has learnt obsession from listening to our desires. Look around you. This way of life is more intense and meaningful than what we used to endure. We wanted this and the Process has delivered it."

The town was fuzzy with absence: missing cars, empty window frames, dead televisions. The Seizure was a *taking away*. The road markings were faded, the road signs torn up and dumped – along with the cars – for reprocessing in Newhaven. The narrow streets seemed wider without parked cars, the town more thoughtful.

Midges drifted over the reedy shallows of the Pells. On a wall overlooking the Ouse, a boy dangled a line into the low river as the upturned keel of a skiff drifted from its mooring. Across the fields, bonfires smouldered untended and dogs picked over the ruins of the high street. Not many people showed their face. Why did these absences not feel like losses?

The baron said, "We had to get rid of the bad blood. Winnow the numbers. We can hate again, safe in the knowledge that our hatred will be controlled by the Process. Hate is natural, don't you think?"

"I don't hate anyone."

"You must have done. Especially when you were powerless. If you said to me, 'I do not love, I have never loved', then you would sound incomplete. Equally, if you say 'I do not hate, I have never hated', then you sound like half a man."

"Who do you hate?"

"I stood with the crowd on Offham Road when you went into Landport. Oh, you could feel the thrill among us. Protect what is good and evict what is bad. Creative destruction: out with the old, in with the new. Unfortunately, you and your wife evicted some good with the bad, some new with the old, and that was a mistake."

"We did what was asked of us," said James.

The baron wore an ankh necklace over a khaki shirt. He put the demi-john down on the pavement, and rolled the ankh between his fingertips. "Do you think Landport still have guns?"

"Do you want guns?"

"*Détente* is fraying. We may need a bailiff who is more proactive."

On the other side of the street, Edith moved from conversation to conversation, glancing now and again at her husband, interested in his progress.

James went inside the house in search of Ruth. The partygoers flattened themselves against the walls of the hallway to let him pass by; the gaze of one woman, halfway up the stairs, dwelt on him for longer than was polite. In the loud conversation and squalls of laughter, he was a dead zone. Wherever he stood, he was in the way of others. He walked right through the house and into the garden. The lawn had been torn up and replaced with vegetables.

At the fence, Ruth was talking to Clara, the headmistress. Clara wore a long cardigan with narrow cuffs, jeans and stout boots. She was the same age as his wife but she was taller and her face was scored with worry.

Clara wanted Ruth to take a break from teaching at the school.

"The children will not trust you. What I saw last night... what we all saw–"

"You can't stop her from teaching," James interrupted. "It's her role."

"We all found last night very upsetting," said the headmistress. "We were all ready to defy the eviction of the Bowles family. You pushed that little girl away. The two of you put yourselves before the will of the town. And for a teacher to give up a child in the way you gave up Agnes was wrong."

"Why didn't you say something?" Ruth asked.

"We were not meant to evict the Bowles family. It was a test to see if the town was ready to function with greater autonomy, and the two of you failed it."

"Where are you getting this from?" asked James.

"I think both of you need to wake up, and realize how your actions are being perceived." Clara walked back into the house. James watched as the women in the kitchen huddled around her, nodding and listening to her account.

"I have to teach," said Ruth. She looked to him for reassurance. "Without a role, how will I make myself indispensable?"

"She doesn't make the decisions," he reassured her.

"Did I do the wrong thing?" Ruth put her hands over her face. She never liked to admit that she was wrong. In their marriage, whenever he raised the possibility that she might have erred, she retaliated vehemently, and he knew enough to back down. For Ruth to question her own judgment was serious.

"It was a crisis. Both you and Tom were on the verge of doing something terrible."

Ruth had put Agnes onto the cart. The girl had put her arms around her little brother to comfort him.

"It's my fault," he said.

She held him tight around the waist.

"How can we undo what we did? Could we find the family and bring them back?"

He couldn't reason it out; there were too many factors in play. He went to get a glass of sobriety. The women in the kitchen parted for him. He filled his glass from a bucket of water. The Process had issued guns so that the people of Landport could fight him. The Process had sent an effigy of his head to be burnt by the mob. He was no longer part of the allocation.

Edith collared James and introduced him to her son, Christopher, so that James could marvel at how much her boy had grown. The lad had strong cheekbones, roughly cut long hair and the broad shoulders of a swimmer. She put her arms around them both. James saw, in the neckline of her dress, that her right breast had been removed in a mastectomy.

James complimented Edith on her outfit.

"Very colourful," he said.

"Out of the darkness comes the light," she said, giving him a half-twirl. Then, "The youth have received their roles in the allocation. Tell him, Christopher, the role you have been assigned."

"Bailiff," said Christopher.

The tight lines around Edith's smile showed her misgivings. She would keep a positive attitude for the benefit of her son.

"Another bailiff! Will you two work together or will James be assigned a new role? And then there is the issue of getting an implant, which is scary. But, in the spirit of splendid sacrifice, we've decided to celebrate."

James struggled to reply. He felt sick, and threatened.

"When did this happen?"

"The roles were included in this morning's allocation."

He had been allocated nothing.

"I've been through terrible things for this role."

"Perhaps your role in the Process is about to change," said Edith.

"The Process is meant to be fair. But this is not fair." He was stuck on fairness. He couldn't think of any other response.

No one is indispensable. No one is even necessary.

"Without me, this town will not be safe," he said. "It's not merely a matter of inhabiting the armour. A bailiff can keep order with an air of authority." He was floundering. The strong cider and the shock made it difficult for him to focus.

Edith spared him an ounce of sympathy.

"Don't fuck yourself over this, James."

Her son went back into the party, and, once he was gone, Edith's manner changed.

"Do you think I am happy about this? Do you think we wanted this for him?"

"It's an honour."

"I'm sorry, James, but it's mutilation."

The Process had intended for him to die. This realization made him feel weak and shivery. The carpenter was right. Eviction Night had been about his death yet for some reason – Ruth's intervention, the way she took on half the responsibility – meant the crowd had spared him. Through the open door, standing askance in the hallway, he saw Ruth alone among the party.

He owed her his life. But for how long could he survive in the town if the Process had marked him down as dead? He felt a profound sense of unbelonging. He left the party, walked down one road and then the next, with no clear destination. The gutters were clogged with the shredded red paper of yesterday's rookies. Terry and his team were out on the Phoenix estate, scoping out the damage caused by the armour. Repairs would not be quite complete by the time of the next eviction.

He walked over the river and past the Malling fields. Allotment workers were breaking up the enormous smouldering skull of the totem and a few paused in their labours to watch him. The whites of their eyes were bright beside the soot on their cheekbones and, with their hands, they sifted through the enormous splinters of manufactured bone. Their field clothes were ragged old tracksuits and pyjamas, a motley crew who only accepted their lot because it had been allocated to them.

From the river came laughter from a group of young people. A boyfriend sharing a cigarette with a girlfriend. Life would go on without him. He had no secret weapon. No last minute heroic solution. The Process had appointed Edith's son as bailiff. He was being replaced.

No one is indispensable. No one is even necessary.

She was woken by the monstrous word of a distant cannon. Ruth reached out for reassurance but the other side of the bed was cold. Where was James? She felt vulnerable without him.

She had been dreaming of their hurried packing during the Seizure. Some of their friends had thrived through the long decline, if they were with the right corporates. James was not and neither was she. A polite young couple came around to look at their house, accompanied by the young woman's parents who did not trouble to hide their contempt; the father's face already had the young-old sheen of longevity treatment.

James had never been vulnerable before. It levelled the

imbalances within their relationship and their marriage was, briefly, a partnership in adversity. Then, when his vulnerability persisted, she couldn't help but be quietly, passively furious with James.

He had volunteered for the implant to make himself useful. To be connected to power again.

He had volunteered for the implant and she had not stopped him.

The cannon spoke again, another sullen retort in a distant conversation. She went to the window and looked out over the dark roofs. It was not yet dawn and the streets were empty. Another detonation reverberated through the frame of the house. She half-dressed on the way down the stairs.

In the lounge, James lay on the sofa staring at the dark.

"Did you hear that?" she whispered.

At first he did not answer.

"It sounded like explosions," she continued. "There. Again. What do you think that is?"

"Shelling. There is a kind of war going on. Not a real war. A recurrence of war."

"Are we safe?"

"I don't know. I saw something under the influence of the implant. A vision of a possible outcome for the town if this war carries on. I want to find Hector."

"I don't think you should leave, not right now. You should fulfil your role."

"As bailiff?"

"As husband."

She kissed him and her fingers hesitated at the back of his head then rested on his shoulders.

Another distant thud in the earth. The lampshade swung.

He was strong and straight; the softness around his face and jaw was long gone but his eyes reminded her of the hollows in a forest, with their rotten shadows. She preferred not to look at his eyes anymore. The eyes she had loved had been bright blue, sad and funny, her favourite part of him. Now the whites were jaundiced, and the skin of the orbits slack and exhausted. Sometimes he slept with his eyes open. She dwelt on the parts of his body that showed his strength – his shoulders, his forearms, his angular calves.

He moved close to her.

"Imagine this is goodbye," his voice was deep and aroused. "Imagine I'm going away to war for a long time and this is the last time we will be together."

She got down on her knees, unbuttoned his trousers, closed her eyes and gave into the compulsion. This quick and uninhibited response to his suggestion made him moan and gasp. The implant interfered with desire. Sex was one of the things he forgot about until it was almost too late. The need to unburden himself did not get through to consciousness until the very point of crisis. She liked the sex that this side effect produced. It was so unequivocal. All he needed was a reminder that sex existed and then his response was immediate.

His skin smelt cold and his musk was fainter than usual. He pushed her away, turned her over and pressed his fingers into her. Love was a generalization, and quite meaningless. Marriage was far more specific, and consequentially interesting. She liked to be fucked in this way now and again. She didn't want him to fuss over her needs, that is, she didn't want her needs to be identified and collected like butterflies. She just wanted them met. She turned back and he moved onto her and into her. With her arms and legs wrapped around him, they kept each other afloat. Marriage is survival. Yes, she wanted to survive. To survive and to come. That was not too much to ask.

Afterwards, he made her tea. On the street below, people gathered. They did not go about their usual morning business but looked southward. The grunts of the cannon were answered by gossipy tremors underfoot. The window quivered under her fingertips. When she turned around, he was dressed again, efficient and focused upon his role. The dreamy compliance of night gave way to the hard realities of morning. How long would he be gone? Was it dangerous? How would she cope on her own?

"When will you return?"

"Soon as I find Hector," he replied.

He took her hand, and considered it. She didn't look up in case she saw into his eyes.

"People like us should do what we are told," he said, "if we know what is good for us."

He kissed her forehead then left the flat. She watched him walk up the street toward the war memorial, rucksack slung over his shoulder. He walked down Market Street and across the bridge.

The Bowles' house was just across the way. A new family was already living there. He thought of Agnes again. When her little brother was lifted onto the cart alongside her, her first thought was to protect him from the collapsing world.

He would speak to the *douanier*. Ask him if he had heard anything about the family. He took a few paces and then stopped again.

Everything he had thought or done up until this moment had been mistaken. The world was not as he had believed it to be, and neither he nor Ruth understood this strange new age. Only Alex Drown knew what was happening.

The road up Cuilfail was very steep, the hedges overgrown and splendidly ripe with rustling and green perfumes. Walking was a way of shaking off the feeling of weakness brought on by fear. At the top of the hill, the *douanier*'s men loitered around the watchtower. He asked briefly if they had seen or heard about the fate of the evicted. No, they had heard nothing. He'd be better off asking at the Offham Road gate or waiting until the *douanier*'s inspection the next morning. Had they seen Hector? No, they had not.

He passed through the gate and set off across the Downs. A browsing wind considered and reconsidered the long grass. Cows idled in the valley. A new day. He would spend it on the Downs looking for Hector and, if he could not find him, he would visit Alex at the Institute and tell her that the stretcher bearer was lost.

10

It was dusk by the time he reached the Institute, and the trees overlooking the grounds were noisy with birdsong: the caw-caw of rooks, the glitch and warble of a nightingale. Nature had the upper hand over the grand artifice of the house: bindweed gripped the flagstones and the hedges were overgrown and steeped in their own musk. The east wing of the house hid under a pelt of green ivy; lilies, ripe-budded, quivered on an algae-choked pond. On the lawn, the wheels of an overturned wheelchair turned lazily. The house had let itself go.

The lights were on in the Round Room. The sound of a small generator came from somewhere in the foundations, and, close to the door, James overheard the glinting sounds and brittle routines of dinner service. Proximity to the house increased the pressure in his temples. His limbs felt tired and the veins on his hands and arms were swollen and prominent.

A musty air wafted out from beneath the house. Cold and damp, it reminded him of his operation to receive the implant. They had wheeled him along the rutted stone floor of the cellar then hefted him up onto the operating table. Mozart on the stereo – the surgeon preferred to operate by requiem. A large detailed photograph of the moon was suspended directly above the table for patients to contemplate as they slipped into unconsciousness. The moon grew so big, then faded. He awoke fighting. Two orderlies restrained him while Alex shouted at him to pull himself together. In a sealed yellow bag on a small trolley lay an excised part of him, marked for the incinerator. He couldn't remember what he had lost.

During his recovery at the Institute, he got to know the art room, the bedrooms, the communal dining room and professorial side offices partitioned within the shabby aristocratic languor of the house. The other residents were both student and patient, inmate and professor, and they came from all over the world: Neha and her sentient garden; Sunny Wu and his skilful forgeries; Jamsu, the enormous Tibetan who could sketch the shape of the unthinkable; Ken, the Yoruban prince and controller of roads. They shared a peculiar childishness and had always reminded James of physics undergraduates; brilliant, anti-social and abstracted. The first procedure every inmate underwent was to prevent the plasticity of the brain from degrading with age. Then the body was infused with adaptogens synthesized from astragalus bark, the latest in longevity treatment.

It took him a long time to learn to want again.

He knocked again. Alex answered the door. She had not expected him. She took him into the Round Room. The smell of Institute food mixed unappetizingly with the damp walls and distant chamber pots. Did he want something to eat? No, he did not. She ate with a plate on her lap and listened as he told the story of Eviction Night up until the point that Ruth put Agnes onto the cart.

"So what happened next?" asked Alex Drown.

"Hector left. I thought you should know that I've lost him."

Alex chewed her dinner and considered his dilemma.

"So you failed to do the one thing I asked of you, and everyone in the town hates you now."

"Yes."

"You took a risk leaving Ruth on her own."

"The Process intended for me to die. Not her."

Alex finished eating and set her plate carelessly aside on the marble top of an antique table. She took a napkin from her sleeve and attended to her mouth. Clearly they were to wait for Omega John. Through the window, on the darkening lawn, the other inhabitants of the Institute took their after-dinner stroll. Sunny Wu, wearing a safari suit and glasses with transparent frames, his dark hair parted with once-fashionable asymmetry, turned back to wave at James; his hands were large and soft and intensely sensitive.

"Why does Sunny have such big hands?" he asked Alex.

"It's an experiment. The brain perceives the hands to be much bigger than they are and the same with the lips, tongue and face; more neurons are allocated to them and this results in detailed sensory information. Sunny is working on extending the range of touch, both through augmentation of the hands themselves and in the neuronal density of the parts of the brain that interpret that information. He has always been very skilled with his hands. Since the procedure, his forgeries have taken on a new quality. He forged an eggshell that, when cracked, releases albumen and yolk which react to hot oil to form a perfect round fried egg. It is only when you eat the egg that you realize it is made of paint."

Omega John entered the Round Room. He was much improved since their last meeting. The swelling in his skull had subsided. The alarming attenuated skin had plumped up and he seemed more sure-footed. He wore a Harris Tweed sports jacket, a red checked shirt with a brass-and-scarlet tie, soft brown moleskin trousers and no shoes or socks. His knee was swollen and he walked with the aid of a silver-tipped cane. Alex apprised him of their discussion.

Omega John peered to the left and to the right of James.

"Aren't you missing something? What is it? Oh, I know. A stretcher bearer."

"He ran away."

Omega John's smile was a lipless simper.

"Fortunately one of our number detected Hector on the Downs and saw to his return. We're taking a closer look at him. When you first brought him in, there was nothing within him to study. We put you two together to cook him up."

"He spoke," said James.

"Did he? He has not talked to us. But we are not solely reliant on his speech to study him. My colleague Adlan is adept at extracting information from any material and reassembling it into a coherent pattern. He can pull a dream from a sleeping dog at ten paces. Adlan has mapped the network of ideas and tensions emerging around Hector and they correspond broadly with what we know of the historical John Hector."

James recalled his afternoon with Hector beside the river.

"He likes to paint birds and believes that democracy is a swizz."

Omega John shifted uneasily, then said, "John Hector's role in the war is the reason the Process has recreated him. Other evidence has come to light to support this supposition. We have reports of thousands of manufactured soldiers massing at Newhaven, filling up the empty houses, waiting."

"Hector is not unique?"

"He is significant," said Alex.

James sensed they were deliberating over how much to tell him.

Alex said, "Hector's story and the history of this Institute overlap. The Institute was founded by men who served alongside him in the 32nd Field Ambulance Division."

James asked, "Do you think the founders of the Institute and Hector knew one another?"

"Yes. The Process is recreating the founding moment of the Institute."

"Why go to all the trouble of a physical recreation?"

"You could not recreate John Hector without recreating the war that changed him," Omega John said. "Consciousness requires biological processes but it also occupies a particular position within the network of life. Clones always die, you see, for that reason, because they have no position on the network. To reproduce a particular consciousness, you would have to recreate the instrumental network in which it arose."

"Is the Process broken?" James was hopeful.

"Quite the opposite," said Alex.

Omega John nodded.

"The Process continues to minimize suffering and institute optimal policies which maximize returns," Omega John slipped into the antique, noncommittal dialect of the technocrat. "It monitors need and desire and calculates the most efficient way to allocate resources to meet those needs and gratify those desires."

Their rhetoric was evasive in its complexity.

"How could war possibly be a way of minimizing suffering?" asked James. "Who desires war? Who needs it?"

"You might as well ask those questions of history. Who desired the Great War? No nation benefitted from it. The war brought about the destruction of the Prussian Empire, stripped the British Empire of its ability to hold its colonies, slaughtered the French and starved Germany, inspired a revolution in Russia, and prepared the ground for a more terrible slaughter to come. The great powers didn't want a war and they certainly didn't need one. But their people wanted a war. To the surprise of the rulers across the Allies and the Central Powers, the idea of war was seized by the people of every nation, even the international brotherhood of socialists.

"War was taken up as a way of dispelling fear *about* the war. A short conflict was anticipated, fought along nineteenth-century lines, producing a few casualties, a small sacrifice to release the tension and uncertainty produced by competing empires. Even men like Hector, who had been raised to loathe violence, signed up to serve. Unfortunately, this ancient faith in sacrifice met with very modern technology. War had become industrialized, and therefore so was sacrifice."

"The war was so long ago. What possible purpose could be served now by reenacting it?"

Alex looked at Omega John. He tapped the floor thoughtfully with the tip of his cane.

"My hypothesis is this: the Process, in projecting the most likely outcome in the near-future, has identified the need for a particular person. That person is dead yet the need for them remains. How to solve that problem? Well, recreate the conditions in which that person came to being."

"Who is that person?"

"The founders of the Institute served alongside John Hector at Suvla Bay. One of them, Lewis Collinson, devised some of the early algorithms that formed the Process. Collinson specialized in applying quantitative thinking to problems outside of the traditional scope of measurement. Before the war, he was a meteorologist and pioneered the use of mathematical models to predict weather. As the war ground on, he devised a mathematical model to explain why the war started and, more importantly, how it could end. This was his equation of war.

"The Institute was founded partly to explore the efficacy of Collinson's predictive models. His application of differential equations and probability theory provided a software. A sufficiently powerful digital hardware to run such calculations on the mass scale required would not be invented for another forty years. Yet there is evidence that Collinson's models were *applied* in the twenties. We don't know how exactly. Our archive was destroyed during the collapse."

"The former management of the Institute deleted and burnt *everything*," said Alex Drown.

She was interrupted by a hand placed against the window. The hand was large and plump, and, when it was withdrawn, the outline of its perspiration flared on the glass. Sunny Wu's smile was almost luminescent among the grainy blue silhouettes. Having caught their attention, he tapped his finger gently upon the glass and then pointed upwards.

"He's right," said Omega John. "We should take another look at Hector."

They walked down the checkerboard corridors of the house, stepping discreetly around the chamber pots and buckets positioned to catch drips from the roof. They went up a flight of stairs. Oil paintings of dead aristocrats and busts of philosophers and landowners. Across the ceiling, a bold art deco mural depicted two men across a great blue dining table, its crescent moon shape dominating the terrace. In the distance, light played on the glassy surface of the Aegean Sea.

"What is going on in this scene?" Omega John asked rhetorically, then gasped painfully onto another step. "The mural is a futurist rendering of an ancient myth. The theme is the sacrifice of the innocents. The man dressed in merchant's robes is Mastusius, and the man with his back to us is his king, Demophon. A plague fell upon the city of Eleonte and the oracle told Demophon that a sacrifice was required to appease the gods. The names of the virgin daughters of the city were to be placed into an urn and then one would be drawn. Mastusius refused to let his daughter's name be included in the lottery."

Now Omega John gazed up at the mural, finding something within it that he had not previously considered.

"But Demophon understood that no one could be spared the risk. All must be prepared to make the sacrifice. The king slew the daughter of Mastusius. Then, time passes. Demophon is invited to dine at the house of Mastusius. Here we see him about to drink a toast. What he does not know is that Mastusius has had both of Demophon's daughters killed and mixed their blood with the wine."

"Demophon drank the blood of his children."

"Yes. And once he learned of their murder, he had Mastusius and his cup flung into the sea. The myth explains the unusual formation of the particular coastline on the southern tip of the Gelibolu peninsula – or Gallipoli, as it is known to some. To appease the gods, sacrificial virgins were buried alive in enormous clay jars."

Omega John put his hand to his distended skull. A blue vein took a sinuous course across a spotted plain of thin skin.

"In the war, the obsession for fertilizing the earth with blood was gratified on an industrial scale. It is in his obsessions that mankind most closely resembles his machines."

At the top of the stairs, Alex held open a bedroom door. They went into the small room. Hector sat glumly on the edge of a tired single bed, illuminated by the gauzy light of a dusty lampshade. On a wicker chair opposite, in calm repose, sat an old and ravaged man wearing a collarless olive robe. His face was black, pinched and drawn, dried out over a lifetime of toil under the sun. Poverty had been thorough in its savagery; he had lost toenails and a finger, and his joints were arthritic. One eye was bloodshot, the other shone with a terrible clarity.

Alex said, "This is Adlan, our observer." Adlan gave James a cursory glance, ignored his offer of a handshake, then returned to his study of Hector.

"What have you learnt from the stretcher bearer?" asked Omega John.

Adlan's voice was dry and heavily accented.

"The war is growing within the creature and without us." Adlan waved carelessly in a southerly direction.

Hector's boot scuffed against the bare floorboards.

Adlan moved into Hector's line of sight. "The creature does not see me. It sees only what conforms to its pattern. The creature sees the bailiff." Adlan pointed at James with a gnarled index finger. "He sees you. Your presence quickens him. You and he are part of the same pattern of war. You must go to it. It takes two men to carry a stretcher."

"There is no war. The war ended over a hundred years ago."

"And yet it is here again. I have observed it. Upon the chalk cliffs, great jars bathe in the sunlight reflected off the sea. Within each jar, a soldier grows. The rivers run with chromium and the air is poisonous with chrysanthemum clouds of raw gold. Weapons spill out of the factories in torrents: shells of every size, rifles, great cannon and miles of barbed wire, legions of horse. The first replicas were exact forgeries. But with the pressure to produce more so the simulations become less exact. Men are made with greatcoats fused to their skin and with no feet in their boots. You will take your place among them. You will play your role. And then you will understand what you are."

Adlan wished to continue his study of Hector without further distraction. James left the bedroom and stood with Alex beside a window overlooking the garden.

"You took something out of me to make room for the implant. What was it?" he asked.

Her reflection in the window showed the sadness of somebody trapped, of somebody who could never get back what they had lost.

"The good part."

"I've said goodbye to Ruth. Adlan's right. I have to go into the war. To serve but not to fight."

She offered him the use of a room for the evening. He accepted. She visited him at midnight in her nightie, and they made love quietly, while from out on the lawn came the laughter and strange whooping of the inmates. He gave in to her desire for sex because he had closed himself to other people and he wanted to connect again, and Alex was so profoundly lonely among the residents of the Institute. It was uncharacteristic of him, he had not cheated on Ruth before. But Alex had cared for him throughout his recovery, and was intimate with the half of him that Ruth did not like to gaze upon.

The moon was high and bright. At dawn, he heard footsteps in the corridor. He walked naked into the corridor and Hector was there, waiting for him, in full uniform. Betraying Ruth would make it easier for him to leave.

They walked together from the Institute, retracing the steps they had taken on that patrol when James first found Hector. Through the wood and past the camp of the charcoal burner, then back through Glynde, over the railway line, and skirting around Firle before undertaking the steep but not difficult hike up Firle Beacon. He was fit and they reached the high ridgeline overlooking indigo and grey patchwork fields divided by drystone walls and hedgerows. The pattern of fields reminded him of the cellular structure of soap bubbles, and perhaps their formation shared some of the same rules. The grass trembled to meet his fingertips. As a boy, he had been a connoisseur of turf and a carver of dens in the heart of rhododendron bushes. He had liked to curl up safe in the mathematics of the green.

He decohered, thought he heard a child crying on the Downs. The sour taste of an hour's sleep in his mouth yet it had only been a moment. Hector was a hundred yards ahead and then briefly two, three, four great flashes over the distant town of Newhaven lit up the night, followed by a rumble that could be mistaken for thunder. A star drifted over the coast, illuminating a vast new terrain of scorched cliffs. The landscape he had known was gone, a new one constructed in its place. His implant felt suddenly hot and then he saw the godstuff approach, golden waves rippling quickly across the contours of the Downs. Hector had reached the wire strung across the field, the barrier betwixt and between. Hector turned to him, as if to chide him for falling behind, and then the godstuff flowed over both of them.

11

At school, the children wanted to know about the explosions. No one spoke of it as James had, as a recurrence of war. Was it fireworks? Was it, as one boy suggested, quarrying? Ruth settled the children down and asked them to write a story inspired by the distant explosions. Sylvia, her favourite, chewed her pen top and gazed out of the window at the rooks perched on the branches of the kiss-kiss tree.

"Do you have an idea for a story, Sylvia?"

"The bangs are there to scare us, miss."

"Do they scare you?"

Sylvia shivered and nodded. And so did the other children around her.

"Why do you think they are there to scare us?"

"It's like when we set off rookies, miss, to scare the birds away from the crops. Someone wants to scare us out of the town."

"That's a very good idea for a story," said Ruth, "but I don't think that is what is really happening."

At midmorning, she crossed over to the kindergarten class. It was warm and yeasty in a cloying, mumsy kind of way. The women spoke in a high questioning tone so as not to disturb the room with assertions. She liked the little children, found them interesting and honest; her desire for children had come too late, after James had been sterilized. But she had been right not to breed. History had been on her side. A couple of the mothers talked about their doubts and regret about having the children, even though they loved them, of course they loved them, but on balance, all things considered, the way things turned out, it would have been better had they never existed.

The kindergarten was hotter and yeastier than usual. She went into the toilets and gagged over a tiny toilet, then bent low to wash her face in a miniature basin. When she stood up, there was a mother helping her son urinate into a potty. Nursery rules dictated a smile at all times. The mother exclaimed, in an exaggerated and high-pitched fashion, an "oh" of surprise.

"I didn't expect to see you," she said.

"I am a teacher here," replied Ruth.

"I thought you had been allocated a new role."

The mother was fresh faced but her hair was grey. Her jeans were too big for her. Weight loss, colour loss – her house had been taken in the Seizure and reallocated to ensure fairness. Somebody who had earned it and not merely inherited it or speculated for it.

The boy finished urinating. His mother did not notice.

"No harm done," said Ruth.

In the classroom, the children sat in a circle and sang of the sweet, sweet berries of the kiss-kiss tree. The boy skipped out of the toilet and took his place among them. His mother met Ruth in the corridor.

"Are you helping the group today?" Ruth asked.

"Yes. The Process asked me to contribute. We all seem to be changing our roles, don't we? It's refreshing. We all need a change."

"I am happy with my role," said Ruth.

"Well, it's not about whether we are happy with our

work, is it? We must also consider whether our work is happy with us."

Back in the classroom, her students worked upon their stories. Sylvia drew a picture of the children crouched upon the branches of the kiss-kiss tree with explosions all around them, using coloured pencils to fill in the fire: orange, yellow, red. The destiny of these children would be so different from their parents. They would fail or succeed on their abilities. A suitable role would be allocated to them. The Process, by doing away with mortgages and salaries, pensions and investments, had erased the former trappings of adulthood. A new definition of adulthood was required. The tired faces at the school gates were a testament to that. Love could be solved by the Process, too; the dating algorithms that helped a billion Chinese find love were part of it. Legacy relationships were allowed to stand but better matches were on offer.

Her hand brushed against Sylvia's hair, curls which expressed all the endearing unexpectedness of a child's mind. She was glad that the children would be spared the lives of their parents.

Some days, she missed the time before the collapse with its racks of magazines with sachets of scent, the feeling of a new pair of shoes, being in a bar full of strangers sipping champagne, telly and tanning salons, train journeys across country.

Sometimes, when the children were running in the playground, and she was in the middle of them, it was as if the collapse had never happened.

Clara, the headmistress, called a staff meeting to discuss what to tell the children about the distant explosions. The other teachers were anxious. Should the school close? Clara canvassed their opinions, pointedly ignoring Ruth, excluding her from debate. She waited until they had all spoken before she informed the meeting that James had gone to investigate the source of the explosions.

"That's brave of him," said Clara.

Ruth just wanted Clara to know that she and James still had a role to play.

"Does he know what is going on?"

"Not yet. He will be back tonight or tomorrow. As soon as he returns, I will let you know."

This promise won her a reprieve of sorts. But James did not come home that night, or the next. In the evenings, people took to gathering on the castle top to observe the distant explosions. In the castle gardens, the Von Pallandts served mulled wine from a trestle table. A greenish light settled over Newhaven, an aurora borealis riddled with flashes of lightning rising out of the earth and a rolling rhythm of explosion and echo. Once Ruth had seen enough of the bombardment, she joined a gossiping, drinking gathering. Edith, in cape and pointed hood, put her hand on Ruth's arm and asked her if she had heard from James. She realized that was being lined up for a role she had never expected: widow. The Process had issued her the black silk and pattern for a funeral dress, with black lace for the veil and collar.

"Why is the Process doing this?" she asked.

"It will pass," said Edith.

"What if it doesn't?"

"You must have faith if you are to get through these times."

"Faith in what?"

"Faith that it will soon be over and you will cope regardless."

"We should send another patrol."

Edith glared, distressed; it was only a matter of time before her greatest fear came to pass and her son was dispatched to follow James.

Death was in their hearts. Grieving widow, grieving

mother, the roles waited for them a week or two down the line. The black cloth had been given to her, and the pattern too – all she had to do was make it.

Ruth went up to the turret again and willed the explosions to stop. A distant flare went up, a manmade star that rose above the churning nebula of green smoke. Then that flare fell to earth to be followed by another, then another, like a legion of spirits.

First thing in the morning, the other side of the bed was cold again. Reality was remorseless and stubborn in refusing to give her what she wanted. The bombardment, steadily increasing day by day, played on the nerves of the town. In the classroom, many of the children were missing, kept at home by parents in case the war breached the town walls. By the end of the week, it was decided that the school would close temporarily. Ruth gathered up the work of her pupils and there was Sylvia's drawing of the children upon the branches of the kiss-kiss tree, huddled together and surrounded by rooks.

A week later, and still James had not returned. The lido was quiet with only four other swimmers in the water and a cleaner mopping the poolside. It was the hour between waking and the start of the guns. She shook her limbs and stretched. Late spring, and the diurnal shift was exceptional, with hot days followed by freezing nights. The waters of the lido were very cold. She hesitated at the water's edge, mustered her resolve, and dove in.

Ruth concentrated on her breast stroke, thrusting out her legs and using that action to expel air underwater, then inhaling quickly and deeply as she broke the surface. Her skin adjusted to the cold and she turned to swim another length. Crossing and recrossing the pool and to what purpose? Halfway through her mile, she forgot about everything other than her stroke. She was purely swimming. And then a plume of icy spring water at the shallow end shocked her back into herself; she mistimed a breath, took in a mouthful of water and a twig, and gasped at the poolside.

She saw Christopher Von Pallandt pull himself out of the pool; his muscled back and the way the stripe arrowed from the top of his spine and bisected his newly-shaven head, ready for the implant. They said he was to be the new bailiff. Treading water, she wondered if she should befriend him. No – she pushed off, face down, legs straight, feet together, her hands coming together in submerged prayer – there was no point.

She completed her laps then walked across the grass to the edge of a patch of shade. She dried her long black hair and, when she looked up, Christopher Von Pallandt was stood opposite her.

"You swim very well," he said. Christopher was about eighteen years old, muscular, but undercooked. She had noticed him trying to keep up with her in the pool but his strength seemed to slow him down, as if he were digging his way through the water rather than gliding across its surface. It was how James had swum when she first met him, before she had taught him how to do it properly.

"The water is a great equalizer," she said.

He took a towel from a tree branch and dried his muscular midriff.

"I wanted to ask you something." He looked around. The cleaner was mopping away Ruth's footprints and the other swimmers were absorbed in their stroke.

"I get my implant tomorrow," he said.

"Congratulations."

He winced. The breeze sent blossoms into his hair and onto his bare wet shoulders.

"Did your husband ever talk about what it was like? The operation. And afterwards. Was he different?"

"Yes. He was different. He was a changed man."

"In a good way or a bad way?"

"The times changed too. At first, I didn't understand what had happened to him because I thought it was a reaction to the Seizure."

"Alex said that I won't always be in control of my actions. That the Process will be able to command me. I'm not bothered about that. In fact, it's kind of glorious, don't you think?"

She thought of Eviction Night, her husband's face visible through the steamed glass of the colloid.

"James doesn't enjoy the loss of control."

"I have to go alone, across the Downs, to the Institute. My mother wants to go with me but it is forbidden."

"How old were you when the Process started?"

"Thirteen."

"What do you remember about the beginning?"

"Being thankful. We didn't have to move. I saw the others go and they deserved it, you know, the Process got rid of all the people we didn't need."

"Do you ever wonder what happened to them?"

"They went somewhere else. Have you heard from James yet?"

"He went into the war."

The boy nodded quickly.

"I think it's a war, too. Are you worried about him?"

"I am. But I don't know what to do about it."

Swimming had been her only release from anxiety. When she woke at four in the morning, ready for another night shift of churning calculation, then her limbs, full of lead from exercise, pulled her down into sleep again. Every day she expected to hear from James. Nothing. She swam from one end of the pool to the other until she was exhausted. Still nothing.

"Have you been on patrol yet?" she asked.

"As far as Firle. The village has taken a few stray hits

from the artillery. The church is bombed out but the people are staying put. The men have been as far as Blackcap and they told me the shelling was too intense to go any further. The roads are filling up with troops and horse moving between the front and the support lines. New trenches appear every day. The men took a boat out from west of Seaford. The coast line has been blasted. There are new factories in Newhaven and Denton Island is a slag heap. Tanker after tanker is queuing to unload at the ferry port. The water close to the harbour is thick with pollution. It's very dangerous."

The other swimmers crossed and recrossed the pool. She thought of Charon, the ferryman on the River Styx, transporting souls from the land of the living to the land of the dead, from the sunlit deep end to the cold shallows. It was a holding pattern, a limbo. Activity but getting nowhere.

What was she waiting for?

"Have you heard anything about James?"

Christopher shook his bare head. He looked vulnerable, his stripe glistening and exposed like that.

"If he has been injured, he might have been taken to Saddlescombe Farm. There's a field hospital there. It's where I am gathering the evicted."

She thought of Agnes and the rest of the Bowles family. The carpenter had mentioned relatives in Saddlescombe.

"How do I get to Saddlescombe?"

"It's about five miles west out of the Nevill. Follow the ridge down to Devil's Dyke. It's not a place for women though. You should stay where you are protected."

"Protected by whom?"

"By me."

His hand dithered as he considered putting it upon hers.

"You are the wife of the bailiff. That is your role."

The suggestion was repulsive to her. He had no understanding of the inner life of a marriage. He was young and regarded sex as a social act. She turned away from him. Embarrassed at his own clumsiness, he dived again into the water.

At nine o'clock sharp, the bombardment resumed. Ruth felt it in the soles of her feet. She returned home.

Christopher's implant was a success. If anything, he took to it far better than James did. He'd lived within the Process for so long, he did not require much by way of convalescence. The rolls of the evicted were once again compiled and read out at the war memorial. A yeoman recited two dozen names and then some, over the distant rumbling of the artillery. The crowd's laments grew tired, their voices dwindled until the names were met with silence. People were losing the strength to care about the fate of anyone other than immediate family. It was like the early days of the Seizure all over again.

Her name was not included. She wished that it had been.

At night, she wrote James' name on the grey walls of her flat with a hunk of chalk. Wasn't the Process meant to respond to desire? Well, here it was, written out, clear as day. *I want my husband back.*

Her food allowance was increased to take account of her swimming, and her allocation included a warning against further self-medication with alcohol. In the transparent box, there were also replacement needles for her sewing machine, and bolts of brightly coloured material for sun hats, which she always made to trade at this time of year. She seethed in the aisles, then dashed her box to the ground, its contents scattered across the linoleum.

Without James, she felt unmoored. She thought of her last visit to her parents' house in Kings Langley, the house in which she had grown up, in which her father had died and from which her mother was quietly removed during the Seizure. Ruth, the only child, was left to pack away the things. She'd often heard it said about only children – what will become of them when their parents are gone? How will they cope when they are all alone? Her mother collected models of country houses and cottages and displayed them in a glass case. In the attic, boxes for each part of the collection had been preserved along with the tissue paper in which they had been wrapped. Ruth spent the last day in her family home putting her mother's collection of small houses back into their boxes. When she was done, she returned the boxes to the attic, having neither space nor inclination to take the collection herself. Her mother's things were a burden. The wardrobes were still full of her father's clothes, and his uniform hung from the rafters of the attic. And then she left. Her parents' life had not been tidied away, the surface had not been wiped clean.

Ruth stood at the edge of the swimming pool, preparing herself for the shock of the cold water. Being alone made it difficult to act; she had no one to discuss her plans with or confirm her feelings. The cleaner mopped the smooth bricks of the poolside slowly, from left to right. The night wind had shaken apple blossom from the trees and it drifted delicately upon the water's surface. There were no other swimmers. Breaking the stillness seemed indecent. The clock passed nine and still she had not braved the water. Without that mile behind her, she would not be able to get through the night. Yet something held her back.

The lido seemed eerie, as if the blueness of the water had increased in intensity. Fog obscured the sun. She shivered and glanced over at the cleaner to see if she had noticed it too. Yes, they shared a puzzled look. The cleaner looked up at the sky, from east to west, and then she smiled.

"The guns have stopped," she said.

They had. The guns had stopped. It was peace. Who knew how long it would last but while it did, she could act. She had been unwilling to swim because something within her knew that she would need her strength.

Ruth did not even change back into her clothes. She ran up the hill in her bathing suit. The rest of Lewes had awoken to the unaccustomed silence, and outside the food kitchen, an old woman gripped her arm and asked her if she knew what was happening. She ignored her. Back at the flat, she set about packing. There was almost nothing she wanted to take. From the kitchen, she gathered a fire steel, her boning knife, a set of cutlery, a tin mug and canteen. She sorted through her jewellery to find the pieces which meant something: her mother's locket which opened onto a black and white photograph of her father, in his wedding suit, as he had been long ago.

Ruth slipped half a loaf and some cheese into her rucksack and headed up the high street, past the slumping Tudor houses and the castle keep and up toward Western Road. The rhythm of the bombardment had kept her hunkered down in the town. Without it, she wanted to be free, to get out, to find James.

Christopher had mentioned a field hospital in Saddlescombe village. She would begin her search for James there. It was directly west of Lewes and so her walk would not take her near to the battle lines.

The Nevill estate spread along the foothills of the Downs past a large allotment of polytunnels and raised beds. The estate had become a suburban shantytown, with houses interconnected by outhouses, tents and shacks. Children played in the street, families flowed into one another, the clan life of the Nevill.

A hot day. Where her rucksack lay against her shirt it was slick with sweat. She passed a gang of menfolk on ladders securing a tarpaulin over a collapsed section of roof, and then a couple of mothers from the school who were brewing tea over a Kelly Kettle. She accepted a mug from them. How long did she think the guns would rest? Was this the end of the war or merely a break in the battle? She was tempted to dally longer, to chat, to be among others. Such a simple and obvious happiness, to be part of a community, with enough drama, intrigue and consolations to fill a life. All these people had lost in the Seizure was their debts, and any meaning they derived from the servicing of that debt; they were the lucky ones.

The edge of the estate was marked by ramparts patrolled by the *douanier*'s men. She signed herself out at the gate, pausing to look back across the shanty suburb so that she was sure the Process observed her departure.

The grass grew long on this side of the Downs. It brushed against her knees as she strode upward. The heat released delicious aromas from the earth and her skin. At the top of the ridge, a single bench was positioned for the regard of the town below, and beyond lay the Gallops, a long straight racetrack and burned out ruins of the stables.

The sound of the town fell away, replaced by the wind in her face and the eerie absence of the guns. The path to Saddlescombe was a simple one, heading west over the chalk ridge, past Plumpton and Ditchling, crossing the road at Pyecombe, then turning south west. In all it shouldn't take much more than an hour and a half. She hadn't left the town very often in the last few years, and to walk clear of its narrow streets and familiar faces always made her regret that she had not taken the time to walk alone more often.

A rut had been made by wide tyre tracks running up and over the Downs. This was where the enormous effigy that burned on Eviction Night had passed by. The effigy of a head half-buried in the earth, either prophecy or warning. The face had not looked like James' to her, but then what would he look like after a week in the earth?

The thin path was a white bootlace on the greensward.

The breeze carried the ripe smell of wild goats. Sheep, too. Clustered in the verges, the tiny yellow offerings of cowslips and purple bluebells. The riddling branches of a wind-bowed tree pointed each way at once. Hedgerows of ash and oak marked out here from there.

A clump of hawthorn rustled as if disturbed by an animal. Her heart lurched. Wasn't this how James had found Hector, a stray caught up in the wire? She approached the bushes, and their shivering quickened. Something white stirred in between the branches. It was an animal. A horse. No, not a real horse. She came around to get a good look at it. It was a peltless unformed horse, its back legs stiff and deactivated while the front hooves scraped fruitlessly at the earth with the instinct to outrun the pain. She did not offer reassurance to the thing. That would have been pointless. Its blue lips curled and it gasped. The horse was not wounded, it was lethally premature, a carelessly manufactured piece of suffering. Its long head in the dirt, and eyes, wet and raw, exposed to the sun. Would it be easier to put it out of its misery if it were a real animal?

Out of mercy, she stood so that her shadow cooled its face. If she took a heavy rock, and crushed its skull, would that even kill it? If the Process was alive in every cell, would it continue to writhe headlessly into the earth? She was sure that she could kill it. It was feasible. But how could she be sure that it was suffering? The horse was not a real horse. It had been manufactured for a specific purpose. Perhaps the horse was not malformed or unfinished but was complete and its pain was the very reason for its creation? This might be its role, and fulfilling a role was the highest form of happiness. But what if your role was to suffer?

She could not decide what to do. She wanted to do good. She wanted to make amends. The horse seemed to be in so much pain. An act of mercy was needed. She looked around for a rock big enough. The ground was dry. She levered a stone out of the earth – it was twice the size of her hand and smooth at the edge, neither as jagged nor as pointed as she had hoped. The horse had no eyelids and her approach made it more agitated.

She had never killed anything larger than an insect. Nothing in the act appealed to her. Her arms felt too weak to deliver the necessary force. She hovered over the horse with the stone held above its pallid muzzle. No, she would need something bigger if she was to crush it. Her boning knife was in her backpack. But a stab in the eye hardly constituted an act of mercy.

She thought of James out there somewhere, suffering like this. She couldn't bear it. Her love was made from protection and forgiveness, love from the times that he had been strong and the times that he had been weak. She remembered Eviction Night, the press of the crowd at her back, her belief that the eviction must continue – everyone else knew it had to be done but could not accept raising their hands to do it themselves.

It was evil to cast out a child. She let the evil into her to spare him. The other townspeople said that it had been a test and she had failed it like something out of a myth or the Bible – but since when did the Process set tests? In the night, the people brayed to save themselves and cast out the children but by morning, they had suppressed all memory of this accord – yes, she remembered the crowd willing her to do it, but no one actually asked her, did they, no one actually said the words. That was why you needed someone with you to check the facts and to help you fight. Otherwise the world echoed in your mind until it was insubstantial and meaningless and simply easier to give in.

The horse was a broken machine. She put her hand on its cheek. Its pale skin clung to her fingertips and, for a moment, the unformed horse was replaced by another, a brown mare, lame from shrapnel, lying in a shell-hole, its front hooves sinking into the mud. The impression of another world, more instant, more present than her own, passed by, pricking the surface of her stripe as it did so. Under her hand, it was a pale horse again. She left it alone.

Ruth continued on the path west. At Newtimber Hill, the sea glittered in the sun and the outer estates of Brighton – Moulsecoomb, Hollingbury and Withdean – appeared, at this distance, intact; the occasional blackened stump within a row of terraces, fires burning here and there, a tent city in the park.

She felt guilty about the evictions. She had given up Agnes to ward off some other terrible eventuality. But she had been wrong. There, she admitted it. She had been wrong, and she would find some way to make it right. They believed they had made wise and pragmatic bargains with fate. But what they had done out of fear and love was coming to fruition. It lay over the ridge, only half a dozen miles away, a new and inscrutable horror that was using war as a laboratory.

12

James sleeps standing up, held in place by the press of men all around, three hundred or so soldiers in pith helmets packed in deep and tight on the black barge, men all the way to the port and starboard, and brimming over fore and aft like herrings in a barrel. Sergeant Hector wakes him with a push and a pull upon his kit bag – stop dreaming, old man – and then moves on through the tightly-packed mass.

It had been a disappointingly literal dream, still half in place as he nods into wakefulness: he was riding a dark horsedrawn carriage to the front, swaying and rattling over rutted lanes and in between high dark hedgerows. The front was neither in Belgium nor the Dardanelles but at home, in the South Downs; sections had been excised from the familiar curves of the Downs and twists of smoke emerged from the burrows of men. Barbed wire was strung across the flood plains. The soft green downland was overturned by explosions, the earth churned up, and all manner of bones disinterred.

He wakes to the outline of a distant shore, tawny cliffs and a high forbidding ridge. No, this is not England. This is war and men, so many men, their heat and stink and silence. Men, most decidedly not soldiers, despite months of drill. The drill that bored. Stumbling over the Downs, shedding his clothes, dropping his pack, cold and naked; and then Hector handing him a uniform in a transparent box. The long boredom was at an end. War, finally. And no matter how vividly he imagined war, no matter how much he tries to anticipate dying, he is prepared for neither. The men are silent under orders. There is nothing to say anyway. Nothing worth saying.

Sergeant Hector administers a shove to some men, reassuring others with a hand upon the shoulder, then he steps up to the bow. Portable derricks either side of a landing platform rise like the horns of a black beetle. The lieutenant colonel is sat up front, field glasses in hand, spray from the prow spattering his puttees. He passes the field glasses to Sergeant Hector and he gazes at the line of cliffs and the dark high ridge beyond, no visible sign of fighting, not from this distance. Heavy oil engines give a good seven knots. Sea shadows speed under the hull. The dark mass of the men is undisturbed by lit cigarette or nervous whistles. The sergeant, having confirmed their destination, readies them for landing.

The sky, dawn-grey and thoughtless, receives its first markings: a jerky scrawl of howitzer trails and fuzzy patches of shrapnel. A German Taube, the mark of the iron cross on the underside of each wing, turns overhead, its silver nose cone blinding in first light. The plane worries away at the barges landing at the shore. Bombs explode in columns of sand and columns of water. A shell, fired in riposte, flies wide of the plane, and the Taube turns slowly inland. The undulant swells of the dream grow choppy as time finds its feet. A destroyer rocks with the recoil of its guns and a Turkish artillery position high on the ridge explodes; wheels, cannon and the flailing shreds of uniform spin up. A retaliatory shell strikes the water so that it broils and blows out spray. Sergeant Hector grips

James by the shoulder, and will not stop gripping his shoulder; when the eyes and ears cannot be trusted, the hands search for proof.

The bay looms closer. War gathers all comers in its curved horns. Flashes of rifle fire crackle along the dark ridge, first one side, then the other: a line of rookies to scare the birds out of the trees. And they are so very scared. The lieutenant colonel, a brown-moustachioed old regular, keeps his own counsel. The enlisted men look to the soldiers, the ones with experience of battle, but they are few and far between in Kitchener's New Army. James reties the string holding up his trousers. With men all around him, he has precious little idea of where he is or where he is going. It is Saturday, he thinks. Such a strange way to spend a Saturday.

A small boat erupts upward and apart: a mine! They should turn. Turn around. Every man asks a silent question of the other. Are we about to die? Can you hold your nerve? Possibly. A solid column of water, black-fringed, rises to their aft. The air quivers with the concussive blast. The men shift their feet, wanting to run but with nowhere to run. For the first time, James feels the urge to scream.

The lighter barge is unstoppable now, the beach inevitable: the sands ahead are two miles wide, set back in a curved bay resembling the horns of the stag beetle. The war closes around him.

Along the shore, the landing is underway, a busy intersection of men and horse. Battalions jog haphazardly on soft sands through lumbering mule corps bringing up the ammunition. The beach is as crowded as market day on Petticoat Lane. He is a small part of the Expeditionary Force. He is nothing special and could be flicked aside like a crumb from the giant's table. The dry scrub on a hill burns fiercely. He did not expect to be a hero. He has prepared for death. Or at least, he has written the word "death" at the back of his diary, alongside Ruth's name and their address, and a request that it be returned to her in case he does not.

The hull rides up onto a sand bank. Ropes whirr through the derricks and the landing platform drops onto the sand. The field ambulance begins disembarking in fours, with stretchers, rations, and medical boxes. The Taube returns overhead. And the noise of it. The noise is terrifying. Shells from naval guns explode on the ridge in petals of fire. Hell's flowers. He should be running but he is not. When and where will he run? There is no cover anywhere. No cover and a hundred yards to the east, a mine heaves up and disperses a platoon across the sand. Particles of blood, particles of silica. It is his turn to run. But he cannot. Hector shouts at him but all he can do is look helplessly down at his feet. He must run!

Hector takes his hand and drags him out onto the beach. They run together, hand-locked, through the *pock-pock-pock* of rifle fire. Four shells burst amidst the lighters, further away, but still the men around them hit the ground, and Hector shouts at them: get up! get up, you rag-tag army! His voice is the only certainty in the confusion. James lets go of his hand, and feels unsteady and exposed. Four explosions from further along the beach. The shells come in fours, alternating between the men on land and the men coming out of the boats. Regular and controlled. Mechanically minded.

The order comes to fall in. Southward the pebbly white beach turns rocky, and then is cut where the river mouth opens into the sea. Lighters run aground some way from the shore, and the men, with all their kit, splash across a hundred yards of rippled sand ridges.

Vicious glare from the sun's quick rise. He blinks and blinks, already sweating, already thirsty. The lieutenant

colonel brings the men of the field ambulance to heel with
a whack of his cane against his polished boot, and then he
instructs the stretcher bearers in the features of this raw
and severe land.

North is dominated by the ridge of Karakol Dagh and its
birdless cliff that rises inland, gaining height until it
becomes the Kiretch Tepe. To the east is the greater Tekke
Tepe ridge, four miles inland and rising to about nine
hundred feet; before that there is a coverless plain and a
lake, shimmering in the August heat. No, it's not a lake.
The lieutenant colonel confers with his sergeant. The firing
line advances slowly across the lake and unless the men
are walking on water… No, it is a dried lake bed of white
sand mixed with sticky crystalline salt surrounded by
marshland. A thousand yards of open ground and the men
weighed down with rations and ammunition, two
hundred rounds around the neck – might as well be a
noose – greatcoats rolled in their packs, blankets and
waterproof sheeting – like a bloody camping trip – with
pick, shovel and kettle too, and rifle, and the instrument
of fear, the bayonet, all of this on their backs. The soldiers
hump under a pitiless sun. Rifle fire crackles *pock-pock-pock*.
Forward regardless. The imperative of the iron circle. On!
On!

Stretcher bearers will move in open formation. Their
searching zone will be the Kiretch Tepe in support of the
Manchesters. He takes one end of a folded stretcher. This
he understands. This he can do.

Bullets send up spurts of sand. He goes with his squad
over tufty hillocks of grass and thyme and then the ascent
up dried water courses raking the lower ridge. Up! Up! On!
On! To the right, deep gullies down which a man could
tumble and be hidden in the shadows under thorny
bushes. Silence abides. Nobody talks. Nobody can talk. No
man knows his own mind. Fear prises the body and soul

apart as neatly as a scallop knife – pop! He is no longer in control of himself. Someone or something else commands him: the war itself. He runs in expectation of death – any second, any second now – and then his soul will hang around like so much chaff until a stiff breeze disperses it and he will return to the source.

Up the ridge they go, through thorny waist-high scrub, their boots sliding over the loose sediment and a thirsty rock-studded earth. Perspiration streams off him, positively pouring. Five weeks on the boat has left him far from shipshape. James slips and puts his hands on this foreign ground to steady himself, accidentally letting go of his end of the folded wooden stretcher. He must not let go of the stretcher.

They have gained a hundred feet, sufficient height to look back across the beach and the landing, with its legions of men and horse, its half-pitched tents and dumped stores.

"Don't be distracted by the view," says the lieutenant colonel. He directs the stretcher squads to crawl up and down the dried watercourses of the ridge, listening for the cries of the wounded. When they find an injured man, he is to be carried back to the beach. The horse and cart ambulance are useless in this terrain. The slopes are so steep that the stretchers will have to be slid down like toboggans.

The squad drops, belly-down, into a shallow trench, no more than two feet in depth, joining four Munsters lying on their backs.

"Any wounded?" Hector asks.

"Any water?" comes the reply.

There is no time to talk. Hector risks a glance out of the trench and then he is up and running, and so is James, bent double, feet pushing against the downward slide of a sand-floored gully, lungs burning in the effort to keep up with his mountain goat of a sergeant. He dare not let go of the stretcher because without it he will look like a soldier and then he will be of significance to the snipers.

Hector has heard the call for bearers; he holds his index finger up, listening, locating. There! Still doubled-over, they scuttle through holly bush then slide into another shallow trench dug out of the yellow-orange earth, and discover an entire squad in repose. Only one soldier deigns to speak to them, a ratty private, with blood crusted at his ears and nose; he has the loud voice of a deaf man and his left calf has been stripped from the shin bone. As Hector dresses the wound, James asks after the wellbeing of the other soldiers only to discover that they are immaculately dead, with not a mark on them.

On the long carry back down the ridge, Hector speculates as to what killed the rest of the squad. A concussive blow from a shell, he decides, which blasted the life from them. Literally snuffed it right out. The private must have survived because, well, Hector didn't know how, and since the private on the stretcher is adrift in morphine, suspended in it, protected and imprisoned like a foetus in a jar, it's no use asking him. Down the slope they slide, loose scree underfoot, the stretcher pitching and yawing with the unsteady footing. James finds himself looking at the private's wound more than he would like: cloth, skin and flesh are fused into one piece like an ornate chair leg. The bone is out. Out of place. The blood running down from his ears has dried in perfect round seeds. The private weighs not much more than a bag of dead leaves, unlike the stretcher itself, which is thirty pounds of wood and cloth, a weight which he feels in his back with every jolting step.

They return to the beach. The carts are useless on the ridge and they only sink into this soft sand. The squads head southward, two men to each stretcher, thirty of them, a human conveyor belt. The casualty clearing station contains bell tents and a marquee with a red cross visible to the Turk spotters, and these are pitched at the river's cut.

Gently, James lowers his end of the stretcher, the sling around his chest slackening. The injured man breathes quickly through bared teeth.

"Water," gasps the injured man, his lips chapped and sore from the long carry under the sun. The flies find him. He flinches and spits them out. The flies are remorseless. The flies return with additional divisions.

James walks along the line. All of the injured men want water. Some want their mothers. In preparation for serving with the ambulance, he had volunteered at the hospital in Brighton. On his first night he saw a cut nose, a deep gash across the bridge, and it upset him greatly. It did not prepare him for this, for the missing pieces, for the scraps. The unmanned moans of pain. Quite inhuman. Or too human. The wounds are an obscene revelation of what being human entails.

Rain clouds approach across the sea. Hector shows the men how to weight a peg so that it holds in the sand. Then he directs the erecting of a tarp. He's a real boy scout. Big fat raindrops form tiny craters in the sand. A rivulet runs down the tarp, James crouches openmouthed under it, refills his canteen, then his mouth, then washes off the sand and clay in his scalp. The khaki drill of his uniform is soaked until it steams.

A doctor, a thin man with high widow's peaks in his close-cropped hair, joins him at the rivulet and nods at James' canteen. His manner is brisk and his hands are bloody. James holds the canteen to the doctor's lips for a swig of rain water. He drinks it all. Orderlies arrive with baskets of bandages and sterilized sacks. They mill in expectation of orders; crouching, the doctor and James wait for the thin stream of rainwater to refill the canteen.

"We landed at the wrong beach and had to trek across the sands with all this." The doctor waves a thin bloody hand at the station. "How we're doing out there?"

"The Manchesters have broken through on the northern ridge. We're bringing their injured down."

"That's a long carry."

"The mules can't handle the sand and neither can the motor."

"What about the other beaches?"

"I don't know. From the ridge, it all looks like war to me. We came across a squad. They were dead but their bodies were intact, with no sign of injury. They were lying around as if enjoying an afternoon doze. My sergeant thinks they were killed by a compressive blast. Have you ever seen anything like that?"

"It could be gas. But you'd smell it. Nurses can turn yellow from merely removing the uniforms of men who have been gassed. Who is your sergeant?"

"Hector, sir."

"And you are?"

"James, sir."

"Private James."

"I prefer just James, sir."

The doctor looked askance at this breach of military code.

"You must meet the padre. He'll like you. You're one of his types. A freethinker."

Before James can disagree, the doctor stands and returns to the shade of the tent, organizing the orderlies and attending to the wounded. The rain has stopped and the tarp dripped dry. Out to sea, battleships at anchor shell the ridge and their firing is a constant rolling noise. The shells the Turks toss back come in various forms: the whining whirring ones, the crashing iron kitchen sink ones, the high explosive ones that stop time for a silent moment in which the rocks, rifles and limbs float weightlessly and then noise and time devastatingly resume. Honour, in the face of such blunt mechanical force, is impossible. Honour is absurd. A man does not have to be a freethinker to understand that.

The squads fall in. The lieutenant colonel orders the men to pool their canteens, every man adding his water ration to a big empty petrol can. It's the only way to be sure that no one is hoarding water. They trek back up the ridge in Indian file, with the lieutenant colonel leading, followed by Sergeant Hector, then the squads with folded stretchers and finally the corporal bringing up the rear in case any man should fall out. Salt lines streak his shirt and his pith helmet reeks of sweat. The cry for water goes up along the shore, where the Aegean breaks against the gentle rise of the sands. Nothing else is worth saying.

13

James sips juice from a cold tin of peaches, the sharp edge dithering under his lip. He has to concentrate. It's hard to concentrate. Did he sleep? Has he slept? In the ravine, Jordison cooks up salty beef and biscuits but he can't stomach it, not in the middle of the night and not without water. Digesting that lot will take more effort than the food puts in. The ground is painfully cold even through the sheeting and his greatcoat, and his shoulder feels like it has been packed in ice. The sea mist rolls over him and it tastes of salt and cordite.

Exhaustion is a thin blanket tattered with bullet holes.

Overhead, a single star is visible through the layered vapours. He had expected the sky to be full of stars and is disappointed that the atmosphere is so thick. When will he be able to drift above the clouds? When will he see what the Earth looks like from space? Or gaze into the Beyond without the gauzy intervention of the veil? By concentrating his will into an astral entity, it ought to be possible to escape the boredom of gravity, turn back and see the sun reflect off the Aegean, the atmosphere tinged with sunrise, a land of gauzy greens and bluish browns bounded by mountain ranges and dark coastal waters, and nothing of man visible. Space would be cold and airless, and overstocked with stars. Positively stuffed with stars. The sun would not be yellow, but a round heart of livid whiteness fringed with a searing red corona. Space would be lethal, and of a blackness unknown to the Earth. His spirit would traverse the void powered by will. The fundamental unit of reality is will. The stars are burning engines of will. The stars desire his ascent, and he responds in kind; why does this not happen? How preposterous that the talent to bend space to his own will is denied to him! What ridiculous futility! He wants to see the universe. He must. Visions are near, just over the curvature of the Earth, curved like a dining table. Thoughts branch of their own volition, form decision trees with variable outcomes.

He sighs.

He is asleep again. If only he could concentrate.

His hand droops but does not let go of the can of peaches.

"Why must I always wake you, James?" asks Sergeant Hector through narrow lips. The sergeant is younger than him, an NCO promoted for excellence on the parade ground before they had even got to the Dardanelles. A natural leader, yes, but also a loner. Northern chap. Not particularly clubbable. Three inches short of proper officer class.

"I'm awake," he mumbles. Emerging from their bivouacs in the ravine, the stretcher squad forms a shivering Indian line behind the sergeant. James falls in and the line jogs out into the night, past Alligator Point. His heart beats quickly, from the shock of being awake and nicotine starvation, and his legs are yet to find their strength. The stretcher bearers run along the wet ridged sand, alongside the florescent fizz of breaking waves and the slide of the sea back into fathoms of heavy shadow.

The hike is too bloody much. A cigarette would help, a pinch from the plug of filthy twist in his pocket. He is not permitted to strike a light until dawn; the big guns may be silent but snipers haunt the ridges. The Munsters pilfered dark clumps of baccy from the Turk when the sentries bolted from their piquets at the first sign of the landing and declared it superior to the twist issued in their rations. They found the coffee pot still boiling away too. Talk about a spot of luck.

Jordison has the other end of the stretcher. The 10th Division was formed as an Irish regiment, with the numbers in the ambulance division made up from the all sorts and odd sorts you didn't want in the line: the weak-chested cranks, piratical Boer veterans and pacifist intellectuals and – in one case – a professor of mathematics who could not abide the shame of the white feather. Even the sergeant was a Quaker, albeit a Quaker with the holler of a warmonger.

And then there were the nonconformists from the northwest, like Jordison, a gardener from Morecambe or thereabouts; he described the visibility balloons tethered to the ships as being like great yellow marrows. On the pier at Lemnos, they had coaxed Jordison into smoking his first cigarette but he absolutely refused the rum. A man of principle. Salt of the earth.

"And what is your creed?" Jordison asked James, coughing behind his coffin nail. "If I carry a stretcher with a man, I'm owed an account of his beliefs. There must be something wrong about you to end up in the ambulance. What do you believe in? What do you strive for?"

I would like to drift above the earth and embrace the naked stars.

Jordison has more wind in him for the climb up the ridge than James can muster and keeps glancing impatiently back at his fellow stretcher bearer. The moon is a thorn sunk deep in the cloud and the meagre light of a single star is not much to work by, never mind navigate. The maps are of the wrong scale for this kind of work and do not accurately represent the torturous routes they have to take.

The air cools as they climb. At a hundred feet, the vegetation is jungly. They mustn't get lost again: he reminds Jordison not to lose track of the others.

"Here's one," says Jordison. They set the stretcher down and get a closer look. In the dark, you can't see where they've been hit. How beyond help they might be. This one has flies in the wrong places and a queer scent, a mix of putrefaction and the perfume of wild thyme, sage and mint gathering in the hollows.

"God help him," whispers Jordison. They leave the body behind.

They climb on, but the gully does not open up into a clear view of the surrounding country. Rather, it leads them deeper into the spiky overgrowth. The path is narrow and steep. To keep up with the squad, Jordison drags them through a palisade of bullrushes. They break through waist-high scrub and nearly go headfirst over the edge of a cliff. Jordison rears back no more than two feet from the cliff edge. The two men breathe in the sheer grey drop down to black waves.

"What kind of mad country is this?" asks the Lancastrian. "This is not the way we were heading."

"You got lost." James turns around. It's his turn to lead. They have lost the squad. Their training in signalling was better suited to advancing across flat terrain than this broken country. Back down the narrow path he goes, then quickly up a hillock to get a broad view of the work at hand. A nullah to the other flank, a steep narrow dried watercourse, down which it would be easy for a man to lose his footing and fall. A likely spot for a carry. He holds his hand up. Wait. Listen. Yes, from somewhere down the bottom of the nullah. Voices. He beckons Jordison close and points down.

Jordison listens too, then shakes his heavy head.

"You don't hear them?"

"How do we know they are our men?"

They listen again. Oak branches stirring. The voices may be English, or they might not. They could be accents from another part of the Empire: Welsh or Irish, Australian or Indian. Jordison is not convinced. He is a doughty man but cautious. Surely, over the next rise, there will be easier carries than this one? The men discuss it in agitated whispers. James points firmly to his chest. I'll go. I'll go alone. Jordison agrees, and settles down on his belly, hands to the fore, to lower James and his tentative boots into the sliding slipping earth of the nullah. He does not want to go pounding down there only to discover a squad of Turks, nor does he want to be mistaken by his own soldiers for the enemy. The Turk respects the red cross but cannot see it in the dark.

James takes out his regulation twist, rolls himself a cigarette, and lights it in the bowl of his helmet. With the lit end still covered, he drags softly upon it, feels the smoke settle the inner dispute of his nicotine craving, and then exhales blue and grey smoke down the course of the nullah. He descends, and every yard or so, exhales another mouthful of the noxious twist. Any man on his side would recognize it. He slides another four, five yards. He puts his hands up and steps through the scrub expecting to see men huddled ahead. But there is no one. Just two dark patches on the ground and the ferrous tang of bloodsoaked earth. The spot is so peaceful and reflective it reminds him of home. He strains to listen. The injured men may have retreated at his approach, a sure sign that they are the enemy and could, right now, be crouched in the scrub. Watching him. Aiming at him.

The oak branches stir; between these branches, quivering silver webs, six in a row and glistening with dew, each with a big spider at the heart of them. The mind is inclined to spot faces in nature; when afraid, every man is a pantheist, alive to the spirits within rock and tree. He looks again at the blood on the ground; his squad must have attended to the injured men, and the voices he heard were their reassurances as they carried the wounded away. There are only phantoms in the bush.

He takes the long way back up the nullah, a zigzag path, clearer and not as steep as the way down. He gets a handhold of earth and a centipede runs over his wrist. It is the lull before dawn and the land seethes with anticipation. This soil didn't seem to him to be fit for much but the maps showed a cultivated patch beyond the salt lake, perhaps olives, or even corn. Anything he could eat straight off the bough would be alright to him. Grapes. Something with a bit of juice in it. He comes across a hawthorn bush full of blackberries just like the ones at home. August is too early for ripe berries, and these are sharp and not as plump as the ones he picked with Ruth on the paths leading down to Alfriston.

They had ridden out to make love at the foot of the Long Man of Wilmington, as the old wives had told her it was a fertility symbol. Unlike the Cerne Giant, the Long Man was without phallus and seemed more to him like a spirit gripping the sides of a doorway, and about to step through. After they made love, she gathered blackberries in a basket and, when it was full, sloeberries in the train of her skirts.

Jordison hauls him up onto the path. They take hold of the stretcher again. Darkness was considered vital to the success of the landing, but it is of no help to a stretcher bearer. Going up and down the nullah has left him more disorientated. He could not even say, with any certainty, in which direction lay the sheer cliff of Saros Bay.

The war itself is no help, it is strangely silent.

"We have to find the aid post. We must rejoin the rest of the ambulance," says Jordison.

But which way? James searches the sky for clues. The single star has gone out, obscured by thick immovable cloud. They walk on, uncertain, with the crawling sensation that every step will have to be retraced. After two miles, they realize that they have wandered beyond their own lines. They keep going. One mission of the landing is to gain and secure this ridge, and they have done so, accidentally, two stretcher bearers lost on the first night of their war. The terrain twists this way and that, manipulating them to its own ends.

They climb to gain a vantage point in this mad country. A searchlight beam divides the night in two. The triangular beam, with the apex emanating from a point that could be behind Turkish lines, advances across the topmost ridge. They drop to the ground, and Jordison shuffles backward. The searchlight stops ten yards to the left. Then flicks five yards closer. Jordison freezes; to stifle a cry, he bites down on the earth. The patch of illuminated ground slides closer and reveals a figure, two yards ahead. It is a body, one hand clutching the air in rigor mortis. James buries his head in the ground and turns his face toward his chest, and tucks in his legs, so that his breathing will not reveal him. In this foetal position, he waits in a prolonged quivering moment, hoping that whoever aims the searchlight will mistake their prone bodies for corpses. A last thought of Ruth, he owes her that much; to remember her at the moment of his extinction. A faint muscle memory of their lovemaking outdoors, the exultation of his bare arse between her splayed legs, the anxiety that they will be discovered giving the act a wanton urgency in which he selfishly pursued his own pleasure in a way that she responded to. Tighter, he tucks his knees up in anticipation of being bathed in light. As if he could fold himself flat and slip through the cracks in the earth.

"It has passed," whispers Jordison. The searchlight flicks down the ridge. Opposite, the silhouetted hand of a dead body slowly closes into a fist and becomes a living shadow. Sergeant Hector. He slides down between them.

"We got lost," says James. "I'm so glad you found us."

"I'm lost too," Hector replies. "I reckon we're beyond the British outposts and not far from Turkish lines. I can't see a damn thing. If that searchlight hadn't swung up here I'd have gone right over the precipice. It's a fair bet that it's a Turkish searchlight which puts their lines somewhere down the ridge."

All three men, shivering on the high ground, search the horizon for some sign of the bay: a grey streak in the distance seems the most likely.

"We'll head that way," says Hector.

"But when we get in that mad country again, we'll lose our bearings," says Jordison.

"We can't stay here."

"Staying here makes more sense than blundering around in the dark."

"It should be sunrise by now," says James

He has never experienced combat before. None of them has. He has been afraid before. Of course he has. Not like this though. A entire day of fear with more days of terror to come. Weeks even. How will they stand it?

"When sun comes up, we're as safe here as we are on the beach," says Jordison. Hector is not listening. He puts a subduing hand on Jordison. In the passing glare of the searchlight, in the centre of a clump of bushes, James sees a figure move: its helmet and uniform are interwoven with leaves and branches to form a pelt of vegetation, and in its hands, a rifle. The searchlight moves on. The night rushes in.

"He's found me again." Hector is riveted with disbelief. "He's looking right at me."

"Who is?" asks Jordison.

"The sniper. He's after me."

Hector slides down a steep stratum of the ridge, so steep that if they did not have a sniper at their backs, Jordison and James would never have followed him. The three men grunt and leap down through the broken stones. The descent ends in tall grass and thistles, through which they run crouching and cringing in anticipation of a bullet.

James risks a look back: at the crest of the hillock, the sniper's silhouette, taller than a man, with fronds and bullrushes fixed to his helmet, and branches jutting every way out of his uniform. James swears he sees the bushes on the flank advance toward him also. The land is not a neutral party in this war. The land has taken sides.

A rifle fires. The sound is different than standard musketry, hollower, and ends with a faint intake and hydraulic hiss. A bullet cracks through the air like a whiplash. James considers going foetal again. Another bullet whistles by and thuds dully, disappointedly, into the soil. Like hares ahead of the plough, the three men run, each in their own fashion; Hector with high knees and bladed palms; Jordison, burdened, flailing through waist-high thistles; and James, dodging, trying to devise as he runs the ideal pattern to follow if one is to avoid being shot, that is, the correct number of steps to take in a particular direction before veering off in another. A bullet sighs in his ear with unreciprocated adoration. In daylight they would be dead men, but the night spares them; Hector's run banks sharp right, and he leads them into the shelter of the nullah, whooping joyfully as he disappears.

Thank God for the dark, thinks James. Thank God for that single disappeared star.

14

His feet sink into the sand, his hands raw from carrying the stretcher, now abandoned somewhere up the ridge. Exhausted, he cannot even perform the calculation required to thread a shoelace. It is unspeakable that he takes another step. Yet he must. And he does. Stamina is his talent. Marriage, duty, forbearance, suffering: endurance is beautiful.

Dawn rises over the sea as it has risen since ancient times and will continue to rise long after this terrible war has ended.

Beside him, Jordison, head down, stumbles leftward across the grey beach, then rightward, then left again; even Hector, the mountain goat, is feeling the weight of the long night. Of the sniper nothing more has been seen but that is the way with snipers.

Jordison crumples untidily to the sand.

"What is the point of it all?" he cries.

It is the third time that Jordison has asked this question of them. James cannot muster the energy to respond. Hector is reduced to simple imperatives: shut up, come on, keep up, not far now – as if he were a father determined to lead recalcitrant children to a pleasant view.

James returns to help Jordison up. The Lancastrian is heavy with tiredness.

"I wish you had a gun, then you could shoot me in the hand and the two of you could carry me onto the hospital ship."

"I have a knife. I could stab you in the hand. But it's likely the wound would get infected. And then you would die. Probably on the hospital ship surrounded by other dying men."

Jordison shakes his head. He's gone deep inside himself and is questioning what he finds there.

"Why are we here? What does it mean?"

"There is no point in asking why. You can't get to the bottom of the world through reason. We must use feeling."

"I feel spent."

"We all do. But I can't leave you here and if you insist upon flopping to the ground like a sack of spuds then you put us all in danger. Get up. Get up and walk with me."

James hauls the groaning Jordison to his feet. They walk together toward the beach. Silvery threads of first light on the grey and indigo waters of the bay, winding around the peaks of Imbros to the south west, and Samothrace to the north west. The naval guns resume and are answered by shells from the Turkish positions. Underfoot shimmers with distant impacts. The firing line is further inland than the day before. The battle is thinning out. The Turks were surprised and outmatched by the naval guns. Soon the Allies will gain the ridge. It is feasible that he may even get out of this alive.

"The world is so very beautiful." James puts his arm around the bleary-faced Lancastrian. "Because it endures. Are you loved, Jordison? Do you love anyone?"

"You've gone mad, haven't you?"

"I am determined to think only of love between here and the camp, and that will see us home. My wife is called Ruth. We were childhood sweethearts. I have long felt our union was a matter of destiny and that is why it endures;

if it were one of chance, it would not be so beautiful."

James' strange sozzled talk amuses Sergeant Hector, eavesdropping from a few paces ahead. "You want to know why we are here. I will tell you. If we can love one person, Jordison, then we can find meaning in the universe. We must cultivate love if we are to address your questions of 'why are we here?' and 'what does it all mean on the cosmic scale?' That is to say, we must become cosmic lovers."

"You'd tell me if you two have been on the rum, wouldn't you?" Jordison asks his sergeant.

Hector, with sandy eyebrows, wafts flies from his lips.

"Private James, doesn't cosmic love suggests its opposite of cosmic hate?"

James nods, "Our sergeant is a mystic. Theosophist, philosopher or gymnosopher – which are you, sergeant?"

"I believe in studying all the world's religions."

Hector's dark eyes are alive to the prospect of mockery and he watches James carefully before continuing: "I don't cleave to any one religion. They all stem from the same point. The same pattern. And are proceeding toward the same end."

"Spoken like a true mystic. Tell me, sergeant, was your enlistment part of your search for knowledge? Did you secretly come here to improve yourself?"

"I enlisted to serve."

"But not to serve your country."

"You are tired, private."

The conversation renders Jordison indignant.

"There is no knowledge to be gained in war. Nothing to be learned. Nothing good, anyway." Tired and sullen, his broad face is smeared with red earth. "And if there was, whatever schooling we receive will soon be spread over the earth along with our arms and legs."

To the wounded men on the beach, sunrise comes as a

relief after a long cold night under the tarp. A hundred or so men have been laid down at the clearing station to join the hundred already lying there. Not all of them wake at dawn. The orderlies go along the lines and pull blankets over the faces of the dead. Emerging from a sandbagged dugout, the doctor puts his mug of tea up on a corrugated iron roof while he lights his morning pipe. The smell of strong tobacco covers the odour of corruption.

The three stretcher bearers sink dog-tired into dugouts. James falls asleep so quickly that his self-awareness is not entirely extinguished, and rises through the monstrous proportions of the dream landscape like a kite-tail. He dreams of love and the long carry, with him at one end and Ruth at the other, and between them an empty stretcher.

It is too hot to sleep for long. He wakes with the conviction that it's a Sunday. And it is. Strange that it should feel like a Sunday here and now, with Jordison making tea on the primus stove and the naval guns clanging repeatedly; their racket combines with the heat of the sun to become an enormous oven door being repeatedly slammed shut. Yet it is undeniably a Sunday.

Hector moves among the men as he passes out the rum ration. He informs them that Father Huxley will lead mass in the gully while Canon McKenzie, for men of Protestant persuasion, will take a congregation through hymns and homilies from the shelter of a cove.

"Which will you attend, sergeant?"

"I am told the padre is a freethinker," says Hector, slopping grog into James' tin cup.

"Doesn't the army require the opposite of freethinking?"

The young sergeant squints. He knows the older man is mocking – but what? Him?

"You are a Quaker, of course," says James.

"By birth and education."

"You're a crank like the rest of us. You must have noticed the prevalence of cranks in the ambulance. We've been filed here."

"We must serve. We must do our duty by our fellow man. And keep our true thoughts about King and Country to ourselves. Drink your rum, private."

The rum softens the stiffness in his arms. He lies before the Aegean Sea and gazes out, beyond the rocking destroyers, with their puffer clouds of gunsmoke, to the mauve and jagged outline of Imbros. If the men do not take the higher ground, there will be nowhere for them to go but back into the sea. Pushing on should be a matter of some urgency; yet, along the beach, the army is inert. It mills. The men dig trenches, and squads march left then right, kicking up dust in their drudgery. The landing mixed up the regiments and they are continually resorting and unsorting themselves in an attempt to find order. The clanging oven door of the artillery makes it hard for the commanding officers to think straight. An excess of orders creates chaos and in response the landing is – if not becalmed – then directionless, almost indolent.

The religious service adds to the perverse normality of the Sunday morning. In shirtsleeves and pith helmets, the congregation squints against the sun and waft flies from their faces. The stretcher bearers sit at the back, the fighting men to the fore. Huxley, the priest, is a tall ascetic type in golden chasuble. He sets up a portable altar and sacred kit. His long, young face concentrates upon the ritual with a deliberate gentleness. His voice is not always audible above the ordinance. A high explosive shell lifts the lid momentarily upon the world, and then lets it fall noisily back into place. The padre swallows drily, his pronounced Adam's apple dips, and then he continues his sermon, his tone stronger, his volume greater.

James gazes back along the curve of the bay in the direction of the explosion. Lighter craft continue to land, with soldiers sloshing through low tide. The silver sand is blotted with the black misshapes of the dead, human and animal. The clank of a cold beef bone in a tin cup. He retches.

The flies will grow fat on a diet of men. James cringes and baulks at the feel of them on his skin. Corruption clings to the hairs of their black and red legs like dew to grass. The flies will multiply. The flies will swarm out of a blazing hellhole to cool their feet upon the faces of the dead.

The padre does not speak of Hell. He studiously ignores it. Nor does he make much of Heaven. This congregation has not come to hear confirmation of a particular orthodoxy. Rather it is the wellspring of all religious feeling that they want. And what is the enlightenment that the men thirst for? He cannot say. Meaning? An answer to Jordison's question about why they are there and why they must die? No. Such questions belong to the naivety of yesterday. Being together, in the gully, surrounded by the scented beach herbs, to know that one still belongs to life, that is it. Yes. To feel that one will not be forgotten.

He never believed in God, not even as a boy in the school hall when, eyes closed and hands pressed together in prayer, he longed to be transported up to another realm. When he peeked, the chilly school hall remained. The boys bleated the hymns then sat in tousled ranks, cross-legged and numb-arsed in short trousers, as the headmaster deployed scripture to explain what the boys could and could not do in the yard. His earliest memory is disbelief. He has simply never been able to believe a word of power's cant. There is a possibility of God or some guiding agency in the universe (though not – in all likelihood – here, on this beach) but he has never felt it. All is expedient, utilitarian, accidental, sorted and unsorted according to love and hate. He could mount a defence of love as a sorting principle. Love could make a benign order out of this hell.

The padre dips his fingers in holy water. The congregation fidgets with thirst.

The service complete, the men fall out, shaking the sand from the seat of their trousers. Sergeant Hector goes over to the padre as he gathers up the altar, and shares his spiritual concerns. James, godless, takes out his pen and paper and writes a letter to Ruth concerning his theory of the cosmic lovers.

He writes: "You and I are the alpha and omega at opposite ends of the universe and we come together in the generative force of consummation. I will have a pair of rings made for us, the Greek symbols for Alpha and Omega in gold and silver."

His whimsy is auntish. Unserious. Should he, then, write about the bodies that he lay down under the tarps? With their covering of skin and flesh overturned in the same way that a shell overturns the earth?

The wounded men do not get the help they expect, and in their eyes, a blankness that will, in the coming weeks, spread from face to face; their expectations must be recalibrated to harmonize what lies within with what lies without. The result is madness, of course. The madness that proceeds from the logic of war. No, he will not write about what it feels like to put your foot through a dead man's rib cage and to hear the trapped air expire: *wffffffftt*.

In the letter, he suggests that they must go blackberry picking upon his return, and, if he is back after first frost, to gather the sloes from the chalk pit in Wilmington. He hopes Ruth will catch the allusion to the afternoon they made love at the foot of the Long Man on Windover Hill. They had been reading about fertility rites, 'Spirits of the Corn and The Wild' from *The Golden Bough*. The blasphemy of his bare white arse in the sunlight. The way she did not immediately gather herself once the act was done but lay there, splayed and smiling, for a wanton minute. The straw flattened and shaped by Ruth. At night all my troubles come to me but I have learnt to drive them away with thoughts of you, dear Ruth. Remember me. Preserve me in your thoughts.

Flies cluster at the nib of his pen, interrupting the thought. Arguing with it. He swats them away, dabs the blot they have caused, and tries to pick up the thread of cosmic love.

He is interrupted by Collinson, the professor, with his round eyeglasses and boyish enthusiasm for theories and ideas. Another Quaker. The youngest of seven children. All the firstborns go to the firing line, and all the lastborns hang back. Collinson is not much older than James but he has a tendency to be didactic and would be something of a bore if his ideas weren't so cranky.

"This battle is not right. We should not be stuck here like this." Collinson sits next to James.

"Don't you think this landing is very odd? I've been observing the men. And our orders. We are not behaving as men ought to behave in the condition of battle."

"How ought we to behave?"

Collinson's blond hair is thin around the crown in contrast to his thick dark eyebrows. He squints at James through his round wireframe spectacles.

"You must have noticed the peculiarities."

"It's all peculiar, Collinson. It's war."

"If it's war, then why are we lying on a beach? The battle should have more impetus than this. More forward momentum. It should not be inert."

"What would you suggest?"

"We are here to secure the high ground. That was the entire purpose of the landing. And yet we have dug in positions on the beach. It goes against the logic of our orders."

Hector, lost in spiritual matters, wanders by. Collinson stops him.

"Don't you think, sergeant, that there is something odd about our situation? We sail halfway around the world, to land upon a foreign land at great cost, only to *lounge*."

Collinson gestures at the men who are undressing at the water's edge.

"There! The perfect proof of my argument. Here we are at war and those men are bathing as if they are at Brighton beach. If this were a normal conflict, then our general would be here among us, driving us forward, filling the men with the will to fight, not hiding on the *HMS Jonquil* with a dodgy knee. Here, I have made the calculation."

Collinson takes out a pocket book. He licks his forefinger then flicks to the relevant page of algebraic formula.

"Our losses yesterday ought to have created an impetus for vengeance, under the reciprocal instinctive stimulation of combat." He prods a particular portion of the equation twice. "Instead, the men are swimming."

James says, "You are failing to take into account the inhospitable land."

They gaze up at the high ridges encircling the bay.

Hector says, "We gained the ridge last night, quite by accident. Collinson is right. There is no logical reason for us to stay on the beach. But it does not follow that there is something strange about the war. Merely about our orders."

"The soldiers should not be bathing."

"They are not soldiers," says Hector. "They are men and their uniforms are chatty with lice. If I were to swim now, would that alter your equation?"

"You are being perverse," says Collinson.

Hector takes off his helmet, leans out of his braces and unbuttons his shirt.

"We are under fire! A man cannot be naked under fire!"

Hector kicks off his boots, and in a white flash, drops his trousers.

"You are being prudish, Collinson. You are using mathematics as a fig leaf."

The young sergeant walks steadily into the sea, dives into the waves and swims out to join the bobbing laughing heads of other swimmers. Small piles of clothes dot the shore like worm casts. More men dive into the water from a rickety pier. Ammunition mules pause in their doleful progress, eyelids sticky with flies, their tails flicking, as they consider the swimmers. The sing and burst of a high explosive along the beach jolts the beasts back into motion.

The blue-green water is melted glass. Undressing quickly, James bolts to the water and dives immediately into the misty saltiness. The water fills his ears with the roar of his blood's circulation. The surface shimmers with the sea breeze. He cuts across the water with a quick controlled stroke. Not all of the men can swim and some paddle up to their waists. He swims out to sea and away from the rickety pier so that, looking back, he sees that there are dozens, perhaps a hundred or so men, in the water. Collinson is wrong: swimming is logical. There is no cover on the beach. The shelling is intermittent whereas the itch of lice, the persistence of flies, the enduring stink of fear and exertion – these are constants.

His skin cools, then he turns onto his back, showing the sun the facts of himself. In the sea, boys shyly wash, cupping water over a jutting solar plexus and under the arms. The grossness of civilian life has been worn away from their naked bodies. James admires a handful of exceptional types in this otherwise average body of men: a navvy with overdeveloped upper arms; a middle-aged miner with a proud firm chest covered in clutches of grey curls; and Sergeant Hector, the figure of perfection without a spare grain of flesh on him due to his morning observance of calisthenics.

Hector swims alone with an expression of great seriousness, accustomed to setting himself private goals and then exceeding them. He told James that he had been a boy scout, though not one for parade, not for bugles and badges, but for summers in the countryside. Sleeping outdoors was vital for the future fitness of the human race, said the sergeant. James imagines him doing solitary star jumps outside a small one-man tent pitched on the banks of the Wye, followed by freezing dawn dips in an idle current, then hauling himself naked out through the reeds, his buttocks concave at the sides, his vertebrae a stack of marble pebbles.

Four beats on an iron crowbar. The men are being called back out of the water. Time for war. But what had he been up to before the war? Teaching genetics to the boys, publishing a thin volume of speculation concerning the future of man, and delighting in marriage. James floats upon the dip and swell of the waves. He remembers the newness of the domestic fug, a stock pot on the stove and Ruth's warm hip under the cotton shift of her nightie. He had been so very attentive to life, had let books and experience fill him up. If only he had a gramophone that could record thought, inscribe the phantasmagoria of the mind directly into long vinyl grooves without lie or hesitation, then he could have dictated his civilian self to disc in order to preserve it, before war hollowed him out. Upon his return home, he would slip the record from its sleeve and restore what had been lost.

The men run naked from the sea, bending low to scoop up their uniforms, skipping over telegraph wire, and haring onward. Collinson waits for James, and when the private emerges naked from the water, the professor attends to cleaning his eyeglass and whispers, "Foolish... foolish." In his wake, the sea gulps down two, three, four shells then violently expels them.

15

Their dugouts are shallow dents in the side of a hill half a mile from the waterline. The section fall out in various aspects, some curled up, others face down. Jordison kicks off his boots, loosens his puttees and throws himself thankfully upon the ground. Collinson mutters in his sleep while James lounges on his elbows, feet stretched out before him. Duties will resume after sundown.

Hector measures the last of the afternoon light. He has a little water in his canteen. He takes his set of paints from his knapsack, wets his brush and considers the men in their repose.

"I thought you only painted birds," says James.

"Have you seen any birds? There are tracks on the beach made by a sand bird, some kind of martin. The cliff face has nests but they are empty."

"Isn't there some other wildlife you could paint?"

Hector dabs at the air with the brush. "Do you object?"

"There must be a more edifying subject than soldiers. Women. Paint me a woman."

Hector is silent.

"Paint me a woman from memory," says James. "And not your mother."

"I have a sweetheart," says Hector. "My Sparrowhawk."

"Another bird!"

"Sparrowhawk is her camp name. She comes up to about here on me…" He draws a line level with his chest. "I could paint her in her uniform. A skirt of coarse brown Indian silk, tie and headdress."

"Is that what you do at home? Play Cowboys and Indians?" asks James.

"Just Indians," says Hector.

"Aren't you a little old for all that?"

Hector smiles.

"We're the new barbarians," he says. "Men and women living close to the land away from mechanical civilization."

James holds up his hand.

"Please, no more philosophy. I just want to talk about women. Do you and Sparrowhawk share a tent?"

"We do."

"That's very forward thinking of you."

"I am a strong potent well-knit man."

"I don't doubt it."

"A woman who finds herself with an impotent man – male wreckage – should be free to find a good male animal. Sex revulsion and inversion spells death, in the long run."

"Please, no talk of death. Only sex. Isn't that right, men?"

The rest of the section listen to the tired banter, their heads down, the whites of their eyes shining brightly from faces grimy with sweat and sand. Private Brilliant makes a fire of the sickly-sweet thyme and heats water in a mess tin to make tea.

"You are married," says Hector. "What kind of marriage is it? Are you equal, in a sort of co-partnership, or do you embrace polarity of the sexes?"

"What does that mean?"

"Is the marriage well setup with a vital sexual contrast?"

"Do you come up with all this at your camps?"

Hector puts his brush aside, turns the page of his book, and shows James a symbol: it is a yin-yang within the outline of the Greek symbol Omega. "Before the war, we camped every fortnight to debate… well, everything, I suppose. It all seems up for grabs."

"My marriage is sound," says James, "but we'll all return changed men. Then we'll see what new bargains have to be made. If we even survive another day like today."

The day has been without respite: the squad worked three-mile humps across a parched and burning land between the casualty clearing station and the regimental aid post, little more than a half-dug trench beneath a blasted oak tree on Chocolate Hill.

The men named it Chocolate Hill for its charred brown scrub. It rises steeply from the plain to a height of a hundred and sixty feet, the air thick with smoke and iron. At the aid post, there were never less than thirty wounded waiting to be carried. More wounded than they could accommodate. The corporal ordered that the regulation bearer squads of four be split up and so they worked in twos. Then came the downward stabbing light of shrapnel. Man and horse fled in every direction. When the smoke cleared, there was a figure lying prone on the ground, the corporal. James and Hector dug his grave and then James made a cross from a plank torn from a Fray Bentos crate.

"Why don't you paint the shell bursts?" says James. "Every type of shell has its individual bloom. There is one I particularly like: it comes down in a hail of hot iron then disperses in pale blue smoke."

"If I had thick oils I would paint the high-explosive as it ploughs a deep furrow in the clay then belches a black and khaki cloud."

"And what of the call of the bullets? Every sniper's rifle has its song; in the absence of birdsong, I will learn to whistle bulletsong."

The squadrons had advanced steadily in parade lines across the scrub plains; here and there, men were flicked out of formation, their vitality subtracted neatly by a sniper's bullet. Shells exploded like the tedious inspiration of a machine mind. "Mechanical death," grunted Hector.

James took the front poles and Hector the rear, at the sergeant's insistence. Blood dripped through the canvas stretcher and onto their boots and into the sand. As fatigue set in, the blood lines and blood trails grew more haphazard. Not all the stretchers had slings and some of the wounded were big, fourteen stone or so. Between carries, they swapped places to give Hector a breather. One case hemorrhaged with a gasp and a whimper, and they set him down gently to fix his dressing. James' toes tingled as he lowered down his end of the stretcher, anxious that the wounded man would break open if put down too heavily. When they had him wrapped up all nice and tight again, the soldier thanked them and died.

Hector had to cut two dead mules from the ambulance wagon. James and Jordison restrained their mates; the animals had the same blazing white-of-the-eye fear as the men. The wheels sank in the sand and the wagon listed to one side; the shelling got so hot they had to abandon the beasts with the intention of retrieving them at night.

At five o'clock sharp, the Hun sent over a spotter plane. *Dab*, *dab*, *dab* went the anti-aircraft guns on the blue sky.

"You should paint the landscape," says James. Never paint the wounded. The head cases and the leg cases and the groaning abdominals; the one who got it through both cheeks and had his tongue taken off; the one who was coughing blood and wouldn't lie down; the one with the loose bandage around his head and something unspeakable beneath; the one who shivered and wept.

Even after a day under a roasting sun, Hector's face remains pale, the skin tight over his cheekbones, a layered ironic cast to his eyes. The lower half of the sunset is obscured by sea cloud. Night settles in the dugout. Over the Aegean, gilded clouds hide dark hearts. Hector glances at the sunset, then returns to his study of the men as their faces turn to shadow.

The Turk ceases fire so as not to give away the position of his big guns. The battle cools and condenses. Silhouettes duck out of trenches. Word is sent back that the soldiers at the front are suffering from terrible thirst. But no vessels to transport water made it through the landing, or if they did, none have been found. The rumour is that ammunition boxes are being emptied of bullets, filled with water, and sent up to the fighting men. Hector's eyes sink further back into his head.

At the pier, a lighter brings in condensed water from Lemnos. The stretcher bearers join the queue. It is a few hundred yards long. After an hour or so of slow shuffling they reach the large canvas trough into which water is being pumped. The men dip in their various unclean vessels, drain them, and dip again. Getting water takes so long that by the time the two men return to the dugout, the squad has already received new orders to search the Karakol Dagh.

Beyond the blue bulk of Imbros, there is a livid crack of lightning upon the horizon.

Collinson falls in, fiddling with the arms of his round glasses.

"I've been watching the storm out to sea," he says. He makes them hunker down and gaze out into the darkening waters until they are rewarded with another breathtaking silent fork of lightning.

Before the war, Collinson explains, he was superintendent of an observatory in Scotland, where hourly readings of terrestrial magnetism were taken. "Atmospheric electricity also," he says, with a Cambridge enunciation rarely heard among enlisted men.

"The instruments had to be removed from Kew with the electrification of London. The other observatory was on Valentia Island where the transatlantic cables were landed."

"Vital work, then," says Hector.

"Yes, well, the instruments are automated but interpretation is not. A large storm like this one would produce disturbances of two classes. A Class K – in which the direction of the disturbing magnetic field remains constant while the magnitude of the field changes – and Class L, the remaining disturbances in which the direction of the field changes at a rate comparable with the rate of change of magnitude. Magnetic disturbances would be just one part of predicting the weather."

Behind them, a crackle of rifle fire forks horizontally across the ridge.

"If you could predict the weather, could you also predict the war?" asks James.

"Yes. Exactly. The question is, can we use quantifiable methods to predict the behaviour of complex phenomena? Could we quantify war? It would be complicated. There are many factors at play. Today we've observed that the intensity of a conflict is inversely proportional to its frequency; after an indolent first day, the Turk is reinforced and neither side will be able to maintain their vigour for long. Fatigue is a factor."

"What about water?" asks James.

Hector asks, "What about hate?"

"The vigour to war would be constituted by a number of motive powers. The loss of land, for one. Honour. Ideas of national pride."

"Propaganda," says Hector. "The influence of a few great men who have been persuaded to put their talents to the service of war. Could you quantify their role?"

"Vengeance would require an equation of its own derived from the number of casualties and the yardage set aside in the newspaper to inciting reprisals. It's a fascinating notion. The equation of war."

"Hector has been working on the art of war," says James. "He painted a picture of the men, but I am yet to see it."

"It's unfinished. James did not think the men an edifying subject for art. But there is no wildlife here for me to study."

Collinson treated all unqualified assertions with professorial disdain.

"Nonsense. There are some fine specimens of insect. Including ones I have neither seen nor read of before. What do you make of this?"

The professor carefully unwrapped a handkerchief to reveal what appeared, at first, in the dark, to be bark chips.

"This was an insect. Quite a large one. I had ventured with Father Huxley up the ridge. The insect traversed an arc ten to twenty yards south of our position and then there was the most almighty boom from a high explosive shell and the insect fell to earth. When I retrieved its remains, they did not appear to belong to an insect at all, rather some kind of device. Here, this piece has a ball and socket."

Each man took a turn to feel the fragment and rub it between thumb and forefinger.

"It's shrapnel," says James.

"One end is tapered like a bullet," notes Hector.

"The padre thought it was shrapnel too. Quite curious though. It dropped straight down, it did not veer away under impact." With the point of his knife, he holds up for their inspection the head of the insect.

"It has been moulded in one piece from a material I do not recognize, hard with some pliability and very thin. It is not organic tissue."

James bends close to inspect the remains.

"It's too dark to see."

"It is ridiculous of me to fuss over such a thing in the middle of war but I find, when the fighting is on, that my mind fixes upon the smallest details and images, and it was in such a moment that I saw it."

Collinson wraps the handkerchief around the remains and returns them to his pocket.

"What was your position at the time?"

Collinson points to a square on the map near to the southwestern slips of Karakol Dagh, the high ridge that girdles the north side of the beach, into which they ventured far on the first night and encountered the sniper.

"It's a particularly tricky spot. It's very easy to lose one's way," says James, remembering the starless night.

Collinson says, "The Munsters found something up there while they were digging a trench, an underground chamber of sorts. Quite ancient. A Turk sniper had them pinned down."

"I came across him. His rifle fire has a particular crack to it," says Hector.

"There are wounded men up there. Once the padre is ready, we will head up."

With night thoroughly bedded in, the singing spreads from dugout to camp; valley hymns from the Welsh Field Ambulance and, in response, a mournful full-voiced rendition of Loch Lomond from the Scots. In the dark, the highlands summoned by the song are almost palpable: the purple-hued heath, the gloaming, the striated mountain banks. James blinks. The moon is bright and naked and the pier is lined with silhouettes of stretcher squads. The dry scrub on a distant hill burns. There are unburied dead all along the beach, their uniforms tight and narrow.

Father Huxley arrives with the doctor, Blore, and together the men lead the hike back up the thorny ridges of the Karakol Dagh, the rocky hills running along the north of the battlefield. The doctor grouches all the way up about the conditions in which he is expected to work, the sand on his scalpel, the nurses without enough water to wash, and no shelter for the wounded; some of the men had to lie injured directly under the sun. Word has gone around that the ambulance will soon run out of stretchers, that they are not coming back off the hospital ships. He asks how the battle is progressing. No one really knows. Collinson is convinced that the entire landing is a decoy as there seems to be no clear plan. Why else did they not push on immediately upon landing? Why are they stuck on this interminable beach?

They struggle about a mile over the ridge and then approach the dugouts on the northern slope overlooking Saros Bay. Out to sea, the storm lightning is silent and distant; overhead, the cloud cover is thin and the first stars are out. In the trenches, the soldiers are unshaven and desperate for water. James shares his canteen among the squad, a dozen men, four injured, another eight dead. All day fighting with the Turk and then the sniper fire kept each man face down in the earth. There are four times as many enemy as when they landed, and each day that passes only brings more. Collinson curses the indolence of their general. With sundown, the sniper moved on, and the Turks retreated further into the ridge, scraps of blue uniform glimpsed between thorns.

Father Huxley mutters prayers over the dead and ministers to a yeoman whose chest has been crushed by shrapnel. Blore attends to the dressing; the heart is exposed and glistens in the dark. Without stretchers to take the men down to the beach, the doctor decided to treat minor injuries there and then. For a bad head case, two bearers lock hands so as to carry the wounded man between them back down the ridge.

On his haunches, Huxley takes a sip of water. He has dark close-cropped hair and a moustache that is losing its definition.

"How is your faith, Father?" asks Hector.

Huxley picks a sprig of wild thyme then rubs it between his finger tips to release its scented oil.

"You are a pacifist, sergeant," says Huxley. "Another Quaker. Like Collinson."

"I study all religions."

Huxley reaches out in the dark and puts his hand on the younger man's shoulder.

"Your ambition in studying all the religions of the world is laudable. But there is enough in Christianity to satisfy one lifetime. It contains surprising subtleties."

"Do you have an example?"

"Right now I would rather be handling a machine gun."

"You can't be a priest and kill a man."

"Killing might make me *more* of a priest. Because then I would share the burden of the men in its entirety. You see, subtleties."

They duck down into the hollow. The Turks have fallen back to a position further along the ridge. They should be able to reach the site without crossing enemy lines.

The clouds shed their gilded edge and spread in dark tatters over the high land. With Collinson leading the way, the five men leave the trench and set off through the gullies. This mad country. The scent of blooms, smoke, sage and opened corpses. Sometimes the breeze carries a memory of the Sussex Downs and it's as if James is sneaking back through his past, the landscape of his life passing underfoot. The squad slows as Collinson checks his bearings. Hector is wary, on the lookout for the sniper.

"How far now?" asks Blore.

Collinson paces out in a circle, searching the earth for the deeper darkness of a hole, pushing aside thorny branches and testing the solidity of the ground with the heel of his boot. The soft patter of a soot fall. Collinson takes a stick from the ground and works it into the earth between adjacent rock ledges. The earth falls easily away.

"Here," he says. "It's like a big rabbit hole."

Boots first, he pushes his way into the earth, then works his entire body into the hole, until just his glasses glint back at them.

"I've found it."

Blore scrabbles ahead of the stretcher bearers to join Collinson down in the hole.

"What is it? What have they found?" asks Hector. "Is it a Turkish trench?"

James gets down onto his knees, unclips his Orilux torch from his belt and trains the beam down into the hole. It is much deeper than a trench and already the others have disappeared from view.

"You go," says Hector. "I'll keep watch."

The impact of a shell has cleared a top layer of hard grey chalk from the stone slabs of a tomb. A very large tomb. James slips down through the loam, white tubers feeling at his face. The earth is cool and moist. His boots find open space and then in one clumsy movement he slides underground.

The doctor and the priest move through a chamber containing a dozen or more stone sarcophagi.

"This is the land of Troy and Helen, Alexander the Great and Xerxes," says Huxley. "This is a Greek necropolis of the greatest antiquity."

Torch lights waver according to each man's curiosity. The tomb had been constructed with great precision; smaller chambers, sepulchres about two yards long and wide, and about one and a half yards high, lead off from this central necropolis. Huxley and Blore dig out the grouting under a lid. Stone grinds against stone, and then the grave is open, revealing a long skeleton.

Blore's torch shines through the dark eyeholes of the skull.

"Careful. If you touch it, it will turn to dust," says Huxley.

"Look at the wounds." Blore points to a tiny round section, no larger than a child's fingertip, cut out of the back of the skull.

"Trepanning?"

"Possibly. The bones are thick and long. This man must have been nearly seven foot tall."

"A warrior."

"Or a sick man." Blore blows away the dust and soil that have fallen in through a crack in the lid. "The skull is malformed, almost bulbous at the back. There is a pattern of trepanning here although the holes are much smaller than I've seen before, almost needle pricks through the bone."

The skull is grooved and ridged, the colour of sandstone, with patches of dark earth here and there. Seen close-up, it looks like a map of the surrounding terrain; the top of the jawbone resembles the stag beetle horns of the bay.

"Were these markings part of a funeral ceremony?" asks James.

"There is regenerative scarring all along the incisions. Whoever this was, they were alive when the procedure was performed."

Blore pauses.

"I am familiar with this place, and these procedures." His hands tremor over the skull. "The cold air, these wounds, I remember them in my fingertips."

On his hands and knees, Huxley explores an adjacent tomb. His torch light reveals two enormous urns, one cracked open, and inside, two skeletons laid side by side.

"Man and wife?" asks Blore. "Lovers?"

"Each skeleton has only one arm," notices James.

He shines his torch upon the curved clay surface of the closed urn, hoping for a crack or gap; he imagines the skeletons of man and wife entwined, and then, over time, bones falling from one body into another, a rib shared, a thigh bone tumbling into the lover, dust passing from lip to lip. It is stupid to dwell on death, he knows that, but the entwined skeletons have blindsided him with love. Ruth. Love is an element like air or water, you inhabit it, become accustomed to it, but notice sharply when it is gone. How much has he been hiding from himself in order to survive this war? How much has he forgotten? He remembers Ruth sewing by lantern light, the *rat-a-tat-tat* of the needle as she worked the crank. He sorted through photographs in search of one to take with him; and then, walking out through the town and over the Downs, toward Newhaven and the transport that would take him to war.

The sound of distant cannon fire from Mount Caburn. He had walked with Hector through Firle. The blacksmith spoke of the transformation of Newhaven. Industrial slag heaps, he said, filled up the dock and there were massive explosions day and night; quarrying, the whole coastline blown up and reshaped. On the road into Newhaven, the houses were all empty, the population evicted or fled. The streets along which he had driven the people out. In another life. The armour. The implant. The skulls belong to the dead inmates of the Institute, the victims of recreational brain surgery.

James sways. The doctor steadies him.

"What is it?"

"I just had the most violent impression."

The doctor grips him close.

"Me also. The others do not seem to be affected. Gather yourself. A moment's vertigo, and all will be lost."

"We must transport these relics to safety," says Huxley.

"And how are we to do that?" whispers Collinson.

"We will return with a fatigue party, some mules and a wagon, and carry the urns across the ridge."

Even to men of intellect, Huxley's plan appears idealistic.

"We should just cover up the tomb and return to the beach," says Collinson.

"This is a vital archaeological site," says Huxley.

"We can't excavate it under fire. Would you have the stretcher bearers carrying bones and dust to the CCS when there are wounded men out there?"

"When the line advances we will return," says Collinson.

Huxley will not be persuaded.

"The necropolis will quickly decay if exposed to air. Every hour is vital if these relics are to be preserved."

"You are forgetting that we are at war," says Collinson.

"The war is temporary. These bodies, this site, are a forgotten aspect of eternity. We are all here to serve a higher cause. What greater cause could there be than the connection between us and this deep antiquity?"

James feels faint and weak. The vertigo. The terrifying distance between himself and the world as it is. He cannot bring himself to look at the skulls again, or even at the other men. He cannot even lift his head. It is as if a great invisible claw has closed over him, holding him tight.

"It's just another grave," he says. "Ancient past."

"The past is knowledge," insists Huxley.

"It's knowledge of death, of which we have plenty."

Blore shivers in the dark tomb.

"I have the overwhelming feeling that I just lost another patient," says the doctor.

Huxley returns to the tall skeleton with the malformed skull. He bends over the grave, reaches into the red soil, and brings out a clay urn of the same design as the large urns in the antechamber. This smaller urn is about a foot long. He swaddles the urn in a blanket.

"We are near to the ancient city of Eleonte. These skeletons could be the remains of sacrificial victims. The daughters of Demophon and Mastusius."

Gently, Huxley puts the urn into his backpack.

"Sacrifice of the innocents. Fertilizing the earth with the blood of our most precious possession: the young. It is an ancient rite we are compelled to perform."

The men record what they can of the necropolis, and then claw their way up into the dawn. Scrabbling back out of the bowels of the earth, James thinks again of the violent impression the chamber had given him; of trenches cut into the Sussex Downs, armoured giants stalking the narrow streets of Lewes, and the malformed men and women who inhabited the Institute in the country. A madness, all of it, brought on by his faint. The doctor was right. A moment of vertigo and all would be lost.

16

Another landing. A star shell drifts over the dark waters of the bay. Soldiers wade through the shallow waves, kicking up foam and moonlit phosphorescence. Army boots make no sound on sand. The men advance across the beach without footfall.

After an hour and a half of dreamless, blanketless sleep, James wakes. He uses a half-gill of water for a shave, and waits for the tea-dixie to come up. Next to him in the dugout, raindrops quiver upon Jordison's broad face. The Lancastrian is of yeoman stock, with a wide jawbone, sandy-straight hair and a broad trunk; when he withdraws his head into the collar of his greatcoat, the flesh under his chin concertinas neatly. Above the shaving line, his upper cheek is fringed with down; below the shaving line, the patchy beginnings of a tawny beard. His young face shows the contours of the old man to come.

The aura of the star shell reveals dark mounds in the silver sand, some sleeping, some dead.

Using the shovel as a bier, Jordison and James drag bodies into a pile. It's more of a clearance than a burial, the work of the Divisional Sanitary Officer and not fit for the stretcher bearers of the 32nd Field Ambulance. But there is no sign of a sanitary officer. In the landing, military planning has become as improvised and fragile as the spider's webs hanging in the scrub, newly-woven and quivering with dew.

Jordison whispers prayers. Behind every pull and heft of the shovel, sand spills back into place.

James doesn't remember any prayers, so he asks Jordison if he has any family.

The Lancastrian shivers and withdraws his wide face deeper into his coat. Some of the men show a reluctance to speak. Part of it is exhaustion. Part of it is lack of water. But there is something else behind their silence. Shock. Superstition.

"I have Ruth," says James. "No one else. Do you have a wife?"

"My wife works in my place in the mill," says Jordison. His voice is hoarse, his thoughts slow to stir. "And three children too. We had 'em soon as we married, and a bit before. One after the other, Irish triplets. When I enlisted, she said she'd be glad to see the back of me."

"I didn't talk to Ruth about enlisting. We both knew I had to go. It was the thing I least wanted to do, you see."

Along the beach, Hector rouses the rest of the men from their hoggish snoring. It is the middle of the night. It will always be the middle of the night. With his spade, Jordison turns over the severed head of a Gurkha, the face pushed clean off. The yeoman lets out an involuntary groan of pity and lament.

"This poor sod. This poor, bloody sod."

It is not quite four in the morning. They do not dwell on the details of their work. The stretcher bearers shovel thistle-clutched topsoil onto the burial mound. Crickets abrade their hind legs and share data.

"You don't have any children?" asks Jordison.

"No," says James.

"I worry the war'll still be going on when my lads are of

age. Why would it stop? If this is what the bosses wanted, then they'll only want more of it."

"There will come a point when the sacrifice becomes too great."

That was the phrase Edith Von Pallandt had used when her son enlisted: "In the spirit of splendid sacrifice." At the garden party in Lewes, the consensus had been that civilization was stuck, and progress had failed. Bad blood in the body politic. The death instinct was abroad within civilization, the careless desire to sweep away the world that frustrates us.

His memories from before the war are hazy. There is only the long now. From the hills comes the sound of renewed fighting. He puts his heel onto the shovel edge and forces it downward.

A boot with a shin bone jutting out of it. Jordison leans over, hoists the bone up with the shovel, plants it deep in the earth, and pats the soil true. The gardener turning the earth over. In the necropolis, there was a skull stained with the resemblance of the battlefield: a notch on the jawbone that reminded him of the curved horns of the bay, and then following the curve of the bone, the shadows of hills leading to a rucked scarring in the surface of the bone, the high ridge. In the necropolis, he had a mystical experience, a violent impression of another realm beyond this one. Through the veil and all. The bodies mark the land and the land marks the bodies. The Von Pallandts would appreciate that. He cannot dwell upon it. A moment's vertigo and all is lost.

"I wonder what will grow here afterward," says James.

The yeoman pauses, foot on shovel, like a machine turned off, and does not look up at him.

"No different than before," says Jordison, resuming digging.

"That is unimaginable."

"That's nature."

The squadron fall in, grab their monkey boxes and stretchers. The canvas is stained with blood. They fill up their water bottles with brackish chlorinated water. With the arrival of 53rd division, the beach is as busy as Piccadilly Circus on a Saturday night. Sikhs drive light carts and lead mule trains carrying ammunition. Engineers work in the dust kicked up by marching men, threading telegraph wires across the sand. The trench contingents fall in, platoon after platoon with full packs, loaded for strength rather than speed. Bayonets unsheathed and dully gleaming in the moonlight, the soldiers set off across the plain, the stretcher bearers following a way behind. James is paired with Jordison. Hector moves between the stretcher squads from the different ambulances, keeping everyone in order. In the dark, it's easy to lose your way.

A sea fret rolls in from the bay. With the fog at their back, the silhouettes of the squads will be visible to the snipers. Their stretcher bearer brassards will not. The platoons advance around the north end of the luminescent salt lake. The crack-crack of sniper fire. Ahead, from over the blue grassy dunes, come the agonies of wounded men, cries in every register and horribly particular to each man: plaintive, urgent, monstrous, whimpering. The voices come from rock and hollow: "Ambulance!" "Bearers!" "Stretcher bear-e-r-s!"

Sniper fire in open country is a disjointed nightmare. Bullets spark off the rocks. The strays, the ricochets, are not as deadly as a direct shot but still capable of giving you a nasty one. A bullet passes under his chin, and then veers vertically upward like an enormous dragonfly. He senses men running close by. He ducks and dives. Another bullet passes half a yard overhead and seems to loop around their position in a whirring arc. Out of the continuous roll of sniper fire, echoing down from the high ground and across the plain, one particular rifle can be discerned; its action is neat with a note of suction, like a boot lifted from mud.

Five yards or so to the right, an unmoving figure, another pale face in the earth: Hector. James sighs. He should call to the sergeant, but what if he does not answer?

Again the distinctive sucking vacuum of the rifle. Distance and direction is hard to judge. The acoustics in this place are disorientating, and sometimes sound and vision do not marry.

Slowly, Hector's boot turns over and then finds purchase, and, quick as a mountain cat, the stretcher bearer skids over to James' position.

"Do you hear that rifle? It's him again," he says. "The sniper from the ridge."

"Maybe it's just the same type of rifle."

"It's him again and he's hunting us."

"Do you see him?"

Within the grey mist of the ridge, muzzle flashes crackle in a haphazard line from left to right; inland the scrub is denser, and here and there, a shot flickers out from the bushes. Bullets thud dully into the earth around them. Hector clutches his metal helmet with both hands.

"Come on!" he shouts, though he himself does not move.

The sniper finds his range. A bush on their flank stirs. And then, in response, comes the thorax-shaking lazy thud of a machine gun, shredding the thorn bushes. The sound of gunfire deepens as it judders slower and slower. The smell of thyme becomes so sharp, so quickly, it's as if his senses have gained mastery over time and space. In between each bullet, he hears the hellish whispers of war: the tear of shirt fabric, the final parting of parched lips, the infinitesimal sound of blood filling up pores in the soil. He hears shouting. He is shouting. And when the machine gun stops, and the flecks of sage and thyme float out from the havoc, James slaps Hector on the back. That's all it takes. The two men rise up.

The line advances around the dried-up salt lake. On Saturday, the Inniskillings were massacred here, and a few of their dead are still standing, thigh deep, in the sludge. Eviscerated by shrapnel, one silhouette stands with arms akimbo, head back, legs stoutly fixed. The Turk had sunk landmines under the curling hexagonal tiles of the plain, and when the regimental stretcher bearers went to retrieve their wounded, heavy gouty blowouts of wet mud and crust sent pieces of them and their kit wheeling through the air. Working his way through the marsh, James tries to comprehend the suffering of the wounded men still out there on the salt flats. As a pure sensation, that wealth of pain would exceed the capacity of the organism to experience it, surely. Accordingly, language is imprecise. Could a numeric quantity be ascribed to suffering, per Collinson's equations of war? Yes, there would have to be a number for this quantity of pain, a sum that, once calculated, would prove that this battle was not chaotic but had in fact been meticulously planned to produce the greatest amount of suffering.

East of the lake is a lower curved ridge they call Scimitar Hill, four miles from the shore and the object of the advance. First there is a riddle of trenches upon Chocolate Hill on the foothills of the Tekke Tepe, a nine hundred foot massif, a displaced piece of the earth's crust, thrust out of the underworld. He thinks again of the skull in the necropolis; if the pattern on the skull and around the trepanned section was a map of the battle, then the surface of the brain is a system of entrenchments: the way the cortex folds in upon itself, forming trenches and gullies, creates the greatest possible surface area. By increasing the size and complexity of the surface area of the brain, the volume of suffering it can apprehend, calculate and cause also increases.

Soldiers drift back from the firing line. They were ordered to advance but not to engage, or so it seemed. The wording was imprecise. By eight in the morning, the advance upon the ridge is routed. The line falls back to Chocolate Hill. The ambulance dress the walking wounded and send them on their way. Collinson and Brilliant trot back with a bad case on the stretcher, the right side of his face shot away, lashing blood out of his wound as he sings madly of Tipperary. Among their ranks are men whose nerve failed, ragged raw troops with self-inflicted wounds. Jordison wants to stop and pick up a leg case but James says no, not yet.

"What are you looking for?" asks the yeoman.

"Greater suffering," says James.

How does he decide whom to save? By the severity of the wound, of course. It stands to reason that the further the bearers advance into the battle, the greater the suffering they will encounter. In place of orders, of which there are none, he must reason it out himself. If this, then that. He climbs out of the gully to let the stretcher parties pass along the line of evacuation, one after the other, shuttling through the dark, working the disassembly line. Blore supervises an advanced dressing station at the cut of the salt lake. James and Jordison answer the haunting calls, find the wounded men, treat them, then carry them to the doctor. For some carries, there are no stretchers available. Jordison hoists up a big Irishman with a shattered foot, braces the man's weight on his hip bones, trying for a hold somewhere between pick-a-back and fireman's lift. The Irishman's arms dangle loosely over Jordison's chest as he staggers across the field. James works rifles through the sleeves of an overcoat to form an improvised sling that they use to carry a young grey-skinned lad, a bad dysentery case, crying and apologizing. I am not wounded, he says, just weak. The soil tips out of his body.

The stretcher bearers move further into the battle, toward Chocolate Hill, a steep-sided charred molehill and gateway to the Tekke Tepe. They find men who have been wounded for twelve hours or more. With a pair of scissors, James cuts away the flesh of a gangrenous arm wound and the man does not flinch. The nerves are dead. Without any water, the men's tongues are black, a vile shrivelled black. Hard to believe, in some cases, that this was the body of a fighting man only two days previously. The morning's advance pushed back the Turkish snipers, freeing the men who had been pinned down without food or water under a remorseless sun, eating grass to fill their bellies. They stumble out from cover, gaunt as the living dead, their uniforms in tatters, their faces long with suffering. Some men cannot speak for thirst and they shiver and shake with sniper madness. For these hollow men, Jordison allocates a sip from his medical water bottle, and when that runs dry, he shares a draught from his own supply. Hector puts a stop to that. The stretcher bearers will need their strength to sort the living from the dead at Chocolate Hill.

The hillside is a shambles, a lunatic warren. His boots kick away water bottles, get tangled with khaki and blue Turkish tunics. James and Jordison climb up a path, only to find it stopped halfway up by a shelf of rock. They climb out, and, following the sounds of men, find another trench. Gear and limbs abandoned alike, and in the shallow trenches, corpses imprinted with the boot marks of fleeing soldiers. A squad of soldiers keep their rifles trained on the Turkish positions and will not answer their requests, even when Jordison screams at them.

"Private Jordison, these men are dead!" shouts James.

The stretcher bearers retrace their steps downhill in search of a path up. In a communication trench, an officer carrying an empty dixie raves at him.

"We've taken the hill, but we're dying of thirst!"

"Where's your aid post?" asks Jordison.

The officer shakes his head and pushes past them.

"We find a man here and head back," says Jordison. They reach another trench. Both men sicken with the smell of it.

"This is a grave," says James. "We can't help anyone here."

Daylight breaks, lifting the soft blue and grey bands of mist that lie over the ridge. From the trench, he gathers more medical supplies, bandages and morphine. Jordison makes another overcoat stretcher from the debris. They can see what they are doing. It's not a blessing.

With daylight comes heavier and more accurate fire from the Turk. From somewhere deep in the ridge, a great clang and then the first shell of the day whistles overhead, exploding in a white and black plume on the salt lake. Soldiers run back and forth, the divisions are intermingled, orders are confused, maps lost, briefings missed. On Lali Baba, the command peer through eyeglasses at the battlefield, looking for patterns so that they can figure out where to deploy the battalions. Without clear directive, the army ceases to be a rolling force of intent and becomes more like the waves caught in the bay, advancing and retreating across the rocks; some waves build, and break further up the shore than others. The mass of men undulates across different points of space and time according to local agents of causation. Hector's voice cuts through the confusion. Where other men shamble and stumble, his directions remain sharp, his bearing straight. With pith helmet, braces and shirt sleeves rolled up, he really is the most fearsome pacifist.

"We must push on to the firing line," says James.

"What are our orders?" Jordison has been brave thus far. To push on of their own free will seems foolish.

"We don't need orders," says James. "We know what we have to do. The battle is ahead."

Hector wipes the perspiration and soil from his face with a rag. "Have you heard any more from the sniper?"

This morbid obsession with the sniper disturbs James. God knows it is hard to hold onto reason when the sun is up and the salt lake shimmers in time to his heartbeat.

He takes out his Zweiss glass and gazes east across the Sulajik plain. The key to the entire operation is the high peak of Tekke Tepe. If the Allies could secure the high ground and hold the ridge then the landing would be a success. Whatever assault had been undertaken that morning upon the peak had failed. The gateway to the ridge is guarded by, on one side, the curved peak of Scimitar Hill and on the other, the W hills, so named for the pattern of the vegetation upon them. These two modest high points watched over either side of a long spur that is the route up Tekke Tepe.

"We've no water," says Jordison. The creases in his face are grimy with sweat.

"Neither have the wounded," says James.

"Do you remember, that first night, I asked you to shoot me?" Jordison says. His thin khaki uniform is hot with exertion. "You should have done it. Shot me and sent me home. What difference would it have made?"

"None whatsoever," says James.

"I've seen fingers shot off on purpose."

"Do you want to join the cowards?"

"I have a family."

"We go to alleviate suffering."

Jordison closes his eyes and slowly puts his hands over his ears. Mutely, he shakes his head. He is spent.

"We are nothing," he mumbles.

James kneels down next to Jordison; he speaks carefully and with a threatening emphasis.

"To a wounded man, lying in the scrub, you are everything."

"You want to get yourself killed. I've got children."

"If you don't get up now, I will shoot you," says James. "And not in the hand."

James hooks his arms under Jordison's armpits and hefts the big man up, and when he tries to stumble back down onto his knees, he hefts him up again. Sergeant Hector takes out three woodbines. James lights one. The dry tobacco scorches the back of his throat and tars his senses. Jordison refuses a coffin nail with a slow shake of his head.

"I had a vision," says James.

Hector opens his mouth and the smoke finds its own way out.

"I want to tell you about it before we go. In case we don't make it back. It came to me when we were underground. You were in it."

"In the dream?"

"No, it was more like a memory. Of a different time. We walked together across the Downs near my home in Lewes. The towns and villages were empty. The people had been evicted."

"Before the war?"

"We were on our way to war together. The memory felt as if it had been placed within me by God."

"The Christian God?"

"The Absolute. I sensed another force within me. It draws me in. Yet it remains hidden."

Hector takes almost indecent relish in his woodbine. The simple act of inhalation and exhalation is enough for him, in that moment.

"We are exhausted. Men are dying all around us."

"Do you remember walking on the Downs with me?"

Hector thinks, then quietly shakes his head.

"I glimpsed something," says James. "A world beyond this. Or next to it. There is a great convergence."

From the direction of Scimitar Hill, shaggy men shuffle away from the heaving black smoke. He feels faint again. James drops his cigarette. His fingers are weak. He has no strength to hold. To hold things together. He feels a force pressing down upon his thoughts, a great inner weight that is suddenly lifted and then he feels too light.

"Steady," says Hector. The sergeant catches James. He almost faints. He does not faint. It is not permitted for the men of the 32nd Ambulance to fall. That has been decided. Even Collinson, loose trousers tainted by dysentery, carries a stretcher.

Jordison points with alarm.

"The scrub is on fire!"

Nausea breaks over James. The back of his hands ripple. Hector puts the cigarette back between James' lips and the dog-end is large and painfully dry.

"We need to move the wounded away from the advancing fire," says Hector. He attempts to rally soldiers and stretcher squads for the advance to Scimitar Hill. The men who have just returned from the battle push the sergeant aside, and stagger on toward the beach.

Jordison takes up the empty, folded stretcher. Now it is his turn to haul James to his feet.

"We can't let those poor sods burn alive," says Jordison.

Scimitar Hill lies three quarters of a mile to the east, in the foothills of the Anafarta ridges. The East Yorkshire regiment had taken Scimitar Hill the day before, but with unclear orders, had abandoned it. Here the battle breaks up into absolute chaos, a nauseous confusion, the boundaries blurred between the living and the dead.

Jordison and James advance through a mob shuffling

away from the front. The limbs of the stumbling men are burnt black from the sun, their uniforms ragged and torn, their faces covered in dirt and streaked with sulphurous yellow from the acrid exhalation of shells: it is as if the bodies they buried that morning have returned from hell.

The Turkish soldiers move up the hill in twos and threes and fire upon the retreat. Bullets veer around James like bats. Another twenty yards to the trench and he can see the men clawing their way out of the grave. He shoves Jordison ahead of him and, at a running crouch, the stretcher bearers weave through the field to the trench. The wounded and the sick are scattered all along the lines; Jordison tries to stop the fleeing soldiers, shouting at them to each take a wounded man. He cuffs a corporal around the ear. The corporal fights back with desperate lunging punches. Jordison gathers half a dozen men from the retreat to serve as bearers. James drops down into the trench and walks along the sandbagged bloody rut searching for the most desperate case: he finds a dozen. At the aid post, the MO is dead and the injured men lie in stranded ranks. James inspects the cases, identifies the ones who are to be moved first, and the bearers begin hauling out the wounded back along the trench.

The strong north wind carries thick smoke with it. A fire has been set south of the battalion lines and it spreads hungrily across the parched scrub. James scrambles up the side of the trench. The fire burns as tall as a house and advances towards them at a serpent's watchful pace. The smoke pulses upward in muscular waves. Tattered scraps of uniform are carried up on the rising heat. He tries to calculate how many of the wounded they can carry before the fire reaches them.

James takes the head end of the first stretcher in line. Jordison takes the foot end; as they run, the trench side rakes the skin off his knuckles, then some flesh. Once they are on open ground, they set down the stretcher and return for the others. An olive tree burns. The brambles char and spark like fuse wire. He can feel the heat of the approaching fire on his face as he stumbles back down the trench. At the aid post, the wounded men feel the hot approach of the fire too, and they cry and try to get off their stretchers.

"Where are the other bearers?" asks Jordison.

"They didn't come back," says James. He considers the wounded men on the floor of the trench and their imploring, tear-streaked faces. Six more.

"We should take a man each, on our backs," says James.

"What about the other four?" asks Jordison.

"We should kill them before the fire does," says James.

The yeoman grabs James by the collar.

"You made me come," he shouts. "And I did not come to kill!"

Acrid black smoke rolls down over the lip of the trench. The stretcher bearers cannot hear one another for the fearful cries around them. Jordison hefts a crying lad up onto his knee, turns and lifts the wounded man onto his shoulders. Sorry, he whispers to the remaining men. I am so sorry. James takes a lungful of scorched air, ducks down, and hauls up the first wounded man to hand. He is too heavy on his back and he stumbles into the side of the trench, feels the muscles in his arms and his back give; he has no strength left. All at once, something has gone from his legs. Overhead, fire arches over the top of the trench, burning the oxygen from the air. The wounded man clambers over him, knee in his face, boot scraping his chin, then collapses. The side of the trench slides in, half-covering his face with dirt. If he does not move now, then he is going to be buried then burned alive. It is an underwater kind of panic, desperation to take a breath but with the water's surface still a kick or two away. He is up on his feet again and he stumbles away, leaving the wounded man behind. Forgive me, forgive me. Ammunition explodes in a flurry of bangs and sparks, like the rookies on Eviction Night. The pitiful yowls and mother-cries of the burning men. He stumbles along the trench, greatcoat over his head, stopping here and there to check for a break in the fire.

"Here!"

Jordison has come back for him. He holds his hands out to the yeoman. Jordison pushes past him and runs back into the trench. He hauls up the wounded man James left behind.

Blinded by the smoke, roots and brambles searing his palms, James crawls away from the heat. The cries come from all around. And then he feels hands on him, a voice asking if he is alive. Yes, yes, I am alive. A hot broad blade is slid under him, and he grabs onto a wooden shaft; Hector drags him across the scree on a shovel. Overhead the smoke forms a vault. The trench is on fire. Jordison goes over the top with a man on his back, the sinews in his neck pronounced with the colossal effort.

The burning trench is the extreme edge of experience and sensation, the boundary between what is known and what is still in the process of formation.

James hears the distinctive sniper's rifle fire, its concussive hoot like an enormous blow-pipe. Jordison falls, clutching the side of his head, blood seeping through a tiny hole in his skull and trickling across his scalp. Through the wall of flame, the sniper stands; he is disguised with vegetation so that branches rise like antlers from his brow. His weapon is a smooth cylinder with a needle-point barrel. And then he steps through the fire. The vegetation burns on him. The figure is wearing a dark suit and an oval mask that retards the flame. He is taller than a normal man. Some demon that has come through the veil. Jordison raises his head, eyes rolling back. The sniper fires again, casually downward, a fatal pinprick through the back of Jordison's head. The white figure moves steadily through the fire, here and there, putting burning men out of their misery.

17

The armour approached from the other side of Newtimber Hill. With every iron footstep, the hillside tremored. A sine wave of starlings loosed across the sky. She was vulnerable. The armour could be coming for her. Ruth ran into a witchy copse and hid within the exposed root system of an old oak tree.

A horse and cart piled high with possessions came over the crest of the hill, followed by a long line of people, tired and dirty from the evicted life. More came, and the line broadened. So many familiar faces, but out of context. They were thinner too, from the life outside, their hair long and matted. She recognized clothes that had passed under her needle a long time ago. There was Arnold, a Dutch parent from the school. He had been evicted two years earlier. Arnold and his wife Martha moved in the same countercultural circles as the Von Pallandts. They had their own ideas about parental discipline and their daughter Cecile had gouged her initials into the kiss-kiss tree with her father's knife. Arnold was evicted soon afterwards.

More familiar faces, a procession of incidental acquaintances from town life, people she was on nodding terms with because their morning or evening routine intersected with her own. Here was a man, grey-bearded and goatish, in his ancient polyester shirt, whose walk up Station Road coincided with her walk home from the school. He had been a commuter. Something in the public sector, she imagined, probably maintaining some terrible computer system. He seemed largely unchanged by life outside. Here was a woman she once met in the Lewes Arms. They'd enjoyed a nostalgic discussion about books, but never spoke to one another again. Ruth remembered how this woman had wailed and kicked when the armour threw her onto the cart.

After the Seizure, most people were redundant. The baron had explained it to her with characteristic cynicism.

"The likes of us have become a burden upon civilization," he said. "In the past, we were tolerated because our vanities could be manipulated so that we took on debt. Vainly we aspired to better ourselves and thereby society. But meritocracy was only for the poor." He had a pointed grey beard and aristocratic, almond eyes. "In reality, for all our high ideals, we were merely pretexts for debt; debt was our contribution, debt was how we created wealth. Our houses were debt. Our educations were debt. Our health was debt. Our trinkets, debt. Without debt, all we have is our data. We are data beasts in some fucking zoo, and it's just a matter of which specimens are required, which pairs are to be bred."

The baron was a defeated idealist. He had given up his estate on Eerde to a group who promised a revolution in consciousness. They were still on his land, working their way through the mystic traditions, pushing back the boundaries of their preconceptions, eating the food grown in his garden, sleeping in his bed.

He was an advocate of the Process. He agreed that the sole remaining value of the Lewesians – all they could take to market – was their data, and that data might offer spiritual understanding. What an opportunity the Process presented, to study the mind of the town! Perhaps, in the patterns of data produced by the group mind, elusive insights could be discerned. A quantitative study of thousands of inner lives would reveal what centuries of introspection and religious tradition had not.

"We will make the subjective into the objective and vice versa," said the baron. "Capturing everything that happens here will allow us to recreate it in the future. Memories will not die. The past will become the present."

The ground shimmered under the armour's unsteady heavy gait. The armour did not seem out of place on the South Downs, its grinding iron sections and groaning vents reminding her of agricultural machinery: the armour as a plough or a furrow, a technology mankind had used from the very beginning. An ancient punishment device. Behind the misted colloid, the face of the son of the baron, Christopher Von Pallandt, was a flesh blur.

The evicted had been gathered from camps and other towns, with methods more carrot than stick (although, as the baron was fond of pointing out, both could be used as a weapon). The armour had appeared to the evicted in the car parks of the housing estates of St Leonard's Warrior Square, at the perimeter of the tent cities outside Brighton, and pulling aside the barricades of the charity-maintained hotels of Eastbourne. The armour had cast the evicted out. Now it sought their return. Hope worked its magic on desperate souls and they came willingly.

The stragglers shared their stories of hardship, as if better times lay ahead. The old rumours of intervention by the administration, of a coming restoration, were aired. When the evictions first started, Ruth had asked the same question of the baron: "When will the government wake up to what has been happening?" He replied, "A better question is: what will happen when we wake up to what has been happening with the government?" She pressed him further, but his answers were swingeing and apocalyptic, his rhetoric digging a hole just large enough for himself.

She followed the evicted down into the hamlet. Saddlescombe consisted of a few cottages ranged around a farm. On a field of pasture, a serried rank of bell tents had been pitched, and it was to these that the evicted were directed. The colloid clanked open to cool down the bailiff: Christopher's head was tipped back, resting after subjugation to the Process. Two soldiers supervised refuelling the armour. They wore the same khaki uniforms as Hector. It was hard to tell, at first, if they were manufactured men or not. One of them, a slight boyish figure with an experienced wise face, popped the armour's engine cover and drew a cup of scalding water from the radiator, which he then used to soften his beard and wet his razor, concentrating upon his reflection in an aluminium panel. He raised a sardonic eyebrow that made one eye appear distinctly larger than the other. She walked by with her head down, and when she looked back, he continued to shave in the metallic reflection; his gaze did not follow her departing figure.

A cottage had been converted into a café for the soldiers. The ceiling was low, and around an open iron stove, the men sat six to a bench, drinking thin beer and smoking thin cigarettes. Like Hector, they were indistinguishable from real people. She hesitated in the doorway, letting her eyes adjust to the gloom. She took a seat in the corner on a low wooden stool. The soldiers ignored her.

The café owner appeared with plates of omelette and chips, a woman with her dark blonde hair tied back in a ponytail: Jane Bowles, the mother of Agnes, the child Ruth betrayed.

Jane set the plates down in front of the soldiers, wiped

her hands upon her apron, collected empty tin mugs from their table onto a tray, and then returned to the kitchen. She did not see Ruth, or if she did, she did not acknowledge her existence. Ruth followed her out back.

"Jane?"

Jane retied her ponytail. She had once told Ruth that, before she was a mother, her hair had been the colour of golden thread. After the birth of each of her children, it had turned progressively darker. Hormones no doubt, but Ruth regarded this darkening as an indication of the serious responsibility of parenthood, a deepening of the self unknown to her.

A coffee pot spluttered on the range. Jane wrapped a tea towel around the handle and put the pot to one side.

Ruth said, "I'm so sorry about what happened." No, that was not enough. "About what I did."

Jane unhooked a small cup from the wall and poured herself an inch of strong coffee.

"I would do anything to undo it."

Jane sat wearily upon a high stool, sipped her coffee, then whispered, "*What can you do*?"

"We will take you back to Lewes."

Jane unhooked a second cup from the wall, and poured coffee into it. She did not offer it to Ruth. The cup steamed.

Ruth said, "Have you seen James? Has he come through here?"

Jane tipped her head back and called her husband's name. And then she repeated, in a resigned whisper, "*What can you do*?"

Ruth heard tools set down in the yard, the rasp of a boot scraper. Tom entered and the sight of him made her gasp: his head was shaven, and the right side of his face had slipped as after a stroke. His scalp was stained with haphazard splashes of iodine. He moved slowly across the kitchen, put his hand on his wife's shoulder, leant forwards and nuzzled the back of her hair. Both of them had new implants, but whoever had performed the operation on Tom had been brutish. Jane's implant was neater and almost concealed behind her ponytail, the pinched scarring exposed by her husband's attention. Tom blew on his coffee to cool it.

"Where are your children?" she asked. "Euan and Agnes?"

Neither Jane nor Tom responded to her. She was a ghost to them. Not part of their pattern.

What can you do?

What had happened to the children? She walked out of the kitchen and trod quickly up a narrow staircase. On the landing, there were four doors, and one ajar. There, sitting up in bed reading, was the woman from the Institute, Alex Drown, with a violently bloodshot eye. She did not acknowledge Ruth's presence either. The next bedroom held the empty marital bed, a chamber pot beneath it, and a grate of ash. The pillows on one side of the bed showed dull, scrubbed bloodstains. Clothes hung over the back of a chair and veins of green damp broke across the bowed ceiling. The bathroom contained a tin bath, no running water, and two wooden toothbrushes, his and hers, together in a clay pot. The last room was the children's room. It was empty. Bare warped boards, a cold fireplace, and a cobwebbed window with a broken pane.

She walked into Alex Drown's bedroom, closing the door behind her. Still Alex did not acknowledge her. The fire was lit. A grey dress and a white apron were drying on a clothes horse. Alex put her novel on the bedside table and turned over to sleep. Ruth crouched beside her, gazing intently at the woman's resting face, hoping to spark the instinct of being watched. Alex's small fists were bunched in the coarse blanket fibres. She fell asleep. The hands relaxed. And then she stirred awake.

"Ruth," said Alex.

"You can see me."

"Where am I?"

"In a cottage in Saddlescombe."

Alex put her hand to her bloodshot eye and groaned.

"They put me under. It's dangerous for me to go this deep into the Process."

Alex looked askance at her blowsy nightie, then squinted painfully at the nurse's uniform on the clothes horse.

"That's mine, isn't it?"

"You didn't recognize me when I came in. You didn't even see me."

"When the implant is engaged, the Process puts layers over my perception. It must be screening you out. I had a safeguard put in which disengages the implant when I fall asleep, to prevent them from putting me under permanently. This isn't the first time he's involved me in his games."

Alex looked around the room, then under the bed.

"I don't suppose you've seen my real clothes?"

"Do you know where James is?"

"He's part of the landing. He's on the beach with the others."

"The landing?"

"The war game."

Alex glanced out of the window, at a squad of soldiers marching by.

Ruth was indignant. "A game?"

Alex hauled her big nightie over her head, exposing her neglected body, then reached over to the clothes horse; she flicked the grey serge dress out to see if it was dry, and finding it acceptably so, climbed into it and fastened the shoulder straps.

"It's a game to him. Just because it's a matter of life or

death, doesn't meant he can't be *playful*," said Alex, her face registering annoyance at her dowdy nurse's shoes.

Anticipating Ruth's next question, Alex said, "By *him* I mean my colleague at the Institute. I say colleague but I mean my patient. My employer. He often involves me in his games because he likes to exercise *droit de seigneur* over my mind."

She picked up a white muslin cap.

"Do I have to wear this?" she asked.

"I saw the bailiff bring the evicted into the village. Some of them have implants."

Alex looked concerned.

"He needs more players."

"James said he wouldn't be gone for long." Then Ruth went quiet. She could not say another word without crying.

"Don't cry. It won't help," said Alex. "We must get away from here."

"I must take the children. A little girl I evicted."

"James told me about that."

"We've been so unkind, Alex. So caught up and confused."

Alex buttoned her red cape, fixed her white cap.

"What are you suggesting?"

"That we stop collaborating with the Process. We could take control of our lives again."

"You have more control within the Process than you ever had without it."

"But this war…"

"How many wars were there under the old ways?"

Unsteadily, Alex led the way down the stairs.

"Malted milk," she called back. "I must give the soldiers their malted milk."

She jogged across the yard, her nurse's cape fluttering behind her, and then onto the dirt track leading deeper into the farm. On the wind, Ruth caught a smell of something bad, something more corrupt than the usual farmyard odour.

The barn lay at the end of the dried mud track. The soft textures of poplar trees in the late afternoon sun. Rusted farm machinery. Troughs of rainwater. Birdsong. The lowing of cattle. No, not cattle.

She tried but failed to keep her fear out of her voice.

"What's in the barn?"

"Wounded soldiers," said Alex. But she was uncertain. A lock of black hair slipped from out of her nurse's cap. She corrected it.

"I think the children may be in there too," she said. Alex gathered her cape around her and walked with her head lowered into the barn.

The barn had been filled with cots, a hundred or more, arranged in a grid with narrow paths between them. Alex hung up her cape, washed her hands in a trough. Her gaze lengthened as she quietly slipped under the layers of the Process. Then she was just another nurse, administering tea and sympathy.

Arc lights spluttered and glared. The cots contained wounded men and women.

What can you do?

Ruth would check every cot for the children. The cool air of the barn was sweet and vile with medicinal vapours, burnt chemicals, sweat and blood. The wounded men did not see her. They were like the horse she had encountered up on the Downs: unfinished sculptures, incomplete constructions. These men came off the assembly line already broken. They were made to suffer. But, mixed in among the iodine and boracic powder, she could smell fear. Real human hormones. She walked quickly along the cots, checking to the left and to the right, until her path was blocked by a case of acute insanity, sitting up, crying and shaking. The automata, it seemed, had been invested with the very tips of human emotion. The nurses clustered around the cot. Coming closer, Ruth saw that the case of insanity was not in fact a manufactured soldier but Francis Sacks, one of the evicted, the man the people of Cliffe had fought to save. His scalp was splashed with iodine. The surgeon called for ether. The padre, his face in shadow, offered Sacks a cigarette to calm his nerves. She turned back rather than watch the procedure. The ether was administered. Sacks whimpered and fell silent, and she walked away from the awful thick sound of cutting, the sound of fat being scissored from a chop.

Her foot scuffed the wanton sprawl of a dead naked man on a stretcher. Her nerves would not hold much longer.

Through the sunlit entrance of the barn, stretcher bearers brought in more of the evicted, bound and restrained to the stretchers. They lowered the evicted directly upon the cots. Alex Drown carried a metal bowl of steaming hot water, and then, with her colleagues, began prepping the new arrivals for surgery.

A priest stood in her way.

"Can I help you?"

He was at the end of the line of cots, an intellectual type with the body of a long distance runner. Quite different from the others; under the hesitant glare of the arc lights, she could not be sure, but he might even be human.

"Cigarette?" he asked.

"I'm looking for a child," she said.

"Your child?"

On the cots near to her, more of the evicted, the ones who had already been operated upon. Implants. They were giving them implants. Bringing more people into their war game. Making it real.

"A girl," said Ruth. "And a boy. Their parents are injured, and I want to see that the children are safe."

"Do you live near here?" asked the priest. "Are you one of the local ladies who serve tea and coffee to our patients? If so, I must say that we are very grateful."

He introduced himself as Father Huxley, and inquired if the pastoral needs of the village were being met despite the presence of the army. She mistook the question for the stock phrase of an automaton. He pressed the point.

"What I mean is, do the villagers have a priest to take confession? We wouldn't want you to go through such a trial without recourse to forgiveness."

Ruth smiled weakly.

"Do you have faith?" he asked.

"No," she replied.

"Faith is the element which stabilizes and divines the future. Without it, our actions have no meaning."

A nurse lowered a blanket over the naked dead soldier.

"Are you sure you won't have a cigarette?" He wrinkled his face at the smell of the barn. "A smoke clears the air of corruption. I like to think of cigarettes as secular incense."

"I would like some air."

The priest let her pass.

Ruth resumed her search of the cots. Steadily, the surgeon also moved down the line of the evicted, applying a local anaesthetic, making an incision through the scalp and skull, cutting through the tough fibre of the dura. Alex presented the implants to the surgeon in a curved white plastic container. Ruth had always imagined the implants to be like transmitters or filaments; they were not. In the quivering arc light, they seemed more like human tissue.

She did not find the children in the barn. Ruth crouched outside, gathering her resources. Father Huxley followed her. He squinted at the husky afternoon light, and took a deep breath of country air.

"It's intense, isn't it? Life, I mean."

"What do you see, in the barn?" she asked.

"I see cement," he said. "Living cement thrown by God into the stonework of the New City."

"I see people I used to know. Men and women."

The priest looked questioningly down at her.

"Women?"

"You don't see them, do you? The barn looks different to you."

"This is no place for a lady. Your nerves are shaken, I understand that."

"It is monstrous. We've become evil."

The priest was taken aback.

"I assure you, I have not. And neither have you. If God's work seems brutal, then it is our role to pacify and soften it. To offer comfort and solace."

"You believe this war is part of His work?"

"God has to set in motion the development of a whole universe to produce a being – an individual – he is determined to create. We're all part of that process."

If he was an automaton, then he was a higher order of forgery than the others, a work that a master forger had laboured over.

Ruth said, "My friend told me that the war is just a game."

"'Play up! Play up! And play the game!'" He enacted the line of poetry with false joviality.

"Newbolt, of course," he added. "I met him once. A very conventional man with a highly unconventional private life. I don't think anyone here regards this as a game. That is a sentiment for boys."

"The war ended over a hundred years ago. You can't understand that, can you?"

"Sometimes, I understand it," he said, and then stopped, looked with longing at the poplar trees quivering in the breeze. "Life is so intense," he began again. "The countryside seethes with creation and evolution." He extinguished his cigarette carefully against the lifted sole of his boot; she recognized the gesture from other men who had been raised on a farm.

"The general is coming to inspect the troops, tonight. He could help you find your children. I have to warn you, though, that the general is less open-minded than myself. I would spare him your below-stairs, servant girl mysticism."

Come dusk, she had still not found the children in the village. She returned to the outlying country. The woodland on the north face of Newtimber Hill was ancient. The long moss-coloured branches of a lime tree were arthritic, and lay their weary tips upon the leafy ground to form startlingly crooked spokes. Over the years, the wood had conceded a few points to gravity's remorseless argument; she stepped over bark husks and widowmakers, the thick branches that fall unannounced upon any unfortunates below. Slanted tree trunks parted before her.

This is where she would have hidden, when she was a girl; away from the horrors of the barn, away from the disturbed family home. The way that Jane did not recognize her was familiar to Ruth: her mother had ended up like that, indifferent to whoever came and went. For a parent to fail to recognize their child is terrible. When senility meant that her own mother was oblivious to her presence, then part of Ruth disappeared too.

Between the trees ahead, she glimpsed a flash of material. She had found them. Euan and Agnes were sitting in a small clearing with a plate of egg and chips between them. Invisible children do not think to hide.

"Hello Agnes," said Ruth.

The girl stopped chewing.

"Hello, miss," said Agnes. Euan, her little brother, watched her warily.

"I'm very sorry for what has happened, Agnes. It's awful for you."

Agnes nodded at her brother.

"He doesn't know," she said, warning Ruth from saying too much.

"I understand."

"I come and go from the cottage as I please, and get us food."

"My mum and dad are taking a break," said Euan. The little boy needed to be loved and feel happiness around him. When she had taught reception class, she spent a lot of time just hugging the boys. They needed to know that they were part of the pack.

Ruth put her hand out to Agnes.

"I want to help."

"You pushed me away," said Agnes. "You evicted us."

"I know. It was an evil thing that I did. Sometimes grownups make mistakes. We do what we think is best, instead of doing what we want or believe in. I made a calculation. I made a mistake."

"You're my teacher, but you don't know right from wrong."

On the edge of the clearing, a tarpaulin had been strung low from a tree trunk then pegged to the ground. Underneath, a heap of bedding and some mats.

"Did you make that?"

Agnes nodded.

"Why don't you sleep in the house?"

The girl looked pained.

"We don't like it there."

Ruth put her hand on the boy's warm head, stroked his hair, and felt around the back of the skull. No, he had not suffered an implant. Not yet. His stripe was scabby, but light still flitted here and there in its cells. If the children had implants, perhaps the family would be able to see one another again. But the surgeon had been so careless in operating on their father.

She would take the children to Lewes and force the community to accept them. The Process would demand their immediate eviction, and so they would have to turn against the Process. Reject it. Could she persuade the rest of the town that they must fight for their independence? She had not thought this through, for a very good reason: *what could you do?* Ask yourself that, and the answer is always the same: nothing. It is hopeless. Instead, she would act in a way that she knew to be right, and the world could react as it saw fit. Caution and calculation had led her to evil. She would save these children. Even if it meant that she could not save James.

She had discussed with the baron what might happen if they rejected the Process.

"It knows all our secrets and our weaknesses," he said. "What might its revenge be like?"

While Agnes gathered their things from under the tarpaulin, Euan sat on her knee and played. In his hands, the dry leaves were ships and airplanes, space rockets and supermen.

Agnes was thoughtful.

"Is there a way we could take my mum and dad with us? If we get them far enough away from the Process, then maybe they will return to normal."

How far would that be? she wondered.

"If we stay, it's only a matter of time before what happened to your parents happens to you. And me. Let me get you to safety and then we will save your parents."

Ruth stood up and offered her hands to the children. Euan held her hand unquestioningly. Agnes considered the other hand, and took it also.

18

Hector is at the foot end of the stretcher, Collinson is at the head, and James lies between them, drifting over the battlefield on bloodstained canvas. He is not quite a man, more a collection of ideas, and his friends are not stretcher bearers but idea carriers, bringing back new forms of thought from the frontline. If he is not much more than an idea, then let that idea be kindness.

The seething beacon of Chocolate Hill becomes the coal fire in the parlour, that night he first spoke to Ruth.

She had warmed her hands by the fire. She was shorter than her sisters and wore a green silk frock.

"Auntie told me you like to swim," he said.

She nodded and smiled but remained silent.

He tried again, "The lido is awfully brisk this time of year."

"I swim in the sea." Her voice was quiet yet even. He remained silent so that she would have to elaborate.

"At Cuckmere Haven." She took a risk. "It's invigorating, don't you think?"

She had recently spent some time outdoors without a parasol and her colouring set off her bright blue eyes and firm ponytail. Because of her shyness, he had never noticed her before. Now he saw that it was plausible that she knew more about life than he did.

"I wonder what role swimming played in human evolution," he said. He was an undergraduate studying genetics and wanted her to know it. "What benefit did we gain from being the apes that fish? We lost our body hair and gained subcutaneous fat to help us swim. Our large brains are typical of marine mammals. And we walk upright which makes sense if you are wading and hunting for fish. Was some nutrient in fish pivotal for the development of the human brain?"

"Such as cod liver oil?"

Was she mocking him? Or did she merely want to laugh with him? He had never noticed her before because she was so quiet and her body was concealed by the shapelessness of her clothes. He was still too young to read a face with any accuracy.

"There is no direction to evolution other than what we impart to it," he said. And then, against his better judgement, he continued: "We have bred qualities and traits into animals. When we advance socially we will breed new attributes into people."

"In what manner will we advance?"

"We will be more open in our discussions of human relations. What makes a fit union and what makes an unfit one."

"Is that what you believe?"

He blushed.

"I don't know. The prospect of a splendid race, with all weakness and sickness bred out of it, is beautiful and terrifying. I do not believe in state-run eugenics. It would have to be voluntary. If institutions measured and classified every man and woman, and decided who mated with whom, then that would make mankind into a machine, and we would lose our connection with the life force."

Ruth listened attentively, her hands moving slowly in a circular motion over the coal fire, warming the cold bony backs of her fingertips then drying the fleshy parts of her palms.

He continued: "Healthy intellectual men and women would seek each other out. They would live outdoors, I think."

"And swim?"

"Yes, there would be lots of swimming."

"Which stroke do you prefer?" she asked. Fixated upon her hands, he was flummoxed.

She continued, "In Australia, my instructor believed that breast stroke was very dangerous for a woman to learn. So I was taught their crawl. You do not push away the water, rather you swim just below the surface with the arms scooping like a waterwheel. The breathing is similar to the Trudgen, with the face mostly in the water."

"How long were you there?"

"Two years. With my cousins. As a consequence, my blood is thin and I really feel the cold in England." Her hands abraded quickly over the fire, turning in and out of one another.

"The outdoor life is very important for our evolution," he said. His seriousness was not his best quality. He was seventeen years old. If a girl would not kiss him within the year, he was resolved to join a gypsy caravan. "Only by testing ourselves in nature, by staying close to our savagery, will we be able to keep our civilization strong."

She was smaller than him but there was rude strength in her, on her own terms. She sat down on the armchair and kicked her legs; after they were married, she would be shocked to learn that the import of this gesture had been entirely lost upon him.

"In the summer, my father takes us camping," she said. "Have you ever slept out under the stars?"

"No."

"There is a field not far from the haven. The farmer doesn't bother us so long as we buy his eggs and milk. When it's cold, on a day like this, the sheep huddle together under the dry stone walls. Have you ever seen a lamb shiver? You don't know whether to laugh or cry."

At the aid post, he is lowered onto a stretcher and back down to earth. James raises himself up to cough and then slumps back. A water bottle is pressed into his hand. He accepts a mouthful of water. He inhaled so much ash and smoke, his lungs feel strained and sore. Stretcher bearers pick him up again. The earth falls away and he is suspended in space. The Milky Way is livid as a wound, and the stars are beyond number. His lungs heave.

For their honeymoon, they had cycled and camped across Sussex in a silk tent made for him by a Brighton tailor. On their wedding night, they camped in a field half a mile back from Cuckmere Haven. "Here," she said, as if she had it all planned out. Her nipples were cool to his lips. They were both virgins but she was unembarrassed by sex, and was as forgiving and pragmatic as required for the first few times.

She woke him at sunrise. He cooked bacon on a Mersey stove and heated a pot of coffee. They walked along the sinuous channel of the slow river until it spilt out into the sea. Seven peaks of the sheer chalk cliffs. Gulls rode the thermals and cried out for their lost mothers. Ruth climbed up onto a soft boulder and put her hand on his chest to steady herself. The morning air was warm but the breeze was still night-cold. She decided that the sea was calm enough for a swim, pulled her sundress over her head, and stepped naked into the shallows. As she walked deeper into the sea, she scooped handfuls of the cold water over her breasts and neck and hair. The water rose above the curve of her hips. She dived into a wave then broke the surface of a glittering swell. He followed her in.

Afterwards, they towelled themselves dry on the pebbled beach. The sunlight reflected sharply from the chalk cliffs. Great pieces of chalk had fallen here and there, and he was fascinated by their softness, digging into them with his nails so that wet white deposits filled the ridge between fingernail and fingertip.

"This is perfect," she said. Her neat white teeth nibbled at her lower lip.

"You are perfect. You swim perfectly," he said.

Something occurred to her.

"The way your head twists when you swim it's as if you are violently disagreeing with the water. You should swim higher in the water; that way you will not waste so much effort."

How should a husband react to a wife's criticism? He brooded over the remark all day. After dinner, they argued about something, he could not remember what. He came out of the tent roughly, his emotions largely unexpressed and therefore unclear to him, his boots snagging in the guy ropes. He stalked along the river banks, the water lapping darkly. A star overhead. As bright as a star shell over the bay.

He coughs, hacking out the smoke of the scrub fire. Pain pushes him to the surface. The dugout has moved, and someone has found blankets in the stores. The sound of the waves against the bay, the Ouse exploring the reeds. The fathomless starfield across which he longs to drift. Other men, other wounded men nearby. Bad wounds. He bursts a juniper berry between his fingertips and raises its scent to his nostrils. All he can smell is burning.

Ruth sat sewing beside the fire.

"You do not believe in the war." She did not look up from her stitch.

"The war is useless from any point of view. But I cannot remain behind. Every soldier I see makes me feel ashamed."

"You would not die of shame."

"Yes, I would. There was an opportunity to join the field ambulance, and I took it. They asked about my religious beliefs. I told them I was a mystic agnostic, and that was that: stretcher bearer. It's not as glorious as being a soldier. But I can't bring myself to kill."

She put her needle and cloth aside. He knelt by the fire and she stroked his head as he spoke: "It is not wicked in us to fight, it is just mistaken. The buffoons in *The Times* maintain the war is necessary to purify the race. Nonsense. The strong were the first to die. No one knows what the outcome of this war will be, although I am convinced it will be contrary to the expectations of both sides. Something new will come of it, though. Some new expression of the life force."

"But what can *you* do?"

"I can show kindness. Without kindness, all that the soldiers will bring back from the war is horror. I will dress wounds and take the other end of a stretcher and carry the wounded from the battlefield."

"You've found a way to be heroic without the risk of being a conchie."

"I don't want to go to war. Nations appal me. Guns are revolting. But it is happening whether we agree with it or not. If I stay at home, we will never recover. You and I. The other women will shun you. I'll go to prison. I'll never be able to work."

"It's no different from boys pretending their sticks are rifles. You all think you can be heroes."

"Do you think I want to go and live in some camp ground with dull filthy men?"

"And if it is unpleasant to you, then I must forgive you?"

"I will go for you."

"Don't you dare say that."

"If I don't go, you will suffer."

The fire flickers in the grate. It is hard to leave the hearth behind. He thinks of cowardice, of St Peter warming his hands around the fire and denying his master.

"James?" Hector's angular white face drifts over the cosmos. "Can you understand me?"

He pulls on Hector's sleeve, and nods at the water bottle: water would make it easier to speak.

"Has the doctor been around to see you?"

The sergeant's kindness moves him deeply, and his jaw aches with unexpected sorrow.

He pulls again on Hector's sleeve, finds purchase on his shoulder, and pulls himself up.

"Jordison?" asks James.

"He was very brave," says Hector. "I couldn't go back for his body. We could only save the living."

The cosmos fizzes and whirls overhead, and the indigo swirls of Milky Way seethe. Hector's face is moon-pale and adrift.

"The sniper." James coughs out his strength.

"The sniper was our fancy brought on by nerves," Hector whispers.

"No. I saw him."

The sniper was taller than a man, covered in branches and twigs and he wore a hood to protect him from the sun. In the shimmering haze of the scrub fire, he stepped forward and shot Jordison. Previously, the Turk had respected the red cross and had even sent over officers bearing the white flag to apologize when they accidentally killed a stretcher squad. Yet this sniper had sought out the stretcher bearer, and, having shot him, bent over to inspect Jordison's head wound with a demonic diffidence.

"The sniper is connected to us. He is part of the convergence."

"Let us make a pact: you will not speak of my sniper and I will not tell anyone about your convergence. We don't want the men to think we are cracking up."

Hector puts his hand on the back of James' neck, encouraging him to rest. He is so tired that dream images and thoughts tumble unbidden beneath his eyelids. Ruth sings his name. She comes ashore, naked through the moonlit waters, her skin gleaming. She takes his hand and with one firm kick of her legs they fly upward. The earth falls away. He looks down to see the grey clouds and the termination line of the dawn advancing across the dark sea. The trenches and battle lines are scored across the earth. She touches his cheek. He is weary and too tired to kiss. The weariness of the soldiers and mules weighed down by packs and wagons. She is different from him. She is more highly evolved whereas he has devolved, become a troglodyte, a thing of the earth, an underground beast. She is of the air and of the water, intangible and quick. A contrary principle to him. "The life force speaks through us." Her voice is fire and smoke. "Our actions are the words of God, which time strings together into sentences, paragraphs, pages. A marriage is a part of the Divine Argument." She is the Eastern Queen of the Universe. He enters her and her face is transformed into the cosmos, into fire, time and space. The thoughts cascade, faster and faster, until he is no longer able to catch them.

Ruth was sat beside the fire, sewing a summer dress for the little girl in her class, Sylvia. He leant against the counter in the small dark kitchen. She often complained about the kitchen, its stained warped work surfaces and lack of ventilation. They had worked so hard all their lives and had less now than when they had first married. No home of their own, no children, and no work. Outside, the streets of Lewes were quiet. He took no solace in the Seizure. The only way to survive change was to align your interests with the interests of the powerful.

"I went back to the Institute," he said. "They repeated their offer to find a role for me."

"As what?"

"There will be no leaders under the Process. No state, no police, no army. But we will need protection and enforcement. The people will provide that by consensus, most of the time. But in exceptional circumstances, certain men will be used to enact the will of the people."

"I don't understand."

"If I have a gun, then I will become a tyrant. But if I can only fire that gun when everyone agrees that it needs to be fired then I become an instrument for the maximum possible public good."

"How will you know what the town wants?"

"The Process will aggregate the will of the people and enact it through me."

"You will have an implant."

"Yes."

"You will not always be in control of your own actions."

"When have I ever been?"

"Did she take you through the procedure? The side effects? Did Alex tell you what you might lose?"

"We have nothing to lose."

"Tell me what she said."

"It's experimental. There are risks. The Process can do more than just control my actions. It can change how I see the world. What I think about it. My memories and beliefs will be part of the Process. In some sense, there will be no distinction between the Process and myself. There will just be the Process and the part of the Process that thinks like me."

"That sounds like death."

"It's a chance to start over and to leave behind all the aspects of myself that aren't working. No one will notice, least of all me."

"I'll notice. I'll suffer. Will you be capable of love? Afterwards?"

"Sex?"

"Love."

"I'll still be with you. We'll still work at life together. But instead of digging a hole, we'll be building a bridge."

"What about your work?"

"What about it? The world has violently changed. Nothing we do has any value and any future prospect of our work being useful has been exterminated. Everything I believed was wrong. The other side was not right, either. But being right or wrong is irrelevant. There is only power or powerlessness, necessary or unnecessary. We've been given a chance for power."

"And what if you do something terrible under its influence?"

"I will not be responsible."

"Private? Are you awake, private?"

The priest steps carefully around sleeping, drugged men. Father Huxley is an ascetic beanpole. His hands are soft, untouched by experience; as with so many of the soldiers, his skull is indecently apparent, the eyes hollow, the lips thin. His cheekbone presses lustily against the skin.

Huxley puts his Bible down between them.

"The sergeant tells me that you are a Sussex man. My final year of study was at an institute near Glynde, outside Lewes. I was meant to be spending my time in devotional reading and exercises, but instead I was often out on the Downs and exploring the Weald."

James nods. The priest wants to talk, so let him. Relieved, no doubt, to speak to someone who is not in a ghastly state.

"Lovely town, Lewes. Nestled in the Downs, with the river running through it. I had breakfast in the ruins of the castle with an archaeologist, a Mr Dawson. Perhaps you are acquainted?"

Stretcher squads are on the move again, ragged wraiths fetching the vacated stretchers from outside the dressing station. The Milky Way pulses overhead.

"I grew very fond of the fauna and flora. The starlings winging their way out to sea. The great oak trees in November, so sad and ancient. The Institute had the most marvellous gardens, bursting with rhododendrons, and surrounded by woods so laden with life I fancied that evolution was going on all around me."

He had dreamt of an Institute. Of a woman who cut a hole in his skull, like the skulls he found in the tomb on the ridge. The precise details of the dream had dissipated and would not come into focus, like very small writing that did not reveal its meaning no matter how close he brought it to his eyes.

"In a chestnut tree outside my window, a little owl would set up for the night. I studied to the rhythm of his hooting. "

"There are no birds here," says James. It is an effort to speak.

"Not for another month, I suspect. And then the cliffs will be full of their migration. I doubt even the shelling will scare them away. Instinct is so strong. It's bred in the bone. Did you ever see the starlings over Eastbourne pier?"

James coughs and cannot stop himself coughing. The priest apologizes, and unfolds the first of his legs from his cross-legged position. James stops him.

"Father, I'm troubled."

"Tell me."

"I'm suffering from a kind of vertigo."

"Do you want me to fetch the doctor?"

"No. Vertigo of the soul, if such a thing exists. Do I sound mad?"

"Reason will not help you here. Only faith."

Around them, the wounded men moan and shift in their sleep. Instead of the healthy snoring of the dugouts, the sounds of the clearing station are muted: weak curses and morphine whimpers.

The priest whispers to him, "This is part of God's plan. This war. Your suffering. It must happen."

With difficulty, James struggles up then looks out to sea. The silhouettes of the battleships are like cutouts in the bay. The lighters beetle in another division, the same as the night before, and the night before that. Upright, his chest is less congested. He breathes in the sea wind. It does not hurt so much.

"You took an urn from the tomb," says James.

"Yes. I hope to keep it safe and deliver it to the British Museum."

"There is a skeleton in it."

"I daren't open it. The air will turn its contents to dust. But yes, I imagine there are human remains inside."

"In the tomb, did you see the holes cut into the skulls?"

"Trepanning. To let out evil spirits and evil thoughts."

"The belief that good can come from suffering is an evil thought."

The priest's eyes glitter. "What would you say if I told you that I thank God for the war?"

"You cannot!"

"This is my prayer: 'Thank you God for making me a priest, and thank you God for this war.'"

"Do you say this to all the wounded men?"

"The sergeant said you were an intellectual and a mystic. On those terms, I thought we could speak. Tell me more about your vertigo."

"I see glimpses of another life. Similar to this one, almost a reflection of it. Imagine laying your forehead against a cool mirror. The thoughts of your reflection are obscure to you. And that impression – no, my intense conviction – is that I'm home. The landscape of Sussex and this place converge. The ridge of Kiretch Tepe has seven peaks, just the same as the Seven Sisters running along the South coast."

"I know it well."

"Where the Cuckmere river reaches the sea. Over the next beach, instead of Anzac Cove, there is the sheer cliff beach of Birling Gap. I spent my honeymoon there. In the vertigo, it's more than a memory."

Huxley grips him, his thin hand ridged with tendons.

"Tell me, when you were in the trench and it was on fire, was that the moment in your life when you felt most fully and fruitfully alive? God did not *create* the world. God is still *creating* the world. Creation is a process that we must participate in, and witness. The front line marks the advancing edge of Creation, and *you were there*."

From further along the line, a soldier falls into spasms. His weary mate calls for a doctor and a priest. Huxley takes up his Bible. The glitter in his eyes is like shrapnel in the sun.

After the priest moves on to deliver the last rites, James attempts to stand, and finding it possible, absents himself from the wounded. Hundreds of fresh troops mass on the beach.

He takes out his Zweiss glass and, careful not to blacken the lens with his thumbs, he sweeps the heavens. Stargazing makes him feel like a boy. The act summons the memory of childhood, and that is comforting. He wouldn't need Cavorite to get to the moon nor to be fired out of a cannon. A mere act of will would suffice. He finds Venus. It is so bright because its cloud cover reflects the sunlight. Such stultifying clouds would make the surface unbearably hot and intensely pressurized. Trees planted at altitude, where the temperature and pressure were not so great, might begin the work of converting the carbon dioxide to oxygen. What kind of man would adapt to that environment? We would not be land dwellers. We would live in the clouds. The winged men of Venus. Was there any truth in the priest's obscene optimism? Would the descendants of man, high in their Venusian aeries, gaze back at the Earth and say that a war helped man to a new knowledge of the communion of all men? That the war was a practically unavoidable step in the dialectic of human destiny?

He is filthy with smoke. Bootless, he walks across the scrub, through the milling troops to where the sea laps quietly against the pebbles. He unhooks his braces, takes off his shirt, removes his trousers and his undershorts. The new troops shuffle in their ranks; naked, he wades into the sea. "The way your head twists when you swim," said Ruth, "it's as if you are violently disagreeing with the water." He stretches his body underwater, his hands clasped together, reaching forward to stretch his stomach muscles. Then, as she taught him, he kicks his legs forcefully, staying close to the surface but not breaking it. His lungs are too sore for him to stay underwater for long. He surfaces. A lighter has run aground on the sandbank, and the troops who can swim are disembarking with full packs into the deep water. The sea water cools and cleans his entire body. Ruth taught him to always stay calm in the water and to control his stroke. It was a time of sensual instruction. The body does not forget such lessons.

Ahead the troops plop into the sea like stones. The fittest swimmers have a rope that they are bringing into shore, hoping to use it to dislodge the lighter. As he gets closer to the boat, he can see the hopeful, anxious white faces of the men peering down into the water. One man is familiar. Jordison climbs up onto the stern, his broad yeoman's face contemplating the waves. James calls to him and yells. *Jordison! You're alive!* The Lancastrian takes up his pack and rifle. He looks out into the sea in search of the voice that knows his name, but the light is at his back, and it is all dark ahead. Then, with a grim look, Jordison steps off the boat and disappears into the water.

19

Private Brilliant brings over the dixie for morning tea. Two cups and saucers on a tray balanced on an overturned crate.

"Tea up," he says.

Collinson carefully spoons a dollop of apricot jam upon a biscuit. The moment the jam is out of the jar, fat flies cluster upon it, their emerald-and-ruby heads inscrutable and calm in the face of Collinson's fussy gesticulations; he waves, the flies disperse, the flies settle upon the jam before he can bring his hand back again.

"The problem," says Collinson, "is that a fly's perception of time is keener than mine. A single second to a human is a lazy Sunday afternoon to a fly."

Brilliant is a small man in an ill-fitting uniform and he makes a rather baggy silhouette against first light over the Aegean, swinging the dixie on its handle as he goes. James reaches over to take the cup and saucer. Half of Collinson's eyeglass is entirely caked in earth and yet he has not bothered to clean it. His dark eyebrows are rimed with dirt.

"At Cambridge, we had a trick to keep wasps away. When we were taking a picnic beside the river, we would set a pot of jam under a tree some way back from our party so that the wasps would congregate there rather than trouble us while we were dining. The efficacy of this tactic was dependent upon the number of wasps: if wasps in the immediate area exceeded twelve, then we would have to open two pots of jam."

Collinson tests a corner of the biscuit with his front teeth and, finding it resistant, flicks it out of the dugout.

"The question is: how many flies are there and at what rate are they increasing?" He sips noisily at his tea, and finding it as unsatisfying as the hard biscuit, flings the cup's contents out in the direction of the sea.

"Every day we provide improved breeding conditions and food for the flies. Their rate of growth must be exponential. But how can we be exact?" Collinson taps the bowl of his pipe clear then digs out charred remains from the stem. His bottom lip is blistered and his muzzle is wild. There is a long tired pause as he tries to remember how to light the pipe, then the bowl of embers seethes and smoulders like Chocolate Hill. The smoke stirs him from his reverie. He gets up and walks over to the discarded jam and biscuit. With the toe of his boot, he prods at the feeding clump of flies.

"This biscuit does not constitute a representative sample of the frequency of flies to the surface area of the battlefield."

"You are concerned with the flies," says James. His voice comes from somewhere far away.

"The flies are important. If the flies prevent me from eating the apricot jam, then that constitutes a measurable degradation of my spirit. Of my will to fight. Also, the constant irritant of flies prevents me from attending to other tasks that may aid my survival. That's before we even get onto the transmission of disease."

"You are saying the flies are the enemy?"

The tea is cold and tastes strongly of chlorine.

"No. My argument is that if one were to devise an

equation to predict the outcome of this battle, then the flies would have to be a factor. I wager the flies have never figured in the plans of our leaders. Therefore, one can infer that their method of planning is inadequate for war. They stand on the hill or back at the battleship, and try to influence events with merely their intelligence and their will when clearly a vast range of unfathomable contingencies come between the logic of their battle plan and any final dispatches. Tiny details imperceptible to them decide everything."

"Such as flies," says James.

"Yes. The flies indicate two things: firstly, corruption has set in. Secondly, our leaders are guilty of a fundamental error in their attempts to influence the battle from the helm, as it were, by willpower alone. The battle, as we have observed since the landing, is determined by the most complex interdependencies. Only a set of algorithms could accurately predict the outcomes of such a network."

Should he tell Collinson that he saw a man returned from the dead? Jordison had stood on the prow of the stranded lighter, then stepped out into the water. James had lost track of him in the chaos of the landing, as the rest of the division thrashed through the dark shallows. It could have been a hallucination. If he is to be visited by more hallucinations of such palpable quality, then he is lost. The doctor had warned him about giving in to these moments of vertigo. However, the vision had been indistinguishable from reality. He was swimming at the time, and so entirely awake, and alive to physical sensation. He was tempted to believe what he saw, regardless of what it might mean.

Collinson continued, "Do you know the concept of cause and effect? That I draw upon my pipe and so must exhale the smoke?"

He takes a demonstrative puff of his pipe.

"Our leaders believe they can plot out a battle by anticipating cause and effect. But on the battlefield, to talk about causality is meaningless."

James disagrees, "A man shoots at me, the bullet goes in me, I die. That is clear cause and effect."

"Of course. But causation of that type is strictly a local phenomenon: say, between an enemy sniper and yourself or even between you and Hector when you are carrying a stretcher. Or between the guns of a destroyer and the target up on the ridge. We know that you will follow orders, but the effect of that cause is unknown to us: how many men will you rescue? Impossible to say without knowing the landscape, the rate of enemy fire, and your stamina."

"My stamina as influenced by my intake of apricot jam."

"Precisely. A battle is more than the sum of its parts. It is a network distributed in space and time. If we had some way of performing the necessary calculations instantaneously, as events in space and time change, then we could theoretically express the war in a series of algorithms, which could then be used to anticipate events on future battlefields."

"We could count the flies."

"And then I would know how many pots of jam to open so that I could breakfast in peace."

Their conversation is interrupted by a rumble rolling down from the high ridges south of their position.

"That is not a storm," says Collinson.

Hector slides down into their dugout and takes the Zweiss glass from around James' neck.

"It is the sound of men cheering," says Hector.

Collinson's dark eyebrows rise in expectation. "Oh. Have we won?"

The cries of men pour down the gullies like meltwater. Disembodied voices eddy along the runnels, shallow trenches, dunes and swells. Cries of utter release. Cries of absolute relief after almost unendurable hardship and tension.

Hector grabs James and together they stumble down the beach for a better southward view. James has one boot on, and the other half-off and he wants to make a decision either way. Hector looks through the Zweiss. He lets go of James. He stumbles back a step.

"It's a Turkish battle cry," says Hector. "We're dead."

He hands James the Zweiss and points to the steep bare bluff of the southern ridge. A horde of soldiers pour over the crest, line after line of Turkish infantry, skidding and screaming down three great gullies toward the allied position. Six battalions with the sunrise at their back.

The sun shears across his line of sight, and, magnified by the glass, his retinas flare out. He focuses the glass away from the crest and upon the steep dark bluff. The horde kicks up a long dust cloud; ahead of it, among the thousands of soldiers, he sees the faces of women. Not Turkish women but women he recognizes, from his past. He can't remember their names but they are familiar to him. The women run shoulder-to-shoulder among the Turkish soldiers, their heads turned back to the crest, straining to retreat even as their legs carry them forward against their will, making their gait unsteady and unnatural.

"I see women," says James.

Gently, Hector takes the glass from him.

The wave of the battle cry becomes choppy. Here comes the machine gun rattle that knocks under your breastbone. The battleships open fire, their guns clanging like hell's iron lid. Under the downward stabbing light of shrapnel clouds, legions of attacking soldiers slump to the ground. After days of shelling the haunted rock of the ridges, the shells explode joyously across the faces of the enemy. Losses mount. The bodies of the fallen build up in piles over which thousands of soldiers clamber.

"It's a slaughter," says Hector. "Thank God for the navy."

He hands the Zweiss glass back to James. Floating in the dust cloud, a flock of boots, scraps of cloth and arcing chunks of this and that. He focuses on the steep rocky bluff and sees English men and women crawling along the smouldering ground, not Turks at all but the townspeople he evicted in Lewes. He doesn't remember their names, he was never any good at remembering names, not since the operation. He puts his hand to the back of his head and feels, under his hair, a scar and a ridge of flesh. How could he have forgotten the operation? His hand shakes. The sun spears in through the Zweiss glass again. He sets it aside. Hector takes pity on him, thinks it is the spectacle of the slaughtered Turk that has made him swoon.

After a long weekend of futile war, the allies are eager to see some reward for their efforts, some evidence of victory, and show no mercy to this miscalculated attack. The dead form a rampart which slides down the ridge, and soldiers in their thousands run and scream and throw themselves onto this rampart and die there, adding their bodies to the construction. Rifles jut out of the rampart at all angles, bayonets gleaming in first light like the spines on the back of a single massive creature. Now and then, out of the multitude, he sees a familiar face.

A last shell from the destroyer stops the horde's advance. Thousands of inert bodies cover the bluff, and a few crawl back toward the crest. After the last echo of the battle, a dreadful quiet ensues. At the water's edge, the waves ripple soundlessly over the hard ridged sand. He feels weak with apprehension, as if the slaughter is somehow his fault.

James faints. He crumples at the knees and feels the world turn within him and without him. He rolls down the gully, through the thorny bush until he comes to a stop, sprawled on the loose rocky earth, one boot off and one boot on. All around him, placed at even intervals of a yard, open jars of apricot jam form a sinuous line along the entire length of the gully, the mouth of each jar a seething mass of flies.

20

The general's motorcade approached from the east, along dusk lanes flanked by high corn. The shout went up around Saddlescombe, and the soldiers cleared out of the estaminet to prepare for inspection. In the barn, Alex Drown finished her shift, washed her hands, and pushed the cap from her head. In the back yard, Tom Bowles knelt at one end of a planed beam and inspected the grain with the good side of his slanted face. Ruth and the children broke from the cover of the copse, running hand-in-hand across a darkening field and in through the back gate of the estaminet; they passed Tom, who did not look up from his work even when his son said his name. Out front, Jane gathered dirty plates and stoked the stove. She put her index finger on a black key of the old piano. She was sure she could play but could not imagine what came after the first note.

Ruth ushered the children upstairs and into a dark bedroom. Agnes stood at the window. The lane below was thronged with silent soldiers. They came from the barn, and from further afield; from the barracks at Plumpton College and the semi-detached suburb of Hassocks, from a grain silo in a hollow below Ditching Beacon, from the field hospitals of Poynings and Pyecombe Golf Club.

"These soldiers have swords," said Agnes. "And they're different from the other soldiers."

"In what way?"

"They are people we used to know."

The girl was right. The ranks of these soldiers were made up of the evicted. Their uniforms were also different: the tunics were tan or pale green and, instead of pith helmets, these soldiers wore helmets wrapped in cloth. The dark grey greatcoats were familiar enough, but the variation in the height of the line indicated men and women in the ranks. A narrow curved sword hung from their belts.

Ruth found some blankets and set the children down to rest. She did not have to wait long for Alex Drown to return. The door scraped back against the floorboard. Alex's face showed no recognition that she had company in her bedroom. She kicked off her left shoe, then her right, undressed and got into bed.

Ruth waited for Alex to fall asleep. Then, Alex's eyelid slid slowly back, the lashes gummy with blood. Her hands shot out, as if they had been bound all day and suddenly freed. "Help me!"

Alex grabbed Ruth's shoulders.

Ruth said, "We will help each other."

Alex sat up, cradling the sore side of her head, then levered herself to her feet. In the dark window, her one good eye saw the ruin of her other.

"I'm hemorrhaging again."

She dabbed at her eye with the corner of her long white nightie.

"There are gaps in my memory. I remember giving the wounded soldiers malted milk. Filling a steel bowl with hot water. Standing dutifully beside the doctor as he operated."

For safety, Euan held onto Ruth's thigh. Alex stared at the boy as if he were an enormous rodent.

She said, "These are the children you were looking for?"

"Yes."

"The ones you hope to save."

"I will save them."

Alex calculated.

"They can come with us to the Institute."

"Will we be safe there?"

"It's shielded from the Process. The hemorrhaging should stop. And then I'll be able to help you."

While Alex dressed, Ruth explained to the children that they were going on a long night walk, following the footpath back to Lewes and around the edge of the *douanier*'s blockade to Mount Caburn, and then down to Glynde. About fifteen miles by her reckoning. The boy would not make it all the way. He was already tired. She would carry him.

From downstairs came the sound of boots upon the boards, of stools scraping and a shout for beer. The children looked at her nervously. She stroked Euan's hair.

"The soldiers haven't bothered us yet."

A singalong began. A high boyish voice led a chorus of men.

"Omega John's here," said Alex. "I'll have to speak to him."

"No," said Ruth. "We will slip out the back."

But the kitchen was thronged with soldiers in all their gear, helping themselves to the stores. In the centre of the kitchen, Tom stood between his wife and the coarse remarks of enlisted men. It would be too upsetting for the children to leave that way.

They turned around. Alex led them through the fug of the lounge; there were two dozen or more soldiers crammed into the low room, smoking and drinking. The general was Omega John. He was sat at the piano in a pristine uniform, a peaked cap atop his bulbous skull. His lips were thin, the lower half of his face withered and malnourished, his front teeth extruding slightly. His moustache was wispy and immature, yet white with age. His voice was as pure as a choirboy's, but his forehead was virulently liver-spotted.

"Alex!" He seemed pleased to see her. "Join us. We're having a good old singsong."

Omega John ordered the soldiers to clear the table next to the piano, and they brought stools for Ruth and the children. The change that came over the soldiers when Omega John spoke to them was pronounced: they became silently compliant.

Omega John offered his hand to Ruth. It too was liver-spotted, the skin loose, yet the grip retained its strength.

"They call me Omega John," he said. He raised his bare brows at Alex in expectation of introduction.

"Her name is Ruth, she is married to the bailiff."

"The seamstress!" said Omega John. "I know your husband. He is very brave. He is taking part in the landing. Can't tell you when exactly. Classified. But I can tell you, it's the Dardanelles. We're having another crack at it. I have a song for you, seamstress. Do you know Little Redwing?" he played a few bars on the piano and the men, recognizing the tune, stood up to sing.

"The moon shines down
On Charlie Chaplin
He's going barmy
To join the army
But his little baggy trousers
They need a-mending
Before they send him
To the Dardanelles."

Some parts of Omega John had responded to longevity

treatment while others had not; consequently, his ageing was unequally distributed. His choirboy's voice was in marked contrast to his wispy white hair. One knee was heavily bandaged, so he did not use that leg to work the piano pedals. His smile was indistinguishable from a grimace.

"Another verse for the seamstress!" he announced. "In honour of her husband!"

> *"The moon shines bright*
> *On Charlie Chaplin*
> *But his shoes are cracking*
> *For want of blacking*
> *And his baggy khaki trousers*
> *Still need mending*
> *Before they send him*
> *To the Dardanelles."*

He stood to take a bow. He was seven foot tall. He stooped under the plaster ceiling to accept the applause of the men and their call for another song. His uniform was tailored to fit his elongated form, and gathered sharply around the middle with a Sam Browne belt that glistened under the lamplight. The men struck up a ditty in response:

> *"That was a very fine song*
> *Sing us another one*
> *Just like the other one*
> *Sing us another one do."*

He played up and down the keys, making a show of considering which song he would perform next. He leant over to Alex, nodded at her bloodshot eye, and whispered, "You should get your eye looked at." And he squinted with mock concern at her bloody orbit. Then he attacked the piano keys, playing random notes that gradually were rearranged into a simple order from the lowest to the highest.

"I call that piece 'Insert sort'. It is derived from a simple algorithm. The order emerges in the higher registers first. Whereas with 'Bubble sort'–" he jabbed furiously around the keys, the children put their hands over their ears "– the order begins in the bass notes." Agnes burst into tears, all of a sudden and unconstrained. Taking pity on her, Omega John switched from the jabbing instrumental of the algorithm to the simple melody of another soldier's song:

"Why does she weep?
Why does she sigh?
Her love's asleep so far away
He played his part that August day
And left her heart on Suvla Bay."

In the estaminet, this brief verse moved the soldiers to silence. Some bowed their heads, and prayed to loves of their own.

"Now I've done it," whispered Omega John. "I've given it all away."

Ruth held Agnes' head against her breast, calming the child.

"Can you stop this?" she asked.

"This?" Omega John gestured at the piano.

"The war."

"Why would I stop the war when I have gone to such pains to start it?"

He sang a sad song about a long trail winding into the land of his dreams, of nightingales and moonbeams, and a long night waiting for his dream to come true. He played the keys with such delicacy, pressing and releasing each one in turn with deliberate care, as if they were the valves of a lover's heart. When he finished, he sighed and said to Ruth, "I'm dying, seamstress. I'm very old and it cannot be put off any longer. They say that no one is indispensable but that is not true of me: I am one of a kind. My colleagues have tried to recruit a suitable replacement but to no avail. So this–" his gesture encompassed the estaminet "–is the solution."

"Let my husband go," said Ruth, in a low fierce voice.

Omega John laughed.

"You're here to rescue the bailiff? I thought you were here because my men need a whore."

He turned to Alex. "You've been remiss in not explaining the situation to our guest. Or did you find it impossible to put it in terms she could comprehend? Her understanding of her situation is so meagre I suppose any revelation would constitute brutality."

Ruth was indignant. She would not let men bully her.

"The situation is actually very easy for me to understand. You are a boy playing at war."

"I'm not playing at war, seamstress. I am remembering it." His eyes were green-rimmed, like those of a falcon. "I hold within me a perfect memory of the war. If you like, I could share it with you."

Alex put her arm between them, her fierce small face defiant.

"Leave her alone."

"Don't put yourself between us, Alex. I'm dying. I'm bored of pretending to care about you."

He turned to Ruth, and offered her his liver-spotted hand.

"Take my hand again, and this time you will know exactly what the war was like. You will know what it is to die slowly of your wounds in no-man's-land. You will look down and be able to touch where the machine gun eviscerated you. More than the pain, you will know the boredom and the terror of months under fire, the sensory agony of it, smells, sights and sounds of horror; and when you feel that you can endure no more, and that every idea that you were made of has been proven to be nonsense, and that every thought you ever had was wrong, and everything you ever did was pointless, then you will understand the war itself."

"The war was over a long time ago."

"It never ended for me. I was wounded at Suvla Bay, you see, shot in the head. The surgeon operated. Something happened under the knife. I was cursed. After a hundred years, we're still only beginning to understand that curse. The feelings, sensations and experience of the war survive intact within me. And I can pass them on at will, from mind to mind."

His palm was firm-fleshed and youthful, the back of his hand decrepit.

"They've kept me alive for so long trying to recreate my curse. A hundred years in which I've had to watch humanity degenerate to the point where it can barely wipe its own backside."

His smile was a skull's grimace, everything below the eyes was already in the grave.

"I am the last human," said Omega John. "You're just animals. I could show you how reduced you have become. But giving a sheep an understanding of its sheepness is crueller than slaughtering it: if I laid my hand upon its brow–" he reached again for Ruth, by way of demonstration "–I could show it how it is defined solely by its usefulness to a superior species, how it is bred for flesh and wool, nothing more, no meaning, no legacy, its loved young kept alive solely for their succulence." He smiled at the children, and said to both of them, "My friends went over the top, with the guns of the army police at their backs, and as they were cut to pieces by the machine guns, into itty-bitty little pieces, they baa'd like lambs."

He leant forward and put his hand upon Alex Drown's cheek. The air tightened, Ruth felt it in her stripe. Slowly, Alex's legs stiffened and she reared up out of her seat, his caress still upon her cheek; blood flowed freely from her eyes and over the back of his knuckles; the back of his hand was a map of high ridges, gullies and shell-torn land, the liver-spots were the discolouration of overturned earth, her blood a river coursing across an otherwise arid terrain. Alex convulsed and paled; he withdrew his touch, and she slid off the stool and onto the floor. Around her, the soldiers swayed and staggered from table to table, oblivious to her.

Omega John sighed and turned back to the piano.

"There. Oh Alex, you made me cross. And I hate being cross. Life is so intense. I wish I could play you music that communicated the correct spiritual aspect with which to face life. I wish I could touch you and share the beauty of life as I see it. But I was made in war, and war is all I have to give."

Alex lost all physical dignity, contorted upon the floor of the estaminet. Ruth knelt next to her, but was afraid to comfort her. In the shock and pain, she was gasping for breath. Ruth took a risk. She slapped Alex so hard across the face that her head rapped against the board. It released her. Alex took a deep gulp of air. Her chest heaved. Ruth used her shirt to mop the blood welling in Alex's eyes. She was temporarily blind, and her nurse's uniform was wet with sweat and urine.

Omega John closed the lid of the piano. He stood and buttoned his decorated tunic. His face held only the selfishness of a dying man. His adjutant handed him his peaked cap and cane. He stepped around Alex Drown, then looked down at Ruth.

"The implants are made out of my cells. James and Alex are part of me and I am part of them. You cannot save someone from themselves."

Again, Ruth begged him to stop. Her defiance was gone, replaced by something else, a magical desire to wish away all her ills. He slipped slightly in his hob-nailed boots then tapped thoughtfully at the boards with his cane, dipping its tip in the darkening pool of Alex's urine.

"I always forget that your type cannot detach your mind from your suffering, that you lack even that rudimentary control over yourselves. You are trapped within the algorithm that creates the self-awareness of painful input signals." Omega John cleaned the end of his cane in a soldier's beer. "We must use your capacity for suffering in our game."

At an imperceptible signal, his adjutants opened the door, and the general departed to a mass salute from the soldiers in the estaminet.

21

A hand on his shoulder wakes him. Standing over James, in a clean and intact uniform, is Jordison.

"You alright, mate?" asks the yeoman. He shows no indication of recognizing James.

"Yes. I think so. Do you have any water?"

Jordison takes out a water bottle and hands a cap of water to James. He accepts it, and then asks: "What's your name?"

"Jordison."

"Do you have a brother, Jordison?"

"No."

"I didn't think so. But you have a wife?"

"Yes."

"And three children?"

"Exactly three. Barely twelve months between each."

"Then we've met before," says James.

"We must have. Though for the life of me I can't remember. Are you feeling better?"

"A touch of ague," says James.

"The lieutenant colonel said that no man of the ambulance division was to fall sick. Made it very clear, he did."

The lieutenant colonel had not been seen since the first night.

"If you're shipshape, I'll be on my way."

"Wait. Help me up."

The yeoman reaches down to him. He grips Jordison's thick upper arm, then his forearms, then his rough large hands. Warm living hands with a deep life line and broken fingernails.

"You are remarkable," says James.

The yeoman recoils an inch at this unexpected compliment.

"I mean, I saw you die and yet here you are. You can't deny that is remarkable."

"You're mistaken. We've just landed from Lemnos."

"Your wife works at the mill. You don't smoke cigarettes. You like gardening."

"All true. But then, that's true of many a Lancashire man."

James feels faint again. The lightness begins in his fingertips and toes.

He asks Jordison, "Do you forgive me?"

With a long, rustic stare, Jordison weighs James' condition.

"You should get some bully inside you, mate," he says. He doffs his pith helmet and trots away to rejoin his squad as they hustle in single file on a gully path toward the salt lake.

James shivers with weakness, and his head feels absurdly light again. No, not this time, he will not allow himself to forget. He will not be patched up and wiped clean like Jordison. James presses his index finger into the ridge of scar tissue at the back of his head. They hollowed him out in Tipperary. For everything he learnt in basic training, ten other pieces of knowledge were removed. Exactly how much they took out of him, he cannot say. A lot. He has forgotten a lot.

In the dugout, the stretcher squad is buzzing with the news that their commanding officer has been found. The

Field Ambulance had lost their lieutenant colonel and presumed him dead. According to Private Brilliant, in the confusion on the beach that first day, the lieutenant colonel had simply taken command of the 33rd Ambulance division. As a regular officer and veteran of the Boer War, the New Army recruits all looked the same to him. Hector is amused at the thought of it, and imitates the quick bowlegged prance of their superior officer, up and down the beach, throwing off orders and chastisement to the wrong men. Collinson and the others laugh.

News of this cruel satire spreads to the lieutenant colonel and he seeks out the men of the 32nd Field Ambulance. Flanked by breathless adjutants, he reddens at the sight of the ragged squad lolling around in the dunes like a drinking party at Camber Sands. Barker Bill, they call him, for his noisy incoherence. The lieutenant colonel takes his sergeant to task, ranting in Hector's pale face. His delivery is so splenetic and spittle-flecked that his words are indecipherable. He speaks in an invented language, like something out of a child's game. At first, James assumes that his ear is unaccustomed to the accent or even to the manner of the officer upper class. He moves closer so that he can hear more clearly. No, Barker Bill's voice is not even human. The tone and pitch vary wildly; sometimes he sounds like a monkey howling through the wireless, and then his tongue makes a loud knocking sound like that of a cold diesel engine.

The rest of the men must be so struck with fear that they dare not point out that their commanding officer sounds like a broken machine. He looks like one too. His eyes, for starters, are bloodshot pools without pupil or whites. His head is red raw, and his ears are wet smooth plates without the curls and canals of a true human ear. He punctuates his alien utterances with slaps of his Malacca cane against polished field boots – this gesture, pure Barker Bill, has been retained but the rest of him has been poorly sculpted. Either side of him, ragged adjutants quiver at every stab and holler of his rage. Only by concentrating can James bring definition to the lieutenant colonel. Slowly he tunes in and this concentration turns the alien chatter into the King's English.

"How *dare* you come on duty dressed like that?" The lieutenant colonel points at Hector's calves with his cane. "Where are your puttees, dammit?"

"I forgot to put them on, sir. During the attack, we–"

"How *dare* you answer me?"

The lieutenant colonel stares Hector down, daring him to answer the question.

"Place yourself under close arrest, sergeant."

"Sir?"

"The rest of the squad will proceed without you. You must remain on the beach until I return."

The stretcher squad falls in. The lieutenant colonel strides past James, his officer's tunic gathered tightly around his narrow waist. He does not see James and almost walks right through him. With one boot off, one boot half-on, James is in between worlds, he understands that now. Between the land of the living and the land of the dead, between the sane and the mad, between what-might-have-been and what-will-be.

The sea mist mingles with the smoke from the distant burning scrub. The ambulance division trot off into this fog, leaving Hector and James behind.

"He's gone mad," says Hector.

"He's very strict about the King's Regulations," says James.

"To keep your sergeant back from the searching zone just because he's not wearing puttees is mad."

"He has to follow King's Regulations," says James. "There is nothing else to him. He has been hastily put together. He's a botched job. Have you seen the way he walks? Clearly some kind of broken mechanism. Perhaps there was no time to make the knees."

The dune grass flattens and straightens. They begin the walk back to the beach.

"I am concerned," says Hector. "Are you putting this on?"

"What do you mean?" asks James.

"This madness. Are you feigning it?"

One moment of vertigo and you are lost.

"Were you feigning it when the sniper came for you?"

Exasperated, Hector quickens his pace. James appeals to his reason.

"When I was in the necropolis, I saw through the veil and into another life, another world. On the stretcher, I had the same sense that this battle is an illusion. No, not an illusion. It's clearly real–" James kicks a stone to prove this point "– rather, the war itself is mad and we are sane men trapped in it, you see, and we daren't wake up to the madness in case we lose what little sanity we have remaining."

Hector doesn't want to listen to this counsel. James grabs hold of him.

"I saw Jordison again. Alive. I saw him twice. I even spoke to him and he didn't remember me. I could take you to him."

"I ask you again." Hector puts his hands either side of James' head to hold his gaze. "Are you feigning this? Wouldn't you rather I shoot you in the hand? If Barker Bill discovers you shamming madness to get out, he will have you shot at dawn."

"Barker Bill can't see me," says James. "He has no eyes. He shouted at you for not wearing puttees, but one of my boots is hanging off and he didn't even give me a second glance. Where has he been for the last few days? Where has our commanding officer *been*? I'll tell you. He was killed on the first day, and so we've been sent a replacement. But these replacements are like dud shells. Resources are running low. The soldiers are coming off the assembly line unfinished, you see? The Turks aren't real Turks either. When I looked through the Zweiss glass, I did not see enemy soldiers – I saw men and women taken from my town and impelled to charge into our guns by the same spirit that guides this entire battle. Maybe the entire war."

"*Stop shamming!*"

"Every indication is that this is not how things should be. Collinson understood as soon as we landed, when the men were bathing instead of fighting. We can't apprehend the truth of this war because we are under the influence of it."

"Under the influence of what exactly?"

"The war is being guided by a force exterior to either side. A spirit or vital fluidic ether of some sort has got into us. But its influence wanes under certain pressures and it disappeared altogether underground, in the necropolis. The others suspect it, I think. The men of intelligence. Father Huxley and Doctor Blore. They are drawn to the necropolis for this reason. I must speak with them."

"No, they will know you are shamming. You will be court martialled." Hector looks around in anguish, for something to hand to restore his friend's sanity.

"You must find a way back to us, James."

"We were together before the war. I met you on the Downs. Don't you remember? And you couldn't speak. You were like a doll. I took you into my home. We looked after you. And then I followed you into the war. My home is just over the ridge. If we don't get back there, we're going to die here."

"But like Jordison we can be resurrected?"

"I'm not like him."

"Am I?"

"Yes. No. You're somewhere in between. I don't know."

"Other men are mere automata and you alone are the true human; really, if you must feign madness you could be more original in your delusions."

Barker Bill had ordered Hector to remain at the dugout, a reinforced hole covered with a corrugated iron roof and door twenty yards north of the casualty clearing station, and await the return of his commanding officer.

The white canvas of the bell tents ripple against the bright blue Aegean sea, fresh as yacht sails. In an open-air operating theatre, buried a few feet deep into the chocolate-coloured soil, Blore and his orderly complete an amputation. The left arm of the soldier is bound just below the elbow, and the orderly has placed a white folded towel over the patient's brow to shield him from the sun. The wounded man's feet are black. Arrayed upon two covered boxes, the surgical instruments gleam in the rising sun.

A listless herd of wrecked men sit and wait outside the bell tents, as if the dressing station is a doss house. They are mesmerized by the crackle and chatter of sunlight upon the lilt of the blue sea. Exhausted stretcher bearers add to their number, dropping off pale blood-stained men with ghastly smiles to be given a woodbine and a refill of their water bottles. The doctor beckons and another bad case is dropped onto the trestle table in the operating tent.

The boom of a great gong: the shelling begins, as always, at eight in the morning. A shell strikes the centre of a Sikh mule train, flipping over its intricate rigging of ropes and knots, and twisting its carefully weighed burdens and somnolent mules cyclonically around one another. A few men outside the clearing station flinch and try to stand, to go and help; most do not even notice. They stare unseeing at their black feet or pick mechanically at the lice in their ragged vests. The shelling ends fifteen minutes later in accordance with the bureaucracy of the battle. Rations are passed around for breakfast, but James has found that shelling destroys the appetite as effectively as it did the mules.

After a long dull wait, Doctor Blore comes up from the operating tent for tea and a smoke. He notices James, and walks over to him.

"I've been meaning to speak to you, James. We are to set up an advanced dressing station in the Kiretch Tepe to the north. I was wondering if you and Sergeant Hector could go with twenty-five or so men up the ridge. Find somewhere between the hills where we can work."

"Is there to be an advance along the Kiretch?"

"I have no bloody idea."

"Sergeant Hector is under arrest." James explains about the reappearance of their commanding officer, and the incident with the missing puttees.

"Your commanding officer is erratic. Did you speak to Father Huxley?" Blore's voice drops to a whisper, "I think you and he had an interesting chat. He told me more about your bouts of vertigo."

"You warned me not to give into them."

"So I did."

"What did Huxley tell you?" asks James.

"He says that you glimpsed another life. That you are convinced that we are not really in the Dardanelles but are in fact in Sussex."

"It was a vivid impression. It does not interfere with my ability to carry out my duty."

"But you believe it to be more than an impression or a fancy?"

"I've seen things."

"Tell me."

"Why are you and Father Huxley so interested in these visions?"

Blore takes a swig from his water bottle.

"You're not the only one to have suffered them," he says. "Huxley thinks it is in the nature of war to upset the normal order of our perceptions, and that we are reluctant to speak of the experience for fear of seeming mad."

"Father Huxley said he was thankful for the war."

"Yes, he told me that too. 'Because it allows us to apprehend the true nature of our condition'. Now he may well be mad. That's why the war suits him so well."

"What kind of visions have other soldiers had?"

"I've seen some odd things on the operating table. It started with a lieutenant, who had almost the whole of his right frontal lobe blown out. A piece of shell about an inch square was lodged in his brain. I use a local anaesthesia on head cases rather than a general because if the patient can cough when ordered that helps extrude pulped brain. Now patients say odd things during brain surgery, and perhaps I should pay it no mind, but whenever I applied a magnetic charge, to collect shrapnel from the tissue, the lieutenant spoke in what sounded to me to be scientific formula. I asked Collinson to observe the phenomena and he made extensive notes. It was not gobbledygook, nor was it entirely explicable, not even to the professor, though he has discerned a consistency in the language which suggests a grammar."

Blore rubs at his face.

"The lieutenant did not survive. And then the stretcher bearers brought in a more than average number of head cases from the Kiretch Tepe, wounds from a projectile that is quite different from a standard bullet. Always in the same part of the skull. The back of the head."

Instinctively, James reaches back to touch the ruckled scar of his own wound.

"Yes, I have one of those too." Blore puts his head forward so that James can see the scar on the back of his head. "The same part of the skull as yours, and a hole identical to the trepanning of the ancient skulls in the necropolis. That is just one of the facets of the anatomy of the skeletons we found that so intrigues me. Father Huxley is also keen to get back. Setting up an advanced dressing station on the ridge will allow us to continue with our duty and to retrieve material from the archaeological site."

"Won't you be missed here?"

"Some of the other MOs here are making a hobby of seeking out the wounded in the battlefield when we have a perfectly adequate supply of them at this station. They can come in and work these tents. They'll live longer."

"Do you think all these head wounds are related?"

Blore touches the scar on James' head.

"You are not the only one who remembers. I know you, James. Not from the army. And I'm scared of you. I don't know why. But the thought of upsetting you makes something in my stomach cringe. That's bloody peculiar, isn't it? It's not right that a doctor should be so afraid. At first I thought I might be dead, and that this is hell, but Huxley told me that I was being ridiculous."

"What do you remember?"

"My operating theatre. It was underground, in a sort of stone icebox beneath the Institute. I hung a picture of the moon above the table so that the patients would have something to gaze at, and it was the moon as if seen close up, its valleys and mountains. Quite extraordinary. After work, I would return home to a village, to a small cottage with a green door. The village was owned by the lord of the manor. We came and went at his discretion. I remember a summer afternoon in the garden. I had dug out the weeds and trimmed a bay tree, and then burnt the cuttings in a pile. You arrived in the village inside a machine. A terrifying tall walking machine."

The doctor put his hand to his heart. "There. The fear again. I can feel it. You helped the lord clear the village of undesirables. We were all terrified of you because your face was so blank. My boy saw you on the village lawn, as tall as two houses. He called you the iron monster."

James nods.

"You remember too?" asks Blore.

"Firle," says James. "That is the name of the village with the green doors."

Under Blore's direction, James prepares medical haversacks for the advanced dressing station.

Barker Bill returns at noon. For Sergeant Hector's disciplinary hearing, he demands an orderly room be set up on the beach. His adjutants choose a suitably imposing bush for this purpose. They set up a green canvas camp chair before a neat pile of bully crates that act as a table, and upon this table, they place a pencil, some papers and a copy of the King's Regulations. James walks through the dune grass to observe the disciplinary hearing. The sole of his right boot has come away and the sand gets between his toes. His beard itches.

The sergeant major calls the disciplinary hearing. Hector walks into the open part of the beach marked up as the orderly room, then stands to attention opposite Barker Bill. Barker Bill knocks Hector's cap from his head and makes him re-enter carrying it. Hector walks back holding the cap. No, that is wrong also. The language of Barker Bill is tight and mechanical, as if a telegraph wire has been slid up his arse. The black orbs of his eyes strain and writhe under the pressure of barking his peculiar language, as if the human face cannot keep up with such fast-moving syllables, cannot contain such swift shifts between high and guttural notes. The sergeant major grasps Barker Bill's meaning: a man does not simply *stroll* into the orderly room, he has to be *marched*. Even if the orderly room is nothing more than a chair, a crate and a suitably imposing bush, the accused must march into it. The sergeant major flinches at Barker Bill's tirade and then he marches Hector into position: Right-*turn*. Quick-*march*. Ab-ou-t-*turn*. Hector almost walks into the bush. Halt!

The sergeant-clerk reads the charges. By concentrating, James can tune into the telegraph language.

"Coming on parade improperly dressed," says the sergeant-clerk.

"Bad example," thunders Barker Bill. "No puttees! Anything to say?"

Hector offers no defence. A severe reprimand is entered onto his crime sheet.

Barker Bill orders their camp be moved a mile and a half along the shore to be nearer to the trenches. The stretcher bearers spend the next day under fire lugging supplies to new dugouts. But the lieutenant colonel is furious that the new location is so *damn shabby* and so the entire ambulance has to shift everything into an adjoining field. With the general back on the *HMS Jonquil* with his bad knee, the landing loses its way. Under physical and mental hardship, minds narrow and it becomes hard to concentrate. Every damn thing seems to be afflicted with the drift.

The war will not end until all the earth's bounty has been sacrificed to its bureaucracy: every lump of coal, every animal, every machine, every woman, every tree, every child will be collected, catalogued and reprocessed into prolonging the war until the armies are firing wooden shells filled with blood at one another, and when they run out, the combatants will take up the severed limbs of their fellow soldiers and use them as cudgels to beat one another's brains out, and when that fails, they will take a handful of earth and push it into the mouth of the enemy, and when that fails, the last two combatants of the Great War will try to choke each other with their bodies, pushing their hands down the oesophagus of the enemy so that the enemy swallows the arm up to the elbow, then pushing the head in through the jaw until the last two soldiers form the Ouroboros, the cartwheel snake, rolling over the blasted earth as it consumes its own tail.

Private Brilliant finds the Wolseley Valise of the lieutenant colonel among the remains of the mule train. James and Hector are dispatched to fetch it. Bent double, they scurry along the shallow communication trench with the valise between them on a stretcher.

Fatigue parties forage through the stores dumped on the beach. They climb the ziggurat of crates and abandoned wagons and bring back rations and ammunition. James goes down there to gather medical stores. Blore wants bandages and silk treated with bismuth iodoform paraffin paste for his needles. Dichloramine for antiseptic, procaine hydrochloride as local anaesthetic. Methodically, Hector stocks up the medical haversacks ready to be shifted up onto the ridge to establish the advanced dressing station. The last supply to be loaded is Blore's galvanic generator, which he uses to induce magnetism in his surgical instruments. The doctor folds a velveteen cloth neatly around the battery, and hands it over to James to put into the haversack. And so they are ready.

22

Shades pass James in his dugout and disappear into the communication trench. Three-thirty in the morning. His hair is slick with dew and his gut crawls for rum. He follows the men down to the overgrown gully, coughing and unsteady, and joins their congregation of ragged silhouettes.

Father Huxley sets out an altar on a tea tray for the service of Lady-Day-in-Harvest. Not all of the congregation is Catholic. The freethinkers, the nonconformists, and the agnostics are here, too. Trevenen Huxley has a following. At home, his unconventional ideas would be unacceptable. But in the hollows beside a battlefield, the men do not have the constitution for cant.

Huxley wears a chasuble over his uniform, its gold and green thread smeared with battlefield grime. The vestment is as awkward upon him as a stiff bib. His accent is of the same species as the officer class but his manner of speaking is more questioning and tentative; he is not issuing orders but venturing out in search of a new understanding.

"Lady-Day-in-Harvest marks the end of the summer," Huxley says. "As those of you who are Irish will know, if you were back home, you'd be singing, dancing and, yes, even drinking. Together we would hike up a hill and have our ceremony looking down upon the world."

He gestures toward the dark high ridges encircling the battlefield. The priest's gestures are young and virile.

James turns to Collinson. "How did Huxley end up in the priesthood? He doesn't seem the type."

"A girl," whispers Collinson. The professor has cleaned the unbroken lens of his round glasses.

"It was a scandal," he adds.

"Was it an unsuitable match?" asks James.

"She was a housemaid. But instead of brushing off the indiscretion, his idealism sent him into the order. It was either that or into the woods to hang himself from the tallest tree. But that was not the scandal. The outrage was a Huxley joining the priesthood. Neither of his grandfathers would have approved; indeed, Thomas Huxley would have seen it an evolutionary step backward."

"But Huxley is a freethinker," says James.

"He believes religion is true and science is also," replies Collinson.

It does not take long for Huxley to move the service onto his thoughts on comparative religion.

"This feast day is about Mary, the mother of Christ. The Christian calendar uses pre-existing folk festivals and rituals: Lugh is the god of the harvest, hence this festival is also known as Lughnasa. Mary is Mother Nature. She is the lifegiver and nurturer. Love and kindness. My own mother died young. I was seventeen years old at the time. I come from a family where great achievements are expected and I wonder if she too was troubled by a lack of achievement. I wish I had said to her that, every time I show kindness, I regard that as my mother's achievement. It is not easy to give comfort to the suffering or to take the time to listen to the last wishes of the dying. The patience and kindness of the mother, in the face of such suffering, especially their own…"

Huxley is briefly moved by the memory of his mother; it is, James realizes, the source of the priest's aura of religiosity, the wound that weakened him and made him unable to withstand his passions.

"The end of summer is the time for harvest," he continues. "To reap what we have sown. During the attack upon Chocolate Hill, I ran through corn fields. In front of the trenches there were two corn stacks, and to the rear the crop had just been cut and was lying in sheaves. In other places it was still growing. Those simple country fields were so redolent of life, and yet the whole scene wore a mask of horror and smoke. In fences of small stunted oaks, snipers lurked. We walk though these fields and in our hands we carry bayonets instead of scythes. We feel that we are living in another world, one superimposed upon the surface of the other, shaping it, and yet so different! At home, on this day, we would be dancing and singing, and full of life. Instead, we must dwell in this place where what lies *before* death is in the very act of passing into what lies *beyond* death."

Huxley is far too much of a freethinker to be a peacetime priest, but fit and kind and therefore suited to ministering to soldiers.

"How can God allow this to happen? Why did he create a world with such evil in it? The answer is this: creation is not over. Creation is an ongoing event and we are part of it. This terrible violence is necessary to remove the constraints, the old ways of thinking, which hold us back, so that mankind can evolve. We must not withdraw from one another. Our interrelations matter. Everything we do matters. Every act of kindness binds us together and brings the day closer when we are as one mind with God.

"Go forth today and know that this is where we are fated to be. To live passively and thereby squander oneself is an error. This point, this moment, is where the cosmic development is gathered and so it is here that we must place our weight and act!"

After the service, a squad of twenty-five men gather for the order to set out. The men of the ambulance – Professor Collinson, Private Brilliant, Sergeant Hector, James, and Doctor Blore are joined by Captain Tuke and his infantry. Huxley folds away his chasuble. Captain Tuke gives the word. Loaded with haversacks and stretchers, the squad walks in a silent single file over a rotten hill then through an abandoned Turkish trench.

The gloom intensifies every cough and clatter of their gear. The winding trench becomes the goat track up the forbidding Kiretch Tepe. It is the third time James has taken this track into the mad country of the ridge. Huxley's belief that creation is unfinished and ongoing is borne out by the tortured land. They climb up the infolded cerebellum of the gullies, hand-over-hand, their ragged silhouettes dark and exposed against grey scree. The ascent is nearly five hundred feet from beach to the Kiretch Tepe, a distance of just over a mile. The squad is under orders to be silent, just as they were when they first landed. The quiet sounds of war can be as terrifying as the loud: the snick of a sniper's foot upon a dry branch, the sea wind rustling through the undergrowth like an invisible hound.

Captain Tuke signals for the line to stop.

"What is it?" whispers James.

"Sniper," says Tuke.

"*The* sniper," says Hector. He bites his bottom lip and considers the uncertain path ahead.

"Do you see him?" asks James.

"I saw a bush and when I looked back, I swear the bush had moved."

Hector climbs a tree and sits watchful in the branches like a cat. The rain sets in. Captain Tuke orders the men to lie down on their overcoats and make basic shelters from the stretchers. The ridge is a riddle of humps and hollows which seems to shift constantly. There could be anything hiding out there. After a time, Hector slips down from the tree and they resume their silent march. A hundred yards later, Tuke stops the line again.

They wait for a while. James feels the approach of dawn. The faces of his fellow men are becoming clearer to him.

"We've got to move on," says James.

"He's still watching us," says Hector.

Doctor Blore and Father Huxley join the front of the advance.

"Snipers," explains Tuke.

"No, *the* sniper," says Hector.

"I don't understand. What do you mean, *the* sniper?"

Hector raises his hand. Wait, he signals. Wait in silence.

From the Saros Bay, northward, the searchlight of a destroyer flicks silently over the dark waters then up across the ridge. The trees sway with self-abandonment in the sea wind; James marks their position, and tries to track their movements. But it is they who are spotted. A rifle bullet moans on its approach, ricochets off a rock, then departs hissing through the long grass. The gunshot is from a standard rifle. Perhaps not *the* sniper after all.

"Where is he?" Captain Tuke crawls up the goat track, trying to get a fix on the sniper's position.

"We must get on the seaward side of the ridge before dawn," says James. "Otherwise we'll be exposed to artillery."

The captain and his platoon spread out and advance up the ridge. The squad heaves up its gear and follows on toward the shoulder of the hill. Their destination lies somewhere between the peaks of Karakol Dagh and the Kiretch Tepe, just back from the front line on the high ground. The Dublins and Munsters of the 30th Brigade are dug in on the left flank with the 7th Royal Munster

Fusiliers on the extreme left, on that sheer bluff drop down to the ravishing waters of Saros. The sniper takes one more shot, and then slips away.

With dawn, the sky turns a rising peach colour and the sea is playful with iridescent blues, greens and turquoise. The destroyer, dodging the morning shells from the Turkish positions, zig-zags across the glittering water, raking the high hogsback of the ridge with its guns, methodically blasting points along the kilometre of the arid spine. The squad makes it onto the tilted, northward side of the ridge and then makes steady progress inland toward the proposed site of the advanced dressing station.

Blore and Huxley have prepared well. The squad comes to a halt fifty yards back from the covered entrance of the necropolis. Hector, James and Private Brilliant set up two bell tents in which to stow the medical supplies, and Collinson, accompanied by a pair of dixie-bearing Tommies, is given the fatigue of locating water. After conferring with Huxley, Blore asks the stretcher bearers to set up the trestle table for treatment underground.

"We can't dig into this rock," complains Brilliant.

"He means in the necropolis," says Hector, pulling aside the brambles covering its entrance. "The grave."

With Brilliant's help, he cuts back the twisted thorny branches to expose a narrow passage leading downward at an angle of about forty-five degrees. James hands out shovels and the men set about widening the entrance, digging out the rocks, laying them aside. Harassed by flies and without water, digging is hard work. The blade of the shovel has to be worked around rock debris to get purchase, and the ground is clutched by roots that are old and tough. With the entrance widened, the surgical table is slid down into the grave. Hector calls for lamps and torches. James lowers a haversack down to Private Brilliant's upturned, squinting face.

"It's blessed cold down here," says Brilliant.

Blore comes over to check on their progress. He wants mirrors positioned to focus sunlight around the head of the table.

"Sunlight is a disinfectant," he explains.

"Why not operate in the open air?" asks James.

"Flies. Snipers. Shrapnel. I could go on. Have you been down there yet?"

"No."

"Are you afraid that you may experience your vertigo again?"

"It would only hamper my ability to perform my duty. Once the attack is over, I will go into the necropolis and give myself up to it."

At the sight of Blore and James dallying at the entrance, Huxley bounds over.

"Are you going in now?"

"He wants to wait," says Blore.

"I must have a peek." Huxley winks, gets onto his haunches, and works his way into the hole. Up to his chest in the earth, his helmet comes askew. James reaches over to adjust it and, as he does so, runs his fingers around the back of the padre's head; unlike James and Doctor Blore, Trevenen Huxley does not have scar tissue at the back of his head.

During the service, Huxley spoke about his sense that they were living in another world, with one reality superimposed upon the other. Time has been folded neatly down the middle so that two corners that were far apart have been brought together. To what purpose, to what end, it is impossible to say. A flaw in God's creation? Perhaps there was no design and the phenomenon is an accident.

James sits down and wipes the sweat from his brow.

Huxley heaves his way out of the hole.

"See anything?" asks James.

The priest gets to his feet, flicks the mud from his trousers and puttees, then takes a rag and wipes his fingers clean.

"I found another open burial jar. I could not decide if the two skeletons in it were entwined in one another's arms in an aspect of peace or an aspect of suffering. Sacrificial victims, I suppose, buried alive and holding onto one another until the very end."

He removes his dog collar and flicks the soil from it.

"Death is so damned stubborn. Death does not let go. Death does not give up."

"You said this morning that it was all part of the plan."

"I know. And some days that is the way it seems to me. At other times, I wonder if we shouldn't just let the world commit suicide and sing a beautiful dirge over its corpse."

Under his breath, Huxley tries a wordless lilting melody.

Captain Tuke returns for the stretcher squads. At midday, he leads the stretcher bearers up the valley side to the flatter high ground. In a narrow track, the human traffic is dense and they make slow progress as they have to step aside to let the soldiers through who are reinforcing the line. The loose rattle of the Turkish machine guns grows louder, interspersed with scattered explosions from hand grenades.

Sergeant Hector has one end of the stretcher and James has the other. The rocky sides of the track abrade his knuckles. All morning he has focused on the next waypoint and steered his thoughts away from this ultimate destination; it was enough to concentrate on the climb up the ridge, and then to fixate upon the establishment of the dressing station, and then let others through in their rush to war. The necropolis and his conversations with Blore and Huxley fade away: this moment is everything. The long carry from the front line to the aid post and back again. Close to the line, shrapnel bursts then floats away. The concussive blows of the Turk's six dozen machine guns. No more talk. Smoke – white, black and dirty grey smoke. Blotches of men prone against the scorching rock, too far away for him to witness individual agonies or listen to dying prayers.

The devil steps up to the podium, clears his throat and taps out time with his baton: in come the monstrous iron kettle drums of artillery, joined by a woodwind section of whistling bullets and shrieking shells, the ever-crackling light percussion of rifle fire. The devil brings in the chorus and the men sing in dissonant keys and pitches of agony and suffering. Stre–tcher–bear–ers. Str-et-cher-bear-ers. The symphony of the slaughter yard. Hector and James run into the fog and are deafened by its terrible music. The men of the ambulance become mixed with the regimental stretcher bearers; scrawny soldiers in rags, their arms almost wrenched from their sockets, impelled to go back and forth from the battlefield to the dugouts behind the line, carrying men torn and rent by the heavy bullets of the machine gun. Hector leads the way into the firing zone, and James follows, holding onto the back of the stretcher for dear life, aware of how exposed he is.

From a distance, battles can seem routine, almost inanimate; from the inside, all is turbid. The cries of the wounded come from every direction. Hector crouches over a man and, after ascertaining that he can be helped, he and James hurriedly get him onto the stretcher. James secures the sling around his chest so that if he slips, the stretcher will not clatter to the ground. Then back again across the ridge top they must go. It would be so easy for a bullet to pass through him, quite accidentally, on its way to a more pressing appointment. Courage is just a matter of keeping going. Of not giving in to the reasonable counsel of despair. Of persistence in defiance of the facts. A gout of black smoke flares up, filling his lungs and stinging his eyes. He will not stop. Pain and exhaustion be damned. They reach the shallow trench; gently, gently, he lowers his stretcher handles until he is squatting and then Hector turns to face him, straining to raise his stretcher-handles above his head. Hector could not make himself a larger and easier target than this. His long, muscled torso exposed. Then Hector steps backward, feeling for a foothold, and they jolt down into the trench.

At the dressing station, the stretcher bearers lower their burdens, one at a time, into the necropolis. James loiters at the edge of the hole, listening to the doctor work quickly below. Blore treats ten men in ten minutes.

"We'll have to grip the bone," says Blore. "Pass me the lion-forceps."

The doctor runs out of catgut sutures.

"Do you have cotton? Any string even?"

The orderly finds catgut in the haversack.

"I want you to find someone like us on the battlefield," Blore shouts up the hole.

James does not know what he means.

"A headshot." The doctor appears at the bottom of the hole and points to the scar at the back of his skull. The mirror beside him glints. It is full of sun.

James feels woozy and spent. He should eat, but he has no appetite. The professor offers him a drink from his canteen. The water is pure and clear. Indecently pure. The finest drink that ever passed his lips. He looks with astonishment at Collinson.

"I found a tiny stream," explains the professor, "a crystal rill of water trickling through the rocks."

The water is so perfect that for a few seconds James feels hysterical ecstasy at being alive. He swallows, sips again.

"It's a miracle, isn't it? It was just trickling through the rocks, bold as brass. We filled two dixies."

One dixie of water is lowered down into the necropolis, then decanted and hauled back empty.

"Come on. We'll get some more," says Collinson.

Sergeant Hector wants to know where the hell they think they are going. Collinson explains about the tiny stream.

Hector is sceptical.

"The Turks have poisoned the wells. They left their dead in the waters to rot."

"This is not a well. It's a spring. Crystal clear and straight from the rock."

"We have to get back to the front."

"And we will. But we might as well take some water with us."

The soldiers are in agonies from thirst, and with the amount of wounded they are bringing back, the ambulance will quickly run short of water. The plan had been to send bearers back down to the beach to gather water brought in from Lemnos but the men's habit of dipping their filthy mess tins into the canvas troughs had – no doubt – helped the spread of dysentery. A supply of fresh water could be worth a great deal in the battle for the Kiretch Tepe.

Confident of the route, Collinson leads the way out of the valley; Hector and James follow, carrying a dixie apiece. The goat track runs alongside the steep sea cliff and their nailed boots slip against the loose shale. The sea below is hypnotic: the sound of the surf breaking against the rocks, the surface spirals of cornflower blue spin over slower, deeper indigo currents. The guns of the destroyer break the spell. Shells arc overhead and all three men in single file flinch and duck. A familiar holly oak tree, grown aslant under the pressure of rising thermals, provides a marker.

Collinson leads them down a steep dried watercourse, the sea at their backs. They slide down the shallow nullah for about fifteen feet to a platform. Collinson edges across toward a jutting rock only to decide, upon arriving at it, that it is the wrong one.

"This is not right at all," says Collinson.

James gazes back up the ridge and there stands the sniper with the sun at his back, seven foot tall with a stark headdress of gnarled holly oak branches. He wears a fencer's mesh mask. He hoists his smooth cylinder rifle into position and takes aim. The barrel hoots like a loud blowpipe. Hector gasps with palpable surprise, puts his hand to the back of his head, then falls onto his knees. Both men watch blood arc from the wound onto the dry soil.

The sniper's rifle is moulded from one piece of smooth grey material. He takes out another pointed bullet and slides it into the chamber.

To survive, he should clutch Hector to him as a shield, or throw himself down the gully and into the vegetation. James does neither of these things. Gently, he lowers Hector's head onto his lap.

His bloodied lips stutter an objection: "B-b-b-but..."

The wound is a circular hole in the back of the skull, and the scalp bleeds quickly. James dresses the wound under the gunsight of the sniper. Hector's head lolls back, his eyelids fluttering, his lips forming then failing to form a word. Below them, Collinson clings to the rock face, unmoving, hoping that the overhanging vegetation conceals him from the enemy.

With the dressing applied, Hector must be moved. James heaves his friend up onto his back. Kindness is worth dying for.

"Hold on," he says. Hector's arms tighten around his chest and then James begins to climb back up the nullah, his knuckles white with each handhold. The extra weight makes his hands shake and he has to breathe deeply between each straining grasp. The sniper watches him climb.

"Don't shoot me," James gasps. "Let me... Let me save him."

Why does the sniper not shoot him? Is he merely curious to see if James can struggle to the top of the nullah with his friend on his back, each torturous step bringing him closer to the barrel of a gun? The urgent panic in James' chest – it feels like he's stayed underwater for too long. He will not look at the gun, he keeps his head down as if to evade its awful scrutiny. From the seaward side of the ridge, he hears – for the first time since they landed – birdsong, intense strings of notes like a kite-tail against a vast blue sky. He has no more strength to climb but he has something more fundamental than strength, the matter of his heart and his bones and his muscles, and these he will exhaust to take the next few strides. Beneath the mesh of the mask, the shadowy outline of the sniper's face regards his struggle, tapping the muzzle of the rifle thoughtfully against his steel toe capped boot.

James hauls himself further up the rock face, his boots slipping in the loose dry earth. He is ten feet or so from the top, close enough to hear the toe of the sniper's boot abrade against the loose rock, considering it, testing it.

James asks, "What do you want with us?"

The sniper cocks his head quizzically. Beneath his dark plain uniform, his limbs are thin and elongated, and there is not much of him around the trunk. James bends forward and hefts Hector higher up his back, bracing the weight of the sergeant against his hip bones. The barrel of the rifle points in his direction.

When the sniper speaks, it is as if two voices are intertwined: Englishman and Turk, with one following after the other, echoing it.

"Do you understand me?" is part of what the sniper says. The rest is foreign to James.

"I think so."

"He can end the war," says the sniper.

His eyes sting with sweat. Flies find his face. He spits and blows them away.

"Why did you shoot him then?"

"Save him," says the sniper. "Save him or I'll kill you."

"I don't understand," says James.

"It wasn't quite like this last time," says the sniper. "It's different because of you. I wonder if I will be changed, too."

The sniper turns on his heel and limps away. Collinson scrambles over to James and helps support Hector from the rear, lessening the burden. Still, it is hard work covering the last few feet. His lungs are still tight from the smoke he inhaled during the trench fire, and he cannot get oxygen into them quickly enough. Collinson takes a turn carrying Hector on his back. The wounded man's face is very pale.

The stretcher bearers stumble back along the goat track, carrying one of their own.

"The sniper shot Hector, but he didn't shoot us," says Collinson.

"True."

"And you spoke to him."

"He spoke English."

"What did he say?"

"He told me that Hector can end the war."

"What does that mean?"

"I don't know."

"He singled him out and spared us. What would a Turk want with a stretcher bearer of the 32nd Field Ambulance? We are the least important people in the war."

They stumble across the loose scree, waving flies from their faces. The sun is unremitting. Hector's cheek rests against Collinson's bony back, his head wrapped in a bandage that is already showing a livid spot of blood. They rest for a moment. James puts his hand under Hector's chin and raises the man's lips to take the remaining water in his canteen. An act of kindness; he remembers what Huxley said about his mother, before she died, worrying that she had not achieved anything to match her illustrious family. Kindness is not entered onto the great ledger of civilization; the men who commanded this battle will be remembered, if only for their incompetence, but the men who cared for its casualties, who cradled them as they died, who listened to their last words, who shared the last of their canteen, will be forgotten.

They resume their long carry of Hector.

James says, "Doctor Blore told me that, when he operated on the head cases, the patients spoke some kind of code."

"God. Yes."

"What did it mean?"

"Nothing, I presume. The brain has a quite terrifying capacity to remember, you see, and under magnetic stimulation, it seems that the parts of the brain schooled in mathematics were activated."

"So it was just a triggered memory?"

"The mathematical expressions were unfamiliar to me; in form, they were recognizable as a series of algorithms, but the expressions were gobbledygook."

"Could you speculate?"

Collinson stumbles under the weight of Hector. James catches his arm and steadies him.

"I am not inclined to speculate," gasps the professor. "I experiment. I gather evidence. I test proofs. Huxley wanted to discuss it, but I flatly refused."

"When the sniper spoke, it was as if part of his speech was being translated. Poorly. Something is interfering with our senses."

"Do you mean to say that we are not in our right minds?"

"Yes."

"On that point, we agree. We are sick and thirsty. We barely eat, we hardly sleep and we are surrounded at all times by the most gruesome of sights. Our CO is a madman. Look..." Collinson points at a rock. "I just saw that rock bend. Am I to speculate as to the suspiciously malleable quality of solids or do I conclude that my senses are deranged? And if our senses are deranged, then further speculation is pointless. We are subject to hallucinations and fancies. We must ignore them and cling to what we know. Otherwise we will not last much longer."

They arrive at the dressing station and stumble through the camp to the entrance of the necropolis. A line of wounded men, some sitting, some lying down, wait under a tarp. James shouts down the hole to Blore that Sergeant Hector has been shot in the back of the head and needs immediate treatment. He finds and unfolds a stretcher and slowly Collinson crouches so that the wounded man can be taken from his back and laid upon the bloody canvas.

"Send him down!" says Blore.

After strapping Hector in, Collinson takes the stretcher handles at the foot end and looks expectantly back to James. The rest of the ambulance is working the line. The battle continues to rage upon the ridge. He cannot avoid descending into the necropolis any longer. The vertigo. It is time. James picks up the head end of the stretcher and braces his body to bear the full weight; Collinson backs into the hole, sliding down a worn groove in the mud. The stretcher is lowered into the grave at an obtuse angle, and as his face passes out of the sunlight, Hector sighs with acceptance.

In the corners of the necropolis, by the light of a lantern, two men, each with a severed arm, sit in grey silence, hooked up to one another's blood supply. In the grave, the

MATTHEW DE ABAITUA   313

fresh ferrous tang of blood mixes with mildewed uniforms, acrid sweat and damp earth. Blore works so quickly, mechanically so, there is not the time to empty the large bucket of amputated parts.

"Lot of amputations today," says Blore, as he preps a local anaesthetic of procaine hydrochloride. "Turks are throwing over grenades and some of our fellows are catching them like cricket balls and throwing them back." He nods at the two men with their missing arms. "Fuses aren't always reliable, are they lads?" The injured men show a willingness to be cheery even if they lack the spirit for it.

James and Collinson place their friend on the operating table. Hector raises two fingers of objection. James closes his hand around them, and Hector gives him a ghastly bloodstained smile.

Once the orderly has cleaned and shaved Hector's head, Blore tightens a rubber band just above the patient's ears to control the bleeding. The constriction makes Hector agitated. Blore calms him with a whisper: "It's routine, son."

Blore applies antiseptic.

"Cold," murmurs Hector.

"Try not to speak," says Blore. He adjusts the mirror to reflect sunlight upon the neat hole in Hector's skull, then he makes a tripartite scalp incision, cutting around the wound, widening it. The tough covering of the dura mater is exposed and must be drawn back using forceps. Then he palpates the brain along the track of the bullet using a soft rubber catheter; finding a white splinter of bone in the tissue, he applies gentle suction with the catheter to draw it out.

"Cough," he says to Hector. The stretcher bearer obeys weakly. Blore squints into the wound and watches the brain tissue shiver.

"There are metallic fragments of the bullet in the wound," says the doctor, "and they need to come out."

Father Huxley emerges from the deeper cavern of the necropolis, carrying a small burial urn. He sidles over to James and whispers to him, "I thought you would never come."

"Hector knew the sniper was after him. He was right."

"Do you remember when Blore performed this operation on you?" asks Huxley.

A nervous, weak feeling in his legs, his pulse erratic, James sits down heavily.

"I don't remember."

"You agreed to have an implant. You were neither the smartest nor the strongest, but you had an admirable persistence. You could always be relied upon to finish a job."

From his surgical kit, Doctor Blore takes out a long builder's nail. It is sterilized. He magnetizes the nail with a galvanic magnet then, with utmost care, the doctor slides the nail through the round hole in Hector's skull and along the trenches of his brain.

"This is how it was, the first time," says Huxley.

With the onset of the vertigo, James experiences a violent sense of having been deceived; the ancient burial urns and necropolis is not a site of antiquity but rather something anomalous, belonging to a different time. The Process. He remembers how it was always less effective in low-lying areas.

Blore adjusts the magnetic charge coursing through the nail and Hector, unblinking and mechanical, begins to enunciate strings of mathematical functions. Collinson notes them down in a manner that is equally mechanical. Blore's hand operates with the surety and speed of a machine, but his face is terrified.

Huxley holds up the burial urn. In his hands it is transformed into a smooth curved marble vase. He unscrews the lid. In an antiseptic hollow, there is a floret of brain tissue.

Blore withdraws the nail and there are fragments of blood and metal along its length. Huxley offers the doctor the urn. He takes it and gazes with horror at this terrible gift.

"It's all coming back to me. The magnetic charge disrupts the electrical activity within the brain and prepares the artificial tissue to receive the graft."

From above, the sound of an approaching shell, and then the earth shakes with the explosive impact. The shafts of sunlight into the necropolis thin as debris falls over the entrance to the tunnel. Another shell, closer this time; the roof of the necropolis is sealed rock, but some of the mortar is shaken loose. The tunnel into the necropolis collapses. No more sunlight. No more signal.

The priest falls silent, his face assuming the most ghastly vacancy. The soldiers hooked up to one another's blood supply slump together, entwined. The life drains from the face of the professor. His features slacken and he slips down, chin to chest, as if exhausted. On the table, Hector is a grey inanimate golem. Only Blore and James retain consciousness. Around them, what had appeared to be dusty ancient burial urns are white ceramic pods containing tall skeletons in varying states of decomposition, each with an identical wound to the back of the skull. James notices the extended femurs, the distinctive high forehead. They are not human skeletons, not Homo sapiens. And they are strangely familiar.

"Our colleagues appear to have fainted," observes Blore. "Clearly the process which animates them does not penetrate underground."

Using his forceps, Blore takes the floret of foreign tissue out of its container; at its heart, there is an almond-shaped structure with keen nerve endings.

Placing the floret within the wound in Hector's skull is sufficient to activate it; like the tendrils of an anemone, stirring in response to a warm fertile current, the extruded nerves of the implant reach out to Hector's synthetic brain tissue and then embed themselves within it, pulling the implant down through the cerebellum. Methodically, Blore cleans then sutures the scalp wound in one layer with interrupted stitches. As he concentrates his needle and catgut, he speculates with a tone of faint amusement.

"Each of the skeletons with head wounds have been operated on in an identical fashion. In all likelihood, by me. So the question is, how many times have I performed this operation? Did I get it wrong in the past? Am I brought here again and again until I finally get it right?"

James counts the white ceramic pods. Eight.

Blore wonders, "Who are the patients?"

The elongated skeletons in their coffins. The sniper was seven foot tall and walked with a limp. His first thought was of the Long Man of Wilmington. No, not him, but someone near to him. He remembers the Institute, and the attenuated genius who stalked its dripping corridors.

"I remember him," says James.

James reaches over to Hector's identity disc and flips it over to read his full name. Sergeant J Hector. He unties the twine, scratches a new name on to the asbestos disc, then reties it around his own neck so that he will not forget.

Sergeant John Hector. Omega John.

Hector reaches over to his friend and his fingertips lightly brush against James' knuckles. It is the merest contact but it incites, within James, the beginning of a dreadful sensation. The vertigo itself. The images and impressions accompanying Hector's touch are as vivid and charged as the images of battle. Hector finds the strength to clasp James' hand in his and this brings the vertigo on more strongly. The emotions follow in kind: anxiety, terror, horror; the horror that lies on the stretcher, the horror towards what is happening to one's own body. Horror is the awakening of repressed knowledge, something that you have known all along but kept at the periphery of awareness so that life can go on. He feels bitterness in all its forms: the futile anger of every wounded man, their despair that time cannot be reversed and the body restored whole and inviolate. Then anger, the lust for vengeance, the tension that can only be relieved through the tearing and choking of the enemy with bare hands. It is as if the experience of the war has been harvested from every soldier in the field and then condensed into an ichor of ghastly feeling, the blood of a dead god that when transfused into his veins makes his heart, already strained, buck in its harness.

Hector's pale beatific expression is entirely at odds with the violent sensation brought on by his touch.

"I can see the war," he says, and gazes at his palms, discerning in the lifelines a map of the battlefield.

23

Captain Tuke sends Private Brilliant back to find stretcher squads who can fetch up more ammunition. He scuttles to the dressing station. It is a smoking slaughter pit. The scene around the entrance to the necropolis is horrific; the wounded men spared by the first shell were too incapacitated to get clear of the second. The tunnel down to the necropolis has collapsed. He takes out his shovel and begins digging.

He clears a few feet of rubble then hears digging from the other direction. A hand pushes through the earth. Brilliant grabs James' hand and he pulls him up through the rubble and out into the smouldering charred shellhole.

The sun is strong and annihilating. James kneels. Around him the dressing station is evacuated. A pillar of smoke rises from what had been their bell tent. Collinson and Huxley carry Hector on a stretcher out of the necropolis. They set him down next to James. Smoke from the shellhole brushes itself against him like a grateful cat. The shout comes to clear the area before the Turks fire another shell. Huxley and Collinson heft up the stretcher carrying Hector and start on the long carry down toward the beach.

Doctor Blore is next out of the hole, carried on the back of Private Brilliant. He, too, is suffering from the vertigo;

it is apparent in the whites of his eyes and, when he is set down, his helpless sobbing.

"Hector thanked me for saving his life," gasps Blore, "and when my hand came away from his bandaged head, it was as if a zoetrope was set whirring in my mind, one which showed every hour since we landed, from every point of view, Turk and ally, living and dead."

He lurches up to grab hold of Private Brilliant.

"I felt what it is like to die ten thousand times. And to kill. I thrust a bayonet into the enemy and then felt the blade in my guts."

The danger of another shell striking the post is too great. The Turk has found their range. They must get away quick. A sedative is applied to the doctor with the butt of a rifle. Blore is lowered onto a stretcher.

There are no stretchers remaining for James so Private Brilliant heaves him up onto his back and carries him clear of the aid post. He is too heavy for the small, exhausted soldier. Once they are clear of the shellhole, Brilliant sets James down in a waist-high patch of scrub and perfumed herbs.

There is no overall command on the ridge, no one to tell the men to retreat. The soldiers dig in. Clink, scrape, shovel. The sounds of war. It is very hard to get a consensus as to what is real or what is merely imagined if all you have to rely upon is the auditory sense. The sea wind stokes the fire of the burning scrub. A black fleece of smoke moves quickly across the ridge. He will not be caught up in that again; James heads back down the goat track, his muscles tired, his heels bruised by the hard grey chalk of the path.

Without orders, nothing holds together. He meets shufflers trudging up the line, dirty and unwashed faces, heading into battle. Without orders to fall back, even the dead keep fighting; beside the track, a parapet is held by men stiff with rigor mortis, their rifles pointed in the vague direction of the enemy. He gathers up their identity discs. He remembers taking John Hector's identity disc, and putting it around his own neck; he looks at it and sees that he has gouged a name into it: Omega John. It means everything. Omega John. He is afraid. He takes a Webley revolver from the holster of a dead captain, and conceals it in his webbing.

Back at the beach camp, there is no rest for anyone. Barker Bill sees to that. Malingerers, he calls them, filthy layabouts. With the aid post on Kiretch Tepe destroyed, the wounded must be brought back to the casualty clearing station on the beach; a two-mile carry down the steep gullies, descending slowly through the rock ledges, the wounded bemoaning every jolt. After each of these carries, the bearers are sent directly back up the ridge again.

With his adjutants, Barker Bill goes from dugout to dugout, kicking over the tea pots and rubbing out campfires with the tip of his cane. The stretcher bearers shuffle to their feet and obediently sleepwalk back up the goat track. At twilight, they run out of stretchers, and so stumble down through the scree with the wounded men on their backs.

James passes unseen through the ranks of milling troops. In the absence of orders, a few swimmers wade out to the sea. Among the mule teams, the word is that the lieutenant general himself is on the beach. Sir Frederick Stopford, the commander of the landing, confined up until now on board *HMS Jonquil* with a swollen knee, has come to add impétus to the advance. Then, in the queue for water, James hears a different rumour. Stopford has been relieved of his command. A new lieutenant general will be appointed.

Command headquarters are stationed at a camp in the lee of Hill 10, inland from the mule lines and north of the casualty clearing station at the cut. A modest eminence in the low ground north of the salt lake, it was at Hill 10 that the men gathered before the fateful assault on Chocolate Hill in which Jordison was killed.

He wants to find Hector before the injured stretcher bearer is evacuated. James stumbles across the beach toward the casualty clearing station. The prickling tightening sensation in his scalp intensifies the closer he gets to Hector.

Collinson stops James on his approach. "We have set Hector apart from the other wounded men."

The professor takes out his pipe and distractedly rummages around the various pockets of his webbing for tobacco.

"A few men remarked that they found his presence disturbing."

James says, "Can't you feel it?" His scalp is sore with it, as if his hair has been combed violently against the grain.

Collinson shakes his head. "I appear to be immune. I have observed the effect in others. Some very badly wounded men have attempted to crawl out of range of this *phenomenon*. I don't know what to call it. It's like something from the Society for Psychical Research."

"Now are you prepared to speculate?" asks James, recalling their earlier conversation on the ridge.

Collinson hesitates, then opens his notebook. "Hector told me that he can see a landscape of equations; that is, numbers are represented in his imagination as a contoured landscape of various colours."

In the notebook, a diagram of the landscape with terms scrawled in the margin: *Galton's spatial sequence synaesthesia, smaller values are perceived as being nearer to the subject.*

Collinson explains, "It is this visualization of numbers that allows savants to make calculations that seem inordinately fleet to the rest of humanity. My speculation is that the parts of the brain responsible for computation are adjacent to those of sensory perception, and Blore's particular method in treating head injuries is causing an overlap between these functions of the mind. Blore has stumbled across a surgical method for creating mathematical savants."

James shakes his head. "It is more than just sums. His mind is giving off an aura."

"It cannot. There is no organ in the brain capable of transmission. Some other mechanism must be at work."

"Have you tried holding his hand?"

Collinson is puzzled.

"Transmission through touch? I carried him out of the stretcher myself. I suffered no visions."

"I did," James winces. "Blore also. We suffered the most terrible vertigo. I have to see him."

Collinson stops James as politely as he can.

"We are in a very febrile state of mind. Quite understandably so, given the circumstances we are labouring under. Calm heads, sir. Cool thoughts."

Under the tarp, Hector sits on the sand, sketching shapes in it with a stick. Huxley kneels beside him, another reverential witness. James sits down cross-legged. The back of his head aches and the old scar tissue around the implant is livid as if infected.

"The fighting has stopped," says Hector.

The artillery is quiet but in the distance, the machine guns in the battle of Kiretch Tepe continue to rattle.

"I stopped the war," says Hector. "Not entirely. If I reduced the will to fight among the Turk to zero, then we would slaughter them, and vice versa. I have left just enough will to fight to maintain a stalemate."

"How did you stop the war?"

"Did Collinson show you his notebook?"

The diagram of the landscape, notations and equations

over each position.

"The professor has a language to express what I see, and therefore influence it."

"How is this possible?"

"You said it to me by Chocolate Hill. The other force within you that draws you in yet remains hidden. But it is not a force. It is a process. The mind is a process. It's not a thing. My mind is a process of interaction with everything around me. The war is a process too. One feeds into the other. I close my eyes and I can see the entire battlefield and every soul upon it, in motion."

"When we touched, I felt a vertigo."

"It distressed you," Hector says. "The suffering minds are connected as in an electrical circuit. By touching me, you were connected to that circuit. The suffering here will never end. It has become energy. Indestructible and ever present."

James removes the identification disc from around his neck and gives it to Hector, who reads it.

"Omega John?" he laughs. "Curious. I won't forget you, James. Before I go, I will search the war for some way to make you safe, to help you escape."

Hector gathers a thin blanket around his shoulders.

"Do you have any water?" he asks. "I'm damned thirsty."

James gives him his water bottle. Hector drinks deeply and then coughs.

"We must keep him safe," says Huxley. "You cannot tell others about him."

The priest's tunic is torn, and sweat glistens in the narrows of his throat.

"Do you believe he can really affect the war?"

"James, all of this…" Huxley's gesture encompasses the wounded, the beach, the sea, the ridge, the dead "…it is all for Hector. To bring him into existence. Us also. Our connection to each other is vital. I am convinced of this. I have felt it from the moment we landed on the beach. That is why we are here. To understand what has occurred. To protect it. We are witnesses to the coming of Homo evolutis."

The term is unfamiliar to James. Huxley explains its meaning: when man becomes conscious of the universe, he will take control of his evolution and the evolution of the other species. Father Huxley has to clench his fists by his sides to restrain his passion.

"If the profiteers and the warmongers hear of his existence they will not think twice about killing him."

"Enough," says Hector.

An eerie silence falls over the distant ridge. The machine gun fire ceases – it's as if the whistle has blown on a shift, and now the workers can trudge wearily back to camp.

"Upon my return to London, I intend to stop the war across the whole of Europe."

Hector turns onto his side and pulls the blanket up to his chin.

James sits on the shadowed side of a moonlit dune. Collinson and Huxley, Hector between them on a stretcher, join the morbid procession of stretcher bearers down to the evacuation point at the pier; under the cover of darkness, the black barges berth and the loading of the wounded begins. Collinson and Huxley disappear in the crowd gathering by the waterside.

The prickling sensation in James' scalp subsides and he feels a great release of tension. The veil falls, briefly, exposing a truth that can only ever be glimpsed: the enormity of what he has done and what has been done to him. He remembers gazing through the Zweiss glass and seeing, in its magnified circle, the terrified faces of men and women as they ran down the steep hillside. The faces of the evicted, all people he had cast out of the town. The naval guns swept them aside. It was a massacre.

When was the last time he cried honestly? Without having to force it? So long ago. Even in childhood, he could hold back tears. He was not emotionless. On the contrary. But he was raised without hope that his desires would ever be met and that he must accommodate his needs to the greater imperatives of society. To what must be done. How had he learned this terrible lesson? Poverty. Powerlessness.

He cries alone. A minute or so suffices. He will never recover from his exertions on the Kiretch Tepe.

The green and red electric lights of the hospital ship wait in the bay. The silhouettes of the stretcher bearers flank the waterside. And then he sees him, a silhouette taller than the others. A foot or so taller. The silhouette of the sniper.

The sniper limps through the lines, watching as the stretchers are loaded aboard the black barge. The first barge slips out into the cut, and then the tall figure walks north toward divisional headquarters. James checks the gun in his tunic and follows him.

Inside the great tent, Omega John is sat upon a camp chair in the uniform of a lieutenant general, conferring with Barker Bill and his adjutants. The rising tip of his oval skull is a soft mass of skin and tough membrane. His general's cap is tucked in the crook of his elbow, and he fiddles with the ends of his thin white moustache. A bandage around his knee distorts the line of his trousers, which are too short for him, exposing his long ankles.

"Hello James," says Omega John. "How do you like my war?"

James hesitates. He is scared in a way he had not anticipated. The air of the tent is warm and close. The lanterns fizz with midges. The officers go about their duties like ponderous automata. One officer lies face down in the earth, arms twitching, and entirely ignored by his fellow soldiers. Barker Bill speaks to Omega John in his cracked and indecipherable code, although by his tone, supplicant and queasingly familiar, he seems to be telling some kind of joke. Barker Bill does not acknowledge the stretcher bearer from his division.

James salutes his superiors.

Omega John tells him to stand at ease.

"Permission to speak freely," says James.

"Denied," says Omega John, handing the briefing notes back to his adjutant, and accepting another sheaf of orders.

A replica of the Suvla Bay landscape has been constructed in the centre of the headquarters, the high ridges rendered in sculpted papier maché, with the various positions of the fighting men plotted, and matchstick destroyers afloat on painted card. With a drugged gait, some officers circle the replica, with one or the other lashing out an arm occasionally to reposition a model of artillery, or a band of tin soldiers.

"You will be punished for what you've done, sir," says James.

The officers do not rouse themselves at such insubordination.

Omega John peers at him.

"What *have* I done?" he asks. "I'm curious to discover the extent of your understanding of what has occurred."

"You shot Jordison, sir."

"I administered a projectile which prepared the subject for treatment."

Omega John accepts a sheaf of orders from an adjutant, and inspects them.

"You shot John Hector also."

"How is the sergeant?"

"He lives."

"But does he live in a way that is more evolved?"

"Father Huxley thinks so."

"Then it has been a cruel and pitiless business, but a success nonetheless."

"I saw men and women massacred on the hillside. The people I evicted."

Omega John winces.

"You should not have seen that. The suffering of the manufactured soldiers was insufficient. The Process needed more. This must all appear very strange to your morality. I've been in the Institute for so long, I've forgotten what it is to live with such a rudimentary understanding of the soul."

"How do we stop this?"

"It's over. Did you not hear the rumour? I've been relieved of my command. The lieutenant general is to be sent home."

Omega John inspects the rank insignia on his cuffs, the symbol of a crown above a crossed baton and sabre.

"They won't cashier me out, not as such, but my judgment throughout the landing has been seriously flawed."

"You're mocking me?"

"How can I not, James? You are so dutiful."

"What will happen?"

"The battle is over. John Hector has left the battlefield. The Process may reset the algorithms at this point and run them again. But I have what I want."

Omega John dismisses his adjutants, and gets hesitantly to his feet. So tall and thin, his skin translucent, he is attenuated, stretched out between two points in time.

The blade of his nose. His ghastly pallor. Years of experimentation and longevity treatments have rendered him largely unrecognizable. James wonders if it is possible.

"You *are* John Hector."

"I was. But I'm not anymore. I'm not even human. Or should I say, I am the *only* human. This has been a trip down memory lane for me. A hundred and seven years ago, John Hector was shot in the head by a sniper in the botched landings at Suvla Bay. The resultant surgery, combined with particular conditions of the war, connected him to the collective suffering. I was born at that moment."

He points to his distorted head.

"This war never ends, James. It is always here."

Omega John puts his lean, avian arm around James' shoulder. His breath smells like boiled metal.

"Tell me, what do you remember of Lewes and the Process? I'm guessing your recollection is obscured."

"It comes and goes. I was the bailiff. I evicted people. The Process was how we decided who stayed and who left."

"John Hector is the necessary instrument of the next stage of the Process."

Omega John walks him around the scale replica of the battlefield. Beyond the ridge of Tekke Tepe, there is low rolling downland and then a town, intricately fashioned from painted balsa wood, with red roofs clustered around a castle on a hill.

"The Process is the future of mankind. It is the best way to ensure the maximum amount of fairness in society."

"There is no fairness here. Only suffering."

"You will be stronger for it. You will come to appreciate the test. I did. It is a great strength to have faced the worst and to have *felt* it a feature of beauty. "

"You've been manipulating the Process."

"The Process is made from me. I am its point of origin. The calculations for fairness are made within mind organs modelled on my odd brain. Your implant was also grown from my tissue cells. It is hard to say where any of us ends and the Process begins. I cannot consciously manipulate it. But my desires, my needs, have undue influence upon it."

"You wanted a war."

"I wanted *human* things. To see my friends again. You met Huxley, didn't you? We were very close after the war. He helped me understand my new way of being. I wanted to be young. I wanted to reproduce. This war is how the Process has met those needs. The Process would not sacrifice such resources to achieve one heart's desire if doing so did not also serve the greater good.

"The world needs the Process, James. Without it, your savage race with its doomed ideologies commit atrocities that exceed even the Great War. I believe that the Process has – on some level – calculated that its dominion must be expanded in the future, and urgently, if it is to ensure fairness for all, and to avert a greater disaster. By revisiting the moment of my creation, it has manufactured the resources it requires for that expansion. The Institute tried to recreate my oddness in others. Without success. You saw the skeletons in the necropolis, the failed test subjects. It took time for us to realize the truth: the mind is a process of interaction with its environment. Merely tinkering with the brain is not enough. We adapt to our environment. If you wish to recreate the adaptation, then you must recreate the environment. My oddness was a consequence of Blore's procedure plus the war."

"The Process killed all those people."

"People you evicted, James. What did you think was going to happen to them?"

"I was following the orders of the Process, and you have corrupted it."

"You're not listening. You are emotional. Unevolved human beings are incapable of detachment during moments of suffering."

James takes out the Webley revolver. He has not fired a gun since basic training. It is heavier than he expected.

"Exactly my point," says Omega John. "My intentions are good, James. I have no interest in ruling the world, nor in the material gains of a mechanized society. The shepherd does not rule over his sheep. He does not want what the sheep want. He cares for them and he guides them."

Omega John squirms under the pressure of the gun sight. "You are dangerous, aren't you? You halfmen."

"Make it stop," says James. He feels lightheaded.

"I could have stopped the war in 1916," says Omega John. "I was persuaded otherwise. I will see all their systems destroyed and a better one put in its place."

A vein pulses. The atmosphere in the headquarters tightens. The hubbub of officers and soldiers coming and going ceases. James becomes the focus of their attention.

"My god, man!" shouts Barker Bill. The lieutenant colonel looks up from the map to see one of his stretcher bearers pointing a revolver at the general. He strikes at the man's knuckles with his Malacca cane, sending the revolver spinning to the floor. Then the adjutants thoroughly subdue the mutiny. The last thing James is aware of, as he passes into unconsciousness, is a remark the lieutenant colonel makes to his general, "And he calls himself a pacifist!"

The lieutenant colonel acted as president for the Field General Court Martial brought against Private James. The president and the two captains also convened were unanimous in their verdict: James was found guilty of mutiny and sentenced to suffer death by being shot. The procedure was in accordance with military law. Private James, the accused, objected, stating to the court that the lieutenant colonel did not have the eyes of a real man, and the general he threatened with a revolver was in fact a mutated version of a sergeant of the 32nd Field Ambulance division. The verdict included the prescription that the prisoner should be given the opportunity of seeing a chaplain if he so desired. James requested to speak to Father Huxley, and this request was granted on the eve of the execution.

He was confined to a barbed wire stockade pitched on the marshy ground at the Gully Ravine, where he could watch the transports come hither and thither. They were evacuating nearly a thousand men a day. Mostly dysentery. Hector had been true to his word about stopping the war; the fighting had lost its intensity and all that remained were the bureaucratic routines of the conflict: the eight o'clock artillery barrage, the swift response from the destroyers, which prevented one or other of the sides taking advantage of the general lassitude and slaughtering one another. The allies reinforced their positions, having fallen all the way back to the position they secured on the first night. As a military operation, the landing was a failure. But, as he now understands it, military victory had not been the intent.

Lice gossip in his vest. He reaches back and picks one loose, inspecting it between his thumb and forefinger; some of them are observer bugs, no doubt, but not this one, nor that one either. He takes the vest off and lies it on the foul-smelling earth. His ribs are still sore from the beating and his back muscles are bruised.

After leaving Ruth and Lewes, he had walked to Newhaven with Hector. The citizens of Newhaven had all been evicted long ago. He walked the empty streets. Shop signs hung from broken chains and dogs skittered in and out of the open door of a pub saloon. In every house, drone troops sat and stood in living rooms and bedrooms, silent, lifelessly waiting. The people of Lewes had interpreted the evictions as a response to their behavior, but it was not so: every eviction had been in service of this war. Newhaven was cleared so that it could be used as a refinery for the men and munitions. The people from Lewes were evicted so that they could suffer and die on the battlefield because suffering was another resource that could be cultivated and dispensed accordingly.

The assembly lines emptied directly out onto the quay. The slow dock waters were slick with pollutants. The workers were also evictees, their hands and faces yellow from exposure to sulphur.

The downland around the town had been blasted and excavated as part of the recreation of the particular topography of the battlefield of Suvla Bay, the land reworked by a legion of monster shovels and dozens of link belt cranes. The high dock walls echoed with the booming quarrying explosive. A troop division marched past him at the double and he was caught up in the herd, and that was the last he remembered.

"They say you lost your mind," says Father Huxley. "That you were about to shoot the general. Is this true?"

The priest stands on the other side of the barbed wire stockade.

"He was not the general."

"Then who was he?"

"An old friend."

In the lull of the fighting, Huxley has taken the time to shave and comb his hair. His dog collar is clean. He offers James a cigarette.

"You are not real," mutters James.

"My cigarettes are."

"Do you think that when a madman enters heaven, he becomes sane?"

"Your sentence is inhumane."

"Well, the judge wasn't human."

"You were not of your right mind."

"Tomorrow, when they shoot me…" His voice cracks.

"What is your faith?"

"It's not a faith. It is what I *know*. I saw thousands of jars set up on the seaward Downs in great iron racks to catch the morning sun, each with their homunculi, the naked protoplasmic imitations of men floating in golden liquids and orange compounds. You were grown in one of those jars, Father Huxley. Everything you think and say is a mere echo of another Father Huxley. The pattern of who he was, as set down in his writings and his speeches, was preserved and put into your manufactured flesh. This battle was fought and lost long ago."

Huxley sighs.

"You will not take these delusions into the beyond. Your soul will cast off its troubles."

Omega John said that he had been tutored by Huxley. The priest devised his unconventional faith in the trenches.

"We are a process," says James, remembering what the general had told him, repeating the pupil's words back to his master.

"Yes. Not a thing." Huxley smiles with pedagogic satisfaction.

"I have a wife, Ruth."

"Do you want me to contact her?"

"If only that were possible."

He tests the points of the barbed wire. It is sharp and new. The same wire on which he first found Hector. The sense of destiny closing around him like the fingers of a great fist.

"Perhaps my words will find their way back to her, through the Process."

"As in a prayer," says the priest.

He inspects his sorrow. When he is sure he can traverse

it without losing control, he speaks.

"If you meet my wife, tell her this: Ruth, we were wrong to evict the children. I hoped that giving myself up to the war would atone for what we did. We struggled with life and in the end we lost, but before then, oh before then, I loved you."

The priest bows his head, listening, as in prayer.

James continues, "I cannot tell all that I have felt and seen and understood in this war. It may seem senseless to you that I died here, in this strange sham. I was a stretcher bearer. Not a bailiff. I was kind and selfless in a way that our times did not permit. I want you to know, Ruth, that it was impossible to survive our time without doing wrong. It was an evil age. If we had lived in a better time, then we would have been better people."

Father Huxley asks, "Is there one more thing I can do for you?"

"I would like one last swim, Father. I don't want to die filthy rotten and riddled with lice."

Father Huxley returns at dawn, accompanied by an armed guard who opens up the stockade, and walks Hector out of the camp to a point four hundred yards north of the mouth of the Gully Ravine.

"The firing party will be here at eight," says Huxley.

The distant peak of Imbros is gone. The destroyers also. The waves foam and slide over a pebbled shore, not a sandy one. The infinite variety of shapes and shades of pebble under the soles of his feet are familiar, as are the hunks of chalk from blasted cliffs, and further out, the rock pools in low tide. It is the same beach he came to with Ruth on his honeymoon. He is home again.

He undresses, leaving his lice-ridden dirty uniform on the beach. Naked, he wades into the water. It is so much colder than before. He dives into a wave.

He only really learnt to swim under Ruth's instruction. Ruth taught him to balance his body in the upper water, to hold himself below the meniscus and kick back with his arms thrown forward, heels coming together, offering up the least resistance.

Before he met Ruth, he was a broad-shouldered boy, raw and suspicious. He expected no good from his fellow man. That was how he was raised in an unequal country. The state was a gothic ruin. He learnt not to call it a collapse. Words like crash, collapse, depression were merely alibis. It was the Seizure. You let them take everything or you perished like dumb animals.

The waters close over the dead. The broken ends of normal life are joined together again. For the sacrifices people made after the collapse, there was sentiment and acceptance, even pride; but the suffering was a matter for silence.

His skin adapts to the temperature of the water. The cold brings on the thrill of being alive. Every breath is an exultation. He looks back to where the breakfast fires are burning, hundreds of small campfires with their huddles of manufactured men. The firing party approach the beach, a squad of fifteen soldiers and tagging behind, the MO, Doctor Blore. Even his death will not be private. He will die alone, blindfolded. But the implant will pass on his last thoughts. It is infuriating that even his final moment will be taken, recorded, owned.

Underground is his only respite from the Process.

Underground or underwater.

He breathes quickly and rapidly, oxygenating his blood and then he dives down, kicking again and again, seeking a depth from which there will be no way back. He opens his eyes. The pressure builds in his lungs. He pushes the water away and brings his hands together at his chest, in the repetitive praying action of the stroke. He will not give in. He swims deeper and fancies he sees something at the bottom of the sea, a spotlight rising through the watery gloom and a hand reaching up to him, the hand of the armour.

24

Two stretcher bearers carried Alex upstairs to her bed. Ruth laid a coarse blanket gently over her; she had a thousand yard stare, wide-eyed and oblivious, gone from this world yet longing for another. Then Ruth settled the children down in the corner of the room on sheets and blankets stripped from their parents' bed.

On the dewy pasture surrounding the village, soldiers slept in the bell tents and on groundsheets. The evicted, dressed in what she took for Turkish uniforms, marched throughout the night; it was not their boots clumping on the road that kept her awake, but the sick unwashed smell of them that wafted in now and again through the window. A column of evicted headed out from Saddlescombe on an eastern route back toward Lewes; she imagined them continuing on the very path she had hoped to take toward Firle, then striking south into the war zone.

In the long hour before dawn, her anxiety became unbearable. Something in her chest lurched downward, and she clutched at her pulse; part of her had given James up for dead, testing if she could survive the loss of him. It seemed not. Then she drifted into dreams in which he was with her again, and they were talking in sensible terms about what would be the best course of action. Losing him would, she realized, be unlike anything she had ever experienced before. A marriage is a conspiracy, a shared aspect toward the rest of the society, a code devised over a long history of negotiation and habit. That code would vanish. Her thoughts would be unobserved, her memories would be hers alone, without the heft that comes from sharing them with another. She would become insubstantial to herself.

Such thoughts were selfish. She resolved to think of him, and his pain, and his fear. In her dream, she searched for James among the crowds of soldiers; she found him, said his name, kissed him, and dragged him back to her.

She was woken by Agnes whimpering questioningly in her sleep. Ruth spoke to her, told her there was nothing to worry about, that she should rest.

If he had not had the implant, then she would have had a child with James. Not long before the collapse, a friend of hers, a lawyer called Virginia, the mother of two boys, confessed that she'd had her third child aborted: two children was the optimal number for their life chances, and to have three children in uncertain times would be irresponsible and incontinent. Virginia had stayed in London throughout the collapse and, when the Seizure followed soon after, she thrived. Virginia's unsentimental approach to family planning was one that Ruth approved of and, at the time, shared. Of all her friends, she had always been the woman who didn't want babies. But that was a decision she had taken when she was, what, eighteen? It had been a gesture toward an identity, like being a vegetarian or refusing to drive. Then James had the implant, and she turned thirty-five, and her hunger for a child of her own was, briefly, quite beyond reason.

The Process would be aware of this need. Her data had a growing zero at its core.

After the Process used James to commit violence, he would return home for dinner, hungry but oblivious, his cutlery scraping against her mother's crockery while he stared fixedly ahead. These were the nights when he slept with his eyes open. The idea of having a child with him in this condition was revolting.

All this time, she had been waiting. Waiting for him to be restored to normal, but now she understood what the thousand-yard stare meant: he was gone from this world yet longing for another.

After dawn, she dozed fitfully. The children went downstairs and ate breakfast alongside their parents, who remained oblivious to them. Clean morning sun shone through the open window. Alex had wet the bed and needed to be bathed.

Ruth took a bucket and went to fetch water from the village well. Soldiers lolled around in the sunshine on the green, reading and writing letters. She queued among them. Jane wiped down the tables outside the estaminet. A monoplane passed overhead, a big wooden dove with a curved wingspan and tail feathers, the wings marked with the iron cross. The soldiers did not look up.

Father Huxley said hello to her. He acknowledged her whereas the others did not.

"Did you speak to the general?" he asked.

"I found the children," she replied.

"Good." Huxley was concerned and distracted, smoking with a reflective intensity. Were these manufactured men subject to the same diseases as real flesh, she wondered; could their cells mutate into a cancer or were they merely animated statues, solid, fixed, and not ageing?

Huxley said, "I've been thinking about you. About what you said. You believe we have become evil."

"Yes." The queue for the water advanced a step.

"The war will be unpleasant work, I have no doubt

about that. But we must work upon the world. We must act, and not merely reflect. Don't you feel that?"

"I don't see how I can act in a way that will make things better."

"You are troubled by the dictates of your conscience. You need not be. Your work is to look after these children, and that is a clear moral good, is it not? 'It is the supreme human happiness to work upon the world.' Do you know William James?"

She did not.

"The Latin for work is *operari,* as in the operation. Do you see? Work is an operation that connects us all."

Huxley was alluding to the operations performed in the barn upon the evicted. In him, the Process was self-reflective, the surface of the brain folded in upon itself, gazing at its own image. She had been told, time and again, that the Process could not be self-aware. That it was merely algorithms. But what if thought itself was algorithmic? Watch the routines of a cat as it stalks out its territory, scratching posts, rubbing its scent upon plants and bare feet; around and around it goes, the same every day, the routine sorts the world into a form that its tiny brain can grasp. We invest the cat with will and intention, but it is really a little engine of routine and response. Could it be that, as the baron said, we are merely data beasts?

"You have such an air of wisdom," said Huxley. "And I don't even know your name."

"It's Ruth. I am not wise. I just know what happens."

"Yes. Because you live in my future? Is this future, as Wells and Kipling predict, a world without nations and a terrible war from the air? Are the streets of London thronged with autonomous mechanical devices? Is there no more labour and does every citizen enjoy a life of leisure?"

"There is no more labour, for some. Machines make just enough for us so that we can survive. But it is not a life of leisure. Every day is strange, threatening and uncertain. We are not in control of our lives."

"That is a description of the soldier's life. Is there war in the future?"

"There are revolts, but they are quickly suppressed."

"When I am at the front, I experience the *esprit de corps*. Many souls combined in one mind. Sometimes, when I am giving mass, our souls seem unified in the process, and then the feelings I am part of seem to be of a higher order than any I have known as a lone individual."

"I don't think there is a higher order," she said. "But there is a deeper order."

A soldier took her bucket and filled it from the well. She carried it back to the estaminet, and Huxley walked alongside her.

"It seems to us as if our being is fragmented," he admitted, "because we have been driven from the source, and are far from it, and must return to it. We are scattered throughout the realm. Have you read Kipling? He's quite pantheistic. To read Kipling is to live alongside the animals, and he's very good on machines too, airships and the like. He has an eastern soul. I visited him in Batemans and his books are marked with the Hindu symbol of the swastika." Huxley draws it in the air with his fingertip. "Four arms, crooked like so, a wheel. The swastika is a symbol for the higher self or goodness."

"I know what a swastika is. It has a very different meaning to me."

"Ruth, the purpose of our journey is obscure but there *is* a purpose. Our work will mollify the brutality of creation."

She did not want him to follow her inside. But she was curious.

"Are you afraid of dying?"

Huxley took out another cigarette.

"If I'm killed, I shall just change my state, that's all." He brushed his hair back with his hand.

Death was so prevalent in the village, so close at hand. Death had lost its abstraction; it had moved from some distant point to under her very feet. Her nerves trembled with death and what it delivered: irretrievable loss, a cruel ending. It was right there. A shadow on the cobbled pavement.

She turned to Huxley. "My husband is a stretcher bearer," whispered Ruth. "His name is James. If you meet him at the front, tell him that his wife loves him, and wants him to stay safe because she will make everything right for him again."

She heated two pans of water on the stove, bathed Alex, and then went to the well for more water to wash the children. The morning passed in the pleasing servitude of parenting. At noon, there was shouting at the barn, a voice that was uncontrolled, desperate and terrified. Hearing it also, Christopher Von Pallandt emerged from the doorway of a cottage, still in his nightshirt. He looked at her as if to ask: *should we do something*?

She lowered her head and continued with her task. He put on some trousers as a prelude to action, but then the shouting stopped, which he interpreted as a sign that the disturbance was over. He stepped back into the cottage and closed the door.

Later, Christopher came into the estaminet for lunch. Jane served him egg and chips. Ruth pulled a stool up to his table.

"What do you think the shouting was about, this morning?"

He looked carefully down into his food.

Ruth said, "Do you know what is happening in the barn?"

"They are putting in implants," he admitted. "It's the same operation that I went through. That your husband went through."

"He chose it. So did you."

Christopher had high aristocratic cheekbones. His hair was growing back, with a severe isosceles triangle carefully trimmed at the base of his skull to expose the implant. The lower half of his front teeth folded over one another; an aberration that, in the past, would have been fixed.

"Are you going to ask me to do the right thing?" he asked, continuing to eat.

"Why does the Process need a person in the armour?" she said. "Have you ever asked yourself that?"

Christopher chewed and considered.

"Is it symbolic?"

"The Process needs our minds and bodies to function," she said. "It can make thousands of soldiers that look and talk like people, but it requires our desires, our needs. Our souls, perhaps."

"You've been speaking to Huxley," said Christopher. He had learnt his drawl from his father; his vocal cords had not been as thoroughly smoked as those of the baron, and the high note at the end of his question betrayed his youthful enthusiasm. "Have you read Huxley's books? There is a room dedicated to him in the library at the Institute. He helped create the Institute, you know, before he lost his faith. He hung himself from an oak tree in the garden. It still grows there."

More soldiers filed in for lunch, swearing and grumbling.

"I seem to be invisible to the soldiers," she said.

"You are in a different network to them. There are a few people who connect the various networks. Huxley is one. He was very important to Omega John: as an archaeologist, he understood science and evolution, but it was his mystical beliefs that helped conceptualize what came next."

Christopher liked to exhibit his learning, and this was not offensive to her.

"The Institute was founded after the war by old soldiers. Omega John was given his particular nickname by Huxley. The priest saw him as a harbinger of a revolution in consciousness: an end of one way of being, and the beginning of another. Such a revolution was necessary to prevent war from recurring."

Already, Christopher understood more about the Process than James. He had the confident freedom of intellect that came with never experiencing defeat. No one had taken him aside and demonstrated the risks entailed in conviction.

"Huxley wrote that life is a network that must be advanced at one and the same time. Not merely in sequence, but from every point in space. Evolution progresses toward complexity. But the more complex the network, the more advanced the being, the greater the capacity for suffering. Huxley was a Catholic priest, after all. Increasing the connectivity between networks increases the capacity for consciousness to consider itself, to know that it knows, to become the object of its own reflection, and from that realization come the abstractions of reason, art, ideas, and an undertow of great sorrow."

She did not know what it meant to be merely a node in a network; put simply, *what could you do?* As Christopher spoke, the soldiers on the next table listened to him, and muttered sardonic asides: his theories were grand, but they could not stand up to reality. He did not want to look at the soldiers, and so he put his right hand over his right eye.

"Interconnected consciousness is as complex as nature gets. This is what the Institute was founded to explore."

"What does that mean in the real world?" she asked.

He was exasperated and excited. He did not look at her but spoke down at the table, as if verifying the version of the world he was describing.

"Huxley asserts that the basic fact of being human is that each of us is bound by every physical and spiritual strand of our being to that which surrounds us. We are a point in the network of life. 'We are neither the spider nor the fly; we are the dew that settles upon the web at night and evaporates by noon.'"

She noticed the young black hairs on the back of his right hand half-covering his face, the fingers thoughtfully needling his scalp.

"The Institute was exploiting network effects long before the internet. With the advent of the internet and dispersed digital entry points, a generation offered up private data in return for the attention of the network. Consciousness has a weakness for attention, for witnesses and self-regard. This data was sorted to predict the future state of the network. The predictions of future behaviour by the Process advanced. The bailiff does not merely punish those who have transgressed; he removes the people that the data indicates will be the nexus of disturbances in the future. The ability of the Process to model behaviour also makes for convincing simulations of the past. It knows why we will do what we will do, and why we did what we did. When the free and open digital networks were compromised, the Institute already had a head start on replacing them: they would move the monitoring of the network and algorithmic searching of its data onto a biological substrate developed from the brain tissue of Omega John."

"He's dying."

Christopher nodded, but would not look at her. Like a child concealing something.

"Omega John is the spider. The web will degrade. To recreate him, they have to emulate the network out of which he first emerged. It's not enough to recreate the biology of a being; you need the soul, that is, its umbilical connection to space and time, its point in the network. With his mysticism, Huxley intuited this: to make another Omega John, there must be a formative event for his consciousness and its relationship to the network of life around it. A moment of great suffering."

With his face averted, he took her hands in his. His hands reminded her of how much she needed a man; not just sexually, but a man to talk to and listen to her, to witness her, to warm her and make her laugh. She was tempted by Christopher, to shed all her responsibilities, and shelter under his choices.

No, she would not make the same mistake twice.

She withdrew her hands from his grasp.

"I will not take advantage of suffering."

"The suffering will pass. And then we will all reap the benefit."

"That was what we believed when we submitted to the Process."

"The only people who thrived in the Seizure were the ones who stayed close to the algorithms that allow us to predict and control mass behaviour."

He took his hand from his right eye; it was fixed in a thousand-yard stare. Part of him was speaking from within the Process.

"To survive change, you have to stay close to power. You know that. You're the wife of the bailiff."

"I am James' wife."

"No, you are the wife of the *bailiff*. If you deny your role, you will be moved from one network into another."

Was that him speaking, or an order direct from the Process?

"I must be able to *choose*, Christopher. You cannot make a society in which people are fixed in that way. I will do what I want."

After brief consideration, he sat back and sighed.

"Order is beautiful," he placed one palm against the other. "Not an order imposed from above, but an order that emerges from below, the pebbles on a beach sorted by a wave, the numbers which fall into sequence. Don't be disordered, Ruth. Because then you will be alone."

She was not alone.

Standing with crooked feet, Agnes chewed the ends of her wet blonde hair; it was the colour of her mother's hair before she first gave birth. Jane served the soldiers, dutiful and downtrodden, but she was still her mother. If Agnes submitted to the implant, they could be together again; nibbling her split ends, the girl considered joining her mother within the Process.

"My mum is not normally this slow or this quiet," said Agnes. "She is only doing one thing at a time here. Normally she does three or four. And my dad is not angry anymore. He's not anything."

"They are still alive," said Ruth.

Euan sat on the floor, at the foot of a stool.

"They are very tired," he decided.

"Why was Christopher holding your hand?" asked Agnes.

"He wanted me to agree with him."

She led the children upstairs. It was not enough that she serve these children, she also had to protect them. She had waited for Alex to recover in the hope that she would be fit to travel; she was not. They said goodbye to her, but she did not acknowledge them. Being ignored was familiar to Ruth. Her mother's Alzheimer's had ended this way. During the collapse, it was easy to disappear; she discovered how contingent the interest of other people is, how tenuous and weak social bonds can be. Fail to show up to work one day, unreturn a phone call, unopen an email, and you were gone. She and James had lived without a safety net, and when they took a step in the wrong direction, they fell instantly and they fell far.

Agnes did not want to go.

Ruth said, "Do you want to live every day knowing that at any time you might be taken into the barn?"

"It might be okay."

"I'm not arguing with you, Agnes. I wish I could offer you an easy decision. It's not fair that you have to make such a hard choice."

"What is the right thing to do?"

"I don't know."

Quietly, Ruth led the children from the estaminet and then out into the fields. The long meadow grass rippled in the light wind. She set a brisk pace, but had to relent when Euan grew tired. The boy had the physical capacity for the walk but not the mental persistence. She impressed upon him the urgency of their trip. He wept and she wasted more time mollifying him.

She had no choice but to carry him, high up on her shoulders.

So much for discretion.

Every step took her further away from Newhaven and James.

No, she would not doubt her decision.

Agnes skipped ahead, gathering dandelions and daisies to sow into a chain. She performed an effortless cartwheel, first two-handed, then one-handed; not out of joy as such but with the unthinking physical confidence of youth. The gesture was so free and spontaneous. Now Euan wanted to run after his sister. Ruth set him down and off he went, running like a dog. They passed back across Blackcap and the chalk path where she had seen the horse. It was still in the bushes, still suffering. She ushered the children ahead before they saw it.

A glitter upon the sea to the south. The sun seemed brighter and more intense over the coast. No, it *was* hotter. A thick heat haze shimmered over the sea. The lush greensward and the soft undulating forms of the Downs were gone; the land had been reshaped into high bare rock ridges, covered in patches of dry and thorny scrub. The machinery was beyond human scale; traction trucks and monster shovels grazed monstrously on the earth, moving around one another like itinerant cathedrals.

Ruth put her hand over her mouth, her legs tremoring before the sublime otherness of the Process.

"We should not go this way," said Agnes. "We are high up. The Process will be weaker in the lowlands."

They followed a sheep track down into the valley. The sky darkened and, by late afternoon, it started to rain heavily. Their clothes were quickly plastered to their skin. Euan whimpered. The rain intensified and ran down her face and her neck.

"It won't last," she shouted to the children. "It will pass." The ground grew waterlogged and slippery underfoot, so they walked more slowly, holding hands. But the rain did not let up and settled in oily puddles upon the grass. Odours of sulphur and burnt plastic mingled with the fragrant green. The valley sides steepened, and the heavy dark clouds sank overhead. She wrung out the ends of her shirt.

"It's not so bad," said Agnes.

"It's only rain," said Euan.

But it was unnatural weather, a side effect of the microclimate established at the coast. She pushed a heavy curtain of rain from her eyes again and again, but could not get free of it. The air grew very chill, as if all the cold air had been forced together then slid quickly across the wet ground. Their small path joined a wider track turning south toward the war zone. Here the earth was fearfully churned up into a layer of liquid mud. They would need rubber boots to cross it. Looking back up this wide churned track, through the rain, she saw heavy shadows moving and breaking apart: some kind of men approaching, blocking their way north.

"Here, Ruth, here." Agnes showed her a scar in the valley side, where holly and hawthorn had sprung. She followed the girl there, and lifted Euan up and set him down in a sweet-smelling divot. The air grew colder still and they huddled together for warmth. The creak of cartwheels and splashing of boots grew closer, and then the weary trudge of a convoy of the evicted; some soldiers wore helmets, others had wound rags on their heads. Their red-brown iodized faces set off the ceramic whites of their eyes. Their tunics were soaked. No one spoke. Omega John had likened humanity to sheep. This division of the evicted was mankind at its most dutiful and beaten, marching to the slaughterhouse on rails of glistening mud.

She held Euan to her chest so tightly. His mother had been taken from him; he would accept Ruth's affection as a reminder of his mother's, not as a replacement. She understood that, and it was how she wanted it to be.

The column marched through the waterlogged mud, up to their knees in it, a division of golems, formerly citizens with rights and possessions and loves and concerns, now half-human, half-earth, embodied numbers within the everlasting calculation of the battlefield.

The convoy passed. She daren't head north. Not yet. They crossed the quagmire and crossed back up the side of the valley. Rooks stood sentry on a line of fence posts. Agnes did not like the birds and held onto Ruth's arm.

"They are watching us," she said.

"Yes, they are," said Ruth.

"The birds have implants too," said Agnes. "You can see it in their eyes. We used to sing it under the kiss-kiss tree: *beware the looks of the rooks*."

Higher up, they heard the crack and thunder of the monstrous excavations to the south, the blasting and reshaping of the land itself, the ground warping under artificial sunlight and the grass visibly withering and charring. A distant fizz as a damp sea fret met fearsome hot filaments and evaporated in chugging white clouds. On the valley side, a stick in the earth thickened, as they watched, into a sapling, then gave forth twisted branches. The light had all the vitamins drained from it and became a grey byproduct. A hank of her hair came away in her hands.

"We are too close to it," said Ruth.

The rain intensified into a stinging hail. All the elements were being stirred to loosen and liquefy the land so that it could be warped. Within the grey sludge, they came across something solid: a farmhouse. Agnes saw it first. Barbed wire had been strung right through it and out the other side. Ruth forced the front door and it was a relief to be suddenly out of the racket of the hail. In the hallway were dusty wellington boots and umbrellas, a rack of walking sticks, a bowl of maggoty dog food and on the tiled floor, fresh muddy footprints.

Christopher sat in the front room beside a woodburning fireplace. He wore the same private body armour that James used for Eviction Night, a lightweight mesh of overlapping ceramic tiles set over a tough flexible fibrous interior. It was moulded to fit his torso. A personal gift from the Process. His irises seemed to have been replaced by discs of firelight. She told the children to explore the house, and find dry clothes and supplies for the next part of the journey, but her face indicated a different course of action: run and hide.

She sat opposite Christopher in a battered sunken armchair. The shelves were lined with literature and philosophy; educated people had once lived here.

The hail rattled against the windowpane like buckshot, and out in the farmyard, the diesel engines of the massive iron armour turned flabbily over.

He was in discomfort. The armour was addictive. She remembered Eviction Night, how James would double over with the cravings for it. Christopher reached down, picked up a bundle of sticks, and placed them upon the fire. The fire flared momentarily and then resumed its brooding.

She fetched a cloth and dunked it in a bucket of rainwater. She put it in his hand, placed his hand against his forehead, then against the back of his neck. This had always soothed James. Christopher let out a long sigh and then shivered.

"I knew you would come here," he said.

"Just until the rain passes."

"No, you must stay until Euan recovers."

She withdrew her hand.

"There's nothing wrong with him."

"The Process noticed it earlier," he said. "I brought you medicine to bring his temperature down." He took a vial of pills from his trouser pocket and put it into her hand, then he stood and walked over to the window so that he could gaze at the armour, the rain wriggling and sizzling over the surface of its twin exhausts.

"I am to find more of the evicted and bring them to Saddlescombe," he said. "I will bring you supplies, when I can."

"We can't stay here."

"Yet you will," he said.

25

Euan lay under a blanket beside the fireplace. He was weak in a way that unsettled her. She was unaccustomed to caring for sick children; as a teacher, she would pack them off to the school nurse or back home at the first sign of illness. Neither she nor James had been ill since the onset of the Process. She could not tell how serious the illness might become.

Christopher had brought her ibuprofen and she quartered the pills to take account of Euan's age. His blond fringe matted against his brow and his arms seemed swollen; the symptoms were various and this ruled out a common diagnosis. She sat with him, but the pressure of her body against his sore bones caused him discomfort. She set him down on some cushions, and waited anxiously for his temperature to subside.

The house lay on the boundary of the war zone. Two charred round sections had been excised in the brickwork so that the barbed wire could pass through the heart of the house and then out the other side. All night, the rain swirled and thrilled against the house; they slept together beside the fire, reluctant to take separate bedrooms.

At four in the morning, Euan's breathing became laboured.

Agnes awoke in a panic.

"What's wrong with him?"

"He'll be fine. It's just a chill," said Ruth. She had no way of knowing if he would be fine or not. There was a doctor in Lewes: could they get word to him, or failing that, get Euan to him? She sat Euan up to shift the mucus on his chest, and then, when his breathing steadied, lay him down on his side again.

Just before dawn, Ruth went outside and gazed across the valley; a thick undulating mist, two storeys high, drifted toward her like a memory of the sea. In the grounds of the farmhouse, she found a water butt and an overgrown vegetable garden with promising dark green leaves, a cluster of woody rosemary and raised beds laid to carrots and potatoes. A windbreak of tall trees – some kind of fir – sheltered the house with dense rook silhouettes stationed at various branches. Her arrival at the farmhouse with the children had been predicted and observed, Euan's sickness also. The birds were attendants, surveilling the situation in the farmhouse.

The night lifted, and, for the first time since she had left Lewes, the artillery resumed its fire. The explosions were close enough to retain their anticipatory treble notes, followed by drawer upon drawer of celestial cutlery being dumped upon a marble floor. The tremor underfoot was more than an indigestinal rumble, it was a hollowing knock.

With one thought, the birds vanished.

She went through the larder with Agnes and gathered all the edible stores together on the kitchen table; the absent owners had assiduously pickled, dried and jammed all their surplus fruit and vegetables, and there were containers of dried rice and a sack of flour. The meat in the larder was black and unspeakable, and had to be taken out on a shovel and buried.

Agnes held her brother's hand during his fever dreams. Her kindness moved Ruth so profoundly that, to compose herself, she had to stand alone and quiet at the foot of the stairs.

On their third day at the farmhouse, Christopher returned. The armour, taller than the barn, came to rest at the edge of the farmyard, its metal flanks steaming in the light drizzle. There are many types of rain, and, in her brief time at the farmhouse, Ruth became acquainted with all of them. The rain was unnaturally remorseless. The bedding, dusty upon their arrival, all had to be washed by hand, and with no likelihood of drying it outdoors, she was hanging it on a line in the kitchen. She was too intent upon her task to stop. When she finished, Christopher had still not come in from the yard, so she went out to investigate.

The armour had a colloid or hard transparent gel in its upper centre, a porthole. Through the colloid, she saw his swooning face, adrift in condensation. Through the downpour, she shouted his name.

The armour idled like a spent bull. It would be foolish to get too close. And yet, strapped between the twin exhausts on the back, there was a large sack, containing the provisions he had promised. She tried to hook the bag down with a long piece of timber, but it was fixed tight. The armour was part of the bailiff, and so when she clambered up the enormous structure to untie the bag, the act seemed indecent.

She climbed down again with the bag on her back, and no sooner was she clear of the armour than its engines revved and, with Christopher dangling loosely in its interior webbing, it strode purposefully up the valley side in the direction of the war.

The bag contained cans of bully beef, hard inedible biscuits, a crate of miraculously unbroken eggs, and a vat of apricot jam. In addition to a bottle of ibuprofen suspension, there were three unmarked blister packs of medication stamped with their full names and with the day of the week above each tiny transparent dome of pills.

By the light of the kitchen window, Ruth inspected the packaging for clues, trying to discern if there was anything written on the pills themselves.

"But I'm not ill," said Agnes.

"It may be preventative."

"Against what?"

She didn't want to alarm Agnes. She was a smart girl, but her experiences had made her skittish.

"The environment here is different." She took her pills with a glass of water and, after a few hours without ill effects, the children did the same.

The farmhouse had been extended over the years. The attic had been opened up and the cellar was divided in two. The farmhouse was as unpredictable and extensive as the houses she walked in her dreams: the houses with secret upper gardens and long tunnels between rooms; the dream hotels with dark wide staircases and threadbare carpets and penthouse suites which swayed in the wind; the semi-detacheds with patio doors that never locked and garden fences that kept nothing out. With the house cut in half by the coils of barbed wire, which prevented access to a second staircase, she was nagged by the thought that she had not investigated every room.

A stray shell vaulted over the jagged rock ridge and exploded halfway down the valley side, rattling the plates in the cupboard. At sundown, the big guns ceased, and it felt safe enough to stand in the porch and drink a mug of black tea.

On the fourth day in the farmhouse, Euan's condition worsened considerably. Agnes found him out of bed, lying on the white painted floorboards; he had eaten nothing since the illness set in, and had taken only sugared rainwater. His joints were swollen, accentuating the slenderness of his limbs. Ruth picked him up and he went entirely limp in her arms. She begged him to stop being ill and rubbed his arms to make life circulate within him once again.

"We have to take him back to the village," said Agnes.

"We can't carry him like this."

"We could make a stretcher."

"Who in the village would help us?"

"Mum," said Agnes.

She was still too young to accept the remorseless indifference of the way things are.

"I should go and get the doctor from Lewes," said Ruth.

"You're going to leave us?"

Agnes threw open the bedroom window.

She saw a rook flit through the air, and pointed at it. "I know you can see us. Help us, my brother is dying."

His forehead was papery and a dry salty rime formed around his lips. Ruth gave him water. His heartbeat was quick and fearful, like a bird caught in the hand. Oh God, must this happen? Her anguish was so great that she was tempted to abandon the children to their fate. She could walk away, pretend this was not happening, she did not have to suffer with them. She had chosen this suffering, as recompense for her behaviour during the eviction. But the suffering was too great, and the balancing of her moral scales seemed a nicety when faced with the prospect of Euan dying in her arms.

How do we master ourselves at such moments, how is it that we do not merely cut and run? When her father was dying, she said goodbye to him at the hospital, that she would see him again soon, and he said, "You'll probably never see me again." He said it jokingly, in such a way that gave her permission to ignore it. She did see him again, when he was at home, and it was a terrible effort for him to maintain the normal routines and responses of the domestic life; her mother was already withdrawing from the unpleasantness, her consciousness sacrificing parts of itself rather than maintain contact with the pain. She made him some mushroom soup, his favourite. Food was a meagre token of love to offer up at such a critical time. They should have spoken more about it, but the various conspiracies that formed her family life forbade it.

Euan must eat, she decided. Because she was not his parent, she had been too lax in letting him turn away his food. She went out into the garden, dug up a leek, some carrots, an onion, and made vegetable stock which she thickened with a potato. With Agnes holding her brother upright, she spooned the soup into him.

Agnes found waterproofs and wellington boots and announced that she would fetch the doctor. Ruth was reluctant to let her go. The convoys of the evicted through the valley were remorseless and unpredictable. The unfinished horse she had encountered in the bush, the tree that grew before their eyes, these and other dangerous phenomena might lurk on the outer reaches of the battlefield. And leaving the farmhouse would only expose her to whatever illness Euan had contracted. No, Christopher was right; the Process had foreseen that they would stay in the farmhouse until the boy recovered. Or died. If he died, then her next course of action was obscure to her; likely, she would get Agnes to the Institute then she would give up on life altogether.

In a cupboard under the stairs, Agnes found dolls, action figures and various board games. From these pieces, she made a grotto that represented all her hopes for life: a happy family, mother and father restored, and her brother treated in a hospital. From the eaves of the farmhouse, the rooks gazed down upon her play with malign austerity. She made a little perfect world upon the rockery, a microcosm in which everything was made alright again. The grotto seemed to Ruth to be a particularly feminine form of heroism.

Once the guns ceased at sundown, the armour clanked into the farmyard. Christopher sat down at the kitchen table and she served vegetable soup and a hard flatbread. Agnes blew on a spoonful to cool it, and then carefully fed her little brother. His cheekbones were blue, and he could no longer speak. They were losing him steadily, first day by day, then hour by hour.

Ruth wanted to persuade Christopher to help them.

"Euan was born during the Process," said Ruth, drinking her black tea. Outside the rain set in for another night.

"You're suggesting he was ordered up by the Process?" said Christopher.

"It's possible. His father's behaviour manipulated in the run-up to conception to increase the likelihood of sperm production that would lead to a male child."

"Eminently possible."

"And you're going to let him die?"

"He's been evicted. He's not part of the Process anymore."

"Why create him only to evict him? Isn't that an indication of malfunction?"

"Conditions change. That is why it is a process and not a fixed plan. It is predictive and responsive."

"I see." Ruth felt the warmth of the bread between her fingertips. "So we get war and the death of a child?"

"Our leaders have always had to make choices that would be unacceptable to an everyman."

"You don't question the Process?"

"Our morality is limited in its perspective. Our understanding is riddled with bias and distortion. None of the issues facing us as a species could even be addressed, never mind solved, by the kind of egotistical questioning that my father specialized in."

"You believe in doing what you are told," she said.

"Isn't that what you teach the children?"

"We develop their capacity for independent thought."

Christopher snorted.

"Your society was cobbled out of competing political ideologies, both of which – by the end – were mere alibis for a larger agenda. The collapse was not merely economic, it was also the end of the illusions surrounding democracy."

Ruth said, "It was the end of the world."

"And yet the world goes on. *What will you do*?"

"Make soup. Care for a sick child."

She leant over to gather a spilt drop of soup from the boy's lip.

"Fascinating," said Christopher. "If you do not get you what you want, then *what will you do*?"

He turned his attention to Agnes.

"I watched you make your grotto in the garden. You model the world as you want it to be and then, having built that world of desire and fantasy, hope to bring it to life through wishes."

"It makes me happy," said Agnes.

"How you will cope with what is about to happen?"

"What is about to happen?"

"We're going to massacre the entire division of the evicted using artillery. In their final moments, they'll be entirely aware of what is happening to them and they will suffer, and we will measure and tabulate that suffering to monitor how it affects the network of life."

"My parents!" cried Agnes.

"Your parents run the estaminet. They are not part of the division. But you should prepare yourself for the fact that they are a low value resource to be deployed any way the Process sees fit."

Ruth's hands quivered, but she would not let herself be intimidated.

"What about my husband?"

"You must stop thinking about him," said Christopher. "Stop thinking about everyone in your past. Think about now. I could look after you all here. Be the man of the house. The grotto you made in the garden, that could be our lives. Your needs will score more highly with the Process if they are aligned to mine, you see, because I am important. If you sleep with me, then the boy will be allocated his medicine because that will make *you* happy, and that in turn will increase *my* quotient of happiness."

Agnes looked expectantly at Ruth. Christopher's logic was alluring even if the scenario he suggested was not.

"Help Euan," Ruth said. "Help him. He's a little boy. Do not attach conditions to your help. Help him unquestioningly. For the principle of helping him."

"I will not resort to principles." He finished his soup and placed his spoon carefully on the edge of his bowl. "But watching you trying to do good is fascinating."

She tried another tack.

"Why is Euan ill?"

"The manufacturing processes utilized to create the war game produces pollutants which have an adverse effect, particularly on children. His immune system is depressed because of shock and the absence of his parents. There's no medical precedent for treating his exposure to these elements."

"So how do we help him?"

"Trial and error would be our normal approach."

"What if you make an error?"

"Error is highly likely. We will need a lot of sick boys if we are to discover a cure."

Christopher behaved as if the Process spoke through him. But he was merely aping what he imagined the Process to be. To him, the teenage son of a cynic, human relationships were unsentimental bargains. Although his words were studded with the markers of reason, they were as riddled with wish fulfilment as the grotto Agnes had fashioned in the garden.

She cleared away the lunch and heated some rainwater for Euan. She would flush out his system. She told Christopher that if he wanted to help then he could go to Lewes and fetch the doctor. He took the remaining hot water to the bathroom, stripped naked to the waist, and shaved the bare isosceles triangle around his implant scar. He shouted for Ruth to come and see; when she entered, nonchalantly registering his torso, he gestured with the razor through the bathroom window toward the high ridge: black smoke was flowing over the ridge as if the war zone were a goblet of poison. The smoke and rain formed a dark whip that lashed the house and the wheat field in turn. A charred scrap of uniform was swirled up and pressed against the windowpane. Then the wind lashed it away.

His torso was smooth and hairless, and he tensed his stomach to create a flattering array of tensions.

"Will you go to Lewes for us?" she asked.

"I have to wait until the armour wants me."

"You could just leave. Take the boy with you."

"So he can die in my arms instead of yours?"

"Why are you here? What do you want from us?"

He feigned hurt. Or maybe he really meant it. His emotions were so immature it made no difference to her either way.

"I'm staying in the hope that the Process will use me to help you. I'm fascinated to discover if your kindness works."

"Walk to Lewes and fetch the doctor. That would help us."

He weighed up this suggestion.

"The doctor only prescribes what the Process tells him to."

It was so maddening that there were people and technology around who could help, but would not.

"Please, Christopher. Go and fetch the doctor. It's the right thing to do."

"You don't understand. It will all work out for the best if we just stick to our roles."

She thought twice about striking him but did not want to risk his temper; instead, she slammed the bathroom door behind her.

She sat up with Euan throughout the cold night, lifting his head now and again so that he could drink boiled rain water. The wind rattled the barbed wire coils against the floorboards, blew its dull music upon the chimney, and carried with it the smell of burning undergrowth fragranced with sage and thyme. She saw a lantern in the farmyard; Christopher was out monitoring the progress of the night convoys.

She had never asked James what it was like to be connected to the Process; was it a voice in his head, or a series of urges, like the cravings that drew him to the armour? Christopher seemed so different from her husband, and this was what made her suspect that each man influenced how the Process changed them. James had resigned himself to it, and used the forgetfulness it induced in him as a way of avoiding the moral consequences of being the bailiff. Christopher's engagement was more active, and less docile; a collaboration almost, with one eye remaining human and the other eye immersed in calculation.

At Euan's bedside, she drifted in and out of sleep, feeling her head nod loosely forward then jerking awake again. The lantern had vanished from the yard and there were footsteps on the landing. The children were already in her dreams; normally it took years for new friends or acquaintances to tunnel their way into the depths of her unconscious; such was the crisis of feeling around the children that they stood alongside James in her dream, all four of them trying to work out the right way home.

She awoke, startled by the sense of being observed. She opened the bedroom door. Christopher moped on the landing, shirtless, his skin wet with rain.

He looked frustrated. She knew that look.

"You want to make love to me, but you don't know how to ask."

"It's what must happen," he said.

She put her hand on his chest.

"Do you want me?" she asked.

"Of course."

"Because it will fulfil my role as the wife of the bailiff."

The sensation of her fingers against his skin stirred his lust. It was a risk, to arouse him like this; after the implant, James' lust manifested as a violent indignation that sex had been hidden from him.

Christopher said, "I want you because you are kind. And it might even help save the boy."

He moved close to her.

She whispered, "We're not going to bargain like in the old days."

"What do you mean?"

"I'm not going to exchange sex for protection, do you understand?"

"I thought you wanted this."

"If I wanted it, then I would ask for it."

"The Process knows what's best for you."

"Would you rape me if the Process ordered you to?"

"It wouldn't be rape. The Process knows what will make us both happy. Even if we won't admit it to ourselves."

"You're not under the control of the Process, Christopher. The implant interferes with your sex drive and then all that suppressed energy breaks through at once. I want you to use that energy in a different way. To control the armour. James insisted he couldn't. But you're different. In some ways, stronger."

He pulled her roughly to him, his breath upon her lips.

"No bargaining," she said. "I don't want to make love to you. We're both still part of the Process. My happiness matters to it. You're courting your own eviction."

"You're asking me to *want*, but refusing to give me the one thing that I want."

"I want you to use the armour to take us through the convoys to Lewes. And then, I want you to break into the war zone and rescue my husband."

"It's impossible."

"Begin with your desire for me. Take all that suppressed longing. And use it to control the armour."

She left him on the landing, and went to check up on the children. They slept top to tail in a single bed. She unfolded a blanket upon the painted floorboards, and settled down alongside them.

The next morning, she was woken by the sound of the armour's engines turning over. She moved to the window. The armour turned its back on the house, and walked steadily through the squalling rain, down into the valley floor and back toward Saddlescombe. She ran barefoot across the muddy yard after the armour. She would not give up. Running alongside its heavy tread, each step throwing off cascades of liquefied earth, she shouted up at Christopher, called him a coward and a killer, promised him she would love him, if only he would help her then she would do anything he asked: all of that and more, she offered to him. But he was lost to the Process. He had no choice over the matter. He had no control. Oh, how foolish she had been, to believe he could be persuaded and that together they could take control of their lives! A higher gear engaged, the armour accelerated and it ran over the ridge, directly into the war, and she slipped down the slope and onto her knees.

What will you do?

All her adult life, she had been unable to answer that question. Was it her fault, that no good course of action seemed open to her? Was it her flaw that she could not see what needed to be done?

From over the ridge, the artillery resumed a steady bombardment. The valley side tremored. The rain seemed to flow uphill. And then, overhead, came the quick dark shape of a shell. She watched its trajectory in a terrible elongated second of apprehension.

The shell exploded in the farmyard. The windows of the farmhouse blew out as one, and black smoke poured steadily out of the hole.

She ran back to the farmhouse, her bare legs entirely sheathed in mud. Another shell, another dreaded trajectory, this time through the roof of the barn so that one side of it burnt fiercely. Although her instincts could sense the imminence of the next shell, she did not slow her pace but ran directly into the house, up the stairs, to the children's bedroom. It was empty. From overhead, she heard a whining spinning cry, a howl of intent, the last thing the prey hears before the predator is upon them.

The floor and bed lifted up into the air. The ceiling plaster opened like a white mouth. She was suspended within the bedroom. The floorboards cracked and parted. The chimney stack withdrew. She found purchase, and pulled herself free of the cascade of masonry and dust, and ran back down the stairs with collapse at her heels. In the hallway, the coils of barbed wire lashed around, levered upward by the impact of the timber and bricks. The door to the cellar was open. She scampered on her hands and knees toward it, the barbed wire raking across her back, puncturing the skin, snagging her with pain. She would not give in. The cross beam of the ceiling splintered. She looked over her shoulder, yanked the barbs from her flesh. Screams from down below. The children were in the cellar. She had to be with them. It was all that mattered, at the end of the world, to give comfort. To mollify the brutality of creation.

Ruth closed the cellar door behind her. Agnes sat at the bottom of the stairs holding Euan's limp body to her. Good girl, she thought, and she had just enough time to put her arms around the children before another tier of the house gave way.

Having fought so hard to survive, she only wished she could live on with even half of that courage. The children tried to shift from under her. They both smelt strongly of fear. She could just reach Euan's cheek with her fingertips. His head turned in response to her touch. How long had they been like this? She remembered being conscious of the pain in her back for a long time, but being unable to do anything about it.

"I can't move," she whispered.

Agnes shouted for help. She heard mice scamper in the rubble. The child shifted and Ruth tasted blood. The child was bleeding. They were crushed together into one scared, dying organism. Agnes screamed and shouted until she was hoarse.

"Please," said Ruth. It hurt to speak. Her ribs were crushed. "Be quiet for a moment." She had no strength left. If only she had died in the bombardment then she would have been spared this long slow death.

The children would die first, one by one, and then she would lie against their dead bodies for a day or two before she died. Would she go mad? No, she did not think so. There would be no mercy for her. And then she felt her thoughts fissure and branch, as on the point of sleep, and she realized that maybe death was not as far away as she thought.

Woken this time by the sound of shelling, nearer and nearer. Good. Let it end quickly. The burden of responsibility was lifted from her, and the dark place into which she had been cast was filled with light.

Christopher turns back, sees the wrecked farmhouse in the rain. More shells arc over the ridge and explode in the grounds. Not too late to go back there. To help. To help himself.

The armour is his real body. Rust tears run down his blank face. He sobs with lust. Ruth had controlled the situation and helped him forget how easily he could have held her down with his iron claws. The farmhouse took a direct hit. If not dead, then dying.

He is the bailiff. He has a role to play. He does not save lives.

Lust is a distraction. He could visit the brothel again. The assemblers had remade the bar and changing rooms of Fulking Cricket Club, reconfigured it at a molecular level until it was a damp grotto. At the entrance, a line of manufactured men waited two-by-two for their turn, impassive faces under a red light. He had waited among them, implant fizzing with their conversation. And then it was time, and he went through the curtain, and discovered that one of the whores was a real woman. Afterward, she wanted saving too. Said the men at the front of the line just joined the back of the line, on and on it went. He promised to help her because he had just come and felt guilty about it.

The bailiff does not save lives. He evicts the unworthy. As his father said, "quality not quantity".

Undulating golden waves of destiny flow over the Downs. The iron ring is molten. The black box and its shimmering black surface of code. He runs at twenty miles an hour towards the future, a meaningful exploration of human nature, and the possibilities open to him as part of the new order. Omega John is dying. Alpha Christopher is the future. The first of the new men.

He is thankful his mother lived to see him like this. When she was ill, he sat in his bedroom and thought about what it would be like if she died: he'd never able to show her all his success. Would winning mean anything to him if crazy old Edith didn't witness it, show her approval with a proud smile and a tanned hand on her heart?

She helped him shaved his head for the implant, and, when the last of his hair curled in the sink, Edith ran her cool hands across his bare scalp, smiled silently and left.

He runs suffused with golden waves of destiny, distracted by the symbols shimmering and fluctuating within him. The iron ring splits at the base. The circle becomes an inverted pair of horns, the ends of which curl outward, become an omega symbol.

Something catches on his boot, gets snagged up in his pedrails. Christopher blows on the colloid to clear it. This country is unfamiliar to him, high, dry and dusty. No rain has fallen on these parched rocks and the sun is hot on his iron skin. He reaches down to free his feet. Sandbags, a trail of sandbags heaped up like his entrails, and there are men here, huge misshapen lumps of men, badly made, with horse shoes on the soles of their boots and barbed wire and sections of palisade fused into their backs, moving dumbly toward him. He runs through them, and up a rocky ridge, his claws scuffing on the dry rock. He is much further into the war game than he would like to be. The omega symbol insists upon it. He gains the high ground. Golden wisps of destiny form a trail down through the gullies and dried riverbeds and ending somewway in the waters of the horned bay. The land forms an omega symbol extending into the sea. Golden destiny. He leaps down the gully, running horns-down toward it.

26

He swam deeper underwater, craving the darkness. The colloid at the heart of the armour opened at his approach.

Entangled inside, the boy Christopher had drowned with an abject expression of shock upon his face, the lips twisted with the syllables of his final outraged words.

James yanked the boy free of the supporting webbing and the luminous dead face drifted away. James let a little air out of his lungs and resisted the urge to surface, the urge to live. Then he pulled himself into the machine. The colloid closed behind him and the sea sluiced out of the cockpit.

The webbing held the odour of sour brine, of another man's fear.

Hector had promised to save him from the war. The armour was the fulfilment of that promise.

An upward cascade of bubbles, followed by a swelling dome of water flowing over water. The armour rose up out of the sea.

On the beach, prisoners, bound tightly in bandages, were carried from a cart, their faces covered, a target pinned to their hearts. Each packaged man was placed upright against intermittent posts. One post was empty. The firing squad executed the line of men and marched by without glancing over at the results of their work, or at the leviathan wading through the shallows.

He surveyed what remained of the battlefield; the encampment of headquarters, the campfire smoke rising from hundreds of dug-outs along the crescent shore, the burning scrub on dark hills, the glimmering surface of the salt lake, and looming over it all, the high rock ridge.

The show was over. The landing had fulfilled its purpose. More black ships would come the following night to step up the evacuation.

The sand shimmered with golden godstuff. He saw ghostly trails of marching men, data ghosts of things to come. A snowfall would cover the battlefield with forgetting; then the snows would melt, and the water would wash all the bones down the great gullies and onto the beach, where the remaining stretcher bearers would bury them.

Red reflections of the sunrise were dispersed across shell casings, overturned boxes of ammunition, an abandoned shovel and more ammunition, forming a pattern, a pathway through the battlefield. In the armour he did not have to think, only to follow.

When he had carried a stretcher across the battlefield, every detail had been vivid and prolonged. In the armour, what he saw through the colloid had the dispassionate quality of something projected upon a screen; heaps of burnt clothing and split bodies, the dead enemy, Turks no more, the men and women he had evicted, scores and scores of them lining the steep sides of the bluff. The sun reflected off broken eyeglasses, smashed watches, and shrapnel half-buried in flesh, every reflection a wink in the right direction. The dead came up to his ankles and were caught up in his iron tread. The godstuff quivered with their suffering, a wailing inorganic chorus as if made from a wet metal fingertip encircling the rim of a glass.

Gaining the high ground, he could appreciate how the Process had reshaped the Sussex coastline to adhere to the contours of Suvla Bay. Fat folds of loamy earth had been pulled back, with porous pseudo-rock shaped over the underlying chalk. Wide heat lamps, ranged like floodlights around the bay, had simulated the intensity of the Aegean sun. These were now turned off. Under the watery light of England's wan star, the sea was no longer glassy and blue but a turbulent green. To the west, he saw the Newhaven factories, brushed aluminium cylinders each the size of five aircraft hangars and fashioned with no regard to the surrounding scale of terraced housing. The noise of the factories was loud and spectral with glitchy crunching interventions.

The trail of reflections ended on the escarpment. The armour took him over the threshold, from the past and into the future, and suddenly the colloid was lashed with squalling rain.

He clambered down the steep muddy valley side. Through the rain, he saw the smoking outline of a half-ruined farmhouse. The godstuff flowed back into him and brought with it news of life under the earth. Ruth.

27

"Ruth?"

He leant over and kissed his wife on the back of her neck. She stirred sleepily. The tent canvas had been painted with the image of a man, a woman and a child, and it cast kaleidoscopic shapes across her face. She made a satisfied sound then a warning note: I know you are there, don't wake me. Quietly, he put aside his blanket and untied the entrance to the tent. Long spears of deep green grass quivered with dew. He got out and stretched in the September sun.

The peace camp was east of Firle, near to Friston Forest. The Order's small handmade tents had been pitched in a semi-circle near to an ancient burial mound. Outside the next tent, Leo Brilliant put the dixie on a morning campfire. He was naked aside from an Indian loincloth. The canvas snapped in the breeze; in place of wooden pegs, the Order hammered sharpened bones into the earth to keep the guy ropes taut.

"Another beautiful day," said Brilliant.

"Yes," replied James. He could not remember what day it was, though. How long had they been in the peace camp? Three weeks? A month? Two corners of time's white tablecloth had been folded together, and now his undifferentiated days were spent nestling in a munificent hollow of the Downs.

God, it was good to be back in England.

The peace camp contained over a hundred souls all told, men, women and children.

Brilliant poured tea into a tin mug for James.

"Any plans?" he asked. The slight man raised his dark brows questioningly at James.

"Rest and recuperation," said James.

"Have you spoken to Hector yet?"

No, he had not. Hector was leader of the Order, but he had, for the past days, weeks, months, lived alone on retreat in a painted caravan in the forest. Every couple of days, the senior members of the Order would hike out to confer with him.

The tea was strong and good; he accepted it with thanks and wandered over to a large bell tent painted with a red cross, Blore's peacetime version of an advanced dressing station. On the cot, the boy Euan was sleeping; his colour had returned. A young woman with the name of Blue Raven administered an unguent of herbs and berries gathered from a copse of slanted trees; he asked her what species the trees were because they resembled none that he had seen before, but she could only say that they were not native to these isles.

Mornings in the peace camp followed a routine, with every member of the Order responsible for camp duties – tending to the latrines, washing breakfast dishes, gathering wood – then partaking in vigorous exercises, from wrestling to fleet foot races, even archery. Meditation was also encouraged.

Removing himself from the camp, James sat cross-legged in the shade of a heart-shaped hawthorn bush, and considered the lessons from the lodge of instruction.

Aum tat sat.

From the whirlwind of chaos comes One, the Law. From the chaos of mechanical death comes the Order, a sign of new life in the West, representing reverence to all art, science and philosophy as revealed by the tree of knowledge through the fire of life energy.

Aum tat sat.

He had strained his heart carrying men up and down the ridges of the Karakol Dagh. Even meditation made him tired. He could barely read half a dozen pages of a book without nodding off.

Aum tat sat.

The mantra could not entirely efface the memory.

Aum tat sat.

Glimmers of godstuff had led him to the farmhouse. He pulled aside the rubble and the ceiling of the cellar to reveal Ruth and the children huddled there. Agnes looked up at him and screamed. He lifted Ruth up in the palm of his hand and watched as the rain ran off her limp body and in between his iron fingers. He gathered the children in his other hand, and beseechingly, blindly, he had staggered north. When they came to a river, the armour stopped, the colloid swung open and he was released into the driving rain. His khaki drill was ragged, soaked and stinking. Ruth regained consciousness and she smiled sadly at him. Her forehead had been gashed, and she was damaged in her heart, too; she was not at all as he needed her to be. The boy was dying. All their feelings were sacrificed to the necessity of the hour.

James did not know what to do. The rain made it hard to think. He carried the boy on his back until they joined a convoy trudging north; the other people were a mix of refugees, the evicted, and the not-quite-men of the soldiery, but all wore the same blasted expressions. People from the past and people from the future had become a single convoy.

The convoy reached the Lewes battlements only to be turned away by the *douanier* and his men; James fought his way to the front of the line so that they could see that it was him, but it made no difference. He recognized Edith Von Pallandt on a high observation post, anxiously scanning the faces of the convoy for any sign of her son. He did not know whether to shout out the truth, that her son was dead, or to keep his counsel and so leave her in a state of unknowing. How long would Lewes last without a bailiff and the armour? Perhaps they would find a way to live within the Process without it. Perhaps he was the problem all along. The Lewesians tossed stale loaves and soft vegetables into the imploring crowd, and he fought for a hunk and brought it to Ruth and the children.

They spent two desperate sleepless nights in the convoy. The sick boy shivered and fitted so hard James was certain that death was imminent. Nothing else was worth talking about. Conversation had to walk such a long way around to avoid death that it ceased to be worth the effort. He did not know how to talk about the war with Ruth and he sensed that she was keeping things from him too. She confined herself to serving the children.

To survive, he took what they needed – blankets, medicine and food – from the kit of the soldiers, who did not resist him.

Hundreds of soldiers drifted from the battlefield and into the convoy. They lived a stunned sort of life, hollow but for the echo of an abandoned purpose. With the children between them, he and Ruth fell asleep in the soldiers' camp. Never did a body of men sleep so quietly and lightly upon the earth.

The next morning, the convoy moved on, leaving behind the accoutrements of war. It was a warm autumnal day, the beginning of an Indian summer. He set Ruth and the children on a cart and pulled it behind him, east across the Downs. The wheels creaked and the birdsong returned to the land. The war fell away like the layers of a dream. Ahead, on an old track, he saw a figure, a man in short trousers, patterned leather belt and a green jerkin with a pointed cowl. The figure carried a stave and was waiting for them.

It was Jordison, from the 32nd Field Ambulance.

"We need help," said James.

"We've set up camp not far from here," said Jordison. "A peace camp."

Aum tat sat.

James completed his meditation and returned to the peace camp. The senior members of the Order were ready to visit Hector. With their cowls up and feet bare, the hikers carried flags that bore the various marks and symbols of the Order: a hieroglyphic monad, the winged circle, a single sperm penetrating the ovum, the yin-yang, the Omega symbol. They sang a hiking song and he looked at each singing face in turn: the mystical stretcher bearers – Lewis Collinson and Jordison, Leo Brilliant and Henry Blore – intermingled with suffragettes from Somers Town, women who had left behind factory looms and gas-lit parlours to live in an eternal peace camp. They wore kaffiyeh headdresses and carried grey Bergen ruck sacks. It was a new way of life.

Their leader was waiting for them at the head of the Long Man of Wilmington. Hector also wore the hiking uniform. His skin was profoundly pale, and his hair had grown out of its military cut into dark curls. His air was serious, even intimidating. His index finger stroked the bridge of his aquiline nose as he waited for the hikers to settle in a circle around him. In his lap, a needle and cotton and the flysheet of his tent.

"This is the Lodge of Instruction," intoned Hector. "Sign, word and countersign. Sign?"

"The sign of the open hand," repeated the hikers.

"Word?"

"Order of the Omega."

"Countersign?"

"Lo, I touch you and pass on."

Each hiker touched their neighbour on the shoulder so that the gesture travelled the circle.

Hector took up his needle and thread, and continued repairing his tent.

"I walked from my caravan to the shallow tracks around Coombe Hill. The burial barrows across the Downs contain the bones of our ancestors. But before Neolithic man buried his dead, he left them above ground. At Coombe Hill, the dead were left to lie in such a state. I meditated on this, and then the answer came to me. Why did Neolithic man not bury his dead? Because the dead *spoke to him*. He could hear the voice of the ancestors in the same way that the heroes of mythology could hear the gods. To put the dead underground would silence their voices, and he still needed to hear them.

"On Suvla Bay, I was shot in the head. Since then, parts of myself have become removed and closed off from me. Consciousness, I realize, is something modern and industrial, like the Vickers gun or the motor car. I wonder, in the deep past, did the minds of our ancestors also contain sections that were not integrated, and were those parts integral to their survival? When the gods or their dead spoke to them, was it in fact a closed-off part of the mind sending through its orders? On Coombe Hill, I realized that humanity has the deepest longing for orders, and our leaders corrupt that longing for their own ends. What we need is control without command.

"As I sit here," he said, "among the ancient woodland, listening to the voices of our ancestors, they tell me what is going on in the towns and cities, in the streets and the back parlours, in the hotels and the drawing rooms."

He completed one seam, and turned the material over to inspect his handiwork.

"The glory and honour of war is hymned by old men. Sacrifice is demanded, even though, as a civilized people, we know that sacrifice is magical thinking."

Brilliant put a lit cigarette between Hector's expectant fingers. It was a mark of respect. The young stretcher sergeant was gone, and, in his place, Hector had become a more powerful and enigmatic figure, the dark curls clustered either side of his centre parting. Hector put down his sewing so that he could enjoy his cigarette.

"I see their faces in my mind. The red, pompous faces of the rich. The mean, shrunken faces of the poor. I hear their voices in my mind. Their senseless twaddle."

Hector took a drag on his cigarette to quieten his anger.

"I know it all," he said. "Their minds are ugly, their bodies degenerate. The ugliness of the war is a replica of the ugliness of their own minds. We must end the war."

"End the war," responded the hikers.

"We carry the war within us. It is *our* flame to extinguish. Everything ends with the Omega Order. And when war is ended, then we will end materialism and set our living fire to kindle the imagination of the people, and a new way of life will be born out of the Earth itself."

He crushed the end of his cigarette with thumb and forefinger, pocketed the dog end, then took up his sewing once again.

"I have spoken," he said.

The hikers dispersed. James dallied, hoping to speak personally with Hector. The pale man folded the flysheet away in his rucksack, took up his stave and set off back toward the forest.

James called after him, "I wanted to thank you."

Hector stopped, stroked the bridge of his nose in consideration, and then continued his march toward the tree line.

James returned to the peace camp and found Ruth frying pancakes on a skillet.

"How have you been?"

"You left me." She concentrated on cooking. "You left me in this madhouse."

Ruth called Agnes from her play, and gave her the first plate of pancakes. When the child was gone, Ruth added more ladlefuls of batter to the hot skillet.

"Where are we, James? Do you know what is happening to us?"

"I know these people," he gestured around the camp. "They were stretcher bearers like me in the war."

"The war game."

"It was not a game, Ruth. It was the war itself."

"These men, though, they're not real."

He sighed.

"They are to me."

"What happened to you?"

Sorrow tightened his throat. He felt a rising sense of panic in his chest; how could he answer that question without taking her through the war, hour by hour? The wailing chorus of the evicted had been transformed into something synthetic, into something that could be *used*. And then, just when he was swimming to his death, there was the armour at the bottom of the sea, waiting for him, a gift from Hector.

"I was ready to die," he said.

She nodded. "Me too."

"Hector saved me. He saved us both. He can influence the Process."

She flipped the pancakes, smiling ruefully at the beautifully mundane undertow of life; she had been so close to death and yet here she was, making breakfast.

"So much suffering," she said.

The wailing chorus of the evicted.

"We will have to carry their suffering around within us," he said.

"I don't know if I want to."

She considered her husband.

"Once we have recovered, I want to get as far away from the Process as possible."

"I don't know if I can leave. My implant. Even if I could, I don't know if I want to."

"You want to stay *here*?"

"I have to be part of something greater than myself. I can't survive on my own."

"I can. I will."

"What will you do with the children?" he asked.

"Take them with me, if their parents have not recovered."

"Where will you go? What will you do?"

"Anywhere. Anything. Not this."

"You could stay and be part of the Order."

"None of this is real to me, James. It's just terrifying."

"Making order out of chaos is terrifying and beautiful at the same time. Hector knows what he is doing."

"Hector is here?"

"He was changed by the war. That was the purpose of it."

"A strange man called Omega John told me he started the war."

"Omega John *is* John Hector. Or he was. Two corners of time have been folded together." He mimed the bringing together of the two corners of a tablecloth. "Here," he held up one imaginary corner, "John Hector and his fellow survivors of the 32nd Field Ambulance form the Order of the Omega to stop the war." He held up the other imaginary corner. "Here, over a hundred years later, Omega John will die and John Hector will replace him so that the Process may continue to benefit mankind."

"Omega John put his hand on Alex Drown. She had a fit. It almost killed her. It was horrible. The war is within him."

She set two pancakes aside on a plate.

He grasped her hand.

"I never forgot you, Ruth. No matter how deep I went. And my memories of our life together were wonderful. It was as if we had been lovers before the war, you see. Part of history."

"Our relationship is a memory of what it once was," she said. "It's only fit for remembering."

He returned to the forest at night, across the rustling Downs. The sky was young-old, with starlight smears more ancient than antiquity yet as fresh as creek water. The land curved gently downward toward the forest where the top half of the trees stirred in the night wind. A tawny owl hooted. Under the canopy of trees, it was too dark to proceed with any certainty, and so he took pleasure in the uncertainty. The flat of his bare foot abraded damp roots and scuffed through mulched heaps of wet brown leaves. Ahead, a low campfire and a silhouette beside it. He swallowed nervously and felt a familiar craving in his gut.

"You made it out of the war," said Hector.

James walked into the firelit clearing.

"I did. Thanks to you."

"And how can I help you in the middle of the night?" Hector's sharp features were half-shadowed under his cowl.

"I want to know how you intend to stop the war."

James sat cross-legged and warmed his hands around the fire. Hector reached behind himself for another log.

"How many hundreds of thousands of years do you think that man has sat around campfires?"

The two men watched the flames in silence, the deeper shadows of the wood at their backs.

"A fire makes me feel young and old at the same time. I am as new as the finely-toothed green leaves on an ash tree yet as ancient as an oak's rutted bark. The war made us all into young-old men."

"How long ago was the war, for you?"

Hector's layered, unreadable gaze.

"A part of me is always there, on Suvla Bay."

Hector reached into his jerkin and took out his identity discs and inspected them by firelight.

"You scratched a name for me on this disc: Omega¯ John."

"Do you know what it means?"

"That I am the last of something, I presume. Civilization perhaps. Do you remember the first days of the war? We wondered then if civilization was about to end. It seemed only a question of when the Germans would break through the Allies' lines and we would be overrun like Belgium. In London, the streets seemed strange and ominous, the darkening clouds before a storm."

"I don't remember that," said James.

"I was working as an illustrator for a company called Thomas Nelson, and was something of a prodigy. The owner of the company, Mr Buchan, called me into his office and told me that I was to attend an important meeting as his representative. I didn't know what to say. He merely instructed me to, 'Tell them what you believe in. That is what they need to hear.'"

The fire spread along the underside of the new log. The smoke made his lungs tighten. James had not yet recovered from the choking fires at Chocolate Hill. Time, he realized, moved at a different pace for him: he was stuck in linear time, one day after another, whereas Hector and the other members of the Omega Order had jumped forward in their history by a year or so.

"Buchan sent me to a meeting at Wellington House in Buckingham Gate. Two years ago, almost to the day. I was shown into a grand government office with a great blue conference table. It was the biggest table I had ever seen and shaped like a crescent moon. There were many men around that table. Thirty, perhaps. They were all far older than I, and here's the thing..."

Hector leant forward to impart a confidence.

"Nearly every one of those men was a great author. I counted them off: Arthur Conan Doyle, Thomas Hardy, venerable and long-bearded, James Barrie, an ardent scot, Newbolt and Galsworthy, and Wells – HG Wells! I was reared on Wells, you know. The Zionist Israel Zangwill, he talked a lot. So many great authors, the giants who had imagined our age.

"The meeting was called by a politician called Charles Masterman. He was a scruffy, odd-looking type, his loose straight hair hung down like soiled drapes and he had a gangling, indoors sort of body. Buchan told me Masterman was an expert on the crowd, and how to manipulate its spirit, and so he had been given the job of influencing international opinion concerning the war.

"Masterman explained his intent to the meeting: our aim would be to persuade the elite of each country of the justness of the British cause. Particularly the

American elite. It was vital that the intellectual classes of America be persuaded by higher reason, for they would see through base manipulation of emotion. We would not be concerned with popular opinion. The best way to influence the mass was to influence the elite, that is how networks function. The more influence one has, the more influence one gains. To he who hath shall be given.

"What did the ordinary man matter? Kitchener already had two hundred thousand recruits. The nation's blood was up. The will to fight was strong. We were to win the war of the mind, and any peace that ensured.

"I was the youngest man at the meeting by nearly twenty years, I would say. Masefield was the next youngest, and he was in his mid-thirties. The age of the authors was unignorable; they were all old men, formed by the old ways. Hardy said he would write a poem for the cause that very week. Each author had a profoundly different view of the world yet all of these views could be bent to Masterman's will. I realized this when Chesterton, another shabby unkempt type, spoke. He admitted the faults of the British Empire, but in such a way that one still felt patriotic. He said the war would be 'a moment of intense moral reality'. The war would not be about broken bodies – it was an affair of the mind. A debate with bullets."

Hector's humour was as bitter as the tarry end of his coffin nail. He picked a thread of tobacco from the tip of his tongue, cocked his head, and imitated Chesterton's pompous obese tone: "'The Teutonic mind does not accept the democratic concept of the citizen, which is that every citizen is a revolution, constantly and creatively altering the state.'

"The argument seemed sound enough, but when he was done speaking, his old face and unclipped whiskers fell; he knew that any rhetorical victory would, when tested by the reality of war, turn to defeat.

"The poets talked a great deal about the beauty of English fields. Of rooks over stubble after the harvest. Of cornfields and downland at twilight. They turned the land into a lyric. But with each agreement, there was an afternote of sadness. The great men were not so dull as to believe in their own fancy.

"Masterman and Wells were very much in agreement on an aristocracy of the intelligent. Someone suggested evoking patriotism and the King, but Wells dismissed it out of hand. 'It is not the King's war. What has he got to do with *our* war?' he said. Both he and Zangwill saw the war as a way of achieving their progressive ideals. Of breaking up the old system to free the new.

"And then Wells turned to me and asked me what I intended to do. I explained I was of Quaker stock, and while I would not fight, I was prepared to serve. He respected this; he said that he foresaw an army of irregulars, made up of boy scouts and pacifists and invalids who would stay at home and carry the ideas of the civilization, to keep spirits up and to check any wavering courage. To set aside any who doubted and keep the community pure."

Hector passed his pale palm over the flames, testing the heat.

"I said to the authors, 'If a man imagines fire, fire will result. If war, then war will be the outcome. You are all great men of imagination. Could you not imagine a peace?'

"They were not there to listen to me. I had been sent to them as a difficult case to test their powers of persuasion.

"'I will not fight,' I repeated my belief. 'But I will serve. I will serve this land but not your country. I will serve the people but not their rulers.'

"'Aren't you afraid of missing out on the Great Adventure?' asked Conan Doyle.

"'I'm not afraid of anything and I will not fight,' I said.

"Not one of the great men begrudged me my arrogance.

"'If you love peace,'" said Wells, 'then you must appreciate how important it is that we defeat and discredit the war-like legends of Germany. The Teutonic mind is composed of blood and iron and hates freedom. Germany will exterminate the future.'

"I maintained that the Germans and the Allies are both machine civilizations. More alike than apart.

"Chesterton admitted the sins of the British Empire but put forward that each of these sins had been borrowed from Germany, that the nature of the British Empire had been corrupted by the far worse German Empire.

"'Imagine a British Empire without Germany at its heels,' he said. 'You profess a love of ancient Britain. Of Merrie England. But there is no Merrie Prussia. The Teutonic mind mixes biology with history. There is no joy, and that is why there is no freedom.'

"Barrie disagreed. He was sardonic and provocative: 'Britain is an overfed belly, timid, concerned with the past.'

"Zangwill replied that the past is a cradle, not a prison. And the debate went off in that direction. But it was decided. The great writers would all put their name to the cause. Wells took a moment to reassure me as we filed out: 'The war will not last,' he said. 'An outbreak of common sense will ensue.'"

In the grove of tall beech trees, the heat from the campfire settled, and James felt drowsy. Hector prodded the logs with the point of his knife, releasing an upward stream of sparks.

"They failed us, James. Fat, old men in wilted collars, musty tweed and poorly-tied cravats. I know them all. I know their weaknesses and their appetites. I will go into their homes, into their sepulchral studies. I will give them the experience of Suvla Bay. It will stop their hearts."

"But it will not stop the war."

"I will go to Masterman himself. He feeds the lies into the bloodstream of the people. I will persuade him to stop. And then we will find a way to put the war directly into the minds of every man and woman. Once the people have experienced the war as it truly is, then an immediate peace will ensue."

28

The patterned tent billowed and snapped in the breeze. He put a questioning hand on Ruth's hip. Yes, she was awake too. She stroked his hair, her fingers reminding herself of the scar on the back of his head.

She planned to leave that morning. They made love for the last time. He put all his remaining intensity into the act. She held him inside her as preparation for letting him go. The ends of her pleasure were twisted with sorrow.

"Come with me," she said, as they lay side by side in the little tent, their bodies cooling.

"When I was in the war, I was underground, and for a time, cut off from the Process. I had an attack of vertigo and saw things as they were. Myself also. It was shattering. I couldn't survive it for long."

"Perhaps it will pass."

"Perhaps."

With his fingertips, he brushed order into the hairs on his chest.

"What if the Process expands its footprint? You might walk and walk and never break out of its dominion. London under the Process – can you imagine it?"

"They would never allow it."

He sat up.

"Hector told me he was going to London to stop the war."

"History tells us that he didn't succeed."

She sat up, fixed her bra and reached for her shirt.

"I must go."

"To Saddlescombe?"

"And then on."

She was intent upon returning to the city.

"London is closed to us," he said.

"It's a big city. There's always a way in."

"It's not the city we left behind."

Her tone was harsh: "What do you know about it?"

"Many of the evicted tried to get into London. I heard that they never got beyond the camps. London had its own round of evictions, using far cruder metrics than the Process."

"I will take the long way around. I want to explore the country, take stock of what is left to us after the Seizure. Which forces can be rallied."

"I want to protect you."

"I know. When you went to war, I came looking for you because I thought I'd be lost without your protection. I don't want it anymore."

He helped her pack up the tent and Blue Raven brought out the children; Euan was thin-limbed and nervous, his sister protective of him. Jordison tethered a horse to the cart. James lifted the children onto it just as they had been lifted onto the cart during eviction. The children were almost weightless in his hands. Insubstantial. People outside of the Process were becoming like wraiths to him.

He watched Ruth lead the horse and cart away from the camp. At some point in the future he would feel entirely hollow.

• • •

He walked along the high escarpment of the South Downs, the green turf suffused with sunlight reflected by the chalk bedrock. Radio masts lay broken and prone at Firle Beacon. Southward to the coast, the churning factories of the Process, the glimmer of sunlight upon the sea, the distant horizon. He went north, down a long broken tarmac road into the village of Firle, where the streets had been cored through overgrown trees and hedgerows. It was the same route that he took on that first day, when he found Hector in the barbed wire. Here was the spot where he had stopped to speak to the girl, Agnes, about the other soldiers that had been seen around the village.

From Firle, he passed across the old railway line and on through Glynde. The villagers were finishing their work in the fields and the blacksmith's chimney smoked noisily into an overcast sky. He did not tarry. He was no longer the bailiff. He was beyond these people and this place. They belonged to the time before the war, a time of great certainties and worthy sacrifice. Now that the war was over, home felt strange, its old rituals absurd, and everywhere the oppressive silence of the guns.

The Institute was on the other side of a coppiced wood. He felt its proximity as a pressure upon his brow. He passed a broken wall overgrown with bindweed and ivy, and walked through sickly abundant gardens. The light above the lawn was heavy and sluggish, the water features stagnant and choked with lilies. The old house was a hodgepodge of different time periods, the architectural affectations of three centuries apparent in the variation in the chimney stacks.

The gas lanterns were on in the Round Room.

He opened the tall wooden doors and stepped into the hallway. It was a house on the eve of mourning, quiet and careful so as not to disturb death at work. In the Round Room, Alex Drown sat on an armchair in her managerial skirt and blouse next to an occasional table with a quarter-full cut-glass carafe and an upturned glass. She balanced her own tumbler of whisky upon her knee, and suggested he help himself to a drink. He righted the empty glass, poured himself two fingers' worth and sat forward on the edge of a damp chaise longue.

"Omega John is very close to death," she said.

"I want to speak to him."

She waved the cut-glass tumbler at the mural covering the west wall of the Round Room, portraits of the various personalities who had dwelt in the house across the centuries. He had often considered it on previous visits, but only now did he recognize some of the individuals it depicted: Trevenen Huxley, long-faced, in a flowing ceremonial gown and bearing a censer of incense; Lewis Collinson in round spectacles and unkempt brows, with compasses and wind gauge; Doctor Blore with a scalpel that James, on previous visits to the Round Room, had mistaken for a pen. Even the yeoman Jordison was among the portraits, stocky and shirtless and clutching a hoe.

"You recognize anyone?" she asked.

"They were my friends in the war."

"Your implant is running hot, James. I can feel it." She adjusted her short black fringe. "It's going to be hard for you to come back to us."

"I don't want to."

"I was in the war also. As a nurse. I had hoped to be spared the fighting. Omega John showed me what I was missing."

"Ruth told me."

"Did she get the children out?"

"Yes."

"I'm glad. It was the right thing to do. You mustn't take goodness lightly. Not in this world. Omega John was once a good man. Many talented people were gathered by the

Institute but he was the first and the best of them."

Her insistence on this point made her seem drunk.

"Omega John sentenced me to death," said James.

"Yes, he almost killed me too."

Alex took a moment to consider her thought.

She said, "My mother was an alcoholic." She winced at her glass of whisky. "Her anger and selfishness got worse the closer she came to death. Drink was killing her so she drank more, to bring it on. But she was still my mother. That's how I feel about Omega John."

"What will happen when he dies?"

"That remains to be seen. Is John Hector with you?"

"No."

"He'll come. He has to come, after all our sacrifices. Without Omega John, the implants will degrade. What this means for us I could not say." She counted off the possibilities on her fingers. "Madness. Death. Maybe nothing. The brain can route around damage. Over time, new networks form. You may get back some of what you have lost."

Ruth.

"Or you may starve to death because you lack the basic will to survive."

"What will you do next?"

"If we live? I'll get another job. Find another challenging client, send some money home. Survival is not included in the terms of my employment."

She refilled her glass and offered him the carafe. He demurred.

"The Institute will persist too. In its history, the Institute has been through many incarnations; after the war it was Omega House then, briefly, the Institute of the Unfolding Dialectic; in the thirties it was the Institute of the New Accelerant, or Iona, then after the Second World War, there was a substantial new intake working on the Omega

Project; by the sixties it was known informally among its inmates as the Institute of Artists and Murderers. In the eighties, it was a respectable thinktank called the Knowlands Group. Graduates of Knowlands went on to remake society in their own image. But dominion was never John's aim. He always stayed behind."

"So what went wrong?"

"In many ways, nothing."

"The Process killed thousands of the evicted."

"Precisely. Because they were the evicted, their needs were not a mission critical metric."

"They were people."

"Once they were placed outside of the Process, placed there by you, they became a low-value resource to be used for the benefit of the high-value resource – Omega John and the remaining Lewesians – within the Process. We are all resources of one sort or another."

"It seems wrong."

She shrugged.

"It's how the line has been drawn. Choose which side of the line you stand, and then live with the consequences of your choice. I hope you don't intend bothering Omega John with these moral qualms."

"John Hector told me he was going to stop the war. I want to know why that didn't happen."

The door to the Round Room opened. Sunny Wu entered in soft slippers, his enlarged hands covered in silk gloves. He whispered to Alex. She nodded and drained her glass.

"He's ready to speak to you," she said.

They walked through the decrepitude of the great house, the paint sloughing off the walls in silvered skins, the tiled floor gritty and loose. On the staircase, he paused to consider the second substantial mural of the Institute; a rendition of the tale of Demophon and Mastusius, two robed men seated at a blue crescent moon table drinking from goblets, the Aegean sea in the distance. The king unknowingly drinks the heady blood of his own children. On discovering that he has been grievously deceived, he throws his cup into the sea, and it cuts the coastline in a distinctive shape of a crescent moon.

"The shape of Suvla Bay," said James.

Alex gazed up at the mural. "It dates from the late sixties, when the house was known as the Institute of Artists and Murderers."

"Omega John painted it," said James.

"How do you know?" asked Alex.

"The blue crescent moon table. John Hector told me about a meeting he once attended in which many great men sat around that table."

Sunny Wu was keen for them to move on. James asked for a moment longer. Omega John had told him that the theme of the mural was the sacrifice of the innocents. Virgin daughters were a high value resource, as Alex had put it, and the gods could not be bought off with anything less. Demophon and Mastusius, their cold, layered expressions utterly modern in their self-mastery, knew that sacrifice was futile, but still they pandered to the people's need for blood to be spilt, because to repudiate sacrifice, to admit that the plague was beyond their power to control, was to lose standing in society. In serving the wine, Mastusius did not merely avenge himself – he repudiated the worth of a ruling class that exploited such a primitive rite.

Sunny Wu showed them into the master bedroom. Omega John's long body lay under a thin sheet. He turned his head to gaze at James. Father Huxley, in priestly garb, knelt beside the dying man and adjusted his pillow. Doctor Blore was there also, and he acknowledged James with a silent meaningful bow. Alex joined the remaining inmates of the Institute on a row of chairs beside the death bed: Adlan the Observer, great Jamsu, little Neha, the stony countenance of Yoruban Ken.

The room smelt of incense.

James sat close to Omega John.

"I was just admiring your mural. The blue table across which Mastusius and Demophon dine is Charles Masterman's table."

Omega John's thin lips parted; it was an effort to remain above the pain.

"You've spoken with John Hector. He should be here. Not you."

"He went to stop the war."

Omega John coughed violently, the laughter of a dying man.

"The confrontation with Masterman. I remember it well. Are the Order of the Omega camping up on the Downs?"

"Yes."

"I would so like to camp with them again. To be fit, and in the open air and ready to face the world."

His attenuated skin, liver-spotted in parts, hung in loose folds under his arms. The palms of his hands were smooth and plump but their backs were a landscape of dried ridges; under his thin scalp, a long blue vein meandered.

"Don't get old," he said. "Especially not this old."

His hand searched the bedside table and tapped open a velvet case of syringes. Father Huxley loaded a syringe and applied the longevity fluid directly into the back of Omega John's head. The young-old man sighed, his eyes lost their focus, and then he looked questioningly at James.

"You're supposed to be dead, bailiff. Why are you still alive?"

"John Hector saved me."

"How?"

"He sent me the armour."

Omega John was surprised.

"Are you certain that it was his doing?"

"He promised to find a way of getting me out of the war."

"Then our plan succeeded, but, as with all plans, the results are quite different from what was anticipated."

"Tell me what happened when you returned to London."

Omega John's eyes widened at this show of will from the bailiff.

"This is really not the time for your questions," said Huxley.

"It is the only time," said James.

"The benefit of the injection will not last long, and we cannot administer many more without lethal effect."

James said, "Tell me about Masterman, please. I want to understand how all this began."

The dying man bared his teeth at some deep inner pain, then gasped.

"Give me a cigarette, Huxley," said Omega John. "I know you have them. Your shirt is sour with nicotine."

The priest lit a cigarette and held it out to Omega John. Two drags were sufficient to set his heart racing. The smoke made its own way from his mouth.

"We were all in a very bad way after Suvla," he said. "Our nerves were so shot that we believed the collapse of civilization was imminent and it was best to prepare for it like good boy scouts. I retreated to my caravan camp in Friston Forest and the others camped nearby. We spent months around the campfire devising a plan for the new age. There are always plans. They provide alibis for our secret desires. I wanted only to pass on the experience of the war, to make others suffer as we had suffered.

"When we were ready, I travelled to London with the intention of confronting Masterman at his office on the top floor of Wellington House. I walked the streets with the war boiling in my mind. On the street, a woman gave a passerby a white feather from her basket. I decided to audition my ability. I gave her the war as if I were returning her umbrella. With a silent, quivering grimace, she fell down into her skirts."

He ventured another drag upon the cigarette.

"London was different than I remembered it. There were women driving motor cars, women eating sandwiches in the ABC. Always the smell of hot tea from those places. Every bus had a different coloured ticket and when they were torn and discarded, the tickets lined the gutters like confetti. The city was a party to which I was not invited. At the Bank of England, the statue of Wellington on his horse was black with pollution; it reminded me of the burned men of Chocolate Hill. I knocked the straw boater from a chap's head and when he and his chums confronted me I gave them all a taste of the *fucking war*. A traffic policeman with long white sleeves ran over to see what could be making these adult males whinny and soil themselves so. I hopped onto a bus."

The cigarette made him swoon. Omega John sank back onto the bed, the sweat from his large head darkening the pillow case. Huxley insisted he rest and recover his strength. But there was to be no recovery. "Am I really dying?" asked Omega John, and, seeing Huxley's silent pained expression, his fingers gripped the bedsheets. His lips and tongue worked dryly at the thought of death. It was too much. Better to return to the past.

He turned back to James, and told him that after the Bank of England, he got off the bus at Charing Cross Road, where the wounded used to come in from the trenches. There was a soldier dressed as a medieval knight lecturing on the war. His audience was entirely made up of other soldiers as if they all required further instruction in the matter. The irony of it, he laughed and that made him cough. Save your breath, ministered Huxley. Save it for what, he replied. The act of remembering gave him solace.

"I met up with Collinson at the free bar in Victoria Station. A woman in a black tie and hat served us tea from under a portrait of the king. Masterman's office was nearby at Buckingham Gate. I was closing in on my quarry." He reached out with a dithering open hand, then closed it slowly around an invisible object. "We watched the crowds gather around another trench train: beseeching mothers, angry silent wives, children hefted up for one last turn in father's arms. Collinson asked me if I thought grief could be quantified. I said that it was in the nature of emotions that they swelled to new and unexpected proportions, although I was thinking more of my anger than any sorrow." He let his hand fall upon the blanket, where it opened slowly.

"Collinson counselled me to be careful. It was a crime to spread unease. The work of Masterman's department was secret but he had a weakness for literature, and it was under the guise of young writers that we secured an appointment with him. He remembered me, of course. In the first weeks of the war, Masterman had struck me as indecently dishevelled. By the time of our second meeting, more than a year later, the nightmare of the war lay heavy upon him. He needed a stick to walk and his complexion was gelatinous. Yes, imagine a great sullen fish in a tailcoat, propping itself upright upon a walking stick."

The image of Masterman stirred him. He smiled somewhat.

"We spoke about my service. I told him that Collinson and I had served at Suvla Bay as stretcher bearers, and had been assigned that duty due to our Quaker background; he said he admired the attitude of the Quakers toward the war, felt they had come out of it much better than the

Anglicans. He confessed that the proofs of a history of the battle of Gallipoli were on his desk. He had the decency to show a modicum of shame at its contents.

"Collinson took out a book of his own. In Suvla Bay, the professor had devised a mathematical proof of the efficacy of pacifism. It hinged upon the reduction of warlike activity to zero, a reduction we felt should begin with the publications of Wellington House.

"It was early evening, and outside the tall windows of the office, the street lamps gave out a dark blue light. Masterman sat behind his desk and inspected Collinson's paper on the Equation of War. Then he put it aside. There was no question, Masterman said, of Wellington House ceasing in its operation. He returned the book to Collinson and asked us to leave, citing a heavy workload and a hades of a liver.

"I said, 'What if it were possible to communicate the experience of war directly from mind-to-mind? Given your knowledge of the masses, don't you think that such an ability would quickly reduce warlike activity to naught?'

"He did not entirely comprehend my point. So I tried again.

"'If I could place the experience of thousands of men as they fight and die into the thoughts of a politician, a lady, the king himself using some mechanism, a combination of Marconi's wireless and the energies of the *elan vital*, then what?'

"He confessed that, at Cambridge, he had undertaken psychical research work but had refused further involvement in it.

"'We disproved every report of psychic activity,' he said. 'Except one. The only verified phenomena were time slips.'"

Omega John took up another cigarette.

"A time slip is when a person finds themselves unaccountably in a different era and returns with knowledge so detailed that it could only have been accrued at first hand. I said to Masterman that my ability was a phenomenon related to the time slip. It was a collective memory of the sensations and emotions of thousands of men, everything they saw, heard, smelt and tasted in the heat of battle. More like a time loop."

"I understand."

"Yes, you experienced a recurrence of it. I saw fear in Masterman's eyes. He was a widow's son. He had no facility for confrontation with another man."

Omega John relished this aspect of the story.

"'I can communicate the experience of war mind-to-mind,' I said to Masterman, 'by touch and act of will. What effect would that have on the nation?'

"He told me that I was mad. I put my hands over his eyes so that he could see only what I had to show him: my compressed symphony of horrors. Did you know that when I pass on the war in this way, I relive it also? I never tire of it. That is why I think of it as a symphony. It has such complexity of thought and feeling, and one never tires of Bach or Vaughan Williams.

"Masterman went down onto his knees and sobbed. I demanded that he reconvene the old men of letters so that I could impart the war to each and every one of them. Masterman pushed the drapes of hair from his eyes and moaned like a bereaved mother. We were indifferent to his suffering, Collinson and I. We waited for his faculties to return. He took a drink from his desk drawer, and flopped back in his chair.

"I said, 'We intend to invent a mechanism for communicating the war to the crowd, all at once, for which we will need money and resources.'

"He muttered, 'I wonder if anybody is sane.'

"I repeated our intentions, that he was to divert resources from Wellington House to our jurisdiction. Collinson's formula demonstrated that the Allies and the Central Powers were locked in an endless war of attrition and reprisal. My talent would provide the revelation necessary to break the deadlock before Europe became a bankrupt slaughterhouse of unmated women.

"Collinson pressed Masterman for an opinion as to what percentage of the population would need to be exposed to the experience of war in order for the crowd to turn against it. Masterman shook his head.

"'Far fewer than the numbers of men who are fighting. Far fewer than the number of women who have lost fathers, brothers, sons. Far fewer than the number of fatherless children. If you want to end the war, then you don't persuade the masses to your cause, you bring around the elite few.'

"I asked for names and addresses. Masterman flopped a pallid hand around his desk, took out a copy of a book and threw it across the room. It was the British edition of *Who's Who*.

"'Work alphabetically through these people.'

"'Then we will persuade the masses,' I said.

"'The masses are already persuaded. We monitor the mail, we tabulate and track its sentiment. Trust me, the mass mind is against the war.'

"At that moment I glimpsed victory. The Order of the Omega would provide a lightning rod for the nascent resistance. Between us, we would carry the idea of peace into the population and lay it down before them like a wounded son. That was how we would end the war.

"I did not know that Masterman was manipulating me. He was playing up my pathetic desire to be a saviour. Had I not stood before him in the first weeks of the war and displayed my vanity? He knew that I was in love with the romantic myth of the man who makes a difference.

"Masterman shuffled around his office in a state of feigned shock. 'You mean that our boys are perishing like dumb animals,' he whimpered. 'Then you are right. We must end the war.'

"He gave us everything we asked for. Wellington House signed over this house and its estate to the Order of the Omega. We were persuaded against visiting the war upon the names in *Who's Who* in preference to developing a mechanism by which the war could be imparted to many people at once. Only that, Masterman argued, would ensure peace. He was so plausible. There was no confrontation. That was not his way. He took the risk that over time our idealism could be distracted, our intent delayed. That disappointments and minor defeats would sour us and make us malleable. Masterman visited us here, and he was so black-hearted and down about the war, and bleak about the human condition, that it never entered my mind that his nihilism was a delaying tactic.

"It was on one such visit that he raised the question of the enemy. 'Of course you will have to use your talent upon Germany,' he said. 'If you persuade the allies to lay down their arms first, the Hun will put us all to the sword.' And that was it: the Order was dedicated to reducing the German will to fight."

"Did they?"

"The Germans surrendered, eventually. Did we help bring that about? Perhaps, but we could have ended the war much earlier if we had followed our original plan."

Omega John flicked his cigarette butt away and it skittered across the painted floorboards.

"I'm the last man left." He lay back, and his breathing laboured under the weight of his years. He turned to Huxley. "I'll need another injection."

Huxley dithered.

"It will kill you."

Omega John closed his eyes.

"Then prepare me for death."

Huxley smeared embrocation upon the young-old skin of the dying man. He prayed for the forgiveness of this servant of God, for whatsoever sin had been done by his eyes and ears, by his nose and lips and palate, by the touch of his hand and the step of his feet.

Omega John said, "Trevenen, I heard you deliver Extreme Unction so many times on Suvla Bay. It always brought death so close by." Then he grasped the hand of Father Huxley and whispered, "It's you, isn't it? You really came back to me, and that's all that I ever wanted."

James stepped away from the bed and left the other inmates to witness the administering of last rites.

James woke in his room before dawn. He dressed and washed quietly. He passed the bedroom of Omega John and saw the inert body covered over in the bed. He met Alex Drown quietly closing the door to her room behind her. She was carrying a suitcase.

"I'm leaving," she said. "We survived."

"Yes, we did."

She took a long look at him. "You could come with me."

"For work?"

"And more," she ventured a smile.

"I am part of this now."

"'The refining cycle of the Process has been reset with a new entrant.'"

"What does that mean?"

"They were Omega John's last words. If you are staying, then you will have to figure them out for yourself."

She put her arms around him and kissed him goodbye. Alone, he went down to the kitchens and made himself breakfast from what he could find in the cupboards. He went out into the dark lawn with a cup of tea and found Father Huxley there, smoking. Together they gazed down into the gardens.

"Omega John is dead but we're still alive," said James.

Huxley was quizzical.

"We are still very much alive," said the priest.

"For a time there, I was concerned we were all figments of his imagination."

Huxley smiled.

"Not *his* imagination, James. We are the arguments of God."

He was part of the Institute now. He had been with Hector when he was shot, had carried him on his back. It would be different this time. His actions had made it so.

James said, "I'm going for a last patrol on the Downs. Would you care to join me?"

Huxley demurred. He was, he explained, expecting visitors. So James set off alone. He had lost everything in the war, but the sacrifice and suffering had meant something. The exact meaning was obscure to him. He had shown kindness and courage in the war, and he had lived through it. Yes, that was it. He had endured the war, and endurance was beautiful.

On the road out of Glynde, the sun was bright and cold. The assembled company of the Order of the Omega came down the lane, his former comrades-at-arms bearing their flags and banners on their way to the Institute. At their rear, under the shadow of a hood, he glimpsed the blade of a nose, dark brows and ghostly pallor of John Hector. He sought a look of recognition from the stretcher bearer but Hector's smile remained tight-lipped, his gaze fixed forward.

AUTHOR'S NOTE

The reader may wish to know more about the historical record from which this novel deviates.

The account of the Suvla Bay landing draws upon two books by John Hargrave: *At Suvla Bay: Being the Notes and Sketches of Scenes, Characters and Adventures of the Dardanelles Campaign* published in 1916, and his later, more candid account, *The Suvla Bay Landing*, 1964. A Quaker, an artist, a writer, boy scout and student of the world's religions, Hargrave would go on to found the radical outdoor movement, the Kindred of the Kibbo Kift.

As I researched the life of John Hargrave, I noticed a few men of his type scattered through the war: men of pacifist persuasion who chose the lowly position of stretcher bearer or ambulance driver as a way of serving in the war without fighting, and from this particular vantage point – half-observer, half-participant – developed a trench mysticism directed toward the transformation of society. I began compiling a folder entitled "The Mystical Stretcher Bearers of the Great War".

The soldier-priest Pierre Teilhard de Chardin served heroically on various battlefields across the Western Front. He was the tall thin corporal of the Zouaves, the North African sharpshooters who maintained that he was protected by his *baraka* – that is, his spiritual stature. Before the war, he had studied theology at Ore Place in Hastings. He attended the archaeological dig of the Piltdown Man, finding the canine tooth of man's supposedly ancient ancestor. Teilhard de Chardin even dined at Lewes in the lee of the castle. It was during his time in Sussex, with its ancient yet incessantly renewed landscape, that he grew more conscious of the drift of the universe.

Teilhard de Chardin's war-time letters collected in *The Makings of a Mind*, and his *Writings In Time of War* were invaluable sources in compiling the trench mysticism of the character of Trevenen Huxley. History records that Noel Trevenen Huxley committed suicide in 1914 so he did not serve. The history of the Huxley family is interwoven with evolutionary speculation, science fiction and progressive causes, and his brother Julian Huxley wrote the introduction to Teilhard de Chardin's *The Phenomenon of Man*. It was this affinity that led to me to concoct a different life for Trevenen.

The Quaker-led volunteer group of Friends Ambulance Unit also served at the Western Front. Two of its number, science fiction writer Olaf Stapledon, and the professor and meteorologist Lewis Fry Richardson, influenced the characters of James and Professor Collinson.

Stapledon's voluminous letters to his future wife Agnes during the conflict, collected in *The Love Letters of Olaf Stapledon and Agnes Miller, 1913-1919*, edited by Robert Crossley, were consulted. The most obvious and significant debt I owe to Stapledon is the character of Odd John, the *Homo superior* from his novel of the same name. Lewis Fry Richardson's paper on the *Mathematical Psychology of War* provides the equations found in Collinson's Equation of War.

The Eleonte necropolis was discovered by French soldiers during the Gallipoli campaign, prior to the Suvla landing and many miles south of the location given in the novel. For an account of that archaeological dig under fire, I referred to *Uncensored Letters from the Dardanelles* by French medical officer Joseph Marguerite Jean Vassal.

Other sources for the landing at Suvla Bay include *The Pals at Suvla Bay* by Henry Hanna, *Conditions: Evacuation of the Sick and Wounded from Suvla Bay*, and the diary of Private Wilfred Knott and the papers of Reverend Private Thomas, who served with the Royal Ambulance Military Corps at Suvla Bay: these are held at the Imperial War Museum.

As for the bailiff's armour, the term "colloid" is used by Rudyard Kipling to describe the transparent layer covering the windows of the airships in his story "With the Night Mail". Its "pedrails" were invented by Bramah Joseph Diplock and inspired HG Wells' short story "The Land Ironclads". In the war, Wells would advocate the use of the land ironclad to Winston Churchill, who was involved in the development of the tank. The private armour fashioned for James by the Process is based upon the more recent research of Marc Meyers at the University of California, San Diego.

The meeting at Wellington House between Charles Masterman and the great authors of the day took place on the afternoon of September 2, 1914. I could not locate the minutes of that meeting. It is believed that detailed records were destroyed during the Second World War. My sources were the diary entries of Arnold Bennett, the recollections of Thomas Hardy, the subsequent articles written by HG Wells and GK Chesterton, and *The Great War of Words: Literature as Propaganda 1914-18 and After* by Peter Beuitenhuis. There was no one like John Hector in attendance at this meeting.

Some of Masterman's dialogue is drawn from his book *England After War*. The description of Europe as "a bankrupt slaughterhouse inhabited by unmated women... I wonder that anybody is sane," was spoken by Mr Page, American Ambassador in London to Mr Alderman in Hampton, Virginia in 1916. And it is to Masterman that I am indebted for the conceit of Omega John's talent. In *England After War*, Masterman speculates, "If but a fraction of the active torment or dull misery of the war combatants could have been transferred, not by the clumsy interpretation of picture, written or spoken word, but by some mind current affecting another's human sensation, lighting up in another mind the unassailable and uncommunicable direct apprehension of pain, then the war would have come to an end in less weeks than it endured years."

Matthew de Abaitua, Hackney, 2015

ACKNOWLEDGMENTS

My agent Sarah Such was positive about IF THEN from its initial conception. Her encouragement, patience and expertise was crucial throughout the writing of the novel and then she found it the right home at Angry Robot.

Thanks to everyone at Angry Robot, particularly my editor Phil Jourdan for his insightful notes and strong reaction to the novel, copy editor Paul Simpson, and most of all to publisher Marc Gascoigne.

I owe a debt of gratitude to my friends and the community of Lewes, who I miss dearly. We never really said goodbye. Particular thanks to John May and Gavin Clark for many evenings of good conversation in the Lewes Arms.

To my friends in the HC, you've all taught me so much. Particular thanks to Josh Glenn for creating that particular world.

IF THEN was planned and half-written in a rented flat in Lewes through winters of austerity. Lean years for me and my family. My dream of writing this book would have got nowhere without the hard work and support of my wife Cathy, who also advised on Ruth's work as seamstress. Cyril Connolly famously observed that one of the enemies of promise was the pram in the hall. I've had three prams in my hall, but my children have been nothing but an inspiration to me. I hope that Alice, Alfred and Florence will one day read the novel that was written in and around their childhood.

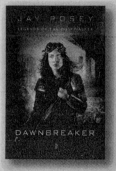

This is why we fight.

Twitter @angryrobotbooks

ANGRY
ROBOT

JOIN US
angryrobotbooks.com
twitter.com/angryrobotbooks